Words of Acclaim

…An exciting new twist to a crime novel. I have to get the first one now ….

….I didn't know where this was going, but I love it! I will read the rest of the series….

THE WAR CONTINUES

Book 2 in the
Hometown Wars Series

D.J. Glawson

Nevada Blue
Publishing

Smelterville, Idaho

Nevada Blue Publishing
P.O. Box 40
Smelterville, Idaho 83868

ISBN: 978164669137-1

You can always tell when you're on the road to success; it's uphill all the way.

Paul Harvey

A special thanks to Wikipedia, Google, Google Earth Pro and Historic Aerials for the help in nailing down certain aspects of the streets of Salt Lake City and Lake Tahoe from so many years ago.

Even though I lived there for nine years, my memory does not always work as well as I would like it to and, I have discovered, it is difficult to find those able to help with events from the 1980's. It seems 30 years is a long time for all of us.

I used the laws governing licensing of the bars and clubs from my time managing the bars in Salt Lake City to guide me. Other laws are stated as told to me by the law enforcement community **at that time**, but this is still a work of fiction and I have used my authorial license to a large extent.

As a work of fiction it is in no way meant to portray any person, place, or event in a bad way. Any inaccuracies are on me and not the fault of others.

Thank you and enjoy the read.

Sincerely,
D.J. Glawson
www.djglawsonauthor.com
Facebook: D.J.Glawson
Blog: DJGlawsonauthor.home.blog

I can also be found on Twitter and LinkedIn.

It has been ten months since George Bonner was imprisoned for numerous counts of murder, Amanda's abduction and minor drug and prostitution charges, and Amanda and Jeremy sit at the usual table at a little café off Main Street on Thirteen Hundred South. The cafe is small, showing its years, but it doesn't reek of stale grease and age. The tables are immaculate, the food and the service, the best in town. Amanda catches herself wishing they were open for more than just breakfast and lunch.

She gazes out the window and smiles. It was a day much like this, four years ago, when she pulled into Salt Lake City driving a U-Haul van carrying all of her worldly possessions, including her lauded filing cabinet full of music and her grandmother's antique china hutch. She rented a room in a cheap weekly rate motel and never looked back. Now, she has a good job, good friends and free reign of Jeremy's retreat replete with dirt bikes, three wheelers and a swimming pool. Plus free vacations at Lake Tahoe, when she decides to avail herself of those amenities.

Following Amanda's abduction, Jeremy quit training escorts, instead, choosing to help the women and girls by teaching them self-defense skills along with how to recognize and avoid being taken in the manner Amanda had, but admits the teenagers act as if invincibility is one of their super powers. They know everything and, until something happens to them, no one can convince them otherwise. Jeremy also admits that in his enthusiasm to help these women it never crossed his mind that they didn't feel threatened.

Then Amanda starts the conversation that elicits the response that stuns them all. Snippets of the next two days are seared into her memory.

"You're awfully chipper this morning," Amanda says.

Jeremy waits and thanks the waitress when she brings their food before he replies. "It is a beautiful June morning," he says.

"Something's on your mind, Jeremy, and I don't believe the beautiful June morning is the only thing affecting that mood."

"What days do William and James have off?

"Usually weekends, except lately. Why?"

"I have something we need to discuss. I am thinking about closing the center."

Amanda chokes on her coffee and stares in surprise, the hot beverage burning the back of her throat as she attempts to keep it from spraying across the table. "What about the classes?" she asks.

"This one should be finished next week. When would be a good time to get together? I thought it might be a good excuse for Mr. Tudor to prepare dinner."

"I'll call William," she replies, noting Jeremy's use of her former nickname for him. "I don't see a problem with tomorrow night."

Jeremy watches her, an unreadable expression on his face. He smiles, but the deep blue eyes don't dance. This is hard for him.

"Thank you. And ask them to have Timothy attend, too."

They finish their meal in silence, Amanda admitting Jeremy is probably right. It's time to close the center. Nobody likes doing these presentations and the girls don't care.

"Are you ready to open those doors?" Jeremy asks. He stands and offers his hand, the ever present gentleman.

Jeremy unlocks the doors and waves for Amanda to step

inside. The sound of tires on gravel draws her attention to a car with two people in it entering the alley. Curious, she pauses to see if they exit the same way. The phone rings forcing her away from the door and Jeremy to run for the alarm, while she races for the office. It's William. The lessons need to be rearranged. He and James are going to be late for their presentation that afternoon.

No vehicles have been heard leaving and, after hanging up, Amanda rushes back to the door. She glimpses a black pick-up pull away from the curb across the street, following it with her eyes. The driver does a quick look in her direction when he makes the left, heading north toward town. He looks familiar.

She turns her attention back to the alley. It's close to fifteen minutes before a group of boys leave, joking and making obscene gestures with they're hips. Then the car pulls out, heading toward town, only one person inside.

Hoping the car didn't drop someone off, Amanda trots for the rear delivery door. She doesn't want them back there alone if it's a student. She reaches for the handle; Jeremy comes from behind her to lift the heavy door. One of the students, Lori, is staring in at them, clasping her purse to her chest. She looks surprised.

"I'm a little early," the girl stammers. "Can I come in?"

"Of course," Jeremy answers.

Lori nods a little too quickly and mumbles an apology in passing, Amanda's thoughts reverting to the boys who exited the alley. Lori's lying, she didn't just 'get here early'; her shirt isn't even buttoned. Amanda debates cornering the girl, but decides to leave it alone. It can wait until after class.

"We're going to be using the front classroom this morning," Amanda says instead.

Lori nods again, blushing as she drops her eyes to the floor. Amanda shakes her head and thinks about her and Jeremy's conversation over breakfast.

Amanda joins Jeremy in the classroom and they start the

morning's session, taking the usual break at ten, but by eleven, boredom is setting in. The girls hate this, and getting them to participate is almost impossible. They want to sit back and watch everyone else while they float through. So why are they even here? Jeremy dismisses everyone for lunch with instructions to meet in the larger rear classroom when they return. As they file out, Jeremy watches Amanda's eyes trail Lori, noting the anger. He understands. Like Amanda, he knows Lori lied. One more reason he's thinking about closing the center.

Amanda broaches her thoughts about Lori. She is only fifteen and turning tricks. "Are these girls that desperate for attention?" Amanda asks.

"I am afraid, I cannot answer that," Jeremy replies. "Now, let's get some lunch."

Several women are waiting when they return, but the teenagers are MIA. Normal occurrence. Amanda waits until the ladies enter then follows Jeremy into the office. The more she looks at this from the other side of the glass, the better she understands Jeremy's decision. It's actually a big relief. Thirty minutes later, everybody's in the larger rear classroom, slideshow and tapes at the ready. Amanda goes through her part of the lesson then Jeremy takes over. As she watches, Amanda realizes Jeremy isn't as enthused as he had been. She hadn't noticed because she hadn't been paying attention.

When William and James arrive, James begins their portion of the presentation, going through the slides, explaining each one in detail. There are a few looks of disgust, at the sight of the room Amanda had been kept in, but the rest falls on deaf ears. James finishes his presentation and introduces William, warning the women about the reality of what they are about to see, reiterating the fact that they are only attempting to help them avoid what Amanda went through. One of the girls laughs from her seat in the rear of the class and makes a snide remark; some of the women –

and a few younger girls – look embarrassed.

"Believe it or not," William says as he steps forward, "there are still women out there who have a little bit of self-respect. You might want to check into that sometime. It makes a big difference in the class of man one attracts."

Ignoring the surprised stares, he continues with his part of the presentation. Once the tape has started, he steps back and leans against the wall beside Amanda. When George has the guard slug her, the women cover their mouths and gasp. When Amanda strikes George with the bench it garners a few cheers. The tape stops and William moves back to the front of the class and pulls up the slides of the bodies they found at Liberty Park and Silver Lake the previous year, emphasizing that that is one of the dangers of the job. William then pulls up a slide of a young girl who was beaten and left in a motel room.

"It's not all glamour and that stuff you see on TV," he says. "This girl was only thirteen years old. The maid found her and called her parents. The girl was afraid to call 911. She didn't want a male officer seeing her. She had been assaulted vaginally and anally, repeatedly. According to doctor's she may never have children. Think about it real hard before you decide to put yourself through that."

William beckons Amanda to join him and reveals the scar on her shoulder then explains she received that at the hands of a man she had been married to. The man told her he loved her. He was the one who sold her to the man who ordered the attack they had just witnessed, and the man who bought her was the man Amanda struck with the bench. He finishes by explaining two police women will be there the following day and reminds them they only want to help them avoid what Amanda went through.

With the presentation over, Amanda approaches them about dinner and they accept, saying they might not be able to stay long, that detective thing. William says he will contact Timothy.

By five p.m. the class has been dismissed and Jeremy sets the alarm, while Amanda waits outside.

The next evening William is early and apologizes for acting like a complete butt part of the time, blaming it on the stress of the detective slot. Amanda doesn't believe him completely, thinking part of it might be the perceived competition from Jeremy. The buzzer sounds signaling James and Timothy's arrival. Amanda lets them in, joking about their punctuality. Timothy teases James about William and him making James look like the center of an Oreo. *Jeremy is running uncharacteristically late and when he arrives Timothy jokes about James, Amanda and Jeremy making the perfect* Vanilla Wafer.

Everyone accepts the jokes for what they are and Jeremy starts dinner. As expected the meal is flawless, but the conversation is stilted. They want to know the reason behind tonight but no one wants to be the person to begin the discourse. Once the meal is over and they move to the living room, William glances between James and Timothy and sees the slight tilt of James head. He has been elected to lead. He scowls at the two, they both shrug.

"Okay, you said you had something to discuss. Let's hear it. You're nervous which makes me nervous," William says.

"I am thinking about closing the center," Jeremy replies. He recognizes the mixture of surprise and relief and sighs. "I have been putting it off for quite some time, but I feel it is time to end this. I wanted this training center to catch on, but the girls don't seem to care. I have also come to the conclusion I don't handle the classroom setting well at all."

William smiles. Jeremy's speech is nervous, he's flustered. So unlike Jeremy.

"I hate doing those presentations," William admits. "It just brings back all the crap Amanda went through last year."

"Well, that has been bothering me, too. I didn't want to bring those memories back and I feel that is all these presentations do.

You have been extremely strong during this experiment, but I don't feel we should continue. I was fine teaching Amanda the finer nuances of defending herself, but trying to teach someone how to avoid what happened to her and protect themselves when they don't give a damn, isn't the same. An incident yesterday morning just made the futility more apparent. Does that make sense?"

"Perfect sense. What happened yesterday?"

Jeremy gives them a quick rundown on the previous morning, and Lori, bringing back memories of another girl Jeremy kicked out of class for turning tricks behind the center. That girl had only been fourteen.

While she listens, Amanda realizes this center has helped her immensely, and the idea of closing it fills her with a sense of relief along with a hint of melancholy and foreboding. She will lose an integral part of herself. It's probably time to move on. She will have to push that fear behind her.

They end the evening with a date set to meet in two weeks. Jeremy says he has an idea that will make it easier for him to pull information and help the police.

1

The shriek of the phone startled William from sleep and he rolled over, checking the clock. Four a.m. Would the bad guys take a break, please? There were definite downsides to this detective crap. A second or third screech – he didn't know which – and he answered.

"Officer Harrison," William mumbled groggily. "Detective Harrison," he corrected himself.

"Hey, buddy," James said with a laugh. "Captain Kirby wants our tails at the residential parking area on Park Street twenty minutes ago."

"Park Street," William repeated. "Pick ya up in a few."

William turned the lamp on and crawled out of bed then showered, debating if he had time to make coffee. To hell with it, he had to have coffee. Toweling off, he picked up his toothbrush and raced for the kitchen, brushing with one hand, holding the towel with the other. Coffee brewing, he sprinted back to the bathroom, rinsed the toothpaste out, did a few quick swipes with the electric razor and paused, running his hand over his kinky hair as he surveyed his reflection. He should probably get a haircut. It looked a little woolly. He didn't want one of those afros he had seen other black guys sporting, and he didn't want to look like a partially burned Tiparillo at a crime scene. One last look in the mirror and he peeled around the door into the bedroom, threw on a clean suit and darted to the kitchen. Slipping a cup under the stream of steaming liquid, he quickly replaced it with the carafe once the cup was full and rushed out the door, taking the steps three at a time. Too early again, but more coffee would be waiting.

He picked James up, automatically checking the clock. They were making good time. James dropped into the passenger seat, coffee in hand, sighing heavily.

Almost as tall as William at six foot with coal black hair and dancing green eyes, James was a damn good-looking man. The gleam in his eyes hinted at a jokester hidden within and William had discovered over the past nine years – there was. James was all into the fun as long as no one got hurt. And William was fine with that. The department couldn't have given him a better partner. The short time they had spent partnered with other detectives during training had felt like an eternity. After several requests they had finally convinced Captain Kirby to put the team of Harrison and Thompson back together, and they hadn't slowed since.

"It's another lovely day in Salt Lake City, Utah, isn't it?" James quipped sarcastically. "Any new girlfriends?"

"Haven't met anyone interesting enough," William answered.

"William," James said, scolding playfully, "as good looking as you are ladies should be lining up at your door. I mean, you're the best looking guy I know."

"Some try," William replied, remembering a woman who had followed him home. He had doubled back behind a Circle K to lose her. "You know I'm looking for more than the bedroom hustle. I want someone I can talk to. Someone who likes jazz. Plus

I have Amanda. I can't walk away from that. How about you and Karen?"

"Same."

William pulled the unmarked up behind a squad car and him and James stepped out, appraising the area. The first thing they noticed was a late model sedan parked along the curb instead of in the designated parking area.

Park Street was one of those older two block north south running streets between Fifth and Sixth East. Close to downtown and convenient for shopping at Trolley Square, it was narrow – some of the homes built prior to the thirties and forties – with driveways barely wide enough to open a car door. With no room for street parking the northern block had added a parking area on the corner of Park Street and Gallacher Place – an access street a half a block long that ran east from Fifth East to Park Street – and it was full to capacity every night.

As they drew closer, the scene melded into the usual assault to the senses, lights flashing and radios complaining while neighbors gawked from their porches or peeked through the curtains. A few yards away, the press of reporters was already jockeying for position. James shook his head. His biggest pet peeve was the press. It was all about those ratings, William had told him once. James didn't buy it, nor did he care.

A female reporter glanced in William's direction and winked with a quick dip of her head.

'Won't work sweetheart,' William thought. *'It will take more than fake eyelashes, a skinny tush and an insatiable desire to be the center of attention to pique my interest.'*

William pulled his attention back to the scene as they approached a sheet covered body, one corner dancing in the soft morning breeze.

Footsteps stopped beside them and Lloyd Farmer, lead tech,

stood next to them, a patrolman approaching from the opposite direction.

"Yo, dee-teck-deeves," Lloyd said. "How are you doing this bright and lovely morning?"

Like William, Lloyd had escaped the swamps of Louisiana wanting to find a better life for him and his family and had found it in Salt Lake City. Lloyd applied with the department the year after William graduated from the academy and had been working ever since. One of the few constants in this world.

Lloyd looked at James and grinned. "Win anymore mullah there cream puff?"

"If I did I wouldn't tell you," James answered. "Last time William and I almost got thrown off the force."

William listened to the two and laughed. James was the only man on the force Lloyd felt comfortable enough teasing like that.

An unexpected gust of wind blew through, lifting the sheet like a catamaran sail. All three men grabbed it, placing it back over the body.

"Damn!" James exclaimed. He had crouched beside the body and looked up at the newly arrived patrolman. "What the hell did they do to the poor girl?"

"She was stabbed multiple times in the abdomen and chest," the officer answered. "According to a couple of the neighbors they heard a commotion, but they didn't see anything, except the car." He did a head jerk toward the sedan at the curb. "Neighbors thought the noise was coming from the car."

William scanned the parking area as the officer talked, it was full. The car probably didn't belong to any of the residents.

"They looked outside a short time later," the officer continued, "because the car hadn't driven off. That's when they saw her."

William knelt and examined her body. She was naked, her arms and her face bruised, she had a cut on her forehead, and one earlobe was ripped where an earring should have been. Her lips were split, trails from the blood running lazily over her chin and onto her neck. Her hands and her arms showed scratches and cuts. The woman had fought her attacker.

"She wasn't killed here, was she?" William asked, glancing up at the patrolman. "I don't see much blood."

"I doubt it," Lloyd interjected. "There's a minimal amount of blood near the car. Not enough for the injuries she's got."

James dropped his corner of the sheet and stood, looking down at William. "I have a question for you."

William stood, looking across at James. "Shoot."

"What if the rumors are true? What if Georgie boy is running this from inside? His nephew and his attorney make regular visits."

"Possibility," William answered. "But if George ordered it, he would have had them dump the girl outside of town. And it wouldn't be this messy. I never knew George to work things this way. Why change it up now?"

"Yeah." James said. "Makes you wonder." James stared at the pool of reporters then back at the patrolman. "Anything prior to neighbors hearing a commotion? Anything more descriptive than, 'a commotion'?"

"One of the neighbors said he heard people shouting about three, three-thirty," the officer replied. "The dude's a little hesitant to talk right now."

"We can come back and talk to him later," William said. He walked over by the car, inspecting the interior and surrounding pavement, James doing the same on the passenger side. If she had fought her attackers, where were the signs of a struggle? He looked back at Lloyd. "And you don't think this was done in the back seat?"

"Doesn't look like it," Lloyd answered. "There's no blood. I know you've seen that."

"It might have been done somewhere in the mountains. Maybe near one of the ski resorts. Those roads are pretty dark at night."

"Possibly," Lloyd said.

William looked back at the body, picturing the scenario that may have played out. Girl meets guys, guys are strung out on drugs – which they couldn't prove, but it was most likely the case – the girl refuses to give the goods the guys are demanding and she is the unfortunate recipient of their aggression. But why kill her?

"If she was stabbed in the backseat we would have found blood in the car," Lloyd added." It isn't adding up to being done here." Lloyd turned to leave. "Well, gotta ditch this party, man. I got work to do."

"I wonder if it was someone strung out on coke," William said, directing his gaze to James. "And the girl was in the wrong place at the wrong time."

"Could be," James replied.

William waved the patrolmen over. "Anything on the car? Is it hers?"

"Plates came back as stolen. It's registered to a girl who works at one of the hotel's downtown. She reported it two days ago. Someone heisted it while she was at work."

William leaned in and inspected the interior of the car one more time. It was almost too clean. He straightened and looked at the officer. "Was anything found in the car? Purse, keys, jacket? Clothes?"

"Nothing," the officer answered.

"You know," James added. "If I was doing this, I wouldn't argue with my accomplice. That would invite the neighbors to check me out. I'd pop him."

After the coroner's van drove out they gave the techs last minute instructions, not wanting anything slipping through the cracks. Once the scene had been processed and the crews had left, they started back to their car, Captain Kirby coming their way.

"Good morning gentlemen," the captain said. "Hear anything through those taskforces?"

"We hear things once in a while," James answered. "Nothing recent."

"You got any ideas about this one?"

"Kicking around a couple of things," William said. "We want to wait until we get the results back from the lab before we jump to any conclusions. She didn't work for the elder Bonner when he was here."

"And his business? Is it still working as usual?"

"We're not sure what has happened to his empire now that he's locked up. Rumor has it his nephew, Jonathan, took over."

"Anything constructive to give the press?"

"Ad lib," William answered. "Otherwise it's the usual. We are fully committed to finding the person or persons responsible. We've been here approximately five hours. We're not going to catch the guy that quick."

They climbed into the unmarked and William looked at his now empty cup then glanced at the clock on the dash. Nine thirty-five.

"Coffee, bro?"

"Read my mind," James answered.

2

William awoke holding Amanda his mind still on the woman on Park Street. For some reason she stuck in his mind with more tenacity than the others. Maybe because her death had been exceptionally brutal.

Amanda moved beside him and he kissed her forehead then brushed a lock of her long dark hair off her cheek, marveling at the scattering of freckles. Her eyelids fluttered open and she smiled, the translucent blue eyes shining. She kissed his chest, his mind wandering to pictures of kinky black hair and bright blue eyes on a dark skinned baby. Maybe it would have her porcelain complexion. Then the alarm barked and he rolled over, turning it off. Time to head out. He didn't want to. He wanted to stay here. Protect her. As if his proximity would keep her safe.

After his shower, William made coffee while Amanda climbed under its warm spray. The water stopped and the closet doors opened then she appeared in the kitchen door. He held his arm out for her to slide under.

"Good morning. Are you ready for breakfast?"

"Of course," Amanda said, snuggling up close. "I'm always up for the famous Harrison omelets."

"Maybe we can go somewhere and find a motel when things get back to normal. You know kind of, get out of town."

"That sounds wonderful."

William arrived at the station and discovered James already behind his desk. James was as big a workaholic as him. He pulled his chair out and sat down and James sighed. This desk duty was hard on James, too.

"What ya thinking, buddy?" James asked, seeing the scowl.

"Just sorting some things out. As usual we got too many loose ends. Too many questions. But…" William paused for dramatic effect, finger in the air. "…I stopped on Park Street on my way in this morning and that old man let it slip that two men got out of that car and then the woman's body appeared."

"So…Maybe someone watched events unfold. Someone saw the whole thing?"

"Maybe. I'm having a problem with that, though. Why didn't the other man try to stop it before it got that far? Now we need to find out who was arguing with who when the woman was killed. Or if she was even in the car."

The phone on James' desk rang interrupting their conversation.

"Officer Thompson, Detective Thompson," James corrected himself, William laughing in the background. "Sorry, sir…No, we're going over that now… Yes, sir."

"What was all that?" William asked.

"Captain Kirby. He wanted to know if we got any new info on the girl from Park Street. I guess he's getting his butt chewed."

"We just got the case yesterday and I put our report in his inbox last night. No wonder the long time goons drink so damn much."

The phone rang again and James answered it, remaining silent, locking eyes with William. James' expression told William everything.

"We're on our way." James was up, grabbing his coat off the chair back before he dropped the receiver in the cradle. "We have two bodies in one of the rooms in that dive hotel on Second South and Second East. Cap wants us there thirty minutes ago. Forensics teams are already enroute." They were racing through the door as James made the last statement. "They say it's pretty ripe in there, too," James added.

"Why us?" William asked. "We aren't the only detectives in the department."

"That taskforce, I guess," James answered. "We get priority now."

"This isn't the type of priority treatment I want," William replied sarcastically, wheeling the car out of the parking lot.

William pulled the unmarked car up to the scene, a few of the patrolmen leaning against the wall, hands on their knees, pulling in huge gulps of air. Others faces were pale, washed out.

They put their masks on and started up. At the top of the stairs, four doors could be seen at one end of the hall. One labeled 'Men's', one 'Ladies', two said 'Showers'. William shifted his gaze in the opposite direction when officers directed them to a larger room near the back. Walking in the first thing that hit them was the putrid sick odor of death. It even assailed their senses through the mask and they buried their faces in the crook of their elbow.

"They weren't kidding! This place is rank!" James exclaimed, his voice muffled by his arm and the mask.

William nodded his agreement then stopped, assessing the space. A small couch sat on the far wall to their left, a nice new stereo system behind the door, a coffee table squeezed into the space between the sofa and the stereo. A bed sat almost directly in front of them, a dresser positioned at the end of the bed to their right, a night stand sat next to the bed almost touching the couch.

A door on the far side of the bed hung half open revealing a closet. A small table had been positioned in the corner beside the dresser holding a coffee pot, a toaster oven and a two-burner hot plate. Two gallon jugs of water sat between the toaster oven and the hotplate. A shelf hung on the wall above with four plates, four mugs, and a pickle jar holding a few utensils. The entire room was maybe twelve feet by twenty feet.

William directed James toward the man on the couch while he checked a second man sprawled beside the bed, pausing to look at the blood on the man's clothing and the carpet under his head. He looked across the room at Lloyd, attempting not to laugh at the alien face painted on Lloyd's breather. James turned away, the corners of his lips peeking out from behind the mask as he fought to hold it together.

"What?" Lloyd asked, staring at William, hands on his hips.

"Area 51 has moved," William said. "You know, wearing that breather with that hoodie, you could pass for the real thing." He laughed, glancing around the room, pulling himself back to the reason for being there. "What we got, Lloyd?" he asked, as he chuckled.

Lloyd shook his head. "Right now it appears to be a drug overdose. There's powder on the coffee table and an empty baggie on the floor. No evidence they snorted. We'll find out more when the lab runs their tests."

"If they didn't snort, did they inject?"

"Doesn't look like it," Lloyd answered. "No needle marks."

"They would have had to ingest it then."

"You'll find out when they do the autopsy."

Lloyd left to help the techs, and William turned his gaze to the victim on the couch and the powder on the coffee table, taking his time, a business card partially hidden under the edge of the sofa. William picked it up. The Landers Corporation – Reno, Nevada.

James moved over to the make-shift kitchen, cockroaches scattering with each step.

"It looks like someone swept something off the table," James said.

William nodded and continued to gaze at the man on the floor, giving an involuntary shudder when one of the insects skittered across the man's forehead. People didn't usually party dressed like that. Why hadn't the guy cleaned up? Changed clothes? Why draw attention to oneself?

William took out an ink pen and pulled out the drawers on the dresser, going through them then flipped through the papers in a drawer in the nightstand. Tons of receipts. He squeezed around James to the closet, bottles filled with urine littering its floor, his mind flashing back to the public facilities at the end of the hall. This building was older, the rooms sharing a bathroom. Usually it was two rooms per bath, but this one – like a few others – had two bathrooms and two showers at the end of the hall and all rooms on that floor shared those.

William made a sweep of the closet, the clothes in disarray; some on the floor and wondered what the person who killed these men had been looking for. He finished his inspection of the closet and noticed the travel size refrigerator wedged under the table, a trashcan on the wall between it and the radiator under the rear window. He lifted the lid on the trash can sending it backwards into the wall. A Driver's License lay on the floor under it. Their lady from Park Street. Holding the can against the wall with the pen, William pulled his keys out of his pocket and slid the license from under the trash container.

"James, make sure these guys go through the john's and the showers real well. I don't want anything missed."

James' eyes locked on the license and he nodded.

William pulled on a pair of latex gloves and picked up the license, studying it. Olivia Holland. Olivia had been a very beautiful girl. The address was an apartment in The Avenues. That was a better part of town than most hookers lived in. Maybe she was a call girl. Then again, maybe she hadn't been either of those.

Once everything was bagged, William and James followed Lloyd outside, his breather balanced unsteadily on his head. Lloyd turned the corner and started down the stairs, the breather sliding off and bouncing down the hall. Lloyd cursed loudly, James joking about the aliens losing their heads on our planet. They could hear Lloyd's voice echo up the stairwell, telling everyone he would be back to get it. William thought about picking it up then admitted his hands were full, too.

"Better hurry, Lloyd," William called. "The mother ship might send someone down for their errant child."

Laughter echoed up the stairwell, accompanied by more of Lloyd's cursing. At the car, they removed their masks, blowing the fetid odor out through their nostrils. William stared in at the stairs, one of the techs making a mad dash out the door and into the waiting van. William hesitated, remembering the driver's license, a hollow nagging in his gut.

He walked to the rear of the building, inspecting the rear stairs and the fire escape, and two dumpsters. William stared at them a tic, did a single quick shake of his head. No way anyone would be dumb enough to throw something in there. He took two steps toward the car, James walking toward him, and backed up, looking at the dumpsters again.

"Let's check the dumpsters before we go," William said.

Stripping their coats off, they pulled on gloves then waded in, each man taking one. Half way through his William found a grocery bag with a woman's purse and wallet in it. He picked up the bag a cockroach scurrying away, thunking when it landed on a box. William jerked his hand back, dropping the bag and cursing out loud. Thank God he hadn't screamed like a girl. James would never let him live that down.

William reached for the bag and stopped, staring at the box. The cockroach continued his escape, the label now in full view. Farberware Kitchen Cutlery. They had found no knives in that room. Not even a steak knife. He grabbed the bag and the box, and climbed out of the dumpster.

Back at the car, William popped the trunk and James covered the interior with a garbage bag then they set the box down and dumped the contents of the bag. William's eyes fell on a business card and he slid the wallet aside with a gloved finger picking up the card, a book of matches catching his eye. Pearls on Main. Olivia, or her assailant, had been in the club where he played. William looked back at the card. The same as the one upstairs.

They put everything into evidence bags then climbed the stairs, combing through the room once more. William started with the couch while James searched the bed, lifting the mattress and going through the dresser and the closet, moving the clothing, checking the pockets and overhead shelf, retracing William's steps, but only found a crack where the chimney ran up the outer wall. When James looked up William was sitting on the floor, leaning against the wall by a speaker.

"Anything?" James asked.

"Nothing. I have another question now."

"Go for it."

"How could they afford a stereo system like this one? I didn't see one paystub anywhere. Not even in the trash." William jerked his head toward the bed. "That drawer in the nightstand was stuffed with receipts so, where'd they get the cash?"

"Maybe we'll find something when we sort through those papers. Let's take one more run at the shit on this table."

An hour later every drawer in the dresser sat on the bed empty, the backs had been taken off the stereo speakers and every item in the ad-hock kitchen had been moved. And they had found nothing. William turned to face James a latch peeking out from behind the refrigerator.

"Pull that fridge out," William said, dropping to his knees beside James.

James rolled it away from the wall, exposing a door. When William unhooked the latch, the door dropped down revealing a cubby between the two by four's. And it contained product. The guys had been peddling drugs. Sometimes that was the only motive anyone needed. Now to discover who they had sold for.

Dropping the evidence in the trunk, William climbed behind the steering wheel.

"I want to go by the club," William said.

"The matches?"

William nodded and checked his watch. This might be another all-nighter. "I want to see if Eddie had those security cameras installed. He mentioned it after Amanda was abducted."

Skipping down the stairs at Pearls on Main, they found Eddie and the bartender at the end of the bar a baseball game on. Middle of the week, the place was dead.

"Eddie," William said. "Did you put those security cameras in after Amanda was taken?"

Eddie nodded, wrinkled his nose and leaned away

"We need to see the playbacks for the last three or four days. Can we do that?"

"You know how long that's going to take?" Glancing between the two and not getting a response, Eddie started down the hall. "Come on. I'll set you up. You're on your own after that, though. I gotta watch the bar."

William laughed. Eddie just didn't want to miss the game.

3

They started their scans at ten-thirty p.m. to save time. Fast forwarding through the third video they saw Olivia at the bar, deep in conversation with two men. The trio finished their drinks then the men waved off a drink, tossed some bills on the bar, them and Olivia backed away from the stools and left. That had been at eleven-fifteen p.m. on the time stamp.

"You notice what I just did?" James asked.

William paused the tape, nodding as he did then rewound it, starting playback a few minutes before ten. Olivia was already there. William rewound it to eight p.m. and started the playback again, dropping to normal speed when Olivia walked in. That had been at nine twenty-five. At nine-thirty a man came in and sat down beside her. He introduced himself. She smiled, giving him the once over with her eyes. William hit fast-forward only seeing the normal chit-chat until two minutes after ten. He dropped it to normal play. A second man walked in and sat down, ordering a round of drinks. They finished those, the first man waved off the bartender, tossed a few bills on the bar, and the trio left.

William leaned back in his chair, his mind working on the

possibility. At eleven-fifteen Olivia walked out with two men. Five minutes to walk up the stairs and around the corner. Maybe six. Add a few minutes to walk to the car. That would make it approximately eleven-thirty. Thirty minutes, depending on traffic, and where they were going put it about twelve a.m. Olivia's address in The Avenues was only a fifteen minute drive away. Neighbors heard people fighting around three a.m.; a couple of minutes for residents to decide if they want to get involved, they call 911 and give dispatch the information. The department's response time is less than five minutes in town. Usually. Patrol responds and makes a call for detectives. They received the call out at four a.m. That gave the guy, or guys, more than two hours with her. And the photos looked like every minute of that time had been used. Striding to the bar, William set the tape in front of Eddie.

"Can we get a copy of this?" William asked.

"Sure. Give me a minute. Where you been, the dump? You smell like you died."

"Something like that," William answered.

They climbed into the car, their radios crackling to life. Both men automatically checked the clock on the dash.

"Detective Harrison."

"Captain Kirby wants you and Detective Thompson in the office. How soon can you be here?"

"About forty-five minutes. We gotta get rid of this funk."

"I'll let him know you're on your way."

They drove to the station and pulled into the lot, each man grabbing a backpack out of the car before going inside. An extra set of clothes for days like today, and they had just cut twenty minutes off their arrival time. They headed for the showers, other officers giving them a wide berth. They tossed their suits into bags, tied the bags shut, ready to dump them in the trunk then showered and changed. They would haul the evidence in and catalog it after they talked to the captain.

"Gentlemen," Captain Kirby said.

"What keeps you here?" William asked.

"Just doing some follow up. You two know how to clear out a station."

"The bodies have been baking a few days. We didn't want to drag that in here."

"I'm glad you cleaned up." the captain chuckled and waved for them to have a seat. "I heard the men talking when you arrived so I appreciate that." He paused, waiting for them to get comfortable. "I want your thoughts on the lady on Park Street. Do you think she was a freelancer? Or was she a hooker at all?"

"Hard to say," William answered. "The preliminary report from the ME says she was raped. Possibly by two individuals, but we have nothing definite. Part of the evidence could be from a customer. We kicking around the possibility she may have been a call girl not your street corner hooker. As for drugs – we won't have answers on that for a couple more days."

"I know you haven't had time to finish working this scene, but did you find anything there?"

"Other than they were partying hard?" James asked. "More than we expected." Then he told the captain about the room being searched prior to their arrival and the Driver's License under the garbage can belonging to the girl on Park Street.

"Her name was Olivia Holland," William continued. "We didn't find any knives, not even in the kitchen, but we found an empty cutlery box in a dumpster. We're going to check with the businesses in the area, see if anyone besides the victims have used the dumpsters recently. According to the tech's the guys have been dead close to three days." Captain Kirby nodded. "The woman's license shows an address in The Avenues. With no keys in her purse, we think whoever swept the stuff off the table took them. We're going to talk to her apartment manager. We might turn up something there. Getting some guff from upstairs?"

"A little and, needless to say, I don't like it. As long as you're making headway I'll survive. Have you seen those men? Do they look familiar?"

"No, sir," William told him.

"We have evidence to process yet," James said. "We might find more when we go through it."

"Keep me posted. I need reports on my desk in the morning."

4

William and James met at seven the next morning, James offering to do the door to door with the businesses near the hotel, already knowing chances of finding anything was slim, but it had to be done. While James worked the area around the hotel, William would search Olivia's apartment. James to join William as soon as he'd completed his canvas of the downtown area.

William pulled up in front of Olivia's apartment at ten minutes after eight. It was an older, well maintained, four-plex. Inspecting the grounds and the building, he noticed the absence of any security panel. A sign at the house next to it advertised it as the office.

The obligatory bell announced William's arrival as he walked in, a very pregnant young woman answering the summons, her left hand massaging her extended abdomen absently. She sighed as she sat down behind the desk and William smiled in spite of himself.

"It looks like you're about due," he said.

"Any day," she answered with a soft laugh. "The last month is always the worst." A curly haired little girl peeked around the door and smiled up at William, running to hide behind the woman. "All of our units are currently occupied," the lady said as she smoothed the curls away from the little one's eyes.

"That's alright," William replied. "I'm not looking for an apartment." He pulled his badge, showing it to her and winking at the toddler.

"Oh, how can I help you?" she asked, a hint of alarm behind the words.

"I need some information on one of your tenants. An Olivia Holland."

"Oh, yes. She's a real sweet lady. Never late with her rent. Seldom has company. I guess because she works too much. She's hardly ever home."

"When was the last time you saw her?"

"A couple of days ago," she replied, a frown tugging the corners of her mouth down. "She's not in any trouble, is she?"

William shook his head. "Not really." He paused a second, not wanting to say anything to alarm her, but not having much choice. "Miss Holland was murdered night before last."

"Oh, my God!" the woman exclaimed, automatically hugging the baby tighter with her right arm while she held her belly with the other. The little girl started to fuss, picking up on her mother's discomfort and the woman picked her up. "Such an awful thing. She was always so nice."

"Yes, ma'am. I was wondering if you could let me into her apartment so I can look around. Maybe find out if she had any family or friends. Someone we can talk to."

"Um, let me call my husband." She picked up a walkie-talkie and called him back to the office, explaining what she could.

William followed her husband out and across the parking lot, asking generic questions about any recent complaints or problems with intruders in any of the apartments, being told no on all counts. The couple worked as on-site management along with maintenance and custodial services in exchange for rent, utilities and a small token salary. The man put the key in the lock and hesitated.

"Come to think of it one of the tenants said they saw someone hanging around last week. We figured it was just some low life trying to case the place and have been keeping an eye out, but haven't seen anything since."

The manager opened the door, a sweet sour odor assailing their nostrils. William recognized it, barred the man entry and called for a tech crew then asked James to switch frequencies. As soon as he told James his suspicions, James headed his way.

The rest of the afternoon was spent going through Olivia's apartment – finding nothing. They stripped the bed, searched the dresser and the closet, and took the bed apart, seeing no sign of blood. They took one last walk up the hall and William noticed the stereo appeared to have been moved. Indentations in the carpet showed where the sofa had sat prior to being moved to its current location.

Crews moved the sofa revealing a stain on the carpet where it met the baseboards, along with a thin line of discoloration where the wall met the trim.

Once they had gathered the evidence and sealed the apartment off they headed back to the station, more questions going through their mind. If she had been killed here, why move her?

Back at the station they detoured past their mail slots, a letter stuffed in their cubbies. James took his, handing William's to him then glanced down the wall of slots. Every detective in the department had a similar envelope. James read his as they walked, a grin appearing.

"What did we get?" William asked.

"A letter from the University of Utah," James said. He dropped the letter on his desk and leaned back in his chair. "They're offering to do DNA sequencing for the department as part of their research. We know it isn't admissible in court, but it might point us in the right direction with some of our cases."

William scanned the letter, laying it on his desk. "We can send samples from these two cases."

Half way through their reports, Captain Kirby walked in. He'd heard the call. William went over what they found and what they hoped to prove, and the possibilities the evidence in the apartment opened up.

"We received a letter from the University of Utah and they offered to work their magic with this DNA sequencing free of charge. Use it for some of the labs for the students. We might get some good info," William finished.

"You know DNA's not admissible in court."

"Yeah, but we need something pointing us in the right direction," James said.

"We have nothing positive yet," William added. "So it'll be better than nothing."

5

It had been the appointed two weeks and tonight was their meeting with Jeremy, and the group met at Amanda's.

With the center officially closed Jeremy had spent the last week at his retreat outside Cedar City pulling everything together. Tonight he would approach them, test the waters, and he was nervous. Unsure of how he should word his query. He didn't want anything happening to Amanda, but she had already proved her abilities. If they were receptive, he would invite them to Cedar City for the full presentation.

By seven p.m. everyone was in attendance and seated, and Jeremy set dinner on the table. He sat down and looked around the table, four sets of eyes glued on him and he was suddenly in front of the classroom once again. He held his breath for a tic, his heart skipping a beat.

"What's this idea of yours?" Amanda asked, breaking the strained silence. "I've never known you to be uncomfortable, but tonight you act like a dog who's learning to fly. What's going on?"

Jeremy smiled as everyone laughed. "I want to continue to

help the women, but I don't want to go back to training escorts. I rather enjoy not being quite so paranoid. I was hoping I could coax you four into visiting me to go over a few things. I trust you more than anybody I have had the pleasure of working with." He paused, fumbling for the right words, debating his sanity.

"So far I think I understand," William said, letting Jeremy off the hook slightly. "So, what's on your mind?"

"Well, here goes nothing." Jeremy leaned back in the chair and exhaled slowly. "I thought with you gentlemen's background in police work, my reputation and connections, and Amanda's intuition, you four might be interested in helping bring men like George Bonner down on a regular basis. I have been asked to pull a team together and I need good people working with me. People I can trust. I cannot go into all of the details here. Everything I need is in my office, but I wanted to throw the idea out there. See if you might be interested. If you are, we will set up a weekend to meet and go over everything. Now, I may have said just enough to scare everybody off."

He stopped seeing only blank stares.

"Anyway, I was thinking about providing an event planning service. I would be the coordinator and set everything up, and Amanda would be the hostess helping set the venues and work with the guests. You gentlemen would work security. It would work as a front when necessary. My concerns are last year. I don't want anyone uncomfortable with the idea. I am prattling away like a nervous schoolboy, aren't I?" He took a deep breath, and watched them smile. "Plus, this will be quite lucrative," he added. "Why do you think I worked as I did for so long? It wasn't just to kiss the pretty girls. Although, that was an extremely nice caveat."

"You're rambling, Jeremy," Amanda said, laughing.

Jeremy shrugged. "I had hoped this would be easier to discuss but, for whatever reason, I find it quite frightening."

The laughter grew louder and William caught himself afraid Jeremy might hyperventilate. This was so uncommon, Jeremy was always in control.

Jeremy composed himself and glanced between the four.

"I've wanted to find a way to bring these people down," James admitted. "But it feels like our hands are tied. We need a lot more help pulling the bad guys off the street."

"I agree," Timothy said. "I've pulled people over that I know were shady and I've had to kick them loose. It feels like we're outmanned and outgunned three to one. How would this team help us accomplish that?"

"I work for an organization that is bound by the same rules and regulations as law enforcement," Jeremy told them. "If I don't do things as I should something as simple as going to the grocery store could turn deadly." He paused, waiting for questions. Not getting any, he went into more detail about the organization, its function plus the monthly stipend for working with the team and the pay for his new proposition. He finished by telling them he would still like everyone to meet at his retreat to go over everything in further detail.

"I'll be available anytime," Amanda said. "How hard it will be for you to take a whole weekend off, William?" She recognized the scowl and leaned back, hands up, palms out. "I meant with your work load, nothing else. You work seven days a week part of the time."

"It all depends on the cases. We'll have to talk to the Cap."

Jeremy excused himself at nine, leaving the four to talk. By eleven James and Timothy had left, all of them in agreement. They wanted to listen to Jeremy's spiel and make their decision from there.

The next morning William was running for the door when the buzzer startled him. He pushed the button, Jeremy on the other end. Allowing Jeremy in, he poured them each a cup of coffee then sat across the table from Jeremy and toyed with his cup, Amanda joining them.

"Timothy's going to talk to Captain Ohlmet this morning. We were thinking about heading your way Friday. This idea of yours is sounding better all the time. We'll let you know if we're interested from there. Can you work with that?"

Jeremy looked up, searching Amanda's eyes, seeing her tiny nod. "I will plan on seeing everybody Friday, then."

Amanda woke Saturday morning to the aroma of Jeremy's coffee. He was up bright and early as usual. She slid out of bed and padded up the hall, Jeremy in the kitchen, a t-shirt molded to his torso and blue jeans hugging his hips. It was good to see him in familiar surroundings. He really hadn't looked comfortable in front of a classroom.

When the men joined them Jeremy explained his idea for the party planning portion while he prepared their breakfast and Amanda sat the table. He left them to eat, going to his office and taking a manila envelope out of a desk drawer, four pagers inside. He stared at the devices, doubts bubbling to the surface, quickly dismissing them. The minute he received the fax he knew these were the people he wanted on his team. He placed the pagers back in the drawer then laid out the information for the presentation. Once everyone was seated, Jeremy pointed to a dry erase board that contained a chart with different colored lines.

"These," Jeremy said, "are the latest statistics in the states of Utah and Nevada for drugs and trafficking. As you can see these numbers are going up and that, in my organizations estimation, is unacceptable. I know, as police officers, you gentlemen feel the same way."

Jeremy continued, Amanda's attention locked on every word he was saying.

"As you can see, these numbers are going up. This trend has to be reversed. Our job will be to make them go down. The red lines are ladies who were abducted, or coerced, into a lifestyle not of their liking, shall we say."

"Trafficking," Timothy said.

"Correct. But we didn't reach these women in time. They were found dead. The black lines are drugs flowing through the Utah Nevada area. The green lines are ladies, or children, we have been successful in helping. The blue lines are women we have been given information on, but have no proof of abduction or trafficking, yet. We are still actively attempting to locate them before anything happens. The orange lines are children who have been abducted or are missing. The yellow lines are children who were abducted and we failed. And that to me, and I imagine all of you, is the most disturbing." Jeremy paused a tic. "We have helped to bring a few independent set ups in for trafficking and unlocked a door that this new computer age is heralding in, but the syndicate, and men like them and George Bonner, are leading the pack."

Amanda dropped her head, remembering being one of those children. Just another number, another statistic. She remembered her father's struggle with drugs and eventual overdose. Her mother working two jobs to support them and one of her mother's employers coming to their apartment with a friend. Her mother hid her in the closet while she tried to force the men to leave. She remembered something hitting the wall and leaving the closet, her mother's body slumped on the floor. She looked up, stared beyond Jeremy, her attention riveted to the brightly colored lines, her mind rerunning Jeremy's words '...*that, in my organizations estimation, is unacceptable...*'. It was unacceptable in her estimation, as well.

"Are you alright?" Jeremy asked, pulling her from her reverie. "You look like you are miles away."

She nodded and smiled. "I was for a minute. I apologize."

"Okay, gentlemen," Jeremy said, diverting his attention back to the men. "This is mostly a formality for you, but I need you to tell us why you are doing what you are doing. Why are you cops? Trust is what you use working with your partners and that trust is also what you need for this team to work...."

Amanda faded out again, remembering the singer at the night club, and her singing along outside for change. Their laughter pulled her back once again. As she gazed around the table, they continued, each man in turn going over his reasons for doing what he was doing, Jeremy giving his account as well. Telling a small amount about his time in Viet Nam and his work training escorts. It grew quiet and Amanda looked up to see Jeremy watching her.

"I have a question for you now, Amanda," Jeremy said. "I ran the same trace on you that I have on everybody here, but I find nothing before nineteen seventy-two. You didn't exist according to official records. Then I discovered a newspaper article from 1965 about a Chicago woman who had been murdered. The police thought it was a robbery gone bad. She had a daughter, but the girl was never found. Her daughter's name was Amanda. Amanda Tyler. Was that you?"

She swallowed hard, sucked in a deep breath and smiled then explained about the men, the money they'd left, and her disappearance into the streets. She told them about her early teen years and conning her way into a community college, ending with the jazz club.

"I met a guy at the club who made fake ID's," she finished. "I convinced him to make one for me under Amanda Granger. He got the name changed on my Social Security card, too."

She gave a half-hearted smile and sideways shrug, William and James both giving her a hug.

"How did you get to where you trust men?" Jeremy asked.

"To quote you, some days are harder than others."

The rest of the day was spent discussing Jeremy's offer and by evening they all agreed. Ease of access to necessary information would help any investigation. William was volunteered as the group spokesman, joining Jeremy on the pool surround to accept his offer.

Jeremy retrieved the pagers, handing one to each person then gave them a quick lesson in the use of the tool, showing them the functions, and letting Timothy know Amanda would use a code to feed information into the laptops in the cruisers. She would only need the identifier for the vehicle Timothy was driving on any given shift. It ended by Jeremy telling them they would start their formal training in the next few weeks. Since none of them had played this game, there was a lot they needed to learn. Amanda not being a member of law enforcement would require more. He also told them they would be in Reno for one of those exercises. Once back from Reno, they would know what areas the team needed to concentrate on. James and Timothy were told to bring their ladies to Reno.

"So," Jeremy said, chuckling, "from me and the commander – welcome to the boys club."

7

It had been a week since Jeremy's proposal and now they waited for the training to begin. Amanda took a sip of her coffee and stared over the balcony railing, the suns brilliance filtering through the leaves on the trees. She closed her eyes, taking in the scents from the flowers below, the blare of the phone startling her. She jumped, running to interrupt it before it screeched again. It was Jeremy.

"You don't sound too happy."

"I received a tad bit of a surprise this morning," he replied. "I heard from that last gentleman you met in Reno. Mr. Layton. Do you remember him?"

"I think so," she answered. "If I remember correctly, we had a nice dinner and chat afterwards. He didn't even want to dance."

"That is the one, madam. He was quite taken with you, but was disappointed when he discovered Mr. Bonner had been arrested. Not because Mr. Bonner had been arrested, but because he didn't know how to go about contacting you."

"And?" she asked when Jeremy paused. He sounded nervous.

"Anyway, he found my contact information and called asking

about you. He is looking for a hostess for upcoming dinners."

"Is that why you're so nervous?"

"Well…Yes, and no. Most of the time they do not work like this. Usually this is all handled through the network. And normally they do not get my personal number." Jeremy sighed. "He also assured me he has no interest in any extra-curricular activities."

Amanda laughed.

"What is so funny?" Jeremy asked.

"Extra-curricular activities," she replied, mimicking him. "I love the way you say things. It's great!"

"I'm glad someone thinks I'm funny. Anyway, I set up an appointment with Mr. Layton for Sunday afternoon."

"An appointment? You mean, like in Reno? Why would he want to audition me if I'm only working with you? Jeremy, I do not like this at all."

"I'm not sure I do, either, my lady. However, I chose to set this appointment as a part of everyone's training. I paged the men. William should be picking you up in the morning."

"So…I have no say in this?"

"Normally, yes. In this case…no. I'll see everyone tomorrow."

There was the staccato hum as the line went dead, and Amanda glared at the phone.

William picked Amanda up at nine a.m. and they pulled through the gates at Jeremy's four hours later, James and Timothy close behind them, Jeremy waiting on the porch.

"Well, ladies and gentlemen," he said, "I made sure the fuel tank is full, so there's three hundred gallons of gas out there. Feel free to use the three-wheelers and dirt bikes at your leisure. Seeing the smile on our lady's face I believe I have made the right decision." He laughed as he directed them inside.

"Always," Amanda answered. "Dirt bikes and nature trails.

You know me too well."

"We have a favor to ask," William said. "It's the weekend, but we might need to pull the reports on the drug screens for the last two callouts."

"Not a problem," Jeremy answered.

They spent the afternoon holding dirt bike races, running the valley on the three-wheelers and playing hide-and-seek with crossbows and suction head arrows, and everyone was exhausted by the time Jeremy announced dinner. After dinner, he pulled the foursome into his office, explaining how word would be spread that Jeremy and Amanda were back. That was the reason he had set this appointment.

The tantalizing aroma of Jeremy's coffee woke Amanda the next morning. She stumbled out of bed and into the kitchen, Jeremy working on breakfast. She put her arms around him, resting her head on his chest. Jeremy returned her hug, her warmth and scent filling his senses.

"Amanda," Jeremy warned, checking the hall, "if we keep this up you will get that gorgeous hind end in trouble. Do you know how hard it was not to join you last night?"

"My apologies. I didn't mean anything by it. It's just nice to see you in more comfortable surroundings." She had to be more careful.

She planted herself on one of the stools at the breakfast bar, Jeremy setting a cup of coffee in front of her.

"And it feels good to be in more comfortable surroundings. You look a tad more relaxed than I have seen you in quite some time yourself."

"I guess that center wasn't such a good idea. I miss working with you, though. Maybe I'll pop down one of these weekends and we can go to Lake Tahoe. We aren't working any longer."

"That is something I could handle."

Amanda dropped her eyes, fiddling with the cup handle, guilt rearing its ugly head. Bad move. Two in a row. She was batting a thousand. Plus today was her appointment with Mr. Layton and she was nervous.

Jeremy recognized the look and sat down beside her, giving her a hug. "It will be alright Miss Amanda. We are all right here if you need anything."

She nodded her head too quickly, the men's voices echoing up the hall.

After breakfast, the men played on the toys again, Amanda lazing by the pool. At eleven Jeremy called the men in and steered Amanda toward her room with the instructions to make herself presentable. When she made her appearance, Jeremy stationed her in the living room to wait. A limo pulled into the driveway ten minutes later and Mr. Layton climbed out.

"We're on," Jeremy announced. James opened the door, Mr. Layton walked through, Jeremy shaking his hand. "Mr. Layton. It's good to see you again. Please, come in. Amanda has been waiting anxiously."

Amanda rolled her eyes and saw William's grin.

Jeremy directed him to the living room, brought their drinks then faded into the woodwork. William remained inside near the doors, Timothy and James working the perimeter, surveying the area around the pool and keeping an eye on the limo and its driver.

Jeremy served lunch, showing them to the dining room then faded into the background once again leaving Amanda and Travis to talk. They exchanged pleasantries, continuing the conversation from the living room. It had been several months and he wanted to gauge her presence in a social setting once again, Travis told her. Refresh his memory.

"Let me know what the final verdict is, Jeremy," Travis said when he stood to leave. "I would like nothing more than to have this exquisite creature on my arm. You, as always, have outdone yourself. Oh, and Jeremy, good luck."

With a wave of his hand Travis bound down the steps, nodding to Timothy as he passed. Timothy continued inside, curious about the man. Why would he drive all the way to Utah from Reno to audition a woman? If he had enough money to ride around in a limo, he should be fighting the ladies off. James joined them off the deck, having the same questions.

"Exactly what was that supposed to mean?" Jeremy asked. "Good luck with what?"

"Travis says you are smitten with me," Amanda said. "It seems you can't hide everything. And what did he mean, 'on my arm'? I thought I was only going to help you."

"Those were my intentions," Jeremy said, adding one more question to the list regarding Travis Layton. "I promise to do a more thorough check on him."

"Well, something isn't right," she retorted. "I felt like he was looking me over like a prize steer."

"I noticed that, too," William added.

"Other than the obvious," Jeremy said changing the subject, "what do you think?"

"Just the obvious," William answered. "I don't understand the interview. If she's only helping you, and Travis has already met Amanda, why drive all the way over here to meet her again?"

"Ditto," Timothy said. "It seems to me this would be a lot more expensive."

"It is. But he requested it and was willing to pay so I thought it would be good experience. Give you an understanding of what will be required if we are asked to do a personal screening. Minus the prize steer part," he added when Amanda frowned. "So you know, I was not totally comfortable with this, either. I feel as if there is a lot being withheld. And I told Amanda on the phone, it doesn't normally work like this." He handed them each an envelope. "Now, these are for you."

"And we will be with her on every one of these affairs?" James asked.

"Yes," Jeremy answered. "Also, Mr. Bonner started quite a few rumors last year. Since Amanda and I are the ones those rumors are circling around, I need to be with her. It doesn't matter if she's playing hostess, or I am showing her off, we have to let the gentlemen know – unofficially of course – that Amanda and I have returned. That 'living the part', role. We have to be together in one capacity or another. Otherwise, it doesn't matter how good we are, or how big the team is, our work will be for naught. That is why I explained the process last night. Now," he said, "the commander called. He wants me to begin your training. Teach you the finer nuances of undercover work. It has to be played tighter than hooking a drug dealer slash pimp like George Bonner. Remember, you have to live the lifestyle.

"To bring the syndicate to its knees, it has to be convincing. We all know taking the snake that is the syndicate down will be a temporary beheading. Men willing and eager to grab the reins of that organization are already waiting in the wings. Power, sexy women and money draw men to its branches like bees to honey. In fact, that is what started me down this path. But that is our ultimate goal. With that in mind, we will work a dinner Friday night for the commander. This will be your introduction to him. His name is Howard Chancellor. William, your services will be utilized to head security. Amanda, you will act as more of an escort for this function – for lack of a better word. He wants to see how well you will be received, and how you will handle yourself in that situation."

"But if I'm not going to work...."

Jeremy raised his hand. "*Our* venture will not be utilizing your services in that way. However, if we are working an operation, we may have to project that illusion. Remember, it is all about appearances. I will repeat that on a regular basis as a reminder to us all. Also, we need to set up that date for Reno."

"We talked to the Cap," James said. "So far we haven't been able to convince him it's a good idea. Any suggestions?"

"You said you had suspicions the call girls murder may be tied to Reno," Jeremy answered, "so we'll check leads while we're there. And you are being paid by my organization so the police department won't be out a thing." He looked up, recognizing William's frown. "Is there a problem, William?"

"Kind of. Amanda, will you step outside?" William nudged her in the direction of the porch then turned to Jeremy. "When we talked to the captain we were told to keep you close. Use you as our friend and mentor. Every officer in the chain of command knows you. What's the real reason you approached us? Why Amanda?"

"You are all extremely good," Jeremy answered. "I need a team that I know can do the job. You have the experience and the abilities and Amanda has proved she can handle herself. She is very intuitive, as well. And that is an integral part of what the skill set. Now, we need to make those arrangements. We will go over a day early to meet with the Reno police, so I am going to have Karen and Janice flown over in my jet….."

"Jet?" Amanda asked. "You have your own jet?" Maybe she needed to rethink this. Private jet or a detective's salary.

"Of course, madam. Don't all self-respecting millionaires?"

"When did you get back?" William asked.

"I never left," she answered.

8

After the impromptu interview, they hung around Jeremy's longer than planned Sunday, playing on the dirt bikes and going over the team, the organization and benefits for the department, and William dropped Amanda off a few minutes before midnight. He debated inviting himself in, but ultimately drove home. This way he wouldn't disturb her if a call came in. He crawled between the sheets glad to be getting some rest. William drifted off, thoughts about the organization and Jeremy's proposal floating through. The department pager's chirp woke him. Turning the lamp on, he checked the clock then called the station.

"Detective Harrison," he muttered.

"How long before you and Detective Thompson can get to the University?" he was asked. "There's been a murder similar to the one on Park Street."

"About thirty minutes," he mumbled, thankful he hadn't stayed at Amanda's. He hung up and called James. "Got one my man. See you in ten."

At the U, William and James made their way to a parking garage, surveying the area as they went. Portable lights had been set up at the scene, the normal beehive of activity.

"What do we have?" William asked one of the officers.

"He actually has it set pretty nice," the officer said, leading them inside.

They followed him behind a curtain where the victim was spread out on a roll-a-way. They hadn't exaggerated on the phone. She had been stabbed multiple times and was naked, one leg hanging on either side of the folding bed. One hand had been posed on the inside of each thigh next to her genitalia, framing her. Wide bands of bruising from restraints on her wrists showed dark and ugly against the fair skin. Bits of yellow fibers from the bindings could be seen in the patterned grooves in her skin.

While the crew took pictures William and James inspected the floor, marks where a ladder had been used to string the curtain across catching their eyes. William patted James shoulder and James nodded, pointing to the back wall. A ladder hung four feet off the floor. William dropped his eyes and surveyed the ground. Tracks led from the bed to a storage room near the rear of the three sided structure. William followed the grooves, skirting a tech removing fibers from the girl's wrists, and saw the trash can beside the rear door, a disposable lantern tossed inside. James had walked to the front of the structure, inspecting the ground as he went, talking to a tech examining the roof supports. Once they had completed their initial walk through, William and James joined responding officers going over their observations then returned to the scene.

"We need samples for DNA sequencing sent to the U," William told the men.

"Will do," a tech answered.

Another scan of the interior and William noticed the absence of fresh vehicle tracks. Sweeping the ground once more, a foot print had been marked off, getting ready to be cast. He turned his attention back to James.

"It looks like it would be easier to get caught in here. What are your thoughts?"

"My guess is he knew when the kids would be coming in from classes, or leaving to study, and when others would be coming in from their jobs then he blocked off the parking area." James nodded toward the posts. "He did this quick, clean and between students. They're going to try and gather prints off that lantern and the bed. Maybe the ladder."

"Think they'll find anything?"

"Doubt it. This was too carefully planned. You said Captain Kirby wants us in his office tomorrow. We're gonna have a long day, buddy."

"Today," William corrected him. "It's after six." *'It already has been,'* he thought.

The techs continued their work inside while James showed William the roof supports and the barricade tape stapled to them. The man had covered his bases and covered them well.

By nine forty-five they were at the station getting comfortable in one of the captains' arm chairs, an extra large cup of coffee in hand. Definitely going to be a long day.

"Any new ideas on the girl?" Captain Kirby asked glancing at his watch. "For obvious reasons, I haven't seen any reports, but I'm getting my ass chewed guys. We need something."

"Which girl?" James asked.

The captain scowled and leaned back in his chair.

"We'll get them to you this afternoon," William answered.

"I know. I just want something to give the higher ups."

"This latest girl was alone and the person went to great lengths to keep things hidden," James said. "According to friends, the last time they saw her was approximately ten-thirty last night. Several of them met after dinner, joking and talking about classes and their professors over a beer on the lawn. When they left, she was fine. One of the girls said she looked back to check on her friend and the girl was half way up the stairs to the dorm. He cased the area quite well before he carried out the assault. He took his time and blocked off the parking garage. So far no one admits to seeing anything so we're going to go back and find out if anyone might have seen a stranger or an unfamiliar car."

"We requested the lab take samples of any and all materials from her and send it to the U as well," William added. "It might lead us to someone."

"Anything on the dealers and Olivia?"

"We had our lab send samples of what we found on Park Street and on the clothes off the dudes who OD'd, along with Olivia to the U," William said. The captain nodded. "When the ME did the inspection of the dealer's bodies he found injection points in the armpit. The ME also said the wound on the guys head was two or three days old, which coincides with time of death. One of the street girls was overheard telling someone she saw the car we found on Park Street snugged into the shadows below the dealer's room the night they were killed. She said there were two people in it when it pulled out heading east. One of the residents on Park Street also told us there had been two men in that car when Olivia's body appeared. Our suspicion is, two men stole a car and attempted to work out a deal to take back the product we found in that hidden cubby behind the refrigerator. They met the guys for the deal, injected them with coke leaving them to die. The problem with their plan was they didn't find the product they went in to recoup. We believe that was what we found in the wall cubby."

"And the lady on Park Street?"

"Two men met her at Pearls on Main. Right now it appears that after they completed their appointment, the men killed her, drove her to Park Street and then ditched her body. Unless the man was extremely large, it would have taken two of them to lift her out of the car. We haven't figured out the connection with Olivia or if there is one. The dealer's were killed two days prior to her murder so it might just be one huge coincidence."

James snickered and Captain Kirby smirked.

"Yeah, I know. Also, we received a call from Lloyd. He said they found evidence that someone had covered the interior of the car with plastic. A piece got hung up on the rail to the front seat on the passenger side. We've searched trash bins in and around Trolley Square for any tarps or drop clothes, but haven't found anything."

"Do you think someone wanted it to look like the drug dealers did it?"

"With the car being seen behind the hotel, we're looking into that possibility," James said. "We don't have enough to know anything for sure, and we don't know why they left her body on the street. We are looking at a possible connection between her and the men because we found the business cards from a company out of Reno, Nevada. The purse we found contained make-up, a wallet and a brush. Hair from the brush matches Olivia's. They didn't find any prints in the guy's room, other than the ones left by the drug dealers. The people responsible covered their tracks well, which points to professionals."

9

Amanda stepped out of the shower Monday morning to the phone's ringing. She picked it up, hair dripping, and toweled her mane off, the receiver wedged between her shoulder and her ear.

"Good morning," Jeremy said. "I apologize for disturbing you so early, but I thought we might do that vacation in Lake Tahoe. My cabin is begging for some company."

"Your cabin or you?" she asked, laughing.

"A bit of both I admit," he replied. "What do you think?"

She thought for a minute, debating the wisdom of this trip, but the prospect of getting out of town for a couple of days was enticing.

"This weekend is the commander's dinner and then training starts. It may be our last opportunity for a while," he continued, pushing gently. "We can play on jet skis and nap on the porch."

Amanda cringed inwardly and sighed. "I can do that. I'll just use the guestroom again."

"As you wish. I'll pick you up shortly."

Jeremy hung up and Amanda stared at the phone. Should she call William? She didn't want him to worry if she wasn't home.

She would get dressed first.

Dressed, packed and waiting, she picked up the phone and called the station, leaving William a message. She had just hung up when the phone rang again. It was Jeremy and she strolled over by the balcony, stretching the phone cord to its limit as she gazed out over the grounds.

"How can you call me from the limo?"

"The privilege of money," Jeremy answered. "The limo comes with a satellite phone, but I'm not calling from the limo. I'm calling from the airport. We are flying. I didn't want to waste two whole days."

A half laugh, almost a hiccup, came out and she sucked in her breath, holding it. A black pick-up, no chrome, tinted windows and non-descript wheels had backed into the space across from her apartment. The truck she'd seen at the center. The window rolled down smoothly and she made a mental note that they were electric then a man climbed out and walked under the canopy of trees, leaning against one of them. She surveyed the area, noticing a pair of boots barely visible in the shadow of the same tree.

"Are you alright, my lady?" Jeremy asked, pulling her from her thoughts.

"There's a guy out here I've seen before," she answered. "He's talking to someone, but I can't see the second person."

"Do you remember where you've seen him?"

"No, but I saw the truck outside the center. The day we talked about closing it."

"I should be there in a few minutes."

The line went dead, the man from the truck walking up the side of it, staring directly at her apartment before opening the door. A spasm of panic stabbed at her and Amanda stepped back, even though he couldn't see her. He continued gazing up at the balcony and she moved back one more step then he drove off. She stood frozen, thinking about where she had seen him. The box of the truck disappeared from view and she took a hesitant step forward, glancing under the trees, the incessant beeping of the call being disconnected echoing in her ears. Not finding the boots, she went back to the kitchen and hung up. She took out the pager and keyed in the trucks description and dialed the station, leaving a second message for William. With the organization's help maybe they could find out who it was.

The buzzer blared and she pushed the button to allow Jeremy in. He grabbed her suitcase and they headed out. A short hour and a half later they were driving out of the airport toward Lake Tahoe, Amanda's thoughts still on the black pick-up and those mysterious boots.

It wasn't until they had left the freeway interchanges and started through the hills to Lake Tahoe that she was able to leave those thoughts behind. An hour later Jeremy slowed and they merged onto Highway 28. Amanda scanned the area for black trucks before gazing across the rooftops at the expanse of blue that was Lake Tahoe. It was another twenty minutes before they left the asphalt in Crystal Bay, bouncing up the narrow road to Jeremy's cabin.

"You looked deep in thought," Jeremy said, unloading their suitcases. "Has it anything to do with that truck at your place?"

"Everything," Amanda answered. "I can't get my mind off it. I know I've seen the driver, too. God, I don't want this to start all over again."

"Relax, my lady. I doubt anyone will find you here. Change your clothes and we'll go play on the water. Then we'll see what your request pulls."

They made a quick stop for lunch at one of the casinos then Jeremy rented a boat and they spent the next couple of hours, lounging on deck, playing in the water and staying away from the tourists as much as possible. Tuesday and Wednesday were spent hiking and lazing around his cabin, enjoying the serenity, or jet skiing on the lake. Even though Crystal Bay was a tourist stop, the cabin was quiet. The usual distractions scrubbed away by the trees.

Wednesday night they sat in matching overstuffed chairs, a fire dancing in the fireplace, a gentle breeze blowing through the screens. Amanda took a sip of her wine and realized she hadn't thought of that truck in two days. One of the logs shifted on the fire and she almost spilled her drink.

"You seem a bit tense," Jeremy commented.

"I was thinking about that stupid truck again. I hope what little I gave in that request was enough to find something."

"I have been told they found several trucks that matched that description. They would like to ascertain if you had anything more definite. You know, a license number or a partial license. Even the state the license had been issued in. Black truck, no chrome, is a bit vague." Amanda sighed. "Are you ready to head home tomorrow?"

"No, but we have that dinner Friday night," she replied.

"I'm not, either, but we have training for four to set up and a mysterious black pick-up to track down. I thought we could sleep in, in the morning. We don't have to be at the airport until three o'clock."

She drank the last of her wine then Jeremy took the glass and set it on the counter beside his. When he returned he took her hand, urging her to stand. Amanda stood and he cupped her face in his hands, kissing her softly

"Jeremy."

"What, my lady?"

"You're not playing fair."

"I know. My motives are not always honorable when we are alone."

On their way back to Reno, Jeremy stopped and grabbed them each a soft drink. Amanda pulled her gaze away from the lake, a non-descript black truck nosed in against the front of the building. Jeremy returned as the driver's window slid down. Electric windows.

"I think we have company," she said taking the bottle.

"I saw that," he replied.

Jeremy checked the mirrors and drove out, the truck following three car lengths behind them. Standard surveillance procedure. A mile from the airport, Jeremy exited, parking behind a motel, and pointing to a dusty old Ford beside them. Amanda glided around the front of the car, clicking the door shut after her. Jeremy climbed into the driver's seat as his rental car pulled out, disappearing around a corner. Their luggage would be on the plane when they arrived at the airport. The black pick-up nosed around the opposite corner then followed the rental. Forty-five minutes later, the ground was falling away below them.

By five p.m. they were in Salt Lake City and at Amanda's. Jeremy paged the men, all three of them arriving before seven p.m. The only information William had found on the truck was, there wasn't one matching that description in the state of Utah.

Well," Amanda said. "If it isn't from Utah, that widens the search area. I'll try to get the license number if I see it again."

10

William picked Amanda up Friday, reflecting on the center as they drove. For all the good Jeremy had meant, it had had a much harsher effect on all of them than they could have imagined and he was glad it had closed. His Mama had told him once that we are all our own worst enemies. And from what he'd seen over the years, Mama was right.

Driving through the gates, William was directed to a parking apron, Jeremy walking their direction. Amanda climbed out, a valet taking the car. She surveyed the home and grounds and noticed, even in the stifling August heat they were perfect and her thoughts drifted between what it would be like to live here and what it would take to keep the place up. Then her eyes fell on the roses. One under each window and lined along the front wall like sentinels. She closed her eyes, inhaling the aroma. Spicy, sweet and titillating, a scent for each color, separate and intertwined. Definitely worth the upkeep.

"Miss Amanda, William," Jeremy said. "I am glad to see you. How are you, Amanda? You don't look too well."

"Just nervous, I guess."

"After what Mr. Bonner put you through, I understand. But we are all right here so there is no need to worry. And the commander won't bite."

"This place is huge," Amanda said, changing the subject.

"Yes, it is, madam," Jeremy said.

"So what do we call him? Commander or Mr. Chancellor?"

"That is up to you," Jeremy replied. "He was my commanding officer. For me it's just natural."

"You were in the Army?" she asked remembering him talking about Viet Nam.

"No, madam." Jeremy gave no further explanation. "William, I will take you to the back patio to meet Mr. Chancellor. James and Timothy are waiting. Amanda, wait here. I will return for you."

'Well, that ended that," she thought as the two walked away.

Jeremy dropped William with the men, introducing him to Mr. Chancellor, returning to take Amanda to her room. Amanda took in the hustle and bustle, people scurrying around like ants, the furniture and dance floor being polished to a high gloss for the evening, amazed there had been no collisions. Harsh words came from the back of the house and she realized it was a carefully choreographed chaos.

An inspection of the interior and the pictures hanging on the wall above the stairs, the dower expressions gazing down at them, and she did an involuntary shiver. Why did people always look so angry? Gazing over her shoulder at one gentleman who appeared particularly frightening and Amanda ran into a wheelchair left. Jeremy waited while she maneuvered around it, dropping her at her door then returned to his duties.

While the men strolled the grounds Mr. Chancellor went over their duties, introducing them to his security personnel, the trio of officers automatically reading the men's bearing and stance. They were professionals, not rent-a-cops.

Mr. Chancellor explained that the dinner tonight was meant to assess the team's readiness. What they would be doing required more constraint in certain areas, but the rules weren't as rigid as the departments. At the same time, as officers on the police force, they would have to know where to draw their line so as not to get them or the department in trouble, if that part of their lives were to ever come to light.

"How do we prevent that?" William asked, doubt beginning to surface.

"We have covers in place," Mr. Chancellor replied. "They include everything to keep any ruse going. When you complete the last exercise, Jeremy will go over all of that with you."

Mr. Chancellor volunteered Timothy as parking valet and mid-range security with one of his men. Howard's regular team would patrol the outlying areas since they were familiar with the property. William and James would handle the area closer to the house, and any major decisions, or flack if something went south, would be on William. By three p.m. they were given the rest of the afternoon to check out the grounds, or hang by the pool. Time to acquaint themselves with the area and relax. With a debriefing after dinner, it would be a long night, so rooms had been set aside for the foursome as well. Safety was always the number priority.

With nothing Amanda needed to be concerned about until that evening, she lazed around the pool. She didn't frequent the pool at the apartment complex because someone invariably tried to hustle her.

Part way down the stairs, she ran into Jeremy. Stopping on the step above him, she rested her arms on his shoulders in a loose hug.

"I didn't mean to put you on the spot this morning. I mean, if I did. I'm glad you'll be here tonight." She sighed recognizing the nervous banter. "I just feel a little flustered, I guess."

"It is fine, my lady. Perhaps you are nervous because this will be your first time playing the game."

"Perhaps."

"Yes, madam," was all he could say. Words escaped him.

Then she removed her arms and the moment was gone.

Jeremy followed Amanda with his eyes as she continued down the stairs. Like him, she slipped in and out of this world like she belonged. It was as much an effortless transformation for her as it had become for him. She had that gift. He stopped on the landing to the second floor, and looked down at Amanda stretched out on a lounge chair, remembering that view sans the bikini. He smiled and thought of the irony. He had finally met a woman he wanted to stay with but he was afraid to act. Was it truly his fears about his job or was he just being a closet coward? Tonight was going to be a glorious torture for him.

"Good day, Jeremy," Mr. Chancellor said.

"Commander," Jeremy said, jerking his head around. "You startled me, sir."

Mr. Chancellor chuckled. "I didn't mean to."

Jeremy glanced back outside and noticed Amanda and William had started toward the house then checked his watch. It was time to finish the preparations. Had he really been standing here that long? Excusing himself, Jeremy chanced a glance behind him at Mr. Chancellor.

"You know…" Mr. Chancellor paused, a half smile lifting one corner of his mouth. "Amanda is an extraordinary woman."

Jeremy nodded, moving on down the stairs, taking the time to think about what Mr. Chancellor had said. He was right. Women like Amanda were rare.

Once everything was set, Jeremy made his way to the security office to meet the men, giving them their ear pieces and radios. Making sure all was working properly he smiled as they fiddled with their ties and remembered the feeling. It didn't seem like it had been that many years ago.

The first few times the ties had been torture, but once he'd gotten used to them, he was hooked. Sexy women and large paychecks made the transition easy and over the years he'd earned the reputation for knowing the minute he saw a woman if she would be successful. Then he started working with George and met Amanda. He knew the minute he saw her, she would be the best. There had never been one like her, and there would never be another after her. She had the poise, the grace, the beauty, but she had a stubborn streak that didn't allow her to compromise her values. Still, he had thought if he could break that stubborn streak, he could make her the best. That duplicity of values people talked about. But instead of him breaking her, she had broken him.

Then he discovered how she had come to work for Mr. Bonner and they started planning her escape. Things went downhill from there. One night in her bed and he was lost. And in that industry sampling the merchandise was tantamount to theft. Hearing about it through rumors and innuendos was even worse. On the flip side, to remain with the one who took you down was definitive proof you were holding yourself to a higher standard. Only the best ever graced his arm, and only the best would keep that attention. And that attention hadn't wavered. He was still smitten as Mr. Layton called it.

Now, he had to worm his way back in and Amanda was going to help him. Amanda was the one who had pulled him off that pedestal so Amanda had to put him back on it. Otherwise this venture wouldn't work. He laughed softly. She was the best and she had never even worked the circuit.

Footsteps pulled him out of his reverie and he looked up to see Mr. Chancellor join them.

"Commander, I wasn't expecting to see you here. Are there any issues we need to be aware of?"

"No, no issues. I was just checking to see how everybody was doing. This is their first time working one of these forays, and I didn't want you to scare them off. I know how into propriety you can be."

"Commander," Jeremy said, in mock indignation. "I would never overstep my bounds."

"Yes, you would," Howard said with a laugh. "When we do these dinners that's your job but, as usual, you have everything under control." He smiled and winked at the three. "And don't let the stuffed shirt rub off on you. The name is Howard. Please, do not call me Mr. Chancellor or Commander. I'll see you gentlemen later."

When he'd finished working with the men Jeremy took his position outside Amanda's door. The butler topped the stairs and nodded, Jeremy tapping lightly, a vision appearing. Being her first appearance playing this role Jeremy had decided to show her off in a strapless, burgundy velvet number that clung suggestively to her curves and sported a slit ending just above the left knee. If they were to work this, she had to be able to pull it off which meant the men had to be interested. Tonight would tell. And she had to hold it together.

"Miss Amanda, you take my breath away."

"You're too kind," she replied. "Do you ever miss the jazz club? I miss the dancing."

"All the time," he answered.

She smiled, her lips quivered and she looked down, smoothing some imaginary wrinkle in her skirt.

"This reminds me of that piece they have in the old movies," Amanda whispered. "You know in the southern mansion where the lady of the house is being escorted down the grand staircase to dinner. You know the one I'm talking about."

"Yes, madam."

"Except the dress isn't as big."

"Are you nervous?"

"Terrified," she answered exhaling slowly.

Jeremy nudged her forward. When they stopped at the top of stairs, he checked the guests surreptitiously, several of the men eyeing her appreciatively. All attention was on Amanda. That was what he needed.

Howard made his appearance at the base of the huge staircase. Jeremy chuckled, as they started down, Amanda gliding beside him, her apprehension gone. When they reached the last step and Jeremy handed her off, he made one more pass, gauging the men's interest.

Once the dinner ended and the guests were preparing to leave, Howard led Amanda onto the dance floor then called for the men to join them.

"I would like to give a special thank you to Mr. William Harrison, along with his partners, Mr. James Thompson and Mr. Timothy Johnson, of the Salt Lake City Police Department, for doing such a stellar job," Howard said. "I would also like to thank my long time friend, Mr. Jeremy Hamilton, for allowing me the pleasure of borrowing the gorgeous Amanda Granger for the evening." Howard stepped back and waved Jeremy over, handing Amanda off to him. "I hope to have the pleasure of utilizing their services again."

Several of the guests stopped on their way out and handed Amanda a business card, requesting she call them. She was officially being given the opportunity to step into a wondrous new world, if she was willing to take that leap. She would have Jeremy beside her as navigator in those uncharted waters, and William, James and Timothy along as security.

An hour later they had changed and everyone met in the main dining area again. The staff had been dismissed and Jeremy had made his famous coffee and set out dessert trays. As they seated themselves part of the evening's guest's returned. Jeremy nodded when the four eyed him then took his seat near the commander leaving no doubt as to his position in the organization.

Tonight the group went over Amanda's abduction and the attack at Jeremy's. Most of it was common knowledge, being in the news, but once Jeremy had completed the official rundown, Howard prodded him gently, going deeper.

"Tell us the details. The news left a lot out and everybody on the services board, and in the organization, has heard the rumors. I find it hard to believe. You are the only man with the reputation for never having gotten involved with a victim."

Jeremy gazed around the table in front of the classroom once again. He cleared his throat, stared at his lap then lifted his eyes.

"I had her in my custody one day when Mr. Bonner attempted to accost her. I walked in the door and he was chasing her across the living room." Jeremy explained the rest of the episode and how he had been afraid she might jump from the balcony. "I vowed he would not do that again. To anybody. The contract I signed made her my number one priority. My job was to protect her, even from him. My position with Mr. Bonner died that day."

"That would have been hard to watch," one of the guests said.

Jeremy continued telling them about George moving her to Reno and giving him one day to have her ready for her first engagement. He could hear Amanda fidgeting in her chair, the memories flooding in. He continued to explain about the men from the syndicate and how her ex-husband had bypassed security and Amanda had shot him.

Howard locked eyes with Jeremy's then closed them tilting his head to the right in a half nod, pushing gently.

Jeremy swallowed hard, his heart racing then looked back at the faces of friends and co-workers, all waiting patiently. He hesitated, nervous, uneasy. No one had delved this deep into his personal business before. He locked eyes with Amanda then past her to William, his tongue stuck to the roof of his mouth and attempted to swallow. Everything would be out now. Nothing hidden. Trust. Isn't that what he'd espoused at the retreat? Make yourself vulnerable in front of your peers? When he spoke, his first few words came out halting, choked.

"I'm afraid I fell off that pedestal as hard as one can fall," Jeremy admitted. "I have never in fifteen years met a woman who tempted me. And there have been many who tried. But I could not resist Amanda. And she didn't try. I walked her to her room...." He paused, glanced around the table once more then exhaled deeply. "...and we kissed. And that was all it took. All manly resolve disappeared."

"Backfired, didn't it?" Howard said. "Women like her are a dangerous commodity, Jeremy. Are you sure you're doing the right thing now? Asking her to join this team, I mean. Won't that make it difficult?"

He looked at Amanda, the heat from his embarrassment burning, her face flushed beneath the make-up. Neither of them had expected to be put on the spot like this.

"I take one day at a time." Leave it to Mr. Chancellor to see things one thought they had hidden. He was successful in this business for a reason. "And she is good," Jeremy added. "She is part of the reason we made it out of Reno without being shot."

"Your report mentioned her being as aware as you were of the tail. Put that with her ability to take down an assailant, she does have the beginnings of the necessary skill set."

"Yes, sir," Jeremy said, unsure if he should say more.

Howard stood and scanned the faces around the table.

"If you'll excuse us ladies and gentlemen." He waved for Jeremy and Amanda to stand and led them into the hall. "My intent was not to put either of you on the spot like that so I wanted to apologize. I promise to be more discreet in the future."

Amanda nodded and he sent her back to the group.

"The rest of this will be said in private, Jeremy." Jeremy's shoulders sagged. "Do you think you'll be able to handle this for the rest of your life? What will you do if William steps up and asks her to marry him before you get your head out of your duff? I cannot afford to have any issues pop up if we are in the middle of an operation." He paused, Jeremy gaping. "I'm head of this organization for a reason. Not just because it's my brain child."

"No, sir. But she is the only woman who makes me feel like she does."

"I have never known you to make a bad decision, and I know emotional decisions are the most difficult to make." Howard patted Jeremy on the shoulder. "I hope this doesn't backfire, too, Jeremy." Howard then directed him back to the group, all eyes on Howard as they walked in. "I think we have covered everything. It's time to hear your decision ladies and gentlemen."

11

The following week Jeremy had another meeting with Mr. Chancellor regarding Amanda's training, timing the visit so he would travel back to Cedar City the following Friday, giving him an excuse to stop and see her. He would have liked to take her to Cedar City, but with her singing Friday and Saturday nights it wasn't always feasible.

Pulling in at her apartment, he was surprised to see William's car.

"William have the day off?" he asked when she let him in.

"No. My car's in the body shop. Someone keyed the passenger door. With him and James using the unmarked car, he left his for me. What brings you back to Salt Lake?"

"On my way home and thought I would stop. Are you looking forward to singing this weekend?"

"We're not performing. Eddie told us to take it off. William and James are checking some new leads or something so he'll have the fill handle it. I get to kick around and do nothing."

"How would you like to kick around and do nothing in the pool Saturday and Sunday?"

"I think that's the subtlest hustle I've ever heard." She had grabbed them each a soft drink and sat opposite him at the table.

"I'm glad you like it. If you're not singing, grab your things. I'll kidnap you and hold you hostage in the lap of luxury."

"And what would we do then?"

"Oh, I have a couple of ideas." He smiled as he looked across at her. "We can always start that training. You will need a tad more than the men."

"Actually, that might be a good idea. You said I'd need more than the guys. I can use the guestroom there, too. Let me pack then I'll follow, if you don't mind. I should call William, too. I wouldn't want him to think someone stole his car."

"Perfect. I'll have the men get things set for tomorrow."

Nine a.m. Saturday morning they were in the limo heading for St. George. The huge car glided onto the interstate as Jeremy went over the exercises. What might happen, what would be expected, letting her know any weapons would be loaded with blanks, but the objective was still to keep from being hit.

Inside the building, Jeremy walked her through a Georgian mansion set for a dinner party then they toured a mock-up of a mini-shopping mall, complete with storefronts, restaurants and restrooms, and a loading dock with full pallets of freight. The first exercise would be handling the difficult client, AKA the dinner party.

Once they had dressed, Amanda and Jeremy entered through a rear door into a beautifully appointed kitchen. Stainless steel and copper pans hung above a gas range in the center island, touches of porcelain scattered amid bone china on the immaculate shelves and a dishwasher stood open, its trays near capacity with cooking utensils and paraphernalia. An older gentleman glided in from the hall, introducing them to the staff as he blew out the opposite door to make sure the dining area was being properly set. Amanda eyed

Jeremy, one eyebrow raised in a question.

"That guy takes this serious," she said in a hushed tone. "How pretentious was that?"

"That's what he gets paid for," Jeremy answered. "His sole purpose today will be to step on toes."

"Can we step back?"

"If you do it extremely politely, my lady."

The gentleman breezed back through a few minutes later and made it plain that Amanda would not be aiding Jeremy. That's why he had the wait staff. Amanda would sit at the table with him, hobnobbing with the guests and making him look good.

Amanda stared at Jeremy. Jeremy shrugged. Just before the man dragged her out the door, Jeremy asked to speak with her and left the gentleman waiting impatiently at the entrance to the dining room.

"Jeremy, this man is pissing me off," she said, her voice tense.

Jeremy signaled for her to keep her voice down. "I know, my lady. That's what he is supposed to do. What are you supposed to do? We are playing, remember."

"Keep quiet and be the gracious hostess. And if necessary, open the channel on the pager."

"Correct. I promise to be hovering close by."

Amanda sighed through her nose to control her anger, forced a smile and joined the gentleman, apologizing for the delay. A half a second later, the channel opened on the pager and the party began, Jeremy getting full dialogue.

After the party ended and they'd changed, they were pulled off for a short debriefing then they were given the scenario for the mall. The play would be her and Jeremy doing a quiet afternoon of shopping and maybe dinner until things took a sudden surprise turn. It would be up to her to figure out if it was a robbery, or a terrorist attack, or none of the above. This exercise was designed to learn where Amanda would need the most training.

She nodded and Jeremy saw the eyes.

"Are you going to be alright, Amanda?"

"I don't know. I'm nervous all of a sudden."

"Just repeat – this is only a game," he instructed.

She nodded and swallowed hard. "This is only a game."

"Repeat as necessary, my lady. You must remain calm. Stay in control, or you will have defeated yourself before you even begin. Got it?"

"Yeah, I got it." She bobbed her head and followed Jeremy through the doors repeating Jeremy's mantra.

They stepped inside and Amanda was immediately struck by how much it resembled a normal mall. As they browsed, Amanda joked about the buyers taste, or lack thereof, then the emergency lights came on and alarms sounded. It only took seconds to transform into a full blown panicked stampede. Security personnel arrived on scene, calming the customers and directing them toward the exits, Jeremy nudging Amanda forward. They stopped for a bottleneck just inside one shops doors when she was ripped away from him, corralled by the press of bodies flooding into the hall. Jeremy recognized the momentary flash of anger then she was gone. He faded into the crowded interior of the store, rolling himself outside the staged area and down the rear wall to the monitoring center. It was up to Amanda now.

In the command center, Jeremy watched Amanda through a video monitor as she extricated herself from the mob, pressing her back against a wall then the second button on the pager activated followed by the comm channel. Muffled sounds of a silencer were barely audible above the den then she dropped, something lodging in the wall where she had stood. She jumped up, bolting through double swinging doors and down a narrow corridor. Her lips moved, *'Jeremy, where are you?'*, the sound drowned out by an officer's radio.

"Shots fired! Loading dock, north end. Officers involved. Respond silent!"

"Officer's already enroute," came the response.

She paused, her words loud and clear. "Loading dock, my rear! I wasn't near the loading dock! If you can hear me, Jeremy, I'm heading for the restroom."

"North or south?" Jeremy asked, nodding for another player to start his part of the game. "Give me some direction. I'm in the main hall."

The man disappeared then another dummy round broke into the wall above Amanda's head and she was flying into the receiving area.

"Jeremy! Where the hell are you?"

Wadding ricocheted off concrete as Amanda covered her head and darted for two pallets, squeezing into the space between them.

"Where'd you go?" Jeremy asked.

"Sorry about that," Amanda replied. "Slight change of plans. I'm in the receiving area."

"Which one?"

He read the facial expressions, she was stressed. That is what this exercise was designed to do, but he had to play his part.

"WHICH ONE?" she yelled.

The interior door opened and Amanda closed her eyes, leaning into the pallet, focusing on tracking the intruder by sound. She opened her eyes when he neared the pallet she had hid behind and pulled a small box off the top. He drew closer, his arm scraped the freight, announcing his position. He stopped; she tossed the box in the direction of a pallet ahead of her, the man darting past. Amanda took a deep breath, drifted around the corner and paused before a narrow opening between two more pallets, peering into the gap. The man stood with his back to the stack of boxes as he peeked around the far corner, his gun hand up, firmed against the uneven wall behind him.

Amanda pulled her knife, her wrist flicked, light glinting off metal then she raised her arm and flipped the knife lazily into the space. Light danced as the blade sliced the air, pinning the man's sleeve to the boxes at his wrist. His trigger finger twitched, but Amanda was already beside him, the safety engaged and knife retrieved. She connected with one well placed kick to the groin and he doubled over air exploding out of his lungs, then she grabbed the pistol. He landed on the concrete floor with a thud.

Green lights bathed the makeshift warehouse as the overhead door raised, Jeremy and the facilitators walking in.

"Excellent job, my lady," Jeremy said. "I must remember guns are no match for your skills with a knife. Now time for the debriefing and we will head home."

Back at Jeremy's Amanda was frustrated. The facilitator's weren't happy with the way she had dealt with the mall scenario. They thought it should have been handled in a less lethal manner.

"What do they mean, less lethal? No one was hurt and he was shooting at me."

"He was shooting blanks," Jeremy reminded her. "And the facilitators are not aware of your abilities with a knife. They were concerned because you could have killed the poor man."

"Only if he had moved wrong," she retorted.

"They were actually concerned you had done some damage with that last move."

Amanda shrugged. "I guess he never heard of that situational awareness thing you taught me."

Jeremy smiled and the deep blue eyes danced then he kissed her, and she could only sigh.

"Now, I think we need to work on this stress of yours," he whispered, maneuvering her to his room.

"Jeremy," she breathed, "you are not playing fair again."

"That is the idea."

Jeremy's soft caress roused Amanda the next morning. "The commander called," he whispered as he nuzzled her neck.

"How much trouble am I in?"

"None. As far as he's concerned you did fine. He thinks the facilitator's were jealous. He did suggest you not use the knife when you know it's an exercise. And next time, try not to injure the man. He would also like me to set up the next round of exercises."

"Suggestions noted."

"Good. Now, where were we? Oh, yes, stress management. I believe one more lesson is in order then I'll cook breakfast before you drive back."

12

Amanda left the retreat thinking about the previous days exercises and this proposition of Jeremy's. It was equal parts exciting and terrifying. Earning the money she would collating information for the team was something she had never dreamed of. But that last exercise yesterday had been a little too close to the frightening side to suit her.

Still, those lines on Jeremy's chart haunted her. Women they hadn't reached in time. And the children. That was especially disturbing. Why would anyone, even a parent, kidnap a child? She remembered news broadcasts about several boys reported missing in the Salt Lake City area recently, too.

Flashing lights ahead caught her attention and she slowed her approach, two Utah Highway Patrol cars blocked the freeway. She checked either side, not seeing any damaged vehicles. One of the officers shoved himself off his car and walked toward her. As he drew closer, she noticed the sideways smile, a bit wider than was necessary, his eyes roaming, thumbs hooked over his belt. The good old boy flirt. She looked away, her discomfort screaming. A glance in the rear view, and a truck was coming up behind her way too fast. A look forward at the officer and he had stopped, legs braced as he pulled his weapon. He took aim then hesitated, confusion crossing his face as he locked eyes with her. Amanda took advantage of the pause, aiming the car around the rear of the patrol car. She blew air through pursed lips, and took one more look in the mirror, the truck screaming toward her. This was not looking good. Opening the comm channel, she scanned the road for possible escape routes.

"William how good's your insurance?"

"Pretty good. Please, don't tell me you had an accident."

"Not yet," Amanda replied. "But it looks like that's a definite possibility. I'm going off the pager now. I may be busy so don't expect any answers if you ask any questions."

"Aman…"

"End," she said firmly.

Amanda checked the rear view mirror once again then pushed the gas pedal to the floor. William's car accelerated, but it didn't have the power of the bigger vehicle and the truck was catching her fast. One more look behind her and the pick-up was sliding sideways then metal crunched. She scanned the road ahead seeing the off ramp for Meadow. One more look in the mirror and the truck bounced off the patrol car, barreling toward her, its left front fender mangled.

"Damn!" she exclaimed, reaching for her purse.

She jerked her purse closer, fumbling frantically for the pistol William had given her. She pulled it out, the magazine not seated.

"DAMN IT!" she yelled, Jeremy floating through. '*It's only a game.*' This wasn't a game but, if it helped, she was game.

"It's only a game," she said out loud. Then she repeated it.

Amanda kept her eyes focused on the off ramp, sweeping through her purse with her hand. She found the magazine and propped the gun between her legs, butt side up; barrel pointing to the dash. She flipped the safety off then slammed the magazine into place. Letting off the gas, she picked up the pistol, released the steering wheel and pulled the slide back slotting one in the chamber then flipped the safety on and slid it under her leg.

She veered to her right and sped down the ramp, hoping no one was on that intersecting highway. There was a flash to her right and she hit the brakes, the car beginning a sideways skid. Amanda steered into the slide the first fifty feet then cramped the wheel to the right. The car spun, momentum forcing it toward the base of the ramp, its rear end sliding onto the cross road. Horns honked and tires screeched as she straightened the steering wheel and hit the gas, the tires screaming to gain purchase then she was shooting down the road. More tires screeched and she checked her mirror, the truck following her onto the off ramp.

A scan of the street, as she sped south and she looked to the right, the truck almost at the intersection. She had to get off this main road and ditch him to get back on the interstate heading north. Her brief glimpse of the town from the off ramp had shown nothing that appeared to offer cover. A side street flew past and she hit the brakes, another street coming up fast. All she needed was a garage. Anything bigger than this car. She cramped the wheel to the left, released the brake and let the car slide, straightening the wheels as she skated around the corner.

Heading east, she noticed a church one block ahead on her right. Another check of the mirror and, not seeing the truck, Amanda slowed the car and pulled into the second driveway, continuing to apply the brakes. She coasted the length of the building, easing over a curb and onto the grass behind it. At the opposite corner, she nosed far enough ahead to see the street and waited.

After five agonizing minutes, she inched across a small paved area onto the adjacent street. Driving north again, she paused at the intersection. From here she could see the pick-up and the mangled cop car one block west, both men gesturing wildly. She eased on the gas, not wanting to draw any attention to the car as she darted across the street to make a left at the next intersection, heading west. Back at the main road, the cop car flew by, going north. She waited for what felt like an eternity then pulled out, hoping she was far enough back the cop wouldn't see her.

A half a block north she checked her mirror, the truck moving up behind her, a block and a half back. She cramped the wheel and hit the gas, sliding into a u-turn. Rolling the window down, she held the pistol above the side view mirror, aimed at the radiator. A deafening roar sounded inside the car then steam erupted from under the trucks hood. She readjusted her aim and blew out his right front tire. The truck jerked to the right. Amanda dropped her eyes to the license then readjusted her aim and fired again. The left rear tire went. The driver ducked, the truck drifting to the side of the road. She fired again, her ears ringing, her head throbbing, his rear window now gone.

Amanda jerked her arm in and dodged a vehicle heading north then spun the car back around, speeding past the truck toward the on ramp. The tires screamed as William's car slid around the corner, flying up the ramp. When she topped the ramp and checked the mirror, both patrol cars were gone.

She set the safety on the pistol then laid it on the passenger seat. How hard could it be to drive home without someone causing problems? Two hours later she pulled in at her apartment complex and climbed out, checking the car for damage. It was a little dirty, but she hadn't hit anybody so it was no worse for wear.

Jeremy pulled in four hours later. She'd had a good long soak in the tub and was finishing her second beer when he buzzed.

"What happened? Why did you go off contact?" Jeremy asked. She scowled and he sat down. "So...It looks like you went four-wheeling in William's car. I'm guessing that has something to do with it."

"That about covers it," Amanda replied. She pulled two more beers out of the refrigerator, handing one to Jeremy.

Jeremy sat across the table and listened as she explained her drive home, his frown deepening the more she told.

William and James arrived at nine-thirty and she went over it a second time.

"I wondered where you took William's car four-wheeling," James said, laughing.

Amanda scowled and crinkled her nose; James held his hands up in mock surrender.

"Forget I said anything."

13

Jeremy spent the next few days interfacing with Howard, making sure things were ready for the trip to Reno. Once the men gave Jeremy the date, everything would be set.

James and William talked to Captain Kirby having few doubts they would be allowed the leeway, now that it wouldn't go on the department's expense account and they would be chasing leads, but they still had their concerns. They wouldn't be available if their rapist struck again. It was nerve-wracking not wanting to push the edge of that envelope.

Timothy was low man with less time in, but he mustered his courage and approached Captain Ohlmet. Once they had been given the go ahead, James and Timothy called Karen and Janice with the itinerary so they could make the necessary arrangements then they notified Jeremy.

Thursday morning, the group climbed into the limo and headed for Reno, Janice and Karen to follow Friday afternoon in Jeremy's jet. Upon arrival Amanda and the men were whisked to Jeremy's floor amid heavy security. The Chief of Police and two of Reno's detectives arrived Friday morning.

Going over Reno's information, they learned that a former Las Vegas muscle man, who had been fairly high up in Las Vegas' hierarchy, Glen Tortino, and a hooker named Katie Landry, AKA Loretta Storey, moved to Reno, but both had skipped town when Reno started investigating suspected syndicate muscle men for murder and racketeering. And that was when rumors had started, saying they moved to Salt Lake City, working under the Bonner umbrella. But, where George had broken ties with the syndicate, his nephew, Jonathan, had started actively courting the syndicate, his base of operations still unknown. This was where both police departments were focusing their efforts now. Were Katie and Glen really working for the Bonner's in Salt Lake City. If so, in what capacity?

Waiting in the lobby after the officer's had left, Amanda was nervous. Private jets. Limos. His own floor at the hotel. It was all overwhelming for her, but Jeremy treated it as casually as buying an ice cream cone. Once Karen and Janice arrived, everyone was ushered into the elevator, emerging on Jeremy's secured floor. Jeremy introduced them to a girl who didn't look much older than they were, ignoring their shocked expressions.

"Ladies, this is Melody," he said. "She will show you to your rooms. Lay out your attire for our outings and generally take care of all of your needs. Once you have had a chance to freshen up, she will direct you to the drawing room. I need to speak with everybody prior to tonight's foray. Now, if you'll excuse us." He did a half bow then turned, leading the men down the hall. "We have some things that need to be addressed before this evening. I want no misconceptions about anything."

"This is your gig," William said. "We trust you completely."

"Thank you, sir." Closing the door Jeremy directed them to the seating area where fresh coffee had been set out. "When we do these exercises you may hear background chatter. It will be the facilitators and players giving their signals. It should not bleed over or be loud enough to disrupt us, but if it is, notify me and we will cut the exercise short and reschedule. Any question so far?"

The men shook their heads.

"Okay, with the syndicate possibly becoming involved with the Bonner's once again, I would like to reintroduce Amanda. This was not part of the original exercise, but I want everyone aware of what might happen. Especially if we need to play it down the road. With that said, things may appear quite intimate. I may even join Amanda in her room. For appearances sake," he added quickly. "We have adjoining rooms for that reason. We can slip into our respective rooms without anyone being the wiser that way. Whoever our target is has to believe we are a couple. There can be no mistakes. I cannot stress that enough. I have already gone over the possibility with Amanda following the exercises in St. George."

"I appreciate the warning," William replied, understanding Jeremy would push those limits farther than he had said. It was part of this game they were now playing.

The next hour was spent working on a plan in case things went wrong. None of them wanted any confusion if things went south. It would be too late then to make that call.

At eight p.m. they pulled up to the restaurant, Amanda smiling at Karen and Janice. This was not the atmosphere they had grown accustomed to. The valet rushed out, Amanda remembering her initial entrance here. Her debut with Jeremy. So long ago and still so fresh in her mind. That was the night she had learned his name. He would no longer be addressed as 'Mr. Tudor'.

"Jeremy!" the maître d exclaimed, greeting them. "I'm so glad to see you and your beautiful Amanda again. It has been much too long since she graced our establishment. I have a premier booth waiting for you and your party."

He eyed William curiously, recognizing the stance.

"Things have changed since we were here last," Jeremy said noticing the look. "There are those who think Amanda would do better with them."

The maître d nodded. "Of course, sir."

"If my other guests come in," Jeremy continued, directing his gaze to the remainder of the group, "at any time, they are to be treated with the utmost attention. Remember them."

"Yes, sir," he said. "We will endeavor to remember them."

"You *will* remember them, I am sure," Jeremy said in warning. "You did not earn your reputation for being the best by forgetting things."

The maître d nodded again, took their drink orders then bowed, William standing discreetly to the side.

"Did I catch the hint of a threat in that last statement?" James asked.

"One does what one needs to," Jeremy replied.

James looked at William and raised an eyebrow. William lifted a corner of his mouth in a half smile and did a slight shrug. Jeremy carried more clout than he let on.

As on Amanda's previous visit, the atmosphere was relaxed and unhurried, dinner was heavenly and dessert over the top, and they quickly found the time had flown. Jeremy pulled a card from his wallet and the waiter rushed over, grinning broadly as he scurried away.

It was mere seconds before he trotted back, bowing as he handed Jeremy the card. Jeremy thanked him and they stood to leave, the limo gliding to a stop when they exited.

At the jazz club they greeted Jeremy as enthusiastically as at the restaurant, being given the same speech. Once they were seated, Amanda understood the location of Jeremy's table. It allowed him a view of the entire establishment while affording any attending security personnel room to maneuver.

Once drinks had been ordered Jeremy checked on William.

"Is the background noise disruptive?"

William shook his head.

"Are you ready then? Remember you have that pager. If you see anything, let me know."

William smiled then lifted a hand, directing Jeremy back to the table and resumed his stance.

The next song started and Jeremy stood, offering Amanda his hand. "Excuse us, ladies and gentlemen. You are going to see Miss Amanda in action." Leading her onto the dance floor, he leaned closer, talking quietly. "I have already warned you and William I will be pushing the limits tonight. Are you ready?"

"If you think it's necessary."

"You are on."

Jeremy took a step back, raised Amanda's hand to shoulder height and directed the men's gaze to her. He did a half bow then pulled her close. As they glided across the dance floor, Jeremy continued scanning, waiting for the exercise to begin. He had heard an order to delay the execution, but nothing since. This was not normal. He took a quick look at William, alert for any signs that something might be amiss, but William was maintaining his stance, dividing his attention between them and the room.

They returned to the table and Jeremy switched his pager to the secure channel requesting status of the planned activity then turned back to the group, seating Amanda.

"Please, feel free to dance," Jeremy told the others. "We are here to enjoy ourselves."

"Excuse me, Jeremy," someone said from behind him. "You wouldn't keep this exquisite creature all to yourself tonight, would you?"

"Mr. Layton," Jeremy said. "I had no idea you would be here."

"Word moves quickly through the grapevine," Travis said. "I had my doubts, but I noticed you introduce her and had to avail myself of the opportunity. I may be an old man, but I'm not dead." He bowed, offering Amanda his hand. "Would you care to dance?"

"Of course," she answered, caught off guard by the remarks. "I didn't know you liked jazz."

"There are a lot of things no one knows about me," he replied with a chuckle. "Jeremy hasn't made it to the husband status yet, has he?"

"No, sir." Amanda laughed, shooting Jeremy a curious glance.

Jeremy shrugged, a puzzled look in his eyes. More questions about Mr. Travis Layton.

"I will do my best to sway your affections then," Travis said. "Do the ladies like to dance? I'm sure your card – as it were – will be full. Especially the way Jeremy just presented you."

"Thank you, Mr. Layton," she replied, glancing in Jeremy's direction, confused. "You need to ask my friends."

"Travis," he said, correcting her once again. "Please, call me Travis."

"My apologies. Travis."

Travis proved to be a good dancer and Amanda followed his lead easily, even though he held her tighter than she cared for. Travis did a spin, the move bringing a booth with a man and three women in it, into view. She glanced back at the table, Jeremy and William lost from sight in the crowd. She exhaled slowly then looked to the booth, two men in it now, both eyeing her intently. Travis dipped his chin, one of the men leaned back and nodded, pulling the woman next to him closer. Travis tightened his grip, working them toward the booth.

"There is someone you need to meet," Travis whispered.

"I don't think I want to talk to him," Amanda replied.

One more scan of the dance floor and the crowd had parted enough she saw Jeremy and William coming toward them.

"It's not what you think," Travis said. "He isn't interested in another lover. His only interest is this new business of Jeremy's."

"Then he needs to talk to Jeremy."

Amanda did a mock curtsy, pulling out of Travis' grasp and running into the couple behind them. A nervous laugh and she maneuvered to her left putting the couple between her and Travis.

William grabbed one arm, Jeremy the other, and they started for the table. Both men scanned the room, their stance more alert. Jeremy pushed a button on the pager and his lips moved, but nothing could be heard over the music. Alarmed, Amanda glanced toward the table. James and Timothy's posture had changed. Then they were beside the table. Travis suddenly materialized beside them, giving Jeremy his apologies for any misunderstanding. William stepped forward, yanked Travis back with one arm, jerking Amanda toward him with the other.

Flustered, Amanda looked away as Timothy grabbed Karen and Janice, laying them on the floor, one hand in the center of each woman's back. He leaned forward and whispered in their ear. Both women nodded then Timothy straightened up, spun and went down.

Jeremy was talking again, his lips moving rapidly, agitated, his countenance a mix of anger and confusion. Behind him, Travis appeared shocked. William switched Amanda into the crook of his left arm and turned to face the stage. She followed his gaze two men stepping from behind a stage curtain, weapons raised. The music stopped and women screamed, pandemonium taking over, people racing for the exits. William and Jeremy pulled their pistols the smell of burnt gunpowder filled the air then the gunmen jerked, stumbling off the stage. Something flashed in the corner of Amanda's eye as James sprinted across the dance floor, dodging patrons and skipping around clusters of bodies in an intricate ballet. Then Jeremy knelt beside Timothy. William's hold loosened and a heavy bump sounded behind her. Jeremy laid

Karen's hand over the cloth on Timothy's wound, pushing past Amanda to where William lay unconscious.

This wasn't how this was supposed to go. They were supposed to work with Jeremy, not die before they started. It was only a training exercise. See what they needed to work on, 'if' they worked an operation. Emphasis on the word 'if'. But it had just turned real.

"William!" Amanda exclaimed.

James returned to the group, Jeremy jerking his chin toward the entrance.

"It's alright, Amanda," Jeremy said. "We'll see you at the hotel."

Amanda nodded absently, staring first at William and then the chaos surrounding them, feeling as though she should be doing something, her mind locked, her feet refusing to move.

James rushed the girls to the waiting limo, Jeremy ripping William's jacket and shirt open and unhooking the bulletproof vest, a spread of blood a quarter of an inch below where the vest had stopped. Jeremy grabbed one of the waitresses, taking a dry towel off her tray and laid it over the growing stain on William's abdomen. Sirens broke through, drawing closer. Then James was leading her away.

Outside, Amanda grabbed the limo door and watched police and emergency personnel hurry inside. One of the patrolmen climbed out of his car, their eyes locking. She had seen the eyes. But where? More police arrived and that officer was jostled to the back. A memory of the black pick-up crashed in and she gasped. Then paramedics rushed William out, Jeremy climbing into the ambulance with him, Timothy being escorted to a police cruiser.

"NO!" she yelled, clawing at James and the driver to reach William before they shoved her into the back and the limo's door closed, allowing it to pull away from the crowd.

"Amanda!" James said sternly. "Don't ever fight us like that again! Got it?"

"James...."

"No!" he said. "When we're trying to get you to safety, you do not fight! You could have got yourself or one of us killed!"

Amanda's fists clenched, her mind screaming. William had been shot and they expected her to remain docile and quiet?

Anger flashed in James eyes, his nostrils flaring as he stared at her, issuing the challenge. Her eyes narrowed as she prepared to hurl a response at him. The limo pulled in at the hotel, the staff waiting to escort the group upstairs so they could secure the floor, and Amanda backed down.

Jeremy and Timothy arrived, Timothy's arm bandaged and in a sling. Nothing serious. Just enough to burn like hell and bleed profusely.

"Jeremy, this was supposed to be a training exercise," Amanda said. "If we worked an event! If, Jeremy, if." She stressed the word 'if', repeating it like a powerful mantra, her breathing coming in short gasps. "Nothing was supposed to happen!"

"I know, Amanda," Jeremy replied. "Let's try to calm down, please...."

"Calm down?" Then she was swinging. All the anger, the fear, the confusion – all of it behind the one blow.

Jeremy caught her fist, holding her while she sobbed. She had to control the emotions. This would be her weak point.

"You have to continue to trust me."

She nodded, her cheek rubbing his chest, her tears warm through his shirt, her shampoo feminine and soft. He closed his eyes and inhaled her perfume, resting his head on hers. She would be his weak point.

"In the morning we will go over everything in more detail, okay?"

14

After Amanda pulled herself together and they had changed, the group climbed into the limo for the ride to the hospital. William was out of surgery and resting comfortably in ICU when they arrived. Even though it wasn't of his doing, Jeremy felt responsible. Standing to the back of the group, the antiseptic odor and sterility of the room, reminded Jeremy of a place many years removed and he rubbed a scar on his abdomen absently.

The elephant grass had served double duty that day. It had concealed them and the Viet Cong. Jeremy had been reprimanded many times for hanging too far back, but that day it had worked to their advantage. The platoon the government had embedded him in for travel had walked right past the enemy not even knowing they were there. From his vantage, Jeremy witnessed the enemy soldiers slip out of their positions and alerted those ahead of him. In the ensuing firefight a bullet struck him and he had almost died. He had been given a stern talking to, but it had been a formality. Without Jeremy in the position he had been in, the entire platoon would have been lost.

Jeremy came back from the memory, listening as Amanda and

William talked, James poked fun at William and Timothy and the girls teased one another. A familiar warmth flooded his body. A rush he hadn't felt in some time. He was on the hunt again, but now he had to keep more than just himself informed and alive. For a second the weight felt heavy on his shoulders. He exhaled softly and pushed those thoughts aside.

He smiled as William grasped Amanda's hand and thought about her involvement. The thought excited him and terrified him. She was good, albeit raw. He couldn't let anything happen to her. Just like Amanda earlier, he had to rein his emotions in. They would cloud his judgment.

Jeremy checked the clock, his mind replaying the evening going over possible reasons for the exercises delay. He had still heard nothing. He was certain Mr. Layton had had nothing to do with the ambush. He'd appeared as shocked as the rest of them, but he was curious as to why the older man had been attempting to lead Amanda off the dance floor. Jeremy shifted his gaze from the clock, locking eyes with William.

William smiled. "Damn, Jeremy, I thought you said this was only a training exercise. I don't think I like your instructional video."

"My apologies," Jeremy replied. "I will make sure to rewrite the script."

"Any idea who's responsible?"

"Not yet, sir. We're working on it."

"So, does this happen every time you go somewhere? Because I don't know if I want Amanda doing this on a regular basis. I don't want to do this on a regular basis."

William tried to raise his hand, but it dropped to the sheets. He was tiring. Jeremy checked the clock again. They had been here almost four hours.

"I will endeavor to remember the next lesson must have less

drama, sir."

A nurse appeared and Jeremy nodded his understanding.

"We need to cut this short," Jeremy said. "They broke the rules allowing us in, and William needs to get some rest. We will return."

"Take care of the beautiful lady, Jeremy."

"James and I will do our best, sir."

Amanda gave William a kiss on the cheek, a flutter of jealousy making its appearance. Jeremy put it down. They had no time for that.

"I'll be back soon," Amanda whispered.

"Promise?" William asked.

"Promise."

While they waited for the elevator, the men reviewed the prior evening. Even with their preparation, things had gone south faster than they could have dreamed. They climbed into the limo while Jeremy keyed in a follow up request for new information on recent syndicate activity. Something was being overlooked.

By the time they made it back to the hotel exhaustion had set in and Amanda had fallen asleep. Jeremy roused her, escorting her to her room then detoured to his. Amanda changed clothes and climbed into bed, Jeremy entering through the connecting doors, a glass of wine in each hand.

"I thought you might like to talk for a few minutes," he said.

"Sit down," she said patting the mattress. She took a drink and sighed then sat her glass on the stand, scooting under the covers.

Walking around the bed, Jeremy set his wine on the night table and sat down.

"I want to apologize for earlier," she said. "I was just stressed, I guess. Stressed and scared. I understand the need for training now." She giggled and snuggled up close. "I was a basket case last night. That isn't good."

"It has been a difficult couple of days," he said. "I want to apologize, too. This isn't what I had in mind."

"I know. This isn't what you meant by hostess, either."

"You are correct, my lady," he said, chuckling.

He lay down on top of the bed by her, her soft even breathing coming from beside him. She was already asleep. He brushed a strand of hair off her cheek, pulling the bedspread over him, as exhausted as her.

Jeremy kissed her forehead and smiled, and thought about what he had involved her in. He didn't want her hurt, but he had signed her onto a team that could possibly get her killed.

"Amanda," he whispered. "I don't ever want to see anything happen to you."

15

A soft tap on the door woke Jeremy. He stumbled around the half wall and opened it to James and Karen's surprised stares, Janice and Timothy walking up behind them. Still disoriented, he did an unconscious look down to see he was clothed. At least he hadn't answered the door in his skivvies. Then he remembered he was in Amanda's room and stepped back so they could enter.

"Please," he said. "What time is it?"

"It's almost ten," James answered.

"Ten?" Jeremy asked, his body tensing. How had he slept that long? "P.M.?"

"A.m.," James said. "We were wondering how Amanda is."

"She's fine," Jeremy answered. "I didn't feel her move all night. I didn't mean to fall asleep on top of the covers, either."

"You're fine," James said. "No need to explain. We were all tired."

"Jeremy," Amanda said as she sat up and clutched the covers, "I thought I heard James."

"They stopped to check on you," he replied. "Get up and dress and we'll eat breakfast then spend the day with William."

Amanda nodded, Karen handing Amanda her robe.

"Now, if everyone will excuse me," Jeremy said. "I need to clean up. Janice, while I'm gone can you help Amanda work on her make-up? I don't want the nurses to think she is the patient when we arrive."

Amanda picked up a pillow, hurling it across the room at him.

"I was just kidding," he said, laughing as he ducked the feather projectile.

Amanda padded to the shower, gazing in the mirror at eyes – red and bloodshot – staring back at her and sighed. William and Jeremy were going to be the death of her. This team might not have been such a good idea.

After she'd showered and dressed she stared at her reflection, the doubt disappearing. They were doing the right thing. They had to help those women. And the kids. She didn't want to see more kids disappear or go through what she had – or worse.

Melody appeared at the door and told them, per Jeremy's instructions; breakfast would be served in the drawing room.

They walked in, Jeremy waiting, looking every inch the gentleman they had come to know. Part way through their meal, Melody reappeared.

"Excuse me," Melody said. "There's a Travis Layton here to speak with you."

"Please, show him in. Will you bring more coffee, as well?" Jeremy stood to greet Travis and shook his hand, an uneasiness creeping into his core. "I'm glad to see you are doing alright, sir. What brings you here this morning?"

"May I?" Travis asked, pointing out a chair.

"Oh, by all means," Jeremy said. "I fear I am being remiss in my duties."

"No, you're fine, Jeremy. Except for a few bruises, I'm good. William moves with amazing speed. I just wanted to check on everybody. How are you doing, Amanda?"

"Thanks to William, I'm fine."

"Maybe I should have been here sooner." Travis sat beside her, patting her knee, Amanda surprised by the move. "I could have enjoyed breakfast with a beautiful woman."

"Mr. Layton," Amanda said. "I'm flattered."

"I came over because I have a business proposition for your team," Travis continued, giving her knee a playful squeeze. "First I have a couple of questions, if you don't mind."

Amanda gently removed his hand, eyeing Jeremy.

"We are not able to answer for William," Jeremy replied, noticing both gestures, "but go ahead."

"Obviously," Travis replied. "How many people are on your team?"

Amanda and the men sat up straighter, more alert.

"I'm not sure if you would call it a team. We were kicking around the idea of starting a party planning service. There would be the three of us..." Jeremy nodded at James and Amanda. "....plus William and Timothy."

"So, these other beautiful ladies...."

"Were guests. They just happened to get lucky."

"The other gentleman seems to have some good instincts. He moved the ladies without hesitation or instruction."

"That's why he's working with us, sir. What's this business proposition?" Jeremy didn't want to push, but his unease was growing exponentially.

"How do you intend to run this business?" Travis glanced at Amanda as he talked, ignoring Jeremy's question, his eyes roving. "Were you intending to work your business in the same manner as the other stables?"

"No, Mr. Layton. There will be no stable and no extra-curricular activities. Amanda is not a call girl. I will make all the arrangements, Amanda will help and act as a hostess. William and

I are security. For larger affairs, we would pull in James and Timothy. After last night, we have a few kinks to work out."

"Call me," Travis said, kissing Amanda's hand. "I throw dinner parties quite frequently and she would be the perfect companion. For the other part of this proposition. I purchased Mr. Bonner's property here in Reno. The one where you and Amanda got things together? I need someone with good connections who would be able to make use of it from time to time. Perhaps when they are in town for an engagement? Do you think you're up to the challenge, Jeremy?"

"Most definitely," Jeremy said, eyeing the older gentleman, his discomfort crashing through the roof. "I love a good challenge. I thought that belonged to Mrs. Bonner."

"A play by George," Travis answered. "Our attorneys got to the bottom of that quite easily."

Eyebrows shot up around the table and Jeremy nodded, noting the phrase, *'Our attorneys'*.

Travis tipped Amanda's chin up and leaned in as if to kiss her, Amanda backed away.

"I will talk to William when he is up and about," Jeremy said, standing to escort Travis out if necessary.

"Please do. I look forward to working with you. Now, I must be going. Have a good day."

All eyes followed Travis as he strolled out then returned to Jeremy.

"That was a little formal, wasn't it?" James asked.

"Yes, and no," Jeremy said. His body shook and he closed his eyes, taking a deep breath, calming himself before looking back at the group. "We are on our way, if we choose to continue. I am curious about some of the comments he made, however. You look like you're thinking about something, James. What is it?"

"Don't know," James answered. "His voice sounds familiar.

But I haven't met him that I know of."

"Perhaps from the retreat. He was there for lunch."

"Maybe," James replied, shaking his head. "No, it was before that…. I think…. I'll remember."

"This isn't going to be the norm, is it?" Karen asked.

"My sentiments exactly," Janice chimed in. "I don't want my man coming home all bandaged up every day. Huh-uh!"

"I don't believe last night had anything to do with any of this," Jeremy responded. "I hope to have some answers when we get back to Salt Lake City. People are already working on it for us."

Jeremy's pager vibrated and he checked the screen, James and Timothy giving him a questioning look.

"So, who do you think is doing what?" James asked.

"I am not sure. I could be wrong, but something isn't right. It is just too much coincidence. Ladies will you excuse us, please?" Jeremy glanced from Karen to Janice, waiting until they had left, before turning back to Amanda. "Amanda, what did Mr. Layton say to you last night? Before he tried to steer you off the dance floor."

"He said there was a gentleman who wanted to talk about this business of yours. I told him to talk to you. Who were those men on stage?"

"I don't know, but I don't think Mr. Layton had anything to do with that."

"I thought Howard had men following the exercise," Timothy said. "Make sure we're working like we're supposed to."

"There were. And the exercise didn't even get started."

"Is that who you were talking to?" Amanda asked.

"Yes. They put a delay on the exercise and then it never resumed. It would be advisable for us to up our game. Watch our backs closer. I would like you gentlemen to think about what Mr. Layton just said. His proposition. Get back with me at a future date and we'll go over it. Something is feeling off."

James and Timothy nodded then Amanda stood, shaking her head.

"Let's go see William," Amanda said. "I've heard enough for one day. Mr. Layton almost got shot last night and he comes over today to talk about business. You men are insane."

16

They arrived at the hospital and James told William about Travis' business proposition only to be smacked in the back of the head.

"Ouch!" James exclaimed, "What are you hitting me for?"

"William isn't even out of ICU," Amanda scolded him. "It can wait!"

"Quit beating on our partners," William said.

Amanda lifted her hand and James ducked.

Jeremy decided, instead of reprimanding James, he would let Amanda handle it, and laughed to himself.

"Are you serious?" Amanda asked. "You just got shot, and you're listening to James talk about work?"

"Yep," he said. "James, I gotta question for you."

"Anything, buddy. Fire away."

"Who does Mr. Layton sound like? I've heard his voice before. Have we met him someplace? Other than the retreat?"

"I was thinking the same thing. But I don't remember."

"Gentlemen," a nurse said, poking her head in the door. "The patient needs his rest. You can come back tomorrow."

"Keep her safe," William said.

"We'll do our best, sir," Jeremy replied.

Dusk was just beginning to feather the clouds when they stepped off the elevator and climbed into the limo, Jeremy locked away in his own thoughts. Between the events at the club and Mr. Layton, he wasn't getting a good feeling.

After a quiet dinner at a small restaurant, they rode back to the hotel, Jeremy offering Amanda his arm and walking her to her door. He kissed her on the forehead, hung the 'Do Not Disturb' sign out then closed it behind them and turned the deadbolt. He slipped past her, patting her on the behind as he went.

"You are an extraordinary woman, Amanda."

"Thank you. You're one of a kind yourself," she answered as he exited through the adjoining door.

Amanda closed the curtains and scanned the room, taking note of the short half wall that ran straight ahead dividing the seating area from the sleeping area, the adjoining door into Jeremy's room on the wall to her right. Her eyes swept to her left, past the bed and stand on either side of the headboard to the door into the bathroom. She gauged the distance to the door, gave a single nod to the room and changed clothes. Turning the light out, she climbed into bed, cocooning herself in the covers.

A click woke Amanda and she looked at the clock. Three a.m. Then the connecting door closed. Jeremy checking on her. She awoke again and glanced at the clock. Five a.m. She reached for the blanket where it had slid off her shoulder then a rattle, like a footstep on the fire escape, sounded and she froze but heard nothing more. Someone pulled the blankets up and kissed her on the cheek. Jeremy again. But that wasn't what she'd heard. She peered over her shoulder as Jeremy stopped in front of the window, checking outside then continued back to his room. She clutched the blankets tighter and listened. Hearing nothing,

Amanda drifted off again then metal screeching on metal grated her ears. The curtains parted and a man stepped into the room between her and the connecting door. She shot from under the covers, bolting for the bathroom door, tripping on the blanket.

Air blasted out of her lungs as she sprawled face first on the carpet then she was rolled onto her back, shadowy images of a man holding a gun coming into view. She arched her back, shoving him off and attempted to stand. He grabbed her leg, pulling her back down. Amanda twisted, kicking with her free leg, striking something solid. The 'thub' of a silencer echoed in the room, her side on fire, her toes screaming. She yanked her ankle from the man's grasp and hobbled through the bathroom door. Flinging the door shut, she turned the lock her body in freefall then her head collided with the tile and everything went black.

The shriek of the window brought Jeremy off the bed. No conscious thought. Automatic response. He grabbed his weapon racing for the connecting door then the muffled 'thub' of a silencer came through. He checked the clock as he flew by. Five-thirty. A door slammed and he threw the connecting door open to the clatter of boots on a fire escape. Amanda's bed was empty, a dark stain on the carpet near the bathroom door. He ran past the window, glimpsing a man sprinting across the rooftop below.

"AMANDA," Jeremy called. He shook the door, finding it locked then dashed for the phone to call James. "I need you at the hospital with William. Someone has been in Amanda's room. Take the limo, and tell the driver to wait."

Jeremy hung up and darted to the window, a man swinging himself over the parapet on the south side of the building. Jeremy leveled his pistol, aiming through the open window and fired. The man jerked, but maintained his grip, clamoring out of view. Jeremy fought the urge to follow, racing back to the phone to call security and Timothy.

"What's happening?" Timothy asked sleepily.

"I need you in Amanda's room," Jeremy ordered. "Someone's been here."

It took less than two minutes for Timothy and hotel security to convene in Amanda's room followed closely by police and paramedics. Security unlocked the door, Jeremy shoving it open to find Amanda unconscious on the floor, blood from a wound on her side pooled on the tile. Jeremy grabbed a towel and slid it under her gown, applying pressure to stop the bleeding. A smear of blood on the floor showed where she had slipped, knocking herself unconscious as she landed. She woke when paramedics lifted her onto a gurney.

"How are you doing, my lady?" Jeremy asked.

"I hurt," she answered. "I thought you said something about a training exercise. Dinner and dancing for two nights, your treat. I don't like your idea of a treat."

"Objections noted," he answered.

"Is William okay?" she asked, still dazed. "God, my head is killing me."

"James should be with him." Jeremy looked up to see Timothy already examining the room. "Timothy, have the police check for anything on the roof or the fire escape to the south, please. The intruder is wounded. Do not allow anybody to touch anything in this room, except for the forensics team until I get back."

James threw his clothes on and raced for the stairs. He didn't have time to wait for the elevator. At the hospital he was out of the limo, sprinting for the elevator before the car came to a complete stop. On the floor for the ICU, the elevator lurched to a stop, James shouldering his way out dashing for William's room and hoped no one had beaten him here. William couldn't even defend himself.

Flying up the corridor, he skated around the corner, a nurse approaching a man staring into William's room. James pulled his pistol and took aim, bracing himself against the wall.

"DROP!" James yelled.

How Hollywood did that sound? Of course, this whole thing was feeling a bit like Hollywood. Then the nurse hit the floor. The man ignored James and pulled a pistol, aiming at William. James pulled the trigger and dived for the corner, hearing a wet thud. Alarms screamed, there was a muffled shot then glass shattered. James poked his head out as another 'thub' echoed down the hall and dust exploded from the wall in front of him. He dodged back, sweeping the chalk out of his eyes then peeked around the corner again. The man was staggering for the stairs, a red blossom growing on the back of his coat, the nurse hurrying after him. Keeping him alive had become her focus.

"NO!" James ordered. "I don't want you becoming a victim. Stay here!"

She backed up, nodding nervously, a second nurse already on the phone to security.

"Check the patient in that room." James pointed to William's room as he ran. "Make sure no one has reached him."

He pulled his badge out, hanging it over his belt. The last thing he needed – the police thinking he was the lunatic.

James raced past the nurses' station, telling the nurse to advise security there was an injured man in the stairwell, wearing a lab coat, blue jeans and dirty sneakers, and should be considered armed and dangerous. Wide-eyed, she nodded and relayed James message. James pushed the door to the stairs open, boots and barked orders sounding below as security and police rushed into the space.

A smear of blood on the wall marked the man's path. James bolted up the stairs after him, using the interior wall for cover. It wouldn't stop a bullet, but it would shield him from view. Peeling around the last section of wall and crawling up the steps James discovered the man collapsed on the landing to the top floor. Police piled in behind him then James squeezed his way out of the crowd, rushing for William's room. He hurdled down the stairs, using the handrails like a Jungle Jim, one of the officers trailing him. They found William alive and being chastised by a nurse while she bandaged his side.

William told James and the attending officer, he heard a shot and woke to a gun pointing at him. Instinct kicked in and he rolled over the bedrail, dropping to the floor which set off the alarm on every monitor attached to him.

Jeremy trotted into the emergency room beside Amanda an officer following. In the exam room, the officer went over what had happened in her room, smiling as he took notes. Jeremy had to turn away to compose himself when she told the officer she may have shot herself without being armed. She kicked and struck something hard, the man's pistol going off.

After Amanda's surgery, Jeremy checked on William then left James to watch the two and returned to the hotel.

"Find anything?" Jeremy asked when he joined Timothy.

"The lock on the window has been jimmied," Timothy said, tapping the top the sash. "There's blood on the parapet and the fire escape, but they haven't found the suspect. I'm wondering why Amanda. Is it possible they had their rooms mixed up?"

"Possible. It still doesn't give us any answers as to the why or the who."

17

Two weeks later, James, Timothy and their ladies, had flown back to Salt Lake City, and William was being released from the hospital. Ten o'clock on a Thursday morning the trio climbed into the limo bound for Salt Lake City, William and Jeremy laughing about Amanda's misadventure in shooting herself without being armed. She slapped at them playfully then got comfortable for the long ride home.

Amanda sat on the rear facing seat, the desert flying by, the engine purring at an easy ninety-five. Jeremy and William talked, while Amanda rewound the previous weekend and the lunch with Travis Layton. He had contacted Jeremy, with Jeremy's security measures in place. How? Her mind raced, remembering the way he had examined her, looking for imperfections. A memory of George making the same move when she had met him the previous year wriggled through. Men on the prowl or men on the hunt? On the hunt for the next piece of property? The next means for making money? She tried to dismiss that thought, not at Mr. Layton's age, but it remained firmly wedged in its crevice.

The events of the last few weeks flashed through on instant

replay. They joined the team. Travis called Jeremy. They meet Howard and go to Reno. She had no proof of anything, but her senses, honed from years on the streets, could feel a draft. There were a few too many cracks in this foundation.

Two and a half hours into the trip the limo did a nosedive, slowing rapidly as it veered to the left. The men braced one hand against the seat in front of them, steadying Amanda so she didn't face plant the seat they were on with the other, an eighteen wheeler loaded with cattle lumbering into traffic in front of them. Jeremy pushed Amanda gently to the floor and reached across the facing seat to slide the glass partition aside.

"Are there any turnouts up here?"

"No, sir. Just the one the truck pulled out of," the driver answered. "I doubt he's going to accelerate very fast. Cows aren't known for being the steadiest."

Jeremy instinctively checked traffic, the driver attempting to maneuver away from the truck safely while other driver's passed them at a hundred miles an hour, the truck continuing to drift to the left. Jeremy's driver continued to slow, tucking the limo back in behind the rig. Cars approached on the left, honking and hitting the brakes to avoid the big rig. The truck floated back to the right, allowing the cars to pass.

"Are there any side roads we can use?" Jeremy asked as he chastised himself for not paying closer attention. He should not have been so wrapped up in his conversation with William.

"We just passed the last one," the driver answered. "There's another one this side of Elko, but it will take us into Ruby Valley. That's the long way to Wells or Wendover via Highway-93."

"And put us farther away from help if we need it," Jeremy said, more to himself than the driver.

"Yes, sir," the driver answered. "We have the tunnel coming up with that wide stretch between it and the bridge. Want me to see if I can swing around him?"

"It's in your hands," Jeremy said. "I don't care how fast you drive or what you have to do, as long as you keep it on the road."

Jeremy sat back in the seat, nodding reassuringly at Amanda where she lay on the floor. "William, join Amanda please, and do not move. Stay down and hang on."

"How much paint you want left?" the driver asked.

"I can replace a car," Jeremy answered. "I cannot replace you or my guests."

"Hold on." The driver drifted to the right, the truck mirroring his move. The driver hit the brakes in an evasive move, avoiding the rear end of the truck, veering back into traffic, the truck following once again. "Sir, our company is moving to block us."

"Do what you have to. Just get us out of here."

The truck braked and the limo swerved to the left, a horn honking as a car screamed past, then the driver hit the gas, the huge engine roaring to life, doing what it was built to do, the limo accelerating.

"Sir," the driver said, "a car that passed us earlier is moving up on our rear and the truck is holding his own. He isn't hauling cows if he can move like this. Those are decoys."

"Floor it," Jeremy ordered. "Just don't put us off this bridge or into the side of that hill. I don't want any civilians hurt."

"You need to duck, sir."

The truck continued to steer to the left in an effort to cut the limo off, force it into the bridge railing. With its size – even empty – it was no match for the limo's speed and they continued to accelerate past him. Then the limo careened to the right, lurching forward, when it was rammed. The driver kept his foot pinned to the floor, aiming the limo for the ever narrowing space between the bridge abutment and the truck. The car backed off then slammed the limo again. The limo driver steered to the left this time to correct the slide, metal screeching on concrete as they scraped between the end of the bridge and the eighteen-wheeler, the truck's front bumper clipping the limo's rear bumper. The highway suddenly yawed open in front of them, the bumpers uncoupling as the limo lost traction on a scattering of gravel, its rear end swerving right.

The driver steadied the car, the truck moving closer readying for an onslaught of its own. The limo driver made the necessary correction, aimed the wheels to the right, the tires screaming as the limo skidded across the highway and into the concrete berm of the tunnel. A fingernail's on chalkboard screech echoed off the ceiling and walls, sparks flying then it was shooting back for the center of the road. The driver corrected putting the car back on its original course.

Jeremy lowered the window, pulled his pistol and fired. The blast reverberated off the concrete, the bullet striking one of the tires on the chase car sending it under the eighteen wheelers trailer. The unholy scream of tearing metal bounced off the tunnel walls, the tires on the trailer crunching the hood of the car. The truck rebounded off the side of the tunnel, Jeremy firing again, taking out its radiator. Tires squealed and horns blared as oncoming cars attempted to avoid the wreckage and each other, the sound magnified in the enclosed space.

"GO!" Jeremy ordered.

Jeremy pulled out his pager, switched to a secure channel to notify authorities then keyed in a message for James and Timothy.

They pulled into the apartment complex three hours later, Jeremy surveying the damage to the limo. The rear bumper hung haphazardly, part of the right side had been stripped of its paint, and flecks of concrete were imbedded in the left rear quarter panel. Not bad for towing an eighteen wheeler, bouncing off the bridge abutment, skimming the tunnel wall and sliding around a few corners. The driver had done amazingly well.

"Holy shit!" James exclaimed.

"It was an eventful trip," Jeremy said.

"How much does it cost to replace one of these, babies?"

"You don't want to know, James," Jeremy stated. "Dinner will be something simple tonight, like make your own sandwiches. This was no accident."

"The car that passed us earlier was the spotter?" William said, recognizing the unintended question after the fact.

"Yes." Jeremy set a six-pack of beer on the counter, helping Amanda set the sandwich makings on the table. "That car was the chase car. He stayed behind us until we got close to the turn out where the truck was waiting. The car passed us, gave the truck the signal and the truck pulled out. I want everyone's thoughts on Reno. Something is off."

"How did Mr. Layton know we were there?" James asked, tossing Amanda her apartment keys. "I didn't think you put this trip on the grapevine."

"I didn't. I only put out that I was starting a party planning service. And no names were given."

"I want to know what he meant by husband status," Amanda said.

Jeremy shrugged and headed for the guest room and the fax machine. "I am adding that to my list of questions regarding the man."

18

The next morning Jeremy stood beside Amanda's bed as she slept then bent, kissing her cheek gently. She mumbled something and rolled onto her stomach. He missed their nights together, even though there had only been a few. Now, she avoided those evenings, and the commander's words echoed. *'What if William asks her to marry him...Are you sure you're doing the right thing?'*

"No," he said out loud, strolling to the kitchen to make coffee.

Padding to the shower he thought about the events in Reno then went back to the guestroom and dressed, picking up the faxes. Work beckoned.

With the holidays approaching, it appeared their weekends would be booked solid. That was something he hadn't counted on. Gathering information on the syndicate was one thing, but doing it while running around throwing company parties was another. But, this just might get them closer to the men they were looking for. They had to put themselves out there, get people's attention, and this might be the easiest way to do it.

Jeremy had just finished his last call when Amanda joined

him. She sat down, leaned her head on her hand, and he reminded himself how lucky he was to know her.

"Amanda, you look absolutely divine this morning."

"You're looking pretty smug yourself. I take it you've been busy. What's happening?"

"You will find out. Once the men arrive we will have a short meeting including the business side of this venture."

"That good?"

"Even better. Are you ready for coffee?"

"Sounds divine," Amanda said, laughing. "What's that mean?"

"The business? We are going to be much busier than I had anticipated."

An hour later the downstairs buzzer sounded and Jeremy allowed the men in while Amanda dressed.

"Coffee gentlemen?" Jeremy asked.

"Of course," Timothy answered.

When Amanda joined them Jeremy began the meeting.

"James," Jeremy said, "I don't want you putting yourself in a dangerous situation, but we need to find out exactly who is doing what. Is Mr. Bonner's nephew behind these attacks or is it Reno? I am more positive than ever these are not random occurrences. We need proof and once we have proof, we will have the why. With your undercover work last year I thought it might be easier if you went into the establishments where things such as this are discussed."

"That shouldn't be too hard," James said. "I have some props at the station. I can always act like I'm looking for a little extra income and see if someone knows someone."

"But we need to do it without you making yourself a target so I do not want William going in with you. If anyone on the force is involved, they will know you two are partners, and I don't want them putting things together. I was thinking, since Timothy is the perfect Joe Citizen, that would allow him to help."

"I can do that," Timothy said.

"We also need to discover where the pushers are getting their drugs," Jeremy continued. "With Jonathan keeping a low profile all we have are rumors and supposition. We are still maintaining a visual on the homeless population, but we are not seeing the activity we saw last year. Jonathan is working things different than George."

"George's old bar was sold, but the 'For Rent' sign is gone from a closed bar north of it on State Street," James said. "That might be a place to start."

"See what you can find," Jeremy said. "Timothy, I want you to follow James routine and drop into the bars between his visits. I don't want you two hanging around together right away. Maybe accidentally run into each other now and then. But we need to get whoever is doing this to tip his hand. We need to find his Achilles heel. We need to know what establishment he works out of."

"We can do that," Timothy replied. "How soon do you want the information?"

"Obviously, the sooner the better. Also, I wanted to tell you, the commander is extremely impressed. You have handled these surprises remarkably well. We hope this last one with Mr. Randall goes as planned."

"I was wondering about the men working these exercises." Timothy hesitated for a minute. "You say they were in attendance in Reno, but it still got out of hand. How are the people doing this getting their information?"

"Yes, well, there were," Jeremy replied. "I am going on the assumption that whoever it is knows we are acquainted, which isn't difficult to figure out. Amanda worked with me, and James and William helped at the center from time to time. I think you just happened to be in the wrong place at the wrong time. And the commander is afraid to up the organization's presence. He doesn't want it to look like the president is in attendance."

"Tell Howard we got it covered," William said.

Jeremy hoped William was right.

"See what you men can dig up without anyone getting shot again," Jeremy said, "then we'll go over everything after our exercise with Mr. Randall. Remember, you have the pager now. With a fax line set up here your information will come to Amanda and she will distribute it. Now, for the business. It seems we have started this little endeavor at the most opportune time. Unfortunately, it will not give us much time to learn our roles. I understand you have your jobs and we will all need some down time now and then, so I made sure to keep a weekend or two free for us. I also thought it would be nice to spend the holidays at home. Until we know exactly what is going on, I would like all three of you gentlemen with us as much as possible, so we are going to have to work something out there."

A quick glance up and seeing nods all around, Jeremy handed Amanda an envelope.

"Amanda, that is for the exercises in St. George. Your time is valuable, no matter what you are doing so all of you will be compensated for the fiasco in Reno and for the upcoming exercise with Mr. Randall. I am not going to bore you with the details. Everything is in front of you."

She took it, her mind going over what they had just been told. Meager pickings for stopping these attacks. But with Jonathan leasing a bar, maybe he was pulling himself out of the woodwork, shedding the cockroach in hiding persona. It might be time for her to contribute more to the team effort, the answers coming straight to her. She dropped her gaze and keyed in an information request, keeping the pager under the table.

"Any questions so far?" Jeremy asked.

"What's this deal James talked about?" William asked. "He said something about George's old compound in Reno?"

"Mr. Layton purchased the building from the City of Reno," Jeremy told them, "and he wants to use it like a conference center. Rent it to companies for business dinners and so on. He thought we could run it for him, have a set fee per day which would include Amanda and my services. We add in you gentlemen for security. Then we would not be running around the countryside. That, I feel will work to our advantage. Obviously, it is too close to use this year, but we can use it for some of our engagements next year. Although, Mr. Layton and the Commander booked it for a couple of parties this year."

"I've missed a lot of work because of the surgery," William said. "I'm not sure I can take that much time off."

"I talked to Captain Kirby when I got back," James said. "He said, as long as we are gathering information for the department that will work for a short time, but he needs both of us in town as much as possible to work our case load."

"Okay. Now, what's this about not leaving us alone, Jeremy," William said.

"Is your apartment a two bedroom?" Jeremy asked.

"It is."

"Good. James or I can stay in Amanda's guest room and the other can stay in yours. It makes no difference to me. I am going to leave that up to you since I will still be making frequent runs to Cedar City."

"You stay with Amanda," William answered. "You're already here part of the time and James and I have been working some strange hours recently. We won't disturb her that way."

19

The next couple of days were anticlimactic and the following weekend would be their exercise with Mr. Randall. But tonight William was looking forward to performing. The only thing better than watching Amanda strut it onstage was making love to her.

Lunch time came and it was William's turn to buy. He walked away from his desk as the phone rang. James finished the call, picked up the portable doing a quick triple tap. Their code for William to switch to an alternate frequency. William changed channels and called James. There had been another assault, but she had escaped. James picked William up in front of the diner, William dropping into the passenger seat as he tossed James his sandwich.

They pulled up to the scene and were introduced to the victim by a female officer. She reminded William of his late wife's sister. A slender build, kinky hair cut short to her head, setting off the fine lines of her cheeks and her jaw. Full, but not pouty, lips, dark expressive eyes. Dark chocolate complexion. A beautiful young woman.

The girl avoided eye contact, clutching the hem of her t-shirt, wringing it like a washcloth or rolling her fists in it, blood beginning to seep through a bandage on her arm. Blood coated the top of her shirt, gauze peeking out above her bra. Blood also dotted her shorts where a female paramedic bandaged what they assumed was another injury.

William gave the paramedic a questioning look.

"She refused the hospital," the paramedic told them.

William nodded. They would push the hospital after she'd calmed down.

They began talking to her, her accent thick. Probably from the Caribbean. She told them she had been loading the washer when the lights went out then something grabbed her from behind. It had a gag over her mouth and a cord around her wrists, before she knew it was there. With her hands bound in front of her, it simply moved her clothes to one side. Then it pulled a knife, sliced her shirt up the back, cutting her in the process. It told her, 'I could enjoy you all night long' and asked if she could handle it. Toward the end of the assault it lowered the knife and that was when she made her first escape attempt. It regained control of her and cut her again then it began a second round of assaults, striking her repeatedly.

They noticed her use of the word 'it' and thought about how she was processing what had happened. She may consider the person responsible as less than human.

"You keep saying 'it'," William said. "What makes you say 'it'?"

"Because it was not a man," she replied, fixing her frightened stare on him. "It had big bulging eyes." She gestured with her hands, moving from her eyes down to her cheeks. "And this big roun' tings here. He talk like through a pillow or a, a, aroun' someting."

"Could it have worn a mask?" William asked, thinking about

Lloyd's breather.

"Maybe, yes, but it was hard. I slap it. I try to find something to defend myself, but only find a bottle of soap." She stooped and picked a large bottle off the ground; one side sliced open, its contents leaked out, and shook it in front of her. "I swing. Smack it in the head. It fall back then I turn light on and shove it into the wall and swing again. I hit it a second time. Then I have to fight the door open to run. It followed, stabbing at me, cutting my arm." She held her arm up showing off the bandage they had seen earlier. Then she turned so they could see the back of her t-shirt and the elongated cut on her back. "It continue to chase me, trying to stab me. I get to top of the steps then run into a person who call 911. Now…" She shrugged and shook her head. "Poof! It gone!"

"If you had to, could you place its accent? Would you be able to tell where your attacker was from?"

"No," she answered shaking her head. "It have no accent. It talked like you do."

William nodded and made a note. A man wearing a mask. No accent. Then they went back over everything, asking the same questions in different words to illicit a different response. It sounded like they doubted the victim, but they had to walk a fine line, dance around a defense attorney's word games. It didn't make it any easier for the victims or the investigators, but they could take no chances. And sexual assaults were the worst. They were intruding on a very personal and private kind of attack. Rape was that way. Even from a presumed alien.

They pushed the hospital, stressing the need for stitches in her back and asking for samples to be sent to the U. After much coaxing, she relented and they pulled the uniformed officers to the side.

"The laundry rooms in the basement," William said. "Officers and techs down there?"

"Yes, sir. They're working on lifting prints." The officer

paused. "She says the place scares her. Reminds her of the catacombs in some of the old movies."

At the top of the stairs they noticed markers laid out by partial footprints. One was a boot. Much larger than the woman's bare footprint. Reaching the bottom of the stairs they turned on their flashlights, using them to augment the lighting. The intermittent fluorescents didn't even give off sufficient light to illuminate the corridors. A quick scan of the stark surroundings and they understood why it scared the girl. The place was foul. The odor of mold and mildew hanging heavy in the damp air. Water dripped from overhead pipes in the distance, William's thoughts going back to the girl's description of the place. It reminded William of one of the swamps he had lived near back home.

Shining their lights around the space, they stood on one side of a huge open room, voices echoing from somewhere ahead of them. Four dirt covered windows ran along the ceiling to their right. A few steps in and they noticed the same prints, much more pronounced, fresher, a line of liquid trailing off into the distance, growing thicker. Her soap. They picked their way around water that had puddled on the concrete floor, finding more markers beside prints and wondered why anyone would come down here.

On the far side of the room a hall ran straight ahead, a shaft of light visible at the end of the darkened hall. A second corridor ran to the left. If not for the trail of detergent and the light at the end of the tunnel, they wouldn't have known which direction the voices were coming from. Tunnel. Strange way to describe the hall. But this was less a hallway than a predator's hunting grounds. Custom made just for him.

William walked back to the markers and squatted, inspecting them. The same boot from the University. The same man? He glanced up at James, James nodded in the affirmative.

They drove back to the station and wrote their report while

they ate. Victim number three, and they had more questions again. The man had left a message but if she had not survived, they wouldn't have known. Messages were usually used as fear tactics. Something to keep their victims quiet. Had he said anything to the other women? William frowned, an image of Lloyds' breather filtering through…the message even more confusing.

"I'm curious about the message," James said, breaking into William's thoughts. "That's kind of counter intuitive isn't it? If he's going to kill her why try to scare her?"

"Don't know, my man." William shook his head. "Unless he thinks it gives him more power over them."

20

At six forty-five William bound down the stairs at Pearls on Main sprinting to the stage, apologizing to Amanda and Eddie, as he dropped onto the piano bench. Half way through the second set their department pagers chirped, James jumping for the phone. James hung up and twirled his finger above his head. Time to cut it short. William bolted off the stage, abandoning Amanda and joined James at the base of the stairwell. Another assault two blocks away.

The scene was the usual craziness with female officers talking to the victim while crime scene techs worked, radios blaring. They introduced themselves to the victim then listened as she recounted her experience.

She had gone to dinner with friends, using the parking lot off the alley because it was close and well-lighted, as parking lots went. She unlocked her car then something grabbed her from behind and tried to bind her hands. She twisted one hand free and punched it in the neck. It slugged her in the back of the head and held a knife under her chin. After it bound her wrists it bent her over the car.

"It?" William asked, her face showing shock.

"I don't know how else to describe it." She glanced between the two. "It had these huge eyes, kind of greenish-grayish skin. Big huge honeycomb looking things for jaws." The same description the previous woman gave. "It did not look human!"

"Could it have been someone wearing a mask? You say it bent you over the car, so..." William hesitated, fighting to keep his discomfort from becoming apparent. He was supposed to keep the emotions in check. He was a detective. "...other than the face, it assaulted you the same way a man would have?"

Her eyes flashed then she sighed and looked confused. "Yes, but it, he, it....was extremely angry. It shoved my face into the car like it was throwing something in the garbage. Then it cut my shirt and my bra off." She turned sideways so they could see the back of the shirt.

"When did you get a look at your assailant?" James asked.

"I kicked backwards when it started pulling my jeans down, but it smashed me in the head again, shoving my face into the car a second time." She continued, telling them about it caressing her cheek with the edge of the knife as it began its assault. Then someone yelled from behind them. Her assailant took a step back and turned then she rolled to the side, shoving it away. The knife plunged toward her and she dropped to the pavement, rolling as it stabbed at her repeatedly. "I kept scooting backwards between cars, this..." She hesitated and looked away, the anger coming back. Then tears were rolling down her cheeks. "...whatever it was, swinging the knife. I remember now, it said, 'I would never remember the finale'." Both men's heads jerked up. "I didn't want to find out what that meant. Then someone was running toward us, the yelling getting louder as they got closer. It bolted between cars toward the alley."

"It spoke English?" James asked. "What kind of accent? Could you place where it was from?"

She shook her head, wiping the tears away.

James thanked her and gave her one of their business cards, his mind stuck on the attacker's statement. A second alien with a message. An extremely angry alien with a message.

One of the responding officers held up an evidence bag containing the section of rope that had been used. Generic nylon, readily available anywhere. William took a second look. Yellow nylon. The girl at the University.

"Have that compared with the fibers off the girl at the U," he instructed the tech. "I'll bet they match."

Paramedics arrived and began treating the woman's injuries, while James inspected the car, William checking the area where she had fallen. There were markers following traces of blood, and scuff marks where she had scooted across the pavement. And a tire on the neighboring car had been slashed. Someone was going to be pissed.

"We got a witness," an officer called from behind them. "The dude lives on the third floor up there." The officer pointed to a building directly behind them, a man standing on the ground near the corner partially hidden in the shadows.

As he and James approached, William thought about how to word this. "Good evening. I'm Detective Harrison," he said. "This is my partner, Detective Thompson. Officer Wendle said you could possibly have some information that would be of help?"

"Yes, sir," he said. "Michael Owens. I don't know if it'll help, but I thought, well….maybe."

"Sure," William said. "What did you see? Officer Wendle said you were on your back porch."

"Yeah," Michael said. "If it's late I just leave my garbage up there and bring it down in the morning. The trash cans are down here and I don't want to get mugged. When I opened the door tonight instead of just seeing traffic on the street, I see this lady bent over the hood of her car."

"What made you think something was wrong? Was there a lot of noise? Was she crying?"

"It looked like he hit her then he pulled a knife."

"He?" William asked. Michael nodded vigorously. A man wearing a mask. "Are you sure it was a knife? Could he have just been gesturing?"

"No, I saw the blade," Michael answered. "It was a big one, too. It would have done some damage. I flew down the stairs and started yelling."

"You could have been stabbed. Did you think about that?"

"No, sir. I wasn't thinking about much of anything. I was afraid he was going to kill her. He started following her between the cars me following and yelling at him. Then he ran, pulling off a sweater or hoodie, or something."

"Is that when you called the police?" James asked.

"No. Well, yeah. I wasn't sure if I should approach her or not and then I saw her hands were tied. She had blood on her face and scratches and cuts on her arms so I introduced myself and told her I was going to call the cops and asked if she would be okay for a minute. It felt a little awkward, ya know. Then I ran up and called you guys and the first cop car came barreling around the corner a minute later."

"Do you remember which way he went?"

"Down the alley," Michael answered pointing south. "Then a couple of minutes later a dude walked up to the Bus Stop on State Street." He pointed to the bus bench due east. "He was carrying a hat or something, too. That's why I noticed him."

"Would you be able to give us a description?" William asked.

"I guess. He wasn't as tall as you guys, but I'd say about my height. Five nine or ten. Kind of average build."

"About a hundred thirty pounds?" James probed.

"About a hundred fifty. He had blonde hair. Real short. Not

crew cut short, but short," Michael answered. "Looked like any dude you might see walkin' down the street."

"So, he turned and looked back this way?"

"Yeah. I was back on my porch by then, but…yeah…he took a nice long look."

"And the clothes?" William asked.

"By the time he got over there…" He pointed toward the bus bench. "….the coat or whatever was gone and he was wearing blue jeans and a yellow and light green t-shirt. And gloves. I couldn't see the logo on the shirt, though. It could have been military or college."

"You're sure it was the same man, though," James said.

Michael nodded. "I'll bet my job on it."

"Thank you, sir," William said, handing him one of their cards.

They started back toward the girl when James hesitated, staring into the darkened alley.

"William, do me a favor and grab a tech. If the dude was pulling a sweater off, maybe we'll get lucky and find a footprint."

When William and the techs joined James in the alley, James was staring at a single boot print where it hugged the edge of the asphalt, illuminating the print with his flashlight. The man had stumbled pulling off the clothing.

William kneeled, inspecting the mark. It was the same as the print at the U and at the basement assault. While techs set up to cast the print, William and James searched the alley, checking dumpsters and garbage cans, shining their flashlights into the cracks and crevices between buildings. At the south end of the alley, William found a dark green hoodie stuffed into a trash can. He called techs and backed out, letting them do their job.

"We finally caught a break," William said.

"Absolutely," James answered.

21

The next morning, William handed James the evidence bag containing the hoodie and picked up the phone. James footsteps receded down the hall while William dialed Lloyd's office number not wanting to believe how things looked. Two girls had been attacked in one day. Both men appeared to be alien, which to William meant he had worn a mask. And at the latest assault, the person had ditched a dark green hoodie. A hoodie like the one Lloyd had worn, and techs found kinky black hair in the seam of the hood. Pictures of Lloyd in the hoodie, wearing the breather in that filthy room came to mind. One of the techs darting outside carrying something after Lloyd dropped his breather, flashed and William's gut nagged him even harder. The description Michael had given them was a blonde man of average height and build. Had Lloyd loaned his hoodie to a friend or lost it?

With everything set, William and James waited for Lloyd to make his appearance. When he stepped through the door they stared wide-eyed. His gait was slow, halting, bandages the full length of the forearm on both arms. His left arm had been bandaged above the elbow and was in a sling.

"I hope this don't take long," Lloyd snorted. "Because I gotta tell you this is inconvenient as shit! Do you know how much it hurts just to stand? Walking is even worse! It had damn well better be good." He quit talking, huffed some air out glancing between the two. "Well?"

"Let's go down the hall," William said. "I want a little more privacy than we'll get in here."

"So am I a suspect or some shit?" Lloyd grumbled, his eyes taking in the empty interrogation rooms, doing a quick look behind them every few steps. "I seen these rooms before, William. What the hell you tryin' to do?"

"Nothing, Lloyd," William answered. "We need to talk to you and I don't want the whole damn station hearing it." Closing the door behind them, William pointed to the chair. "If you need to prop your leg up, feel free."

Lloyd nodded, staring between them. "Am I under arrest?"

"Why would you be under arrest?"

"I don't know, but you bring me back here and jam me into one of these places." He stopped, looking around the barren walls. "It's been years since I seen one of these, but they still look the same." He gave a short chuckle then snorted. "What's goin' down, William?"

James laid the evidence bag with the hoodie in it on the table.

"That looks like the one I lost," Lloyd said. Then he leaned back, inhaling sharply as he did. "That wasn't used in a crime was it?"

"Actually it was," James answered. "Last night. When did you see yours last?"

"The day them dudes OD'd. I went back upstairs to grab my breather after getting the shit in the van straight. The mask wasn't on the stairs, or in the hall, and when I got back to the van my hoodie's gone. I made another trip up the damn stairs while you two were goin' through the dumpsters. You don't really think I would do something stupid, do ya?"

"No, Lloyd, we don't," William replied. "That's why we're talking to you." William hesitated, not wanting to use the wrong words. The last thing he wanted was to alienate a friend and co-worker. He nodded to Lloyd's arms. "So, what happened? Your arms, I mean."

Lloyd moved and William noticed the darker splotches on his chin and left cheek. Bruises. They were the correct size to have been caused by a large bottle of laundry detergent.

"My neighbor was playing football with some friends. I was outside with my son. Barbecuing. We don't have a fence between the yards and one of the men ran into the grill. My son was standing a foot away and I dove for him when I saw the direction the dude was moving. I saved my son, but I caught the brunt of it. Burns on my leg…" He chinned toward his left leg. …"my side…" He turned to accent his left side, grimacing as he did. "…and both my arms." He lifted his chin. "The platter with the meat caught me in the cheek and the bowl of barbecue sauce smacked me upside the jaw. You're lucky you caught me. I was heading out. Going home early. The pain meds they gave me are killer. Knocks me on my butt."

"When did this happen?" James asked.

"I am a suspect, aren't I?" Lloyd attempted to stand, his legs unsteady, and gave up anger blazing. "What the hell happened? What am I being accused of doing?"

"Nothing, Lloyd," William stated firmly. "That's why we're talking to you. Neither one of us think you're good for it. Now, when did this happen?"

"Yesterday afternoon. And before you ask what time, it was at about three or three-thirty. You can check with the hospital. I got there just before four p.m. I wasn't released until about eight. I was just stupid enough to think I could work this morning, like this." He raised his arms, emphasizing the point. "And my wife and boy were with me the entire time before that."

Lloyd struggle to stand, but William nudged his shoulder, holding him in the chair.

"Please, Lloyd. We just need to know a couple of things. Okay?"

Lloyd nodded, his mouth firm, eyes smoldering.

"Thank you. You said the last time you saw your hoodie and the breather was the day we worked the scene with those two dealers?" Lloyd nodded. "That was the last day you saw either one."

"Yeah. Pisses me off, too. I mean the breather ain't worth nothing. I got it at an Army Navy store because the ones we get from the department ain't worth shit. But my son painted it for me. He's a real good artist." He looked between the two. "Is my breather part of this thing that happened, too?"

"Yes," William replied.

"Tell me what happened, William. What am I facing?"

"We have two women who were assaulted."

Lloyd groaned and leaned back in the chair. "Shit! When?"

"One was yesterday about noon and the second one was last night." William held his hand up when Lloyd opened his mouth. "You are not a suspect," he repeated. "It's just this hoodie with our kind of hair in it was dropped at last night's attack." Lloyd sighed. "And both women said their attacker looked like an alien. The description they gave matches your breather."

"Fuck!"

They talked to him for another thirty minutes, getting the doctors name and the name of the hospital he'd been taken to, promising to let him know if they learned anything more, and stressed again they weren't entertaining the thought he had done it, but they had to dot all the i's and cross all the t's.

"Lloyd didn't do it," James said as they watched him hobble to his car.

"I agree," William said. "We just have to figure out who did before someone he works with finds out about the breather."

"You think they would do that to Lloyd?"

"Since we moved to this detective slot.....I have no idea what anyone would do anymore," William answered. "But just to cover our asses I told the Cap not to include that information in any of the press releases. If it comes out, it's more apt to be the man responsible."

22

The guard arrived early, pulled up the secretary's messages, copying one containing release papers for an inmate. He redirected the copy to himself, deleted the electronic trail then went to his office and pulled up the message, deleting the trail on his end as well. Once the necessary changes had been made, he forwarded the message to an attorney, deleting the outgoing trace.

The attorney checked that all necessary changes had been made and deleted the incoming trace then sent it to the prison's secretary. After he'd received notification it had been received, he did a wire transfer to two bank accounts. One for the guard and one for him. Once everything had been completed successfully he deleted those trails and called the prison to set up an appointment with his client for that afternoon. The prison would contact him and notify him of his client's impending release. Beautifully simple. Simply beautiful.

By three p.m. the inmate heard the locks disengage then the thunderous slam echoed along the corridor of the cell block. The guard's footsteps made a hard heel-toe plod as they came his way, each step one step closer to his freedom. The guard stopped just outside the bars and smiled, the cell door grating open.

"How does it feel, Mr. Bonner?" the guard asked.

"You have no idea," George said. Sweet freedom was finally his.

By four-thirty George sat outside his apartment in Salt Lake City. He nodded a 'Thank You' to his attorney and climbed out of the car, looking up at the front of the building as the car drove away, laughing out loud. He still had connections and he still had plans.

Inside his apartment, every flat surface was covered in layers of dust thick enough to disguise the black fingerprint powder, and latex gloves littered the floor. No one had been here since his arrest. George walked to the closet, pried a piece of molding loose and peeled back the carpet, uncovering his safe. One of many things his nephew, and the cops, knew nothing about. He took out sufficient funds for a hotel and food for the night then laid the carpet back down, tucking it against the baseboard. Replacing the molding, he snugged it in with his fist. He would spend tonight in a hotel then it was back to business.

He changed windbreakers, grabbed his Utah Jazz baseball cap and put a set of fresh cloths in a backpack then walked to a payphone. First call, a cleaning service then he would contact the man who had worked this magic.

Receiving the expected response on each call, George called a taxi and headed north on State Street.

As George rode he saw his old establishment had been sold. Jonathan had told him, but he wanted to see for himself. Two and a half blocks north the 'For Rent' sign no longer hung in the window of another poor suckers lost dreams and George had the cabby drop him off, the darkened space beckoning George closer. Jonathan had leased it so George would reopen in almost the same location. Cupping his hands around his eyes, George leaned against the glass and looked to both sides. No one had been here for a while, either. He stepped away from the building a police car starting south on State Street. George pulled his collar up, ducking his head like a turtle, pulling the baseball cap lower on his forehead to avoid being seen, perusing the street for his next goal. A woman. A willing and pliable woman to handle the worst part of prison life. No women.

The prostitutes had relocated a half a block north and he approached the gaggle, eyeing them appreciatively. One pushed her way through the crowd to let him know she was the one who would fulfill his desires. He pulled her close, caressing her breast roughly, his body responding.

The next morning George stroked the woman's breast and rolled her onto him. A shower forty minutes later and he slapped her rear then dressed and closed the bedroom door to the two-room suite, a knock coming from the entry door. He opened it and waved the man in, double checking the door into the bedroom.

"Good morning. Good to see you, George," the man said.

"Good morning, Glen," George replied. "Was everything taken care of as instructed?"

"Yes, sir. Set it just like you said complete with powder on the coffee table so it looks like they OD'd. We planted the business card, took the cash, but didn't find any product. Reno should take the fall."

"What else did you find?"

"This is it," he replied handing George a grocery bag.

Opening the bag, George flipped through the stack of cash. Eighty-five hundred dollars. He pulled out two hundred dollars and gave it to Glen.

"You called the cops?"

"They've already been there."

"What about Jonathan?"

"He's doing exactly like you said he would. He's sniveling to

Reno. He's also whining about getting help with the drug flow. It seems he lost some."

"He lost some?" George snapped. "How the hell could he lose some?"

"I think it's what the guys sold." Glen chinned at the cash in George's hand. His mind returned to the hidden cubby and he fought to maintain his gaze, not wanting George to see he had lied. "We found nothing in the apartment."

"Good. This organization is going to be revived, but it is going to be worked the right way. I want no more of Jonathan's shit. I can't afford the mistakes." George stuffed the rest of the money inside his pack. "Meet me this afternoon." He handed Glen a paper with the address on it.

Two hours later, George walked into the bar, taking in every filthy inch of it. The place had, indeed, been empty a while and the stench was even worse than he had imagined. The hinges on the back door screeched and Glen walked in. George motioned for him to sit down.

"Start looking for more men," George said. "Take your time and make sure you hire good men."

"I know some guys who are just waiting for the chance," Glen said. "What are we offering them for pay? Standard rate?"

George nodded. "If they keep their noses clean and follow orders, I'll up the rate sooner than usual."

Glen smiled, heading for a payphone, winking at the hooker as she walked in. She returned the wink with a slight chin lift, mouthing the words *'Day after tomorrow'*. George frowned. He hadn't been out twenty-four hours and Reno was screwing with him.

She strutted up and George took her hand, stroking the inside of her thigh, his body coming to life. He pulled her down so she straddled him on the chair, the bartender disappearing.

George moaned, kissing her eagerly. "Let's finish this in the office. It's been a while."

Glen made several phone calls, the first of the possible recruits arriving as he dialed the last number.

"Target has been acquired," he said once the phone had been answered.

"Thank you. Keep us posted."

"Katie said day after tomorrow."

"Yes, I'll get back with you tomorrow evening."

Glen hung up, heading back to the bar and George. He stepped inside and George handed him a set of keys then nodded in the direction of his office.

"Get rid of her. Not in one of the lakes near here, either."

Glen scanned the bar, not finding the hooker. His countenance fell, panic setting in, the unspoken question in his eyes.

George glared up at him, his eyes cold. "Hurry back. We have work to do."

Glen walked toward George's office, his heart racing. At the door his hand hesitated above the knob. He already knew what he would find, and George's message had been clear. Glen turned the knob and stepped inside, his breath catching when he saw her.

"Damn it, Katie," he whispered. "It wasn't supposed to end like this. We were supposed to get married and disappear."

23

Jonathan answered the phone expecting it to be George. With his uncle's recent release, George would be amping things up for the business once again. Instead it was Glen.

"We have a problem," Glen said.

"Has something gone wrong?" Jonathan asked, realizing the stupidity of that question too late.

Glen choked back a sob, swallowing hard.

"George killed Katie." He stared at the pavement, his toe digging a hole in the dirt between sidewalk sections. He could feel the tears, wiped them away angrily. "She wasn't supposed to die, Jonathan! This was our last job!"

"Hold on," Jonathan instructed. He closed and locked his office door, then dropped into the chair, exhaling slowly before he picked up the phone. "Okay, say that again. He killed her?"

Jonathan listened as Glen recounted making a few phone calls for George then going back to the bar and being told to dispose of the body. The more Jonathan heard the more his anger grew. Glen and Katie had only been loaned to him. How was he supposed to tell Mr. Landers that George had murdered one of them? That he had lost one of Reno's best assets?

He stood, paced the room, his mind racing, grasping at ideas, only to dismiss each one quicker than he had thought of it. He stopped, stared at the solid oak desk and warm chocolate brown leather of the chair, the carefully staged trappings of a successful man, and thought about Reno's inevitable reaction when he told them about Katie. He turned and stared out the window at the park like surroundings, then blew his breath out. Uncle George was not going to win. As long as George thought he was the drunken sot, Jonathan Bonner was not going to lose.

"What am I supposed to tell Mr. Landers?" Glen asked, pulling Jonathan out of his musings.

"Do you have her now? Are you at the bar?"

"She's in the trunk of the car. I'm using a payphone."

"So George gave you the keys."

"Yes, Sir." Glen said, a plan coming together. "I think I got it."

"Exactly," Jonathan said. "Dump her off George's balcony. You know how to make it look. Have your flunkies clean up the mess and take her up one of the rivers where the kayakers hang out to ditch the body. Give it a couple of days and file a missing persons report. We'll point it straight to George."

"But…"

"Just do it!" Jonathan snapped. "It has to look like you're following orders and that should do it. And don't say anything to Reno. I'll handle them."

"What if they call me? Everything was supposed to go down day after tomorrow."

"Obviously that won't happen. If they call you, don't lie. Just don't volunteer anything. I'm working on an idea so I'll call Mr. Fielding tonight. I sure as hell don't want to talk to Mr. Landers."

Glen hung up picturing the perfect drop off point. Have them put her in on the Price River and let her float downstream. There was a sweet little sandbar and beach at the confluence of the Price and the Green Rivers. It would take two or three days for her to float that far. Maybe longer. He made one more call, lining up the men then pulled out.

Glen drove to George's apartment, the men already waiting. When he pulled into the garage one of them dropped the door behind the car.

"I called in a phony distress call," one of the men told him. "It should pull the men away from the security desk long enough to get her upstairs."

Glen nodded a 'Thank You' then they lifted her out of the trunk, using a maids cart to wheel her past the unmanned security station and onto the elevator. Upstairs, Glen unlocked the door to George's apartment and flung it open.

After they lowered the laundry bag holding Katie, Glen posed her; the men helping him walk her onto the balcony. He leaned her against the railing and held her, kissed her cheek then brushed her hair back, tears threatening.

"I'm sorry, Katie," Glen whispered, his mind flashing to the kitchen cubby hole once again. "George Bonner is going to pay for this. I promise. I love you."

He balanced her on the railing, holding her an extra minute then pushed her over, running back inside. He didn't want to hear her land.

Inside the apartment Glen braced himself on the wall, sliding into a crouching position, his head buried in his hands, tears staining his shirt and pant legs. What the hell had he just done? He told her he loved her then threw her off a balcony. He was as crazy as George and Jonathan.

Glen lifted his head and chinned at the door. "Get her out of here," he choked. "George will have your money tonight."

The men nodded, backing out.

Glen took a few minutes to pull himself together, walking the apartment. George lived like this and Katie paid for it. His anger raged, the pain merciless, but he held it at bay. It wouldn't help Katie now.

A picture of the coroner taking Olivia's body from the news popped in, front and center, his mind not wanting to accept that she had been murdered, too. Had George ordered that?

Standing in the door to the walk-in closet Glen shook his head and took a step back, his eyes falling to the floor. Half way across the room, Glen stopped and backed up. He surveyed the carpet not sure what he was looking for, but something looked odd. His eyes moved slow, methodical, scanning every inch. At the door, he reversed his scan, pulling his eyes back when he reached the far corner, locking on a spot where the corner of the carpet was folded over.

He kneeled, pulled the carpet out, the loose section of molding coming with it and found the safe. Laying his ear on the cold steel, Glen turned the dial, listening for the tumblers. When the last number fell, he turned the handle and lifted. George's cash stash. He pulled a stack out. Forty thousand dollars. Not all of the stacks were the same denomination, but there was still plenty here. He dropped the money back inside, noticed the bags of drugs then closed the safe, repeating the combination to himself. Three people would pay handsomely for this information, Travis Layton, Robert Fielding and Thomas Landers. And so would Jonathan Bonner and the cops. If he had his say, George Bonner wouldn't be running Salt Lake City for long. Glen Tortino just might switch allegiances. He had nothing to lose now.

24

William sat on the sofa, popped the top on a can of beer and flipped the baseball game on his phone ringing. It was Captain Kirby. The Emery County sheriffs office fished a woman out of the Green River. How soon could he pick James up and be there?

"Why are we being called to Green River?" William asked staring at the wasted drink. "They should be able to handle it."

"It's reminiscent of the ones from last year, complete with panties around her ankles. You'll see when you get there."

"We nailed Bonner for those."

"I know. Just check it out. How long?" Captain Kirby was irritated. The words coming out short, clipped.

"About three and a half hours," William said. "Maybe sooner. We have the light."

"Head that way. Techs and the county sheriff's are on the scene. I'll see if they can hold it for you. Try to make it less than three."

William called James and gave him the news, telling James he would be there in ten minutes.

When they pulled up to the scene, portable lights had been set up turning the beach into a movie set, everyone scurrying around like industrious rodents. She was laying where she'd been found, at the water's edge; panties hanging around the top of the feet more than constraining her legs, but it was the same pose as the others.

"Glad you could find us," the sheriff said when he introduced himself. "We called because you had a couple of murders similar to this last year."

"Yes, sir," William answered, crouching next to her.

There were scratches on her neck and up the left side of her jaw. She had not gone without a struggle. William moved his eyes down her body, no bruises, fragment of bone poking through the skin on the right side, scratches covered the full length of that side. Her right arm was shattered as well. Scanning back up her body, a small amount of blood had dried in her hair on one side.

"Any ideas yet?" William asked walking around her.

"The tech seems to think she was held in a choke hold. There's no sign of strangulation. Kayakers found her. We think she's been dead between forty-eight and seventy-two hours."

William listened as he looked down at her. Three women last year. One of them had worked as a hooker. All three had had one person – and only one person – in common. And that person had been George Bonner. But George was in prison at Point of The Mountain, the Utah Correctional Center in Draper. Now they find this woman but she's showing a significant amount of trauma to one side of her body.

"It looks like she tried to fight," the sheriff continued. "Until there's an autopsy we can't say a whole lot, but since she's naked we assume she was assaulted."

"Can we get samples of the fluids sent to the University of Utah?" James asked. "They're trying to help us connect some crimes. And we need copies of the findings."

"She's all yours," the sheriff answered. "We told Kirby we'd ship her that way for you. She'll leave as soon as we're finished here."

Slipping on a pair of gloves, William looked at the eyes then checked a tiny discoloration under her chin.

"Find something?" James asked.

"Just checking some things." William pointed to her eyes and then her jaw. "Notice the mark?"

"I noticed that," James answered, looking closer. "That jives with the choke hold."

"Yeah, she's also had a hard landing. Lots of broken bone. She was dead when she fell."

"And by posing her, the perp makes it look like last year's ladies. An attempt to keep us running in circles."

"Appears that way. Throw us off if she was found. I can think of several possibilities."

They backed away and the sheriff nodded for the techs to take the body. Once it was clear, William and James joined the sheriff, getting as many details as they could.

They drove back to town, ordering something to eat while they worked on this new twist.

"It's been almost a year, James. What the hell's going on?"

"We both know this was carefully staged," James said. "On the flip side, George is still in prison so whoever's responsible for this is bound to get careless."

"We can't let it go that far. I'm going to page Jeremy. We need some answers."

William walked to a payphone near the front doors and paged Jeremy. Less than a minute later Jeremy called.

"Is there a problem?" Jeremy asked.

"You could say that. It's more of a great big question. We have a woman posed like the ones from last year," William said. "And the ones from three years ago. Whoever's responsible tried to make it look like she died from a fall. They're shipping her to Salt Lake City and we'll perform the autopsy there."

"Is there evidence to support that?"

"Everything except the panties and the pose. She has scratches and multiple broken bones the full length of one side of her body. Blood beginning to pool on the opposite side. There are signs of asphyxiation, but no sign of strangulation. Evidence of a struggle. She fought and fought hard. I'll get you a copy of the autopsy when we get it."

"I appreciate that. Have you requested information on her?"

"Thought I'd contact you first," William replied. "I'll do that as soon as I'm off the phone."

"I'll meet you in Salt Lake City," Jeremy said.

William used the organization's pager, keying in a request for missing persons matching the woman's approximate age and description. James had their food put in to-go containers and they hit the road, pulling into the station just before midnight. William received the page from Amanda as they strode in and hurried to the fax machine. Picking up the papers, it was a return on their inquiry. Their search using Jeremy's sources had already pulled up several possibles. William slid them into a manila folder and divided the pages as soon as they reached their desk. Half way through his stack, James found her.

A recent transplant from Reno with known ties to the syndicate in Las Vegas, she had been arrested in Las Vegas two years prior for drugs and prostitution, under the name of Katie Landry and was looking at a stint in the county jail. She moved to Reno and subsequently disappeared. According to sources Ms Landry had moved in with a man named Glen Tortino. Shortly thereafter they moved to Salt Lake City. Mr. Tortino had former Las Vegas roots as well and had moved to Salt Lake City taking a job as a bouncer at a bar previously operated and owned by George Bonner. A short time later Katie disappeared then reappeared the month prior rooming with a girl in The Avenues named Olivia Holland. At that time Miss Landry had been using the name Loretta Storey. James dropped the paper on his desk and exhaled loudly.

"I wish we had gone to Reno sooner now. Do you think she was still working with Reno or Las Vegas?"

"That could be why she got iced," William answered. "If she was, and George found out, she'd be toast. George would think nothing of ordering her execution. We just have to start pulling things together. And we have to find Glen. He might still be working for George. Who's to say he's not running things from inside just like we've heard."

25

William and James arrived at the station the next morning, immediately getting a summons from Captain Kirby regarding the call in Green River. After going over what they knew, Captain Kirby admitted it was disconcerting having a possible copycat for Bonner.

"That's part of the reason I called," the captain said. "We had a citizen call and say they saw a man and a woman on a balcony in the building across the alley behind their house two or three days ago. They thought they'd had a lover's spat and were making up. The man was hugging the woman; her head laying on his shoulder. The couple went to the kitchen and when they looked back out, the man and the woman had both disappeared."

"Did they see the woman after that?" William asked.

"No. This person went on to say they got nosy and continued to watch through the window. Two men pulled into the alley in a blue pick-up truck, wrapped something in a tarp and were putting the tarp in the back of the truck. They said the tarp looked like it was heavy …."

"Like a body. Did they call 911?" James asked.

"They assumed if there had been an accident, the man would have called 911."

"But he didn't?" William asked.

"No. We didn't receive any 911 calls from that area," the captain replied. "When the men got the tarp in the back of the truck they put an aluminum boat over it and tied everything down then they took a hose and proceeded to clean the alley."

"Let me guess. They couldn't see what was being washed off."

Captain Kirby did a half shrug. "Whatever was there, it wasn't much."

"That helps a hell of a lot," William said sarcastically. "And the only something on the asphalt had been the woman's body."

"We don't know that," Captain Kirby corrected him. "No one saw anything fall."

"She just disappeared and the man had been holding her." William's tone was condescending and he looked away. "Why did they wait so long?"

"They said they called the non-emergency number and was told the department would have a squad drive by. We did and the patrol reported seeing nothing suspicious and no one was in the apartment. They checked with neighbors and were told no one lives there. It has been empty for almost a year. Something on the news reminded the couple of it this morning and they decided to follow up. See if the woman was alright or if we had found out anything."

"Where was this at?" William asked.

"A building off Nine Hundred West and Two Hundred South," the captain answered.

"That's near Bonner's old building."

"It is," Captain Kirby answered.

"Have you dispatched another unit?" William asked. "What about techs? Did you send techs out? Have them pull sewer grates, if there are any, in the alley. See if they can find blood?"

"We sent a squad out, but they didn't find anything, either. Whatever had been in that alley – the guys were thorough about cleaning it up. According to the men manning the security desk, the apartment is empty. Has been…"

"…for close to a year," William said finishing the sentence.

"There are two grates," Captain Kirby continued, "one at each end of the alley. We're working on getting a city crew to accompany the techs and pull the grates tomorrow morning."

"I wonder if that was George's old apartment."

"Possibly," Captain Kirby replied. "We called Provo, and the park at the Great Salt Lake, and asked if there was any way to verify who had put a boat in the water. We were told only if someone happened to be there and saw it. Provo went through their call logs and they aren't showing any calls in that area. There was nothing at the Salt Lake, either. Both agencies are checking the perimeter of the lakes for us, but it doesn't mean the guys went to either place. They could have driven to one of hundreds of locations. A lot of them more remote and harder to be found in."

"I know," William said with a sigh. "It's just frustrating."

"I understand, but since we don't have a victim, we don't have a picture to show the people who called. We don't even know there was a victim."

William was quiet for minute then looked across the desk at Captain Kirby.

"Any missing person's reports filed recently?"

"We received one this morning. A man called and said his wife left to visit friends in Idaho a couple of days ago and hasn't been heard from since. He grew concerned when she didn't notify him of her safe arrival and he called to check on her. Their friends told him, they haven't seen her." Captain Kirby handed the men a copy of the bulletin.

"We may have the victim." William slid the picture across the captain's desk. "We requested information on Jane Doe's in the area and we have a hit."

"So, you think it's the woman in the Green River?"

"It would have been easy to make it look like she fell. If she was working for Reno and George found out, all George would have to do is tell the men how to stage it. Maybe he's taunting us, flaunting the fact that he still wields the power from inside. We know he has a major ego problem."

"Have you learned anything on her?"

"They did the autopsy this morning," William replied. "We're sending specimens from her to the U along with the others. According to the ME she'd had intercourse with someone before she died. It doesn't appear to be rape. It was consensual. The broken bones were from a fall, like she was dropped or thrown off a balcony or roof. But, she was dead when she hit the ground." William continued, giving the captain what information they had on Katie and Glen.

"I think I'm getting the picture," Captain Kirby said. "Keep me posted."

26

Mr. Randall's exercise was coming up and Jeremy disappeared for a couple of days to go over the scenario with Howard. He returned to Salt Lake City, Amanda's discomfort growing. With her propensity for feeling when things weren't right, the men drove to Park City prior to the event. Once they had checked the venue, they were concerned as well. Money was the magnet undesirables were drawn to so if Mr. Randall had the amount of cash on hand Jeremy had been told there would be, this would be a nightmare with only the four of them. And the recent uptick in activity gave them more concerns.

After he'd conferred with the men, Jeremy brought two of his guards up from the retreat. They needed the extra eyes. Further discussion and Jeremy rode up early with William and James, leaving Timothy to ride up in the limo with Amanda.

Saturday arrived and the closer the limo drew to Park City, the worse Amanda's trepidation grew. She hated these feelings, but had learned to rely on them as much as the men. At the venue, Amanda pushed the second button on her pager which told Jeremy she wasn't comfortable with the festivities. Jeremy met her and Timothy outside and ushered them in, dropping Amanda in the dressing room, Timothy stationed outside the door.

"You have ten minutes, my lady."

"Got it," she called back, a pair of blue jeans flopping over the top of the dressing stall, a shirt following. A vision of her sans the clothes popped in and he backed out, handing Timothy a spare magazine. This was not the time or place for that.

"The magazine in your weapon, with the pink band, is blanks. This one is not."

Timothy nodded, slipping it in his pocket.

Jeremy left him, joining William in the main dining area and waved for James to join them.

"Amanda doing okay?" William asked.

"No, I am afraid not," Jeremy said. "As you can tell, the commander has set this up perfectly for this test. It is not the most secure venue. Some of the doors don't even have adequate locks and the room is wide open. That makes it a tad easier for us and for anyone else. And since Amanda said she is not comfortable, that gives me more cause for concern. Every time she says she doesn't feel right, something happens."

"You do seem a bit uptight there, dude," James replied. He was feeling uneasy himself. The saving grace for the building was also its biggest drawback. "He doesn't give you any hints? Clues so we don't get shot?"

"Every person involved in this exercise has been issued blanks, just like you gentlemen. You will know by the pink band on the pistol grip…"

"Except you?" James said, pointing to Jeremy's pistol.

"That's in case something does go south and we don't catch it in time. That's also why the facilitators and the precautions. No citizens get hurt." He handed them each a spare magazine." As you can see, these aren't blanks. This is also in case things go south."

"Timothy?" William asked.

Jeremy nodded and hurried away, making one last trip outside to confirm his men were ready. The evening was set to begin and he wanted no surprises reminiscent of Reno.

When Mr. Randall arrived Jeremy went over where the men would be posted and what signals they would use if anything were to happen then went back to check on the staff. Amanda should be dressed and aiding them. He walked into the kitchen, Amanda wearing a form-fitting mermaid cut number covered in gold sequins, a matching shawl draped languidly over her shoulders, and Jeremy's breath caught. She never ceased to amaze him.

Timothy followed Jeremy to the front, all of his senses kicking in then people started arriving and the wait staff began their rounds. Timothy and James each took one of the main doors, William floating the perimeter, monitoring the growing crowd.

As the evening progressed, Amanda checked on guests, helped wait staff, and aided Mr. Randall when necessary. A run to refill pitchers and Amanda was back, gliding between tables, checking on guests and making sure the staff had everything once more before resuming her station behind Mr. Randall. When dinner was over and the entertainment began, she was the most popular lady on the dance floor again. Things were going smooth.

Jeremy's pager vibrated. 'New driver?' showed on the screen. Jeremy looked up, confused, Amanda visibly agitated, clasping her shawl tighter in front of her. Mr. Randall took her hand and pulled her down, asking her a question to which she smiled, patting his arm gently.

"Are we doing alright, Miss Amanda?" Jeremy asked leaning closer so she could hear him.

"She said she's scared," Mr. Randall answered, looking up at Jeremy. "I assume that isn't normal."

"You assume correctly, sir."

"So why is your driver inside?" Amanda asked, staring at one of the entrances.

"My driver shouldn't be inside."

Jeremy remembered the message and followed her gaze to a man in full driver livery just inside the doors, his eyes falling to a conspicuous bulge on the man's side. One of the guests bumped the man and he raised an arm, sweeping the jacket aside, giving a glimpse of the weapon. It didn't have the pink band denoting blanks and his drivers didn't wear theirs in shoulder holsters. This wasn't part of the test.

Jeremy opened the channel on the pager. "Gentlemen, switch magazines. We are hot." He gave the command for the channel to close then turned to Amanda and pointed to the chair next to Mr. Randall. "Sit tight until you feel me move. Mr. Randall…."

"Jeremy," Amanda said. "Give me your gun, please."

"Amanda…"

"Jeremy, you have a large amount of cash to return to the safe and a room full of people to help the men monitor. It's my turn. Slip me the damn gun! I know you aren't loaded with blanks and you have a back-up piece." She smiled over her shoulder at Mr. Randall. "My apologies, sir."

Mr. Randall nodded and winked at Jeremy.

"Very well, madam." Jeremy put his back to the crowd and pulled his weapon, slipping it to Amanda then turned back, giving instructions to Mr. Randall. "Would you be so kind as to end this event as quickly and calmly as possible?"

Mr. Randall headed for the dais.

Jeremy pulled his back-up piece and locked the comm channel open.

"We have uninvited guests," he said. "Things are changing. Timothy, James, remain where you are and continue aiding the guests. Make sure that driver does not get out. Amanda will join you from the rear hall. William, move to the stage and join Mr.

Randall, please. He is your responsibility." Jeremy leaned in and whispered to Amanda. "The cash is under Mr. Randall's chair. Grab it and secret it in your dress."

Amanda scowled, letting her eyes follow the skin tight number to the floor.

Jeremy shrugged. "Do the best you can."

Amanda nodded and slid the satchel out, crossing her arms to cover the case with her shawl and followed Jeremy. Once they were in the hall, Amanda shoved the case into Jeremy's chest and ran for the front.

"Lock it up, Jeremy," she called over her shoulder.

Jeremy was already peeling around the corner, racing for the office.

Amanda slipped her heels off, the shawl pooling on top of them. A woman couldn't run in those things. She grabbed the dresses hem and peeled the skirt up, gathering it in her left hand as she raced for the front, leaving everything where it lay. If the damn dress had been any tighter she wouldn't have pulled that off. Just short of the main hall someone darted to her left. Timothy appeared, steadying his pistol against the corner of the wall. Amanda froze. Jeremy was alone. She turned to the rear of the building, movement at the end of the hall catching her attention. A second man in driver's livery raced toward the office.

"Jeremy!" she called, sprinting for the rear hall. "You've got company! Timothy, James, your man's a decoy. Take him out."

She hurtled toward the office, her shoulder scraping the wall as she ran. When she reached the intersecting hall, she dropped her skirt, pivoting around the corner, fabric ripping and sequins flying as she braced her legs, weapon raised. She rolled her eyes. *'Who the hell did I piss of in a previous life?'*

"DROP!" she yelled.

Jeremy thrust the office door open and dropped. The man

wavered, his eyes locked on Amanda. Then they dropped to her leg, the thigh highlighted by gold sequins.

"HANDS OUT!" she yelled.

The man glanced at Jeremy, back at Amanda, then took a step forward. Amanda pulled the trigger. A second shot came from the front of the building and she prayed it hadn't been one of the men.

The double 'thub' of the silencers echoed through the space as Jeremy scrambled for the safe praying Amanda hadn't been hit. He tossed the money in, slammed the safe door, spinning the dial as he did then raced for the hall, weapon drawn. Amanda knelt beside the prone figure of a man dressed in driver's livery.

"Are you alright, Amanda?" he asked.

"Yes, thank you," she said.

Amanda grabbed her skirt, holding it together as she followed Jeremy. William had covered the other man where he laid in the main hall, Jeremy's men stationed outside the main doors. Timothy worked his way among the guests, calming them and checking that no one had been hurt. Saluting Timothy, Jeremy headed toward the rear entrance. That would be their weak link with only the driver. He opened the door the driver giving him a thumbs up. Jeremy started back up the hall, Amanda trotting toward him, followed by William and James.

Jeremy now admitted Amanda was going to be an even bigger asset than he had originally thought. His goal was always no injuries to his men and tonight – in big part to her – he had succeeded once again.

"I paged 911," she said when they reached him.

"Thank you," Jeremy replied, the sirens growing louder. "Go back to the main entrance; my men will need to disappear rather quickly. William, I'm going to have you and James work with the police. Amanda, you help Timothy with the guests. Go. I'll check on Mr. Randall. I am so proud of you, Miss Amanda."

Amanda smoothed her dress and returned to the dining room, slipping her heels on and tying her shawl to cover her left side on the way. When the three reached the front, Jeremy's men were gone, the doors had been locked and Mark Willis from the Park City Police Department stood tapping on the glass with a key. William opened the door, allowing Mark to enter, but barred the rest of the officers' entrance.

"Good to see you again," Mark said.

"I wish it was under different circumstances," William replied.

"As long as you guys are okay it's fine," Mark answered. "No crutches." He nodded at James. "Are you legal this time?"

William and James laughed remembering their visit the year before looking for Amanda. A good cop with a sense of humor.

"Always," William answered, flashing him one of Jeremy's cards.

After William had explained the incident, Mark instructed his men to fan out on the grounds in an attempt to locate any possible accomplices. Amanda and Timothy continued working with the guests and James made sure nobody made it inside who didn't carry a badge. William and Mark joined Jeremy and Mr. Randall in the office.

27

The second night went without a hitch and when the last of the guests left and Amanda changed, Jeremy had William accompany her to the limo, joining them a few minutes later. Safely inside, Amanda should have been relaxing, but only had a deeper sense of foreboding. She looked out the rear window, James and Timothy following in James car. They had only driven a couple of blocks when she started playing with the hem of her shirt. She looked over at Jeremy, eyes wide.

"Is there any other way to get back to Salt Lake City?" she asked.

"Yes, my lady," Jeremy replied. "We can drive through Big Cottonwood Canyon. It's a rather scenic route, and takes a little longer or we can take Highway-189 through Heber City. That one is a tad longer still, but will be easier in the limo."

"Whatever you think is best," she answered, with a dismissive wave.

"Why don't we try the interstate?" Jeremy asked. "If there's a problem we can turn around and head back. It will be much faster. Does that sound alright?"

"I guess," she said with a shrug. She sighed and scanned the road, her eyes flitting between cars. "I just don't think that's a good idea. I wish I could explain it."

Jeremy looked across the seat at William. "Thoughts William? It isn't too late to change our mind."

"I think we need to listen to her," William replied.

Jeremy slid the partition aside letting the driver know they would need to take the right at the intersection with Highway-248. He had barely sat back when a truck appeared behind James' car, following way too close. The truck veered to the left, weaving dangerously then pulled back in behind James, narrowly avoiding an oncoming car. Jeremy turned, looking out the windshield. Another vehicle had nosed across the street ahead of them, two men striding toward the limo.

Jeremy tapped the driver on the shoulder. "We need to get this car out of Park City," Jeremy said. "Do you have room to slide this pig around that corner…" He pointed to an intersection only a few yards away. "…and onto that street?"

"Yes, sir."

"Do it," Jeremy said.

He pushed the button opening the comm channel on the pager, warning James and Timothy about the change of plans.

"Put the lady down," the driver instructed. "It might get a little bumpy."

Jeremy directed his gaze to the floorboards. Amanda obeyed, William leaning over her. The driver hit the gas, cramping the wheel to the right. The rear of the limo swung to the left, the tires screaming. They bounced over the curb then hurtled up the narrow road.

"James, if you are still alright do a single chirp on the second button to verify, please. There have been a couple more surprises so do your best to follow us."

A single beep echoed in the rear compartment and Jeremy moved to the rear facing seat so he could talk to the driver, the driver concentrating on the road ahead.

"You will need to turn right up here. It will connect with Main Street which will take us the back way to Heber City on Highway-224."

"I don't think that's an option, sir," the driver replied.

Jeremy looked out the passenger window, a twenty-six foot refrigerated truck aiming at them. And it didn't appear to have any plans on slowing. The limo driver hit the brakes, its tires complaining, the huge car shuddering, and cramped the wheel to the left then swerved to the right and back left, narrowly missing the oncoming vehicle. The rear of the limo continued to the right, the rear tire slammed the curb, losing traction then they were flying toward another intersection.

"LEFT!" Jeremy ordered. "And keep it floored!"

It was less than ten minutes before the limo slowed again. The road making a left, a familiar truck flying around the corner at them.

"Our company is back," the driver said.

"There is a road on the right up here," Jeremy said. Take it." The driver nodded. "It should take us to Highway-248 and then 189 to Heber City." Jeremy opened the comm channel on the pager. "James, are you and Timothy still alright?"

"We're still here," Timothy answered. "We see him. Do what you gotta do. We'll keep up."

Jeremy watched the oncoming car, his driver counting backwards from some unknown point. Seconds before they met, the driver swerved into the opposing lane, bypassing the vehicle then he steered around the corner to the right.

"Keep going," Jeremy instructed the driver. "Do not slow until you know we are no longer being tailed."

The driver did a single nod and accelerated.

The group pulled into Amanda's two and a half hours later, joking about the cost of keeping Amanda clothed, and climbed out of the vehicles, Jeremy inviting them upstairs for a beer. They had earned it.

They walked into the apartment to the fax squealing. Amanda gave each of them a kiss on the cheek and walked to her room and the respite of comfy clothes.

"What was that for?" Jeremy asked.

"A thank you for all you do. I appreciate you guys more than you know."

Amanda reappeared, curling up in an armchair and relaxed.

"I am thinking about requesting guards for you and William's apartments," Jeremy said, handing everybody a beer. "Just until this is over. What are your thoughts?"

"God, I hate that!" Amanda said irritably. "Isn't there some other way to handle this crap?"

"Getting a tad testy, Amanda?" he asked. "But in answer to your question, no. I cannot watch the perimeter and the interior of this building at the same time. And I cannot watch this building and Williams."

"Just tired," she answered, leaning her head on the back of the chair. "And you're right."

"William?"

"I would prefer you didn't," he answered. "But if you think it's necessary….Do what you have to. My concern is, it will draw even more attention to us."

"Understood. We'll hold off then."

Jeremy moved to the guest room slash office to retrieve the fax sheets, scanning them quickly.

"How are you holding up, Timothy?" James asked.

"Hanging in there. So, is it always this entertaining when you guys get together? Or was this just for my benefit again?"

"It's Amanda," James replied. "Everything was smooth sailing until she stuck her pretty little neck into it."

"You might have something there," William said. "It was pretty boring until she showed up."

"I guess when you're good, you're good," she responded.

Jeremy returned and raised his beer in a salute. "Tonight's planned exercise was interrupted again, but the commander said, as far as he's concerned, you passed with flying colors."

Amanda sighed, taking a long pull on her beer. So much for things working as they should.

After Amanda finished her beer she headed for the bedroom. She had discovered the men liked to talk. Kind of compare notes. And they had already started the rundown on this evening's activities.

"If you will excuse me, I think I'm going to retire. I'm exhausted."

"And I need to make another run to the retreat," Jeremy said. "I will return in a day or two."

James and Timothy followed, neither of them wanting to be last man up when it wasn't their home. William followed them to the door then slipped into Amanda's room.

"Think you might like some company?" he whispered.

28

With the party season officially gearing up and the exercises over, Jeremy scheduled another meeting. He wanted everyone on the same page when the parties started.

"I have a very serious question for you, Amanda" Jeremy said, once everyone arrived.

"About?" she asked, realizing she sounded like James.

"I want to make sure there is no confusion. What if you are put in a situation where you are pulling a civilian out of harm's way, but you are stopped. You have been uncovered. Your true identity discovered."

"With Amanda all she'd have to do is flash that shirt," James said. He grinned, mimicked a flasher and raised his eyebrows. "I mean, that would stop most dudes in their tracks. That might even leave some memories."

"James...." Amanda said.

"And how would you know?" William asked, staring at James as he laughed.

"He doesn't," Amanda said angrily.

"Let's get back to the meeting," Jeremy said with a grin.

Amanda glared at James, the others continuing to laugh.

"Jeremy, that's one question that can't be answered unless I'm actually in a situation," Amanda answered. "I could sit here and tell you I would die pulling these people down, but if I were staring down the barrel of a gun, would I be able to do it? I don't know."

"I'm going to stand up with second thoughts now," William said, wiping a tear from his eye. "After these latest attacks I don't want her out there."

"William!" Amanda exclaimed. "You can't be serious. How can you do this? I have never tried to dissuade you from doing anything for you job. I joined this team for a reason."

"How could I what? Tell you I don't want someone to hurt you? What the hell do you expect me to say? Hop to it? Go ahead and get yourself raped? Or shot maybe? Didn't you learn anything last year? I don't want to hurt you, but somebody has to make you think. You're pushing. You're part of a team, and every man on this team will go down before you do, but it isn't going to do any good if you do it to yourself."

"I don't want to sound like I'm arguing, but this is up to Jeremy and me. You didn't say anything at Mr. Randall's exercise."

"No, but just so you know. It scared the hell out of me."

"I'm not taking sides," Timothy interjected, "but I think I understand where he's coming from. No one here wants to see you hurt, Amanda. No one. He just wants you to be more careful." He looked across the table, searching William's eyes. "Am I right?"

William nodded, giving Amanda a sideways glance.

"Okay," Amanda said. "I'll take your ideas into consideration, but…."

"Why are you so damn angry?" William asked. "What did Royce do to you?"

"It wasn't just Royce," she said. "It's every man who has ever told me, a woman's *place* is under his thumb or only good for something in the bedroom. It's every person who told me I *can't* do – whatever it is – just because I'm a *woman*. It's every lecture I've ever received because I don't fit the ideal of how a woman should act, or agree with the belief that we are only good for *one* thing.…"

"Step out of that grave, Amanda. It wasn't dug for you. You're too strong a woman for that. But that's why I didn't play the bedroom hustle and end up married to the first bimbo who got pregnant. That's part of why I left the cockroach infested streets of Louisiana. I had to get away from the same old grave."

"Did you do it?" Amanda asked, recognizing the challenge in her tone. She paused and softened her voice "Escape the grave, I mean."

"Some days I have my doubts," he answered. "I still have the moments."

Everyone remained quiet, waiting for the next volley, Jeremy eyeing the two.

"Is everything under control now?" Jeremy asked. "No more of these tiffs? We are going to work together like adults?"

"Yes, yes and yes," Amanda said.

"William?"

"Yes. And I'll try not to sound like the jealous husband. Especially since we aren't married."

"Good. Now back to the meeting," Jeremy said. "There are more stories going around about George working the organization from his prison cell. Nothing concrete yet. We are also hearing rumors about underage prostitutes working under the Bonner umbrella. Obviously, that needs to be verified, and quickly. Plus two of Mr. Bonner's supplier's have suddenly turned up MIA. I was told by one source the reason they are unaccounted for is they were trunking off the syndicate's distribution lines instead of purchasing their product from the syndicate."

"They were stealing from the syndicate? Those dudes had some cajones!" Timothy said.

"William and I pulled up the initial reports on the lady from Park Street and the preliminary report on the blood work from the gentlemen who OD'd," James said, sliding a file across the table to Jeremy. "The guys OD'd on uncut cocaine. It was raw."

Jeremy took the folder, going over the reports. "No one does this much at once!" Jeremy said, surprised.

"Not normally," James agreed. "And there's no indication they mixed it with anything."

"One of the men had a business card in his back pocket," William said. "A company out of Reno, Nevada. It matches one we found in their room and the one from Olivia's purse. So far they appear legit. They have their fingers in a lot of different pies. And last report, said that the guy with the gash on the back of the head, the one with the blood on his clothes – the blood was his. It looks like he fell."

"Maybe they were high." James looked at William, puzzled.

"It still doesn't add up," William answered. "I think something is being covered up."

Jeremy listened, watching the two. This is why they were so good. They bounced ideas off each other. Found the flaws as they worked the leads.

"I noticed your reports said someone had searched the room prior to your arrival," Jeremy said, placing the folder back on the table. "Any ideas on who that might have been?"

"Nothing yet," William answered. "Still looking."

"Anything else before we adjourn this meeting?"

"I did some snooping," Amanda interjected. "Put that women's intuition to work." Everyone looked at her. "I remember, right after George went to prison, William and James said George had to have a much more in depth set up than the department knew about. He was bringing in too much money for a penny ante pimp. He drove a limo, had the compound in Reno, the condo in Park City, the house outside Cascade Springs, where did the money for all that come from?" She paused and everybody nodded. "So I drilled that hole deeper with the help of Jeremy's organization..."

"Our organization," Jeremy said correcting her.

"Our organization," Amanda repeated. "Anyway, a George Thomas Bonner was born outside Las Vegas, Nevada and raised by his father; a retired Vegas pit boss turned security guard. His mother died from a drug overdose when he was young. Shortly after George's seventeenth birthday, his father was shot in some kind of dispute at the poker table."

She glanced up, Jeremy nodding.

"We knew about that, my lady."

"There is no record of him ever working a regular job," she said. "It shows two arrests before he turned eighteen, but no charges were ever pressed."

"Let me guess," Timothy said. "Drugs or prostitution."

"Actually both. I also found a large ..." She paused and smiled broadly. ".... 'hotel' – and I use that word in the broadest sense if the word – on the Nevada side of the Nevada Arizona border that shows one hundred percent occupancy every single week. The hotel is owned and operated by, GTB Enterprises out of Laughlin, Nevada, under phony Nevada incorporation papers."

"Money greasing some official palms," William said. "And that's not all. I see that glint in your eye."

"You're right," she said. "According to a few of the town's residents it's an escort service. A high priced brothel. A few of the local officials are entertained, off the books, for helping them stay off the gaming commission's most wanted list."

"So....They're running games off the books, too?" James asked. "That explains the money, buddy!"

"Anything else?" Jeremy asked.

"They're still digging," she replied. "There hints that it may not be the only one. I have one question for Jeremy now. Is that why the training center is in Arizona just outside of Laughlin, Nevada?"

Jeremy smiled and hiked his left shoulder. "Possibly. I never bothered to ask." Then he laughed. "We knew George had things working better than the operation here in Utah showed. And for George to pull in the money he does there has to be more than one location. We just haven't made it any farther than that. We have enough leads teasing us, that a few of those undercover think George is leaking just enough to mock us. Give himself a feeling of power."

Amanda smirked across the table at Jeremy. This organization put that training facility where it was for a reason. Its proximity to Nevada and the syndicate was that reason. She would guarantee it. And George Bonner's rise to power had only been an added benefit.

"You're not off the hook, yet, Jeremy," Amanda said. "And I promise to keep nagging until you spill."

29

Jeremy met everyone at the club the next weekend. Like William and James, he couldn't get past the feeling some important tidbit of information had been overlooked, or hadn't been uncovered. And the information that was coming across wasn't giving them what they needed. When William and Amanda finished the last set, they set up a meeting to go over their ideas then William and James left, promising to be at Amanda's the next afternoon.

Sunday morning Jeremy awoke and brushed the hair away from Amanda's face. He had decided to back out. Let Amanda and William have a chance. Be there as their friend and mentor. But last night, he had not been able to. He had pushed and teased until she'd relented. She moved beside him and he kissed her, running his hand around to her back, pulling her closer, starting the dance again. She had the softest skin.

After making love, he nuzzled her neck, breathing in the scent of Amanda. Amanda rolled to the edge of the bed, sitting up, back hunched, head in her hands. Jeremy recognized the posture. She was feeling guilty.

"Amanda." He pulled her back down beside him. "There's no reason to feel bad. Maybe we need to sit down and talk about it."

"Nothing to talk about. I feel so guilty sometimes. It's not like I'm engaged or married, or anything. And now I feel bad because you're taking the blame."

"Don't. It will be fine. I'll shower and start coffee. Join me when you're ready."

Jeremy heard the sigh as he walked out, cursing himself for not being stronger. When Amanda joined him, he poured her coffee, taking the seat beside her, giving her a hug.

"I promise to control myself better," he said. "Okay? I don't want you feeling bad."

"Same," she answered.

"William and James will be here within the hour." He toyed with his cup, glancing her direction. "I am curious…" He dropped his gaze then locked eyes with hers. "….are you and William thinking about getting married? Perhaps that is why it bothers you when we're together." He sighed and looked away. "He loves you Amanda."

"No, we are not getting married," she said in mock disdain. "He hasn't said anything. It just feels strange." She shrugged, playing with her cup now. "I don't know. Maybe William's right. Maybe I should just quit the team and get a regular job and let you guys find someone who cares for only you…"

"Amanda, that isn't the answer to anything," Jeremy replied, irritation seeping into his voice. "Damn it!" He sat back, waited, watching her then he leaned forward. "I don't want to quit seeing you….."

The buzzer announcing the men's arrival startled them, Amanda jumping.

Jeremy sighed and stood. "I will get it," he said, the perfect gentleman once again. "Get dressed, my lady."

Amanda bobbed her head.

Jeremy let William and James in, being told Timothy was on patrol then started lunch, making more coffee. They ate a leisurely meal then he brought the paperwork out.

"Have you gentlemen learned anything knew about Mr. Bonner's nephew?" Jeremy asked.

"Not directly," James answered. "A bar two and a half blocks north of George's old establishment has been leased to Jonathan. The business license and all liquor licenses are in Jonathan's name. We peeked through the front window. It's been repainted and they've started tearing the carpet out. An antique bar and back bar have been put in so it's beginning to look pretty descent. Someone has moved into George's old apartment and there's a steady stream of ladies going in and out again, the rooms on the main floor are rarely empty."

"What's the word on your call in Green River? I saw you were able to get some help."

"It's a duplicate of the two from last year," William replied.

"Any blood in the alley?" Jeremy asked.

"A tiny amount was found around the edge of the grate behind George's old apartment building, and in a crack where the asphalt meets the building. One of the techs said someone was watching them from one of the apartments, but when officers went to talk to the tenant they were stopped at the security desk and told that that particular apartment was vacant."

"Even though they saw someone in it?" Amanda asked.

William shrugged. "I don't know Amanda. They pushed until a tech was allowed upstairs with an escort. The apartment appeared to be lived in. He said there were dishes in the sink and clothes tossed over the back of the sofa. But they weren't allowed any further than the balcony. He checked the balcony and found a small amount of tissue on the railing. Samples have been sent to the U. We hope that will point us in the right direction. We won't know if it was from Katie or someone else until they complete the tests. That building is under Jonathan's name also, but Jonathan doesn't live there. He lives in a new complex on Forty-Five Hundred South and State Street."

"Any word from the university?" Jeremy asked.

"Not yet. They warned us it could take a while."

"Jonathan's name isn't on any of the paperwork for GTB Enterprises," Amanda said. "A fax came through last night while we were at the club. If anything happens to George any business endeavors including GTB Enterprises are to be turned over to his estate to be handled by the designated trustee. If no one has been assigned that role, all assets are to be liquidated and funneled into an account in Arizona. That trail has turned into a dead end."

30

A nightmarish dream of Katie shocked Glen awake. She stalked him, hair flowing behind her wild and loose, her arms misshapen, legs twisted, mouth open in a silent scream. He ran, her eyes locked on him, dead black hollows following his every move.

He sat up, gasping for air and hung his legs over the edge the bed, sweat covering his body.

"I'm sorry, Katie," he whispered.

Drunks argued and staggered in the hall, falling into the wall, their cursing and yelling growing louder. He checked the clock, wishing they would fight somewhere else. Disturb someone else. He groaned as he stood, glanced at the clock again and stumbled toward the bathroom. He needed to talk to George about his dearly beloved nephew anyway.

At eight fort-five Glen sat a block north of the bar, surveying the street. A black pick-up with one occupant sat across the street by the main door. Glen recognized the driver. He'd worked for George last year.

Glen slid the cash and the photos out of his jacket and studied them then slid them back in. He looked up, the truck gone. Parking behind the building, Glen climbed out and closed his eyes, taking a deep breath to calm his nerves. He had no idea how George would react to what Jonathan had planned.

Glen approached the rear entrance and the door swung open George staring out at him. Inside, the first thing Glen noticed was the man from the pick-up at George's table, a cup of coffee in front of him.

"I'm glad you joined us," the man said.

George directed Glen to a chair and waved for the bartender to bring more coffee. "Sit down," he said. "Have you met David?" George chin pointed to the stranger as he sat.

"I've heard of him." Glen sat down and thanked the bartender for the coffee, laying the pictures on the table.

"Ah, yes." George picked them up then tossed them onto the table. "I knew Jonathan was up to something. I just didn't think he would approach two of my best assets. But now I'm getting the idea. Let me guess, he wants you to get these to the cops. How unoriginal."

"I have a better idea," Glen said.

"Continue," George said.

"We know Jonathan is courting the syndicate."

George almost nodded.

"We also know the syndicate isn't into the underage girls."

George leaned back, listening as he crossed his arms.

"I was thinking," Glen continued. "Instead of getting these to the cops to implicate you and Reno, I deliver them to Reno and implicate Jonathan."

"You would do that to Jonathan?" George waited, but received no reply. "You're a smart man, Glen. That can be dangerous."

"I'm not stupid enough to think I'm that smart," Glen replied, following George's train of thought. "I agreed to work for you. Jonathan only assumes that if he throws money my way, I work for him." Glen tossed the cash onto the table beside the pictures. "I didn't ask him for a penny, nor did I tell him I would do it. Your nephew thinks he can better you by playing the same game you do, but I'll bank on experience over self-importance any day."

"Keep the cash," George said. He slid the money along with the pictures back to Glen. "Deliver the pictures to Reno, kiss a little ass, but keep me out of it."

Glen nodded. "I'll make the call this morning."

"Wait here." George stood, striding down the hall.

David leaned forward and picked up the pictures, studying them closely then set them back down. He looked up, eyeing Glen, the slightest hint of a smile lifting one corner of his mouth.

"You know George didn't hire those kids."

"I know," Glen answered, sliding the photos and the cash off the table. "I also know what George will do if I follow Jonathan's instructions. That's why I'm here. What difference does it make to you?"

"I have a suggestion this morning," David said ignoring Glen's question.

Glen nodded, took a drink of his coffee, setting it back on the table. David's eyes were disconcerting. Empty pools one could drown in.

"Choose your next move very, very carefully. In some ways Jonathan is much worse than his uncle. He won't just you set up for a fall then celebrate that fall; he will dance on your grave after the fall. He learned a lot from his uncle. Problem is... he didn't learn as much as he thinks he did."

"And why are you telling me this?"

"Because you're good Mr. Tortino. Too good to allow a drunk and a wannabe bad guy to screw things up for you. The cops are already nipping at you and Jonathan's heels. If they get those pictures, George isn't the one who will go down. You will. George already has things in place for just such a contingency. His nephew does not. Jonathan hasn't thought that far ahead." He flipped out a business card and handed it to Glen. The Landers Corporation – Reno, Nevada. "I believe we have the same goals."

George had started back up the hall and David gave Glen a mock salute then leaned back in his chair. George sat down and handed Glen five hundred dollars.

"A bonus for staying loyal," George said. "I also want you to know I'm sorry about Katie. She was a special lady, but she shouldn't have crossed. I'm confident I won't have to worry about that with you. Will I?"

Glen took the cash and shook his head dumbly, the words he wanted to say stuck in his throat. George sorry about Katie? Bullshit! George wasn't sorry about anything he'd ever done or anyone he'd ever hurt!

Back in his car, Glen stared at the back door of the bar. *Who was playing who?* Whichever way it was going, the odds didn't appear to be in his favor. He was stuck on the fifty yard line playing the teams against each other, and the fans.

"Katie," he said out loud. "If I don't make the right move, I might see you sooner than we expected. I miss you so much."

The door closed behind Glen and George turned to David, the conversation with Glen already forgotten.

"So, what do you think, David?" He gestured around the bar, smiling broadly.

"I'm impressed," David admitted taking in the place.

George had made some changes. He'd removed the old carpet, dispensing with the last vestiges of the previous establishment's stench. The addition of the antique bar and back bar gave it a touch of class. Men had put the new pool tables together and were hanging racks for the pool sticks, and putting the last of the glass shelves in place.

"I'm curious, though. I thought you were ensconced at Point of the Mountain for many years to come. How'd you luck out?"

"It seems one of the guards got greedy." George laughed and raised an eyebrow.

David chuckled and looked at the floor. "So, why did you call, George? It wasn't to exchange pleasantries. Or have me listen to you talk to Glen."

"I am in need of someone to run the girls and collect from the peddlers again. You're usually up for earning a little income on the side. Think you can handle it?"

"Of course. Jonathan not working out?"

"When did Jonathan work?" George sniped, sarcastically. "But you already know that. He's angling for my best people so he doesn't have to leave the comfort of the bottle." George paused, chinning at David's hand. "How's the finger? Still not as good as new, I see. Want another go at her?"

"You withheld valuable information on her, George. I learned my lesson, though. Never trust you, or the women you procure."

"Here's an incentive to get you started." George said, ignoring the barb as he slid an envelope in front of David. "There should be five grand in there. I'll let you know about the lady."

"When should I plan on starting this new position?"

"How about tonight? The girls are using the same rooms they did last year. The only thing Jonathan changed was his residence."

"And the age requirements?" David asked.

"We're still working on that," George replied. "Start shoving the younger ones out. I damn well don't want to get arrested for that."

31

William and James returned from lunch and were given a message from a woman who lived on Third Avenue near N Street. According to the woman an alien had been observed by several individuals sneaking between houses on the south side of Third Avenue the night before. Several of the women's husbands had taken it upon themselves to attempt to capture the creature. The call had been forwarded to them due to the latest assaults. William called the woman, setting an appointment for two that afternoon and called the captain, letting him know they would be out of the box. They pulled up, several neighbors in attendance as well, and William scowled.

"Why do people always have to include the whole damn neighborhood?" James asked.

"Don't know," William said, opening the door and climbing out. "But this shit's getting to me."

"You got that, buddy. I could use a few days at Jeremy's," James said, shaking his head.

William frowned. He wouldn't mind hanging around the pool, but he didn't want Amanda near Jeremy.

Finishing the interviews, they climbed into the unmarked, their portables squawking. Another complaint of an alien off Foothill Drive on Parley's Way and Pasadena Street. James wrote down the address and the information and William pulled out. They were greeted with the same scene, but this time the woman's husband claimed to have cornered it then the alien came at him with a knife. James made a note that the alien appeared to have traveled from Third Avenue and N Street to Parley's Way and Foothill Drive, and when confronted he did not beam up, or disappear. He attacked and ran like any human would have.

With the interviews concluded they pulled onto East Parley's Way where they could merge onto westbound 80 out of Parley's Canyon, exiting on State Street.

As they approached Interstate-80 William checked traffic maneuvering through vehicles merging from Parley's Canyon and Park City. William took a quick look at traffic on his right, pulling up next to two teenagers. A flash of light drew William's attention and he glanced behind the teen's car to a vehicle following far too close, momentarily locking eyes with the driver. A blue pick-up truck with an aluminum boat in the bed. William turned his gaze back to traffic, giving James a soft back hand, pointing to the right as the truck accelerated, passing the kids and merging in front of the unmarked car. An explosion kicked dust in their direction, James automatically ducking as rocks and debris bounced off the passenger side window.

William glanced to the right, the teen struggling, the front end of his car bucking and wobbling erratically then William looked back at traffic ahead of them, the truck fading from view. He slowed, horns blaring behind him, the teen's car swerving into their lane. The cars collided, the other car careening back into its lane, the driver continuing to work feverishly to regain control. The girl in the passenger seat sat frozen, her face locked in terror.

"Hold her steady, buddy," James said. "We got a parking lot in front of you and someone's eating your tail. You're doing good."

William smiled at James play-by-play, continuing to slow the unmarked car, blasting the siren to warn other motorists. More horns honked and tires squealed as drivers hit their brakes. Then the teen's car jumped lanes in front of them, the smaller car spinning, facing oncoming traffic before bouncing off the divider on the left and slamming into William's door, the unmarked car knocked into a sideways skid. William applied his brakes more aggressively, doing a nosedive to avoid vehicles in front of them, those driver's rubber necking through their mirrors.

William checked traffic then looked to his left, the rear end on the teen's car swinging in a wide arc, its tires screaming. Horns blasted once again as other drivers skidded to a stop to avoid the teen's car. William did one more blast of the siren to warn motorists and a space opened up on the right. William slowed further, maneuvering into the right lane away from other vehicles, checking his rear view mirror.

Then James yelled, his voice tense. "YO, BUDDY!"

William jerked his gaze from the mirror, the teen's car coming at them head on. The impact propelled the teenage driver through the windshield, that car jumping backwards, spinning out of control. William flipped the lights and siren on, continuing to steer away from traffic. The teen's car hit the barrier on the right side, coming off the pavement, the heavier unmarked car ramming its undercarriage. That impact sent the smaller over the barrier. While William fought their car to a stop, James gripped the door handle, wrestling his instinct to abandon ship and follow the smaller car down the embankment. Their car came to a stop, its right front fender mangled, wrapped around the tire.

William's head had tipped to the left, resting on the driver's window, his breathing labored coming in heavy gasps.

"William!" James called. "Damn! Hang on buddy."

James grabbed the mike, calling for assistance; telling dispatch an officer was injured then tossed it onto the dash and pulled out his pager, alerting Jeremy, giving him their location.

James wrenched on the handle, his door jammed. He reached across William and disengaged the locks for the rear doors then squirmed over the seat rolling out the back. Traffic was backing up, drivers craning to see. James placed flares along the road, waving oncoming traffic into the far lane then raced back to check on William. He was having trouble breathing, but beginning to stir.

"I think our reports are going to be late," James said.

"I think we have a good excuse," William wheezed.

Timothy pulled up along with two other squad cars and began directing traffic. With Timothy there, James scrambled over the barrier, hurtling down the embankment toward the teens. By the time Jeremy and Amanda arrived, a tired and dirt covered James had climbed back onto the highway.

Jeremy pulled up, rushing toward James, directing Amanda to stay in the car. "Are you and William alright?"

James nodded, palming his eyes. He lowered his hands, dirt streaked his cheeks where tears had trickled down and he'd wiped them away, a thin line of blood from a cut on his forehead leaving a trail.

"Where's William?"

"In the car." James jerked his head toward the unmarked then followed Jeremy.

"James," William wheezed in a barely audible gasp. "What about the kids? There were two kids in that car."

"They're gone," James answered.

"Damn! They were only kids!"

James could only nod. "The driver's body is part way down the hill, but the girl is still inside." James paused, finally choked out, "It's not pretty."

Jeremy began an inspection of the scene, following the skid marks to where the smaller car had swerved. Paint chips from the initial impact littered the highway, glass crunched underfoot, Jeremy's mind working on the possibilities, visualizing the event as it might have unfolded. A horn honked behind Jeremy causing him to stop and wait for oncoming cars before continuing into the lane of traffic. He moved farther east to where they would have merged, spotting an area that appeared to have been burned. He kneeled, touched the outer ring of discoloration then put his fingers to his nose, recognizing the distinctive odor of explosives. Jeremy looked behind him, assessing the distance between this mark and the collision.

Jeremy joined the others, pulling James back with him. "Can you tell me what happened?" Jeremy asked. "Did another car ram the other car first?"

"There was a bang then they hit our car. The next thing I saw was the teen's car spin out and hit us head on."

Jeremy gazed behind them at the battered car, then beyond it to the crane and the girl's body being lifted to the waiting van. This was intentional. This was no accident. What could those kids have done in their short lives to warrant this? When he looked back, William was being loaded into a waiting ambulance.

"Climb in, James. It's time to see what's going on."

Jeremy walked into the emergency room with Amanda and James still thinking about the wreck and the explosives residue. The bang James had mentioned. The door whooshed open, two nurses and a doctor attempting to work on William. Jeremy pushed past James, a nurse nodding his direction.

"What do we know?" Jeremy asked.

"Other than he's fighting everything the doctor is trying to tell him?" She smiled, seeing Jeremy's grin. "So far, his vitals are good. He's having difficulty breathing so..." She raised her voice a hair and stared pointedly at William. "…if he'll cooperate we'll take him to x-ray to get some pictures." She lowered her voice to normal tone. "Hopefully that will shed light on his condition. His lungs sound clear and he's not coughing up blood, so we're suspecting broken ribs. Is that his wife?" She nodded in Amanda's direction, continuing to work.

"No," Jeremy replied. His eyes dropped to William's hand and the wedding band. "He's a widower."

They wheeled William out for x-rays, Timothy appearing in the emergency room. One of the nurses tried to deny him access. Timothy glared at her angrily and directed her gaze to the exam room. The nurse locked eyes with Jeremy, Jeremy dipped his head and she pushed the button, allowing Timothy in.

It was over an hour before William was wheeled back in.

"Do you feel up to answering a couple of questions for me?" Jeremy asked. "Only nod yes or no." William nodded. "James said the other car swerved and hit you."

"There was a bang, crap blew against the passenger window, then the car started weaving all over the road," William said.

"Please, try not to talk," the nurse chided William. "You need to save your breath."

"That won't happen," Amanda said. "It will be easier for us to save our breath."

Jeremy shook his head the others laughing. "Their car swerved into yours after the explosion? Was the driver looking at you? I know you were busy, but did you notice anything?"

A nurse interrupted, pointing toward the waiting area. Karen was glaring through the doors, her arms out like 'what the hell', Jeremy told them to allow her in. An hour later they had bandaged James cut and the two were signing their release papers.

Jeremy smirked then looked at Amanda. "It may not be a good idea to try and make babies for a day or two, my lady. You need to be gentle with the man."

"I don't think I could handle that." William gasped trying not to laugh. "Breathing is even hard."

"Then you're doing it all wrong," James said, laughing.

Karen smacked him on the back of the head, Amanda glaring across the bed at him.

"Ouch!" he exclaimed. "What was that for?"

"You know exactly what that was for," Karen answered. "One of these days you're going to get that rear end in some serious trouble."

"I think everybody needs to meet back at Amanda's," Jeremy said. "We have some things to go over and I have probably caused enough trouble for one day."

Back at Amanda's, Jeremy set snacks out then looked across the table at William and James.

"Any ideas gentlemen?" Jeremy asked.

"No," James replied. "Not without going through all of our old cases. But I think everyone we sent up is still in prison."

The rest of the meal was spent going over what Jeremy had discovered at the scene, William and James adding bits and pieces from their returning memory. By nine p.m. the pain meds were getting hard for William to push aside. It was time to go. As much as he wanted to stay, he wouldn't do it with Jeremy there.

32

It was a quiet weekend at home and William and Amanda were on stage, William and James' department pager's chirping as they started the last set. William looked over the piano as James rushed for the phone. James hung up, gave an upward tilt of his head and William abandoned the stage, Amanda letting the hand holding the mike drop. William noticed the move and wondered if she was upset. Amanda locked eyes with the soundman and gave a twirl of the index finger on her left hand. It was time for the taped music.

Possible reasons for tonight's summons flooded through as the two gave their apologies, bounding up the stairs to street level.

They pulled up to the scene, William examining the derelict old building, its side door hanging open. Except for the current hum of activity, the ladies experience was probably the only thing that had disturbed the structure in years. Even the vegetation covering the exterior bore witness to the neglect. They ducked under the police tape, the floorboards groaning, their complaints barely audible above the din of the police radios. Inspecting the interior, it didn't appear much different than the outside. Tendrils from vines poked their heads inside, directing ones attention to the broken windows at the rear of the building while layers of dust and the smell of mouse droppings and age permeated the air.

William continued to skim the area, his eyes coming to rest on the woman. She sat on a hay bale, clutching her arms across her chest, rocking in place. A man sat beside her, holding her while she talked. Bruises were beginning to show on the woman's jaw, a cut on her neck. The man took a piece of gauze and wiped blood from his nose, a large area of swelling and discoloration on his cheek, his right arm bandaged.

They approached the group, introducing themselves, listening while the woman gave her account of the attack. Five rapes, two women murdered during the commission of the crime. How did Olivia fit in? Or did she? Rape was usually about control. Fear and sex were only the components used to gain that control.

After she had completed her story, William kneeled in front of her, looked at the man beside her then back at her.

"Forgive me. I hate to put you through this, but we arrived after you started giving officers your statement. Can I ask you a few questions?" William kept his voice calm not wanting to enflame her already raw emotions.

She nodded and leaned into the man.

He and James took turns asking questions, not wanting to grill her but still make sure they had missed nothing. William hated interrogating them so many times, but they couldn't miss a thing.

"Why were you out alone this time of night?"

"My boyfriend and I had an argument," she answered. "I left to cool down. I walk this way every time we fight so I didn't think tonight would be any different."

"Did you see anybody? A neighbor or maybe someone you didn't know?"

"A jogger passed me. He smiled and nodded. But that was the only person."

"Have you seen this jogger before?"

"I've never seen anyone before," she answered. "It's usually pretty deserted."

"Did you see which direction he went?"

"He turned south on Eighth East, I didn't see him after that. The guy grabbed me before I reached the corner."

"Were you directly in front of this building?" William asked, continuing to probe gently. "Was it before or after you passed the garage?"

"I had just passed the corner out here." She pointed to the northwest corner.

"What time? Do you know?"

"Maybe around ten-thirty…."

"She isn't normally gone very long," her boyfriend cut in, defending her. "Ten minutes or so tops. Tonight she'd been gone almost an hour so I got worried. I heard shouting and ran in. One of her hands was tied to the post and she was kicking at some psycho swinging a knife."

"Thank you," William answered, turning his attention back to the woman. "Did you see anyone before or after the jogger? Could there have been someone else in the shadows?"

"I guess," she said. "I suppose anything is possible. I know he'd been drinking. I could smell the alcohol."

"Did he get farther than tying you up?" He thought of Amanda and how she would react, being as discreet as possible. "Was he able to…"

"Are you insinuating she didn't fight?" her boyfriend interjected angrily. "You think she would have…"

"We aren't insinuating anything," William said. "We have to have all the facts. I understand this is hard for both of you, but *you*…" He emphasized the word 'you' as he pointed at her boyfriend. "…have to understand this was an attack, not a romantic interlude. There's a big difference."

The man backed down and William turned back at the woman.

She nodded, the tears flowing again. "Yes. That's when he cut me on the neck. He wasn't gripping the knife real tight. I kicked him in the shin and got one arm free and slugged him. He fell over backwards and I pulled my jeans up then he came at me and my boyfriend showed up."

"We need you to go to the hospital," William said. He looked over at her boyfriend hoping to convey the importance of that. "We need samples of any fluids. I'm sorry, but we have to have some tests run. Can you do that?"

They both nodded and she buried her face in her boyfriends shoulder.

"Thank you, ma'am. We appreciate the help. You've been very strong." William nodded at the man's arm. "Did you get that when you came to her aid? You should have it checked."

Her boyfriend smiled ruefully. "I didn't think about anything except stopping him from killing her."

"Remember that if this ever bothers you. Remember what she's going through right now, and how much you care for each other." William stood and waved a female officer over. "We need samples sent to the U."

She nodded and knelt by the woman.

"James, I want to go by the club and check Eddie's videos again. This one is farther away, but a jogger or runner could have made it this far easily. I'm banking on the perp and the jogger being the same."

"Agreed. I want to take a short walk first," James said. "I have an idea."

William followed James to the corner, James jogging south on Eighth East until he reached the end of the building. Three long strides off the pavement and James was gone. William sprinted to where James had disappeared, but saw nothing. He trotted back to

South Temple, rounding the corner at the precise moment James stepped into a halo of light created by a streetlamp west of the police tape. No one had noticed him. Their suspect was as clever as he was opportunistic.

"The officers didn't even know I was there," James said when they met.

Once the scene had been processed, they headed to the club. There had to be some correlation. A jogger this late at night who'd been drinking. Plenty of establishments along Main Street and State Street now had surveillance set ups and if they saw a man jogging on any of the cameras, and the victim ID'd him, they would be one step closer to catching their man.

They pulled up in front of the club, rushing down the stairs, James pounding on the door.

"It's almost three a.m. We're closed," Eddie called. "Come back tomorrow."

"It's us, Eddie," William replied. "We need to look at your security tape again."

"Why can't you guys do this before the club closes?" Eddie grumped opening the door. "It's bad enough working until two or three a.m. It's no wonder I don't have a girlfriend!"

"We love you, too, Eddie," James said.

Eddie let them in and led them back to his office, dropped the night's receipts and rewound the tape to ten p.m. as requested, William and James watching the ebb and flow of customers in fast forward. At fifteen minutes after ten on the video, a man of average height and build with short blonde hair left a table near the back of the room. William slowed the playback. The man could have easily been at the victim's location by the time her boyfriend said he'd interrupted him. And he matched Mr. Owens description.

"Eddie…"

"Yeah, I know. You need a copy. Give me ten."

Fifteen minutes later they were scouring the facades of the buildings on Main Street working their way north to South Temple. Completing the sweep, they used the same procedure east on South Temple. If their man had come this way, they had a suspect. The next couple of hours were used checking for cameras around buildings as far east as Third East, as far west as Third West and as far south as Tenth South.

They met at the station early the next morning and headed out for the first of many stops. Now that they knew which buildings had cameras they had to locate the runner.

The first two cameras on Main Street showed nothing of any use. The trees the city had planted interfered with the camera's angles. The third camera showed a man running. He moved quickly and easily and once around the corner, disappeared. The fourth camera showed even more promise. The man they had seen on the third camera, stopped at a traffic light, leaning with his hands on his knees like he was winded, catching his breath. The light changed and he moved off heading east. Now to see if the victim could identify him. He had passed her, acknowledging her with a nod and a smile.

Calling the woman at work, they set an appointment for the next afternoon then they called Michael. They spent the rest of that afternoon checking other camera locations, finding nothing of any importance.

The next morning they were at the station early to make sure the video was set. They had just finished setting everything when footsteps echoed in the hall, Captain Kirby approaching.

"Hey, Cap," William said.

"William. James," Captain Kirby said. "Did you look at your package from the University?"

"We haven't been to our desk yet. Did they get back with us?"

"I thought you could tell me. I don't open my detectives' mail.

Last I heard tampering with mail was a federal offense. Let me know what you find out." Captain Kirby gave them a sideways grin as he turned to leave. "There's some good info from the lab in there, too."

James stared at William. "Last I heard tampering with mail was a federal offense," James said mimicking the captain. "Yeah, right!"

At their desks, they went over the packet, hoping it would give them the lifeline they needed. They set the reports from the current rapes aside, concentrating on the woman found in the river and the two from the previous year. On the last page of the report, markers showed they'd had intercourse with the same man. A felon named George Bonner, currently serving time at Point of the Mountain.

"William, this makes no sense," James said. "How could George do the woman from the Point?"

William shook his head. "I don't have the answer to that. Put a request through Jeremy's channels. Let's see what kind of hit we get."

James keyed in the request then they went over information on Olivia, the possibility hanging out there that she had been working and her murder had only been the outcome of an outraged john. By the time they had gone over the reports both men were convinced there was a connection between the drug dealers deaths and Olivia's murder. There was too much coincidence.

"I want to check the drug dealer's room again," James said. "There's something there we missed."

33

Scratching on the wall woke Amanda and she lay motionless, sensing someone in the room. She opened her eyes and a shadow, movement in the darkness, drew her attention to the foot of the bed. It slipped out as quietly as a specter. Crawling out of bed, she padded into the hall. Empty. A peek into the living room and the first rays of sunlight could be seen coming through the blinds. The bottom of the curtain on the French doors fluttered gently and Amanda turned back to her room, smiling at the roses on the dining table. At the mouth of the hall she stopped, checking the camera above the door. If anyone had been here Jeremy would know. She closed her bedroom door and climbed back into bed, replaying the roses.

Jeremy stirred in his room then the front door closed. Amanda slipped on her robe and trotted back down the hall, finding the front door unlocked, a morning breeze blowing through from the French doors. Another memory flashed of the roses.

She leaned against the wall, closed her eyes, listening, forcing herself to stay calm, the possibilities flooding her mind. She hung her head, her mind battling her emotions. Jeremy stepped into the hall and she clutched her chest, covering her mouth so she wouldn't scream.

"Jeremy! Scare me half to death!"

"I am sorry. I didn't mean to."

Amanda rested her head on the wall blowing her breath out between clenched teeth. "You're fine."

"I heard someone in the hall. Was that you?"

"I walked out once and went back to bed, but something felt strange so I got back up." She directed his gaze to the front door.

"Did you lock the door last night?" He slipped his pistol in his waistband and checked his pager, resetting the alert that had woke him. "There's no way you could have accidentally left it open."

"No. I never unlock it. And you checked it before we went to bed."

Jeremy returned to his room and pulled up the cameras. Power was out. He walked back to the hall, checking the wires, they had been disconnected.

"We need to call William, my lady."

They walked into the living room, Amanda freezing in her tracks. One of the French doors stood open, the sheer panel blowing gently in the summer breeze. She turned to the table, a bottle of wine sat chilling in the center, two glasses in front of the ice filled bucket, a dozen red roses strategically placed behind it and off to one side. The memory from earlier flashed again. She raised an eyebrow, asking the question with her eyes.

Jeremy shook his head.

"You didn't put these here?"

Jeremy shook his head again.

Amanda turned back to the table. This had been staged quite nicely. She squeezed Jeremy's hand as he led her into the kitchen, calling the station. If someone had wanted to scare her, it was working.

William and James arrived within ten minutes of Jeremy's call. Amanda directed their gaze to the table and the balcony door and they called for a print crew.

"Were the doors locked when you went to bed last night?" William asked. "There's no way you could have accidentally left them open."

"No. Jeremy even checked them."

"What about the cameras, Jeremy?" William asked. The frustration was bleeding over. His voice curt, the words sharp. "You said they were unhooked. Did they catch anything?"

"They caught about three minutes total and that only shows the man's back," Jeremy answered, biting his angry retort back. "All the cameras were trunked off that one." He led them to his room, pulling up the short segment of video, pointing to the screen. "Here you see the man enter and move up the hall to Amanda's room, checking the guest room first. He returns, but he's walking backwards, his collar turned up. That tells me something tipped him off to that camera. He wasn't aware of it at first. Now, he disappears under the camera and they go down. That shows a familiarity with these set ups. According to the time stamp that was approximately five minutes prior to Amanda being awakened. When he disabled the camera it set the vibration alarm off on my pager. I got up and walked out, but saw nothing so assumed it was Amanda and came back in and dressed. When I opened the door the second time, Amanda was in the hall and told me that that had been the second time she had left her room, and the intruder was gone. I'll get you a copy in case you need it."

William turned to Amanda. "Did anything about him look familiar?"

"No," Amanda said nodding her head 'yes.' She had seen the back of that head too many times before.

"Yes or no?" James asked.

"No," she answered. "I'm sorry.

They were quiet for a tic, William turning back to face Jeremy.

"You took the time to get dressed," William said, his tone now accusatory."What if she had been raped or killed while you were taking this time?"

He turned away from Jeremy, Amanda gaping from the door. He stormed past her, striding back to the dining room, angry footsteps behind him. William turned, Jeremy glowering at him, James and Amanda a few feet behind Jeremy.

"William, I understand your concern," Jeremy said, "but this is not going to help. I don't want to have to worry about this macho, testosterone fueled bullshit if we're working an operation. Maybe your problem is my being here, not the intruder."

Jeremy's hands had balled into fists, his breathing heavy, the anger overriding his wisdom. His voice had risen in volume, he felt confused, his thoughts broken, disjointed and took a deep breath to calm himself.

James turned Amanda and thrust her toward the hall and her bedroom. "Go. I'll handle this."

She opened her mouth, James' anger flashed and she backed up, stopping at the entrance to the hall.

James stepped between the two men, his head swiveling between them, eyes skewering them both.

"You two need to get things straight, and do it now, because this won't work. If you don't, we are not going to have a team. You're acting like a couple of dogs in heat. Work it out and SHUT up!"

Jeremy turned away from William, William pulling his gaze away from Jeremy, both men locking eyes on Amanda, tears running down her cheeks. She shook her head slowly, backing away then her bedroom door slammed.

"AMANDA!" both men called in unison.

"Work it out," James repeated. "I don't care if you beat each other to a bloody pulp, just don't destroy the evidence." He nodded at the table. "I'm giving you ten minutes and then I walk. I will quit this team and I will go to Captain Kirby and request a change of partners."

James strode to Amanda's room, tapping on her door then he stepped inside. She was sitting on the edge of the bed, and wiped the tears off her cheeks then looked back at him.

"I…uh…I've been thinking about quitting the team and going back to work at Berringer & Hardy," she said quietly. "I never meant for this to happen. I don't know what else to do."

"I can't help you there," James answered, sitting beside her and putting his arm around her.

Amanda sniffled and nodded, then wiped her cheeks again.

"I don't think that will help, though," he said. "You have two men out there who love you very much. I've seen you attempt to keep things on an even keel, but you need to be more forceful, firmer. I don't love you like they do, but I care, too. You and William have become like a brother and a sister to me. I don't want to see any of you hurt. Right now, all three of you are."

"I know," she admitted. "I thought maybe…I don't know. I mean, I've never been treated with the respect you three treat me with." She sobbed a quick intake of air then pulled her thoughts back into order. "I enjoy being with William and I stay in the guestroom on the mini-vacations with Jeremy."

"I believe you. But until you tell one of them, you are making a commitment to the other, they will continue to fight for you."

Amanda buried her face in her hands again. "I never dreamed this would happen. I mean, if I was dating both of them…."

"I understand." James gave her a hug then glanced down. He picked a leaf off the floor, twirling it as he inspected it. It looked fresh, still holding moisture from the dew. "Where'd that come from?"

"I haven't got a clue," she replied. "It wasn't there last night."

The buzzer sounded and they walked out, William directing the print crew to the items on the table. He backed up, positioning himself in the corner opposite Jeremy. Both men were still angry, but smiled sheepishly.

Amanda stood at the entrance to the living area, focused on the two, her arms crossed defensively in front of her.

James walked onto the balcony, doing a sweep of the floor then stooped. He stepped back in, a second leaf in his hand. They were the only things that proved someone had come into her apartment from outside.

William pulled Amanda aside and apologized then he and James left. Jeremy waited for William to leave before apologizing then Amanda dressed, waiting for Jeremy to get in the shower. When the water came on, she grabbed her purse and tapped softly on the bathroom door.

"I'm running to the store," she called. "I'll be back soon."

Amanda drove to the nearest payphone and dialed directory assistance, asking for the number to a bar that had recently opened on State Street. She wrote the number down then stared at the phone, debating if she should call. Just to see if they were open. Of course, this might be the wrong bar. But according to the operator it was the only new bar on State Street. She dialed the number, George answered and she almost hung up. Amanda clasped the receiver to her chest and took a deep breath, lowering her voice, hoping it sounded as gruff as she wanted.

"Hey what time you guys open that joint?" she asked. "I been by there two times this morning and the place is closed."

"We don't open until noon," George answered. "I'm only here to accept deliveries so you have something to drink."

"Tanks!" she said gruffly, slamming the phone down.

She got back into her car, her hands shaking. *'Get control of yourself,'* she thought.

Amanda arrived back at her apartment her arms loaded with bags, pushing the buzzer for access.

"Will you do me a favor?" she asked. "See if the guys would like to come over for dinner. I know you are going to want to hold a short meeting."

"I have already called them," he replied peeking into the bags. "What am I cooking?"

As expected everyone was punctual and when they finished eating, Amanda set a dessert tray and coffee on the table purposely setting farther away from the group.

"Miss Amanda," Jeremy said. "Please…"

"No," she replied.

"Very well. As we all know, Miss Amanda had a visitor this morning who knew enough to disable the cameras. I have rewired them so that cannot happen again. Do we have any ideas – besides the obvious – about who we think it is?"

"Only the boys from Reno," James said. "George is in prison."

"That was George Bonner," Amanda interjected. "I saw the back of that man's head enough times last year, I will recognize him anywhere. I want him back behind bars worse than any of you."

"What do you mean, back behind bars?" William asked. "And why the hell didn't you say something this morning? I asked you if you knew who it was."

"And what would have happened then?" she shot back at him. "More of this testosterone fueled bullshit? No thank you!" She sat back, crossing her arms. "Besides, I wanted no doubts, so I got the phone number from Directory Assistance and called the bar. George answered."

There was collective intake of air as they sat back.

"Well, that's a whole different ball game," Timothy said.

William scowled at Amanda. "We will talk about this later."

"Anytime," she replied.

34

Amanda and Karen met for lunch the next day. Once or twice a week had become their routine. The girls talked and laughed until Karen had to return to work, leaving Amanda alone. Amanda finished her drink then stood, George walking her way. How long had he been here?

"Good afternoon," George said. He recognized the momentary flash of fear and halted, stuffing his hands in his pants pockets. "I promise to behave myself. I learned a lot since I last saw you."

"Forgive me if I don't believe you," she replied.

"Can I ask a question?" George asked.

Amanda hesitated then nodded and took a step away from the table. "I suppose."

"Why wouldn't you give me a chance? I really am a very nice person."

"Maybe it had to do with those phone calls when you planted the camera at my desk. Maybe it had to do with the way you just bought me like a piece of meat. There are a lot of reasons I can think of. I think I need to go."

"Can I ask you another question? I see there are no rings."

He nodded at her left hand and she instinctively covered it with her right.

"I still see William, if that's what you're wondering."

"Actually I was thinking about Jeremy, but that answers that. Did you just dump the poor man once you were home? That makes no sense. Jeremy has more money than a police officer will ever make. Maybe Jeremy just wanted the benefits without the added inconvenience." George paused, waiting, not receiving an answer. "If I remember right Detective Harrison is a widower. So, was he more open to the possibility?"

"That's more than one question," she retorted. "But I think we've had part of this discussion at a prior meeting. Money isn't everything."

"You still haven't mentioned poor Jeremy."

"I still see Jeremy. We worked together for a while. Now, if you don't mind, can I ask you a question?"

George dipped his head, his eyes glued on her.

"What gave you the right to barge into my apartment? I don't think you're any different at all."

"I wasn't in your apartment. I don't even know where you live. Give me your address and I'll be more than happy to stop by." He paused, a smirk forming. "I slept in my office the past couple of nights and was up at seven-thirty when my bartender arrived."

"You were in my apartment, George," she said. "Yesterday morning. And I have footage of you checking out the guest room. At five minutes to seven to be exact. It's on the tape from the camera you disabled. A dozen red roses, two excellent examples of stemware, and a bottle of wine – conveniently chilling on ice – were left on the table. How do you explain that?" She paused a second. "Oh, and I mustn't forget the leaf on the floor beside my bed."

George laughed and glanced at the opposite wall. "I guess I screwed up." He took a step closer. "I promise not to be that stupid again."

Amanda took a step back, George stopped, looked toward the rear of the mall and dipped his chin.

"One more thing, princess. Ask William about the significance of how his wife was shot. There's a lot of meaning to how it was carried out."

Amanda froze, unable to move.

George smiled, bowing ever so slightly. "I guess there is a lot you still need to learn. I'll leave you alone. If you decide to meet the real George Bonner, I can be found at the bar. I'm sure you know which one. You really are special, Amanda."

Amanda nodded, stunned, as George walked away. The doors closed after him, Amanda remaining frozen, a jumble of thoughts tumbling through her mind. She reached for her purse, her hands trembling then trotted for the service corridor. She needed to use the restroom.

Amanda hurried around the corner, steps approaching from behind her. The sound was distorted, bouncing off the walls and high ceiling, but it wasn't a woman. The shoes weren't heels and the sound was more driven, in a hurry. She glided into an inset in the wall, and pressed into it, thankful for the meager cover. A man peeled around the corner, weapon drawn, scouring the empty hall ahead of him and she remembered the dip of George's chin. The man glanced behind him, drifting her direction. Then he was standing in front of her, looking back the way he had just come. Amanda clasped a hand over his mouth, driving the thumb on her other hand into the flesh under the man's chin. He choked involuntarily as he went down, hitting the floor with a resounding thud. Amanda planted her foot on the man's gun arm, the bone in the wrist cracking, the pistol clattering on concrete the floor. He reached for the gun with his left hand then froze feeling pressure on his testicles. Amanda stood over him, his pistol aimed at his forehead.

"I suggest you behave," Amanda said. "One wrong move and I go down on something you would probably like to keep intact."

"Hey, dude! Where the hell'd you go?" a second voice called. "Come on, man, we gotta go."

Amanda drifted around him and melted into the shadows of the wall once again, the muzzle of his gun aimed at the top of his head.

"You say one word," she hissed, "and there will be an extra hole in your head."

Not receiving a reply the second man took a cautious step around the corner and sighed when he saw his partner laid out on the floor.

"What the hell, dude?" the second man asked.

"I'm good," the man said. "I slipped on something."

"Up!" she whispered, tapping his skull with the gun. "And don't try a damn thing!"

"I think I broke my wrist," he said. "Go get the car so you can take me to the hospital."

"Where's the girl?" his partner asked.

"She went around the corner," he answered, jerking his head the opposite direction. "Just go get the damn car!"

He did a quick nod backwards to where Amanda crouched, her body pressed against the wall, confusion reigning. A silent curse and she flipped the gun and smashed him on the head with the butt. She lunged forward, twirling the gun back into a firing position, bracing for a shot at his partner. The man's head hit the concrete and his partner dove for the corner, Amanda following his body with the muzzle, firing as he went horizontal. The man yelped, a spray of red coating the floor. She wiped the weapon down, put it in the unconscious man's hand and sped for the far exit. As she neared the end of the corridor, heavy, hurried footsteps raced toward her. She started around the corner, running head on into a security guard.

"Are you alright, ma'am?" he asked, pulling her around the corner after him, pressing her against the wall beside him. "I thought I heard a shot."

"Two guys pulled guns on each other," she said, her voice high, almost hysterical.

The security guard peered around the corner being joined by a second guard. He explained what had happened to his partner then moved cautiously toward the man on the floor. The second guard peeked around the corner, Amanda taking the opportunity to slip out, her mind stuck on George. He had been so self-controlled, so calm. He was behind this incident so, was he the one behind the other surprises? She activated the pager, angry because she took a cab. She should have driven.

"Jeremy," Amanda said. "Can you send the limo? I'm at the ZCMI Center. The rear entrance."

"We are on our way," he replied.

She hurried through the doors, police and paramedics pushing in, Jeremy climbing out of the limo.

"I'm sorry," she said. "I should have driven, but I didn't want to look for a parking place."

"It's alright. I noticed you didn't drive." He held the door and gave her a questioning look. "Are you alright? You look a bit frazzled."

"I ran into someone," she said, her voice betraying her anxiety.

"Miss Amanda, are you sure you are alright?" She nodded. "Good, I invited the men over for dinner."

35

After dinner Jeremy cleared the table and hurried to the guest room. He picked up a manila folder and returned, sitting opposite where Amanda sat next to William.

"First," Jeremy said, "I want to thank William for allowing us to go over his late wife's death. Is this still alright, sir?" William nodded. "Take your time and begin whenever you are ready."

William stared at the table his throat tightening. He pulled in a deep breath and glanced at the others.

"It was just over three years ago. We were going to dinner before the club. I got home from work and didn't see her. I went to the bedroom to change and she'd already been home. I thought it was strange, but not too serious. She liked those CERTS breath mints so I thought she'd gone to the store. I waited until almost time to be on stage. Then there was a knock on the door. I opened it and it was Captain Jakes and James, along with the chief. Her body had been found at the mouth of Big Cottonwood Canyon. She was in the back seat, naked, her wrists bound. Her clothes had been folded neatly and laid on the floorboards on the right hand side of her car so they assumed she'd been sexually assaulted. I noticed when I identified her body, she had been crying. That added to the supposition, but the autopsy showed no signs of rape. There were no bruises or marks of any kind. She'd been stripped and then shot. A single tap .45. A single tap to the heart."

"We all know," Jeremy said, "but I'll explain it for Amanda's benefit. A single tap is one shot."

Amanda nodded and put her arms around William, rubbing his back while she held him. A flicker of something, maybe jealousy, crossed Jeremy's face then it was gone, and she remembered their confrontation.

"A single tap to the heart is meant to hurt a person," Jeremy explained. "The police assumed whoever shot her knew she was married to a police officer. I remembered a case from a few years ago where a gentleman in Laughlin, Nevada had been shot with a .45. I requested an analysis of the bullet taken from William's wife and that unsolved case. They match. Whoever shot William's wife was the same man who shot the victim from a few years ago....."

"How the hell could you do that?" William asked, his head jerking up. "No one knew we had the bullet for comparison!"

"I can access police department files anytime I wish," Jeremy reminded William, his voice calm. "That is how I get information to local agencies. Now, back to the rest of this. The case in Nevada was a local trouble maker who had recently been released from prison for embezzlement. At one time he had worked for GTB Enterprises. In fact George Bonner was the man who filed the charges and had him put away. You don't look surprised."

"Not much Bonner does will surprise us," James replied.

"Were you two gentlemen involved in anything in particular at that time?"

"No, we rode in the squads. Responded to calls. There were a few assists with known drug deals."

"We had just helped with a drug bust," William said. "We had been called in, with two other cars, to aid responding officers. We took two of the dudes in and booked them."

"And we were the only officers who got their pictures in the paper," James finished. "At the time, they wondered if that had had anything to do with it, but they compared the slug found in William's wife against any and all .45's used in a crime going back eighteen months and no one found anything."

"Why wouldn't it show?" Amanda asked.

"Not all agencies are tied into the same databases yet," Jeremy answered. "In some cases it can be hit and miss. Laughlin is a small town and probably didn't have the funds. Do you remember an officer who left the department in early nineteen eighty? An Officer Gary Menendez?"

James nodded, William shrugged.

"I think we worked with him a few times," William answered. "He didn't seem to be too into the job. He barely made it through the academy from what I heard."

"He was the trouble maker," Jeremy said. "He was recruited by Bonner and moved to Laughlin then George had him arrested. George may have thought Mr. Menendez was undercover and would be done away with in prison. There is also the possibility it wasn't George who had him killed. Now, anything new on the woman in the Green River?"

"We requested DNA from her be compared with DNA from the girls from last year. We just received the results. The woman had had intercourse with the same man as the other two…."

"Let me guess! George Bonner," Amanda sniped.

William gave her sideways glance. "The blood found on the grate behind George's apartment came back as hers," William said. "The flesh the tech took from the balcony railing is also hers, and comes back as belonging to a Katie Landry from Reno, Nevada. According to DNA Olivia had not had intercourse with

George. Right now both men are unknowns. The lab is going through our database of known offenders to see if they can find a match. They are also attempting to confirm whether the recent rapes were carried out by the second person who assaulted Olivia."

"And the other person with Miss Holland? You said the lab found semen from two individuals."

"Until we get confirmation from the lab, we're leaning toward one being a john. She was a call girl."

"Okay, I received several faxes today," Jeremy said holding the papers up for them to see. "It looks like Amanda was correct." Her head jerk up and he held a hand up. "Not that I doubted you, but it gives us confirmation. One of the faxes is from Captain Kirby and is a copy of Mr. Bonner's release papers…"

"Damn!" William said, leaning back in the chair.

"I understand, sir. The papers appear legitimate. According to this he was released two months ago. My sources are showing the same thing…."

"What about Amanda?" Timothy asked. "Is that why someone tried to run her off the road?"

"Possibly. She was driving William's car," Jeremy answered. "They may have staged it and assumed it was William when the car drove up. Remember, the highway patrol said they had not set up a road block."

"And by having officers on scene they could guarantee the people they were looking for would stop," Timothy said. "Even phony ones."

"And without the highway patrol actually being involved, it would have been a wreck caused be the driver's untimely death," Jeremy added. "If they were caught they could claim they just happened upon it." Jeremy passed the fax around for everyone to read. "The plate number Amanda gave comes back as stolen and a truck that matches that description belongs to a part time hoodlum out of St. George."

"All these surprises make sense now," William said. "Reno, the trip home, Mr. Randall. We may know who's behind them." William stared at the fax then handed James the papers. "How could a judge release George Bonner without saying a damn thing to anybody? It looks legit, but it stinks."

"I called the judge this afternoon," Jeremy said. "He admits he signed release papers on several inmates, but doesn't remember George Bonner being one of them."

"Then that paper has to be bogus," William said. "But how? Even if they transmitted the release papers electronically, that leaves an electronic signature we should be able to trace. Unless they know a lot about computers."

"We have men working on that already," Jeremy said. "It isn't much, but it is a start." He picked up another folder and laid it on his lap. "For the last order of business. The men in these photos were well-known suppliers." Jeremy handed them two 8 x 10 photos. "These are the men who were trunking off the syndicate's supply lines. Do they look familiar?"

"I think that guy worked for George last year," Amanda said. She tapped the picture of the larger of the two men.

"And Reno," William added. "That's Glen Tortino."

"That means they're still alive," Jeremy said. "At least one of them anyway."

"I'll bet anything he's working for George." Amanda said.

"Please explain," Jeremy said.

"That's why I was so flustered when you picked me up. He was there." Every man in the room sat back and she shrugged. "He wanted to know why I hadn't given him a chance last year." The men laughed. "Yeah, my sentiments exactly. That was about the extent of our conversation."

"Was that why the cops?" William asked. "We heard there was

a shooting in the service corridor."

Amanda shrugged. "I noticed them when I left."

James and Timothy chuckled, William locked eyes with her, Amanda dropped hers.

"Anything else?" Jeremy asked. Everyone shook their head and he rose to leave. "In that case, I'm going back to the retreat. I need to get our attire set for the dinner this weekend."

Once everyone had left William guided Amanda gently into the bedroom, nuzzling her neck as they moved. Inside, he pushed the door closed with his foot. He didn't have to, but he kind of liked it that way. He picked her up, her legs wrapping around his waist, and laid her gently on the bed. He'd met the sexiest woman alive because of a psycho and a pimp.

"FYI. I think you left something out," he whispered.

"You have that right," she whispered.

Amanda woke part way through the night, William sleeping peacefully beside her and thought about his late wife. She needed to get to know 'the real George'. But she couldn't tell the team. With Jeremy out of town, tomorrow would be perfect for her first scouting foray. Then they would be gone for the weekend. And the men would never know.

She kissed William's head where it lay on her chest and he pulled her close.

"You okay?" William mumbled.

"Never better," she answered.

36

David sat at the intersection of Main Street and Second South and watched Amanda cross Main going west, carrying several bags. It had been almost a year, but he would recognize that beauty any place. That was the woman who had broke his hand. He glanced down at the appendage, not completely straight, but functioning quite well, and smiled. He had never met a woman who fought like her. He thought of the syndicate and wondered if they were looking for another fancy lady then shoved the thought aside. His job description did not include working as Reno's talent scout.

A car honked its horn signifying the lights change and David continued north on Main parking in the first empty space he found then walked inside to a payphone. Pulling a card out of his pocket, he dialed the number, skimming the crowd hoping he could pull this off. This would be the trickiest play of his career.

The call was answered on the third ring and he released the breath he'd been holding.

"The Landers Corporation."

The woman sounded efficient. In her forties or fifties. Nice cover for an illegal operation.

"Thomas Landers, please."

"And who may I say is calling?"

"Just put him on," David said.

She put him on hold, David using the time to rehearse his speech. It took a full two minutes for the phone to be answered.

"Mr. Landers," David said. "I have some information I think you could use. Information about George Bonner."

"And why should I believe anything you tell me?" Thomas asked. "You haven't even seen fit to introduce yourself."

"My apologies," David said. "The name is David. Officer David Haus with the Reno P.D. I am currently employed by Mr. Bonner." There was a quick intake of air and David laughed. "I thought that would get your attention."

"How do I know you're not lying to me?" Thomas asked. He gave one of his men a nod and the man walked out. "The last I heard, George was at Point of the Mountain and would be there for quite some time. I'm also curious. What would stop you from contacting me for Reno? How do I know you aren't trying to earn a few brownie points by pulling me in?"

"Please, sir," David said. "Let's dismiss with the posturing. I am not a new man on this ladder. I know one of your men, a Mr. Glen Tortino, is already feeding you information. And I know that that door closing is one of your men leaving to run a trace on this call. He won't find me. If you want to check on me, the name is pronounced 'house', but spelled H-A-U-S. Now, here's something for you to think about. Because of the previously mentioned, Mr. Tortino, we both know George Bonner is no longer at The Point. He has been released."

Thomas hesitated, considering if he should concede. "I'll admit to knowing that, but that is old news, Mr. Haus. Give me something new. Something I can use."

"Have you talked to Jonathan recently?" The question was met with silence. "That's what I thought. How about Glen?" More silence. "I assume that's another no. I was in on the meeting where Glen told George that Jonathan wants to frame you and his uncle for the underage girls Jonathan brought in. Think real hard about that, Mr. Landers. I'll call back in a day or two. Enjoy the rest of your day."

Thomas listened to the dial tone for a few seconds, thinking about whether Officer Haus was on the up and up, or baiting him. Every law enforcement agency in the state and some on the federal level were hunting for him. He stared at the phone then dialed Robert Fielding's number. He needed answers and, as his second in command, Robert should have them.

"Good day, Robert," Thomas said. "Is Travis with you?"

"Yes, sir. We were just going over some new information."

"I received a very interesting call," Thomas said.

"Regarding what, sir?" Robert asked.

"A man who calls himself Officer David Haus of the Reno P.D. called. He confirmed the report that Mr. Bonner is out. I also want to know how much you know about this officer."

"Officer Haus is a known associate of Mr. Bonner's. He works both sides of the fence. Rumors have it, he has been staying in contact with George's nephew Jonathan, but with George in prison he wasn't working very much. That is what Travis and I were discussing. Glen called. He had a couple of interesting tidbits for us. One is that Mr. Haus is working with George again, but baiting Jonathan. The other is that Jonathan has asked him to supply information to the cops regarding underage prostitutes. Jonathan wants Glen to tell the cops the girl's were supplied by us at George's request. We all know that won't happen. If I hear anything further, I will let you know."

"Well, speed shit up," Thomas ordered. "I don't want to be the fool behind the eight ball if anything comes down the pike. This

Mr. Haus is supposed to call again in a day or two and he will probably want to set up a face to face. If he does, I will expect you and Travis to be available."

"Yes, sir," Robert replied. A click as Thomas hung up and Robert stared across his desk at Travis. "It seems the Grand Poobah received a call from an Officer David Haus of the Reno P.D who verified the information about George. He wants to make sure we will be at his disposal if this officer pushes for an in person meeting. How soon will you have things set?"

"They're set now," Travis answered. "I just need the go ahead from you."

"Good. I'll let you know when I get the summons."

Travis walked out, leaving Robert to his musings.

The door ticked closed and Robert stared across the sapphire blue expanse of Lake Tahoe. "What the hell happened, Katie?" he whispered.

37

With William at work and Jeremy in Cedar City, Amanda rose to an empty apartment. She showered, her mind going over George's return. He had invited her to visit and – on the phone – he had said he would be at the bar to accept deliveries. So he would probably answer the back door and he would have people inside with him. Well, should.

Amanda put on a snugger pair of jeans than usual and a midriff top, slipped on a pair of heels then surveyed her reflection. Men liked it when the tush was rounder and firmer, and the heels definitely did that. A peek at the derriere and she grabbed her purse and her jacket, checked for the pager and switchblade then headed out. She was all about the attention today, but she was driving. She didn't want to get stuck.

Choosing a spot on State Street between Fifth and Sixth South, Amanda leaned on the hood of her car, waiting for the first beer truck to pull in. One swung around the corner at eight thirty-five and she slid her ID and money into her back pocket then parked on Sixth South, tossed her purse under the seat and jogged to the rear door. The driver smiled, eyeing her appreciatively as she approached. A half a second later, he stepped back and George poked his head around the door. Perfect. Exactly what she wanted.

"Princess," George said. "I was hoping I'd see you."

"After meeting you at the mall, I decided, what the hey." She giggled nervously and slowed her approach. "I admit the man I met in the mall was totally different than the man I met last year. I wasn't sure if you'd be open yet, but I saw the truck so I decided to stop for a minute. I'm on my way to do some shopping."

"Are you nervous?"

"Yeah." She shrugged, bobbing her head a little too fast. "I'm not sure if I'm doing the right thing now. Maybe I should go. I can come back later when you're open. I'm babbling, aren't I?"

The driver winked as he handed George a receipt then opened the side doors on the truck.

"I promise to behave myself," George said. He opened the door wider and nudged her arm gently. "Plus, we won't be alone, so I will have to be a good boy."

"Well…Okay," she said. So far so good.

Amanda stepped through the door and scanned the interior. It wasn't open so the lights hadn't been dimmed. A man, probably in his early to mid-forties stood behind the bar. Not bad looking. Sported the drinker's Buddha belly. Glancing over her shoulder at George she noticed he had a nice physique, soft brown eyes and a welcoming smile. Under different circumstances she might have been attracted to George.

"Cliff," George said, "will you get the lady a drink?"

"Oh, no," she objected. "I don't want anything. Not this early."

"We have soft drinks and coffee. In fact, Cliff has coffee made. If not, it will only take a minute."

He led her to a table near the end of the bar and pulled a chair out for her.

"I got coffee," Cliff said wearing that eager smile men had

when they saw something they liked. "I have to have my coffee before I even think about talking to anybody. Cream or sugar?" He sat the cup on the table in front of Amanda, dropped his hands by his side, crossed his arms in front of his chest then stuffed his hands into his pockets still grinning like a Cheshire Cat.

"No. Black is fine," she answered. This was suddenly scary.

"You look scared," George said. "I wish you weren't. I would like you to be comfortable with me."

"That's why I stopped. I wanted to see if it was possible. I don't know if this will work. Maybe this wasn't a good idea." She saw the twinge of disappointment. "I'll just finish my coffee and maybe we can try again some other place." Then watched it fade. Men were just too easy. "Maybe if there were more people. I guess it's because it's just you and me, you know?"

"Why don't you stop one of these nights when I'm working? I actually tend bar now. We wouldn't be alone then. How about tonight?"

"Tonight won't work," she said shaking her head. "I'm leaving town in the morning. I won't be back until Sunday. What nights do you work?"

"I help Cliff Friday and Saturday's and give Cliff Sunday and Monday off. What about Monday?"

"Maybe. Then we'd have time to talk." She paused unsure of her next move. Was she pushing too hard? "I'm not sure about this Monday, though."

"Your decision, gorgeous."

Amanda finished her coffee and stood, moving quickly toward the door. George's hand came from behind her, reaching for the handle, her breath catching as the thought of what he might do floated across her mind. He turned the knob and pushed the door open.

"Afraid I was going to pull something?"

"Actually, yes," she said with a sigh. "I don't know why."

She laid her hand against his jaw and he took it in his, kissing the palm as he gazed down at her.

"I want nothing more than to take you home and make love to you all day long, but I won't push that until you are comfortable. I just ask that you try to trust me. Can you handle that?"

"I think I can handle that," she answered.

George put a hand behind her head and pulled her in for a kiss.

Amanda backed out of the door, took a step to her right then strutted up the alley. A glance over her shoulder as she swept her hair behind her ear and George's eyes dropped to the tush. She smiled. He was hooked.

She climbed into her car and exhaled, leaning her head on the headrest as she started the engine. This was going to be harder than she thought. Now to get the smell off her.

Three hours later, she'd cleaned up, Jeremy had returned and they had started the last of the pre-event packing.

"Relaxing day?" Jeremy asked.

"Eh," she replied with a shrug.

38

What would have been an eight hour drive to Denver had been an hour and a half flight and by Sunday evening they were home relaxing.

Monday morning George's question ran unrestrained through Amanda's mind, along with what they'd learned about William's wife. She was convinced George knew something and she wanted to find out what it was.

Karen called a few minutes after noon. Another girl had given her notice. Amanda was guaranteed the full-time position if she took the part-time position now. HR would like her to come in and fill out the papers so they could get her in the system. She would be there, Amanda squealed. Give her a time. Hanging up Amanda ran for the bedroom and started rummaging through the closet.

She was nervous. What if she screwed up the interview? Well, it wasn't really an interview. It was just one of those formalities they had to go through. After she changed and put on her make-up, she pulled her hair back with a clip then surveyed her reflection. It would have to do. She didn't have time to fool with it.

"Miss Amanda!" Jeremy said. "What are you all dolled up for?"

"I just got a call from Karen. Berringer & Hardy has a part-time opening and they want me to take it. A full-time position will be available in two weeks and I'll be up for it, if I want it. I told her I'd be there."

"Amanda, are you sure about this?"

"Jeremy, I know I don't have to work, but you guys all have your jobs. You have something to do. With you here all I do is sit around and watch TV or stare off into space from the balcony. I just want to do something."

"That is up to you, but what if I'm not here? Collating the information is your job with the team."

"I know. I can come home at lunch and handle that. I sound like a whiny five year old, don't I?"

"Something like that," Jeremy said. "You look absolutely stunning. I have to go back to the retreat. The commander has set up some conference calls. All that garbage I detest. I may not be here when you return."

He gazed at her, taking in the freckles, the line of her chin, the brilliance of the eyes. The intoxicating scent of her perfume even from here. He had to go. If he didn't, he would never make it out of town. Why did she have to be so perfect?

"I'll be fine," she said. "I might not take the job anyway." She grabbed her jacket and rushed for the door. "I might stop and have a drink with the girls on the way home. Tell William not to worry if he calls."

She walked as quickly as she dared in her heels, abandoning them totally when she reached the stairs. Now she needed to work something out for her time in the bar. If the girls didn't want to stop for a drink, she was screwed.

When the short interview was over, Amanda approached Karen's cube, the beginning wisps of a plan began to unfold. Like the petals of a Rose, soft and fragrant until you reached the thorns. The idea was to avoid the thorns.

Amanda pulled in a chair and sat down behind Karen.

"What time do you take your afternoon break?" she asked. "I have a huge favor I need to talk to you about and I don't want to interrupt your work."

"You know, it scares me when someone says *'huge favor'*," Karen said.

"I've never said that before," Amanda said, defending herself. "I've only asked you for help a couple of times since I moved here."

"I know, but usually when someone says *'huge favor'* it means borrowing money or helping them move, like last year. That third floor apartment of yours was a killer. And this year's is no better."

Amanda's frown deepened.

"I'm getting the uncomfortable feeling you're working on a way to do whatever this is without my help," Karen said. "I don't like it when you do that. You are going to get hurt one of these days."

"I'm not going to do anything dangerous," Amanda countered. "I finally heard how William's wife died and I think I know someone who might know who did it….."

"Amanda! Don't do it, okay? Just let the police handle that. You're not a cop, or an investigator. There are the days you scare the hell out of me."

"I'm just going to talk to someone. That's all. Besides, I've never done anything like this. Who are you thinking about?"

"Humph! Famous last words." Karen plopped the file she was working on, on her desk and frowned, staring at Amanda. "Why don't I believe that?"

"Honest." Amanda raised her hands in mock surrender and

leaned forward in her chair. She had her alibi. "All I want to do is stop and have a soft drink at a bar on State Street. I'm driving so I won't be drinking. There's a new place…."

"What's wrong with Bourbon Street?"

"Karen! There's a new place on State Street. It used to be a dive, but it's got a new owner and he cleaned it up. It even has an old fashioned bar like the one at The Dead Goat Saloon. I peeked inside the other day. I think the guy who owns it knows who shot William's wife."

Karen's frown deepened, Amanda chiding herself for stretching the truth. She dipped her head and locked eyes with Karen, shrugging her left shoulder in a 'what do you think' move, then smiled as Karen did one slow nod.

"And you're just going to waltz in there, bat those ferocious blue eyes and he's going to tell you the whole sordid story. Amanda…"

"No, Karen. It isn't going to be that easy," Amanda responded. "I am going to have to go in there several times. But I don't want to go in alone. It has to be a person I trust. You and Janice are the only two I trust that much and Janice is too tall. It would draw too much attention to us. It's supposed to be two friends having a drink after work. Not girlfriends looking for a place to hold a clandestine make-out session."

"Okay," Karen answered, scowling. "When and what time?"

"I'm heading there now. Meet me when you get off. It's on State Street between Sixth and Seventh South. I'm not parking out front."

"Afraid William will catch you?"

"You could say that," Amanda answered. "I told Jeremy not to worry. That I might stop on my way home. I just didn't tell him where. Please, trust me, okay? I would never do anything that would get us in trouble, or hurt."

"Amanda…." Karen said then she shook her head. "I worry about you, and now I'm letting you drag me into this."

Amanda gave Karen a hug and rolled the chair back into the unused cube. "Thanks. See you in a bit."

Karen watched Amanda's retreating form and debated calling James. The last thing she wanted was for Amanda to get in trouble and she didn't want to get in trouble. She looked at the clock then at the phone, then turned to her computer and leaned back in her chair, looking at the telephone again. She picked up the file she'd been working on then checked the clock once more. *It wasn't like she was doing anything wrong. But if anything happened to Amanda….Crap!* She slapped the file closed and called James, hoping Amanda would forgive her. When he answered she almost hung up.

"Detective Thompson," he repeated. "How can I help you?"

"Sorry," Karen managed to force out. "I hope I'm doing the right thing."

"Karen? What are you talking about?"

"You sitting down?"

"Karen!"

"Sorry," she said again. "I think Amanda is going to get her butt in trouble. And don't you say a damn thing to William."

"Number one, you already know I will. Number two, what the hell is going on?"

Five minutes later James slammed the phone down and headed for his locker.

"What was that?" William asked.

"Your almost fiancée is going to get her ass shot!"

"How would she manage that?" he asked, following James.

"Amanda is going back to work for Berringer & Hardy…"

"So?"

"So. She has enlisted Karen's aid to find out who shot your wife."

"What the hell is she doing? How does she expect to do that? I am going to paddle that gorgeous hind of hers when I see her next!"

"You have to stay out of this for now," James told him. "Karen said Amanda thinks George knows who shot your wife and she is going to get him to spill. Amanda didn't say George's name, but she told Karen the bar was on State Street. An old dive that has been given a new life. She didn't want to go by herself. She thought it would be safer with Karen riding shotgun. I'm glad Amanda thought that far ahead, but it still pisses me off. I'm going to go in and keep an eye on them. If you want to wait outside in case something goes down, you're welcome to. Just don't use the unmarked car and stay out of sight. According to Karen, Amanda isn't parking on State Street."

While he talked, James had slipped off his suit jacket along with the shirt and tie, changing into a ratty pair of blue jeans and a t-shirt. He laced up a pair of work boots, stuffing a pair of gloves in his left hip pocket and checked his right pocket for the wallet with his fake ID and cash in it, then he pulled on a dirty work coat that said 'Dickies'. Last, James pulled a baseball cap and a pair of glasses out of his locker and put them on.

"Why in the hell is she doing this?" William asked.

"Because she loves you, stupid! Give me twenty minutes if you decide to join the party." James stopped as he closed his locker. "Look. I'm sorry. I shouldn't have said that. You're not stupid. I'm just pissed at her, too."

William nodded his understanding, leaving five minutes after James.

39

Amanda parked on Sixth South, undecided about leaving the car on the street. It would be seen too easily. She trotted down the alley, an unpaved parking area coming into view behind the bar. The beer truck had blocked her view before. She jogged back to the car and pulled in, parking between two pick-ups. Hurrying to the rear door, she grabbed the handle and pulled, the heavy door swinging open. Inside she waited for her eyes to adjust to the dim interior, George walking her way, a broad smile crossing his face.

"Well hello, princess," George said. He put his arms around her shoulders and pulled her into a hug. "After our last meeting I wondered where I stood. You leave because you're scared then tease me with a kiss."

"You teased yourself," she replied, draping her arms around his waist. "I'm still nervous. A friend is joining me when she gets off work. I thought it might be safer. Does that sound stupid?"

"Slightly," he replied. "Come on, I have to get back to work. I deserted my post to greet my guest." He took her hand, leading her to the bar. "What can I tempt you with? I stock both domestic and non-domestic beer. I even have a bottle of whiskey on the bar.

It goes down nice and smooth."

"Just a coke. I'm driving. I don't want to take a chance on getting pulled over." She hesitated a minute then giggled. "Um… I won't get in trouble for parking my car on that parking area back there?" She pointed behind them.

"Nope. That's why it's there. You should be fine."

He put a finger to her lips before pulling her into a long gentle kiss and smiled down at her, patting a stool she assumed was next to his. Several wolf whistles and cat calls came from the pool tables.

"I will never live this down," he said with a laugh.

"Oh, I imagine you'll adjust."

"Are you sure I can't tempt you with something a little more in keeping with the environment? I have wine coolers, too."

"You mean something that will make me relax my guard? Just a coke, George. Thank you, though."

"You hurt my feelings," he said, joking as he pulled a can of coke out of the cooler. "But coke it is. Perhaps I can tempt you later."

"Perhaps," she replied as she sat down.

James parked across State Street a half a block north and sat in the car, surveying the street in front of bar, allowing himself to cool down. A last scan of the area and he pulled the bill of his cap down, sliding the glasses back up then climbed out. If Amanda kept this up, he was going to paddle her gorgeous hind end before William got the chance!

He walked in, readjusted his glasses and pushed the baseball cap back off his forehead a fraction, planting himself on the opposite end of the bar, eyeing Amanda with a smile.

"You have your first admirer," George said, walking away.

"Second," she said, correcting him. "I thought you were one, too."

"Touché." George smiled over his shoulder at her as he walked away. "Name your poison," he said when he reached James. "I have most major domestic brands and a few for the more discerning taste."

"Coors Lite draft," James replied. "What's the lady drinking?"

"Coke," George answered. "She's driving. If you buy her one I bet she'd take it, though."

"She probably said she's meeting a friend, right?" George smiled and James chuckled. "She's not the type I usually see in a street bar. She probably likes the private clubs. She looks like a St. Pauli Girl." James dropped a ten on the bar. "Ya got that one?"

"I got that one," George answered. He picked up the money and pulled James draft then gave him his change and his beer, and opened the beer for Amanda, laughing at her surprise. "From the gentleman at the end of the bar. Did he guess correctly?"

"As a matter of fact, he did." She raised the beer in a thank you, James tugged the bill of his baseball cap down a hair.

Karen walked in forty minutes later taking the stool next to Amanda. James jerked his head requesting George's presence, George moving over to check on him.

"She looks like a Miller Lite girl," James said as he slid a five across the bar. "One for the new lady and another draft for me. Keep the change."

"What if she wants a coke?" George asked.

"Maybe," James said. "Give her whatever she wants."

George pulled James another beer, opened a bottle of Miller Lite, sitting it on the bar in front of Karen. "From the gentleman at the end of the bar," he said.

"He guessed mine, too," Amanda said. "I guess he's psychic."

The sideways grin and left shoulder shrug gave James away and Karen smiled, dropping her eyes. They had their back-up.

Amanda noticed the exchange, locking eyes with James. Her

best friend had set her up. A quick glance at the back door and she took a long drink of her beer giving herself time for the anger to subside before she turned back to Karen and George. She had two counts to get even with James on.

George kept his hands to himself, talking casually as he filled the infrequent drink requests. The three of them and a few regulars being the only people in the place, but Amanda checked the fancy Budweiser clock frequently, deciding it was time to leave at seven-thirty. She had been here long enough. This was only one step of many on the road to where she wanted to go.

Amanda drank the last of her beer then thanked Karen for joining her and complimented George on the decor. Outside she scanned the parking lot before trotting up the alley to Sixth South. If James was here, William was here. She reached Sixth South, surveying the street in both directions, spotting William leaning against his car between her and Second East. He keyed his portable, looked both directions while he spoke then stared back at the alley before he climbed in and pulled out, heading north on Second East. Amanda melted into the shadows and crept along the side of the building to State Street, peering south. Karen walked out followed by James. A glance north on State Street and William took a left off Fifth South, parking behind James' car. Karen drove off while James trotted back to talk to William.

Amanda jogged back to the parking area and climbed into her car, still fuming as she backed out of the parking space. At the mouth of the alley, she drove east to Second East then followed the route William had taken to State Street. She turned south on State Street, keeping to the left lane, passing William and honking her horn as she drove by.

James rolled over the front fender of William's car, popping up on the sidewalk, William following her with his eyes.

Amanda laughed at James reflexes then glanced in her mirror, a patrol car behind her. William merged into traffic behind it. The patrolman picked up his mike, then turned to his partner while he talked and hung it up. They had probably reported to William.

A left onto Twenty-One Hundred South and Amanda checked her mirror again, the convoy still behind her. A block east, the cop car turned south, William's car still there. She did a check for oncoming traffic and swerved into her apartment complex, screeching to a jerky stop then climbed out. William pulled in alongside her, walking around to her side of the car.

"Here," she snapped, throwing her car keys at him. "Give me the damn ticket! I haven't done anything wrong and I have two cops following me."

William laughed as he caught the keys. "Except drinking and driving. Besides, I don't do tickets."

"Oh, lucky me!" She paused and held her hand up. "I'm sorry. I shouldn't have said that. Karen and I stopped and had one lousy, stinking beer. I wasn't even going to have that, but that jack ass at the end of the bar knew what brand of beer I drink. When I see him again, he is mine."

"And what makes you think you'll see him again?" William asked. He dropped her keys into his coat pocket and put his arms around her.

"Because I know who he was. It was your beloved partner. He is mine!"

"James has been with me all day. Anything else you want to talk about?"

"No. James may have been with you all day, but he was in that bar tonight and you were sitting out there waiting when I left. Now, I want to go up those stairs, beat the hell out of something and take a nice long soak in the tub. Then I think I'll have another beer and sit on the balcony while I decide how to dismember James."

William pinned her against the car and kissed her, Amanda sighed.

"You know if we find James' body dismembered somewhere I'll have to tell the department you threatened to do that."

"William. You wouldn't."

"Well…Maybe not. Maybe we can work on that anger issue of yours. Jeremy called and said he was going to the retreat. Maybe we can take that soak together? What do you think?"

"Want to see who can get up the stairs first?" she breathed between kisses.

"I got you beat. I have longer legs."

"Maybe not. You go get more beer and drive real slow. I'll be waiting in the tub." She pointed to his pocket with her chin. "You have a key."

"Bubble bath?"

"Lots of bubbles," she said.

"That's the best offer I've had in a long time."

40

William woke Amanda the next morning with a gentle kiss. "How did the interview go?"

"It went great," she answered. "I start next week, if I take the position. It'll be five hours a day Wednesday through Friday. An occasional extra day if someone calls in sick. In two weeks I go full-time."

"Are you sure that's what you want to do?"

She wrapped her leg over his side pulling him closer. "I'm not sure about full-time. I might stay part-time. Then I can still collate information for the team."

Amanda rose, debating if she should talk to William about her idea. He was already fighting her involvement in the team. It might be better if she let the police handle it. But it had been three years, if they didn't know anything yet would they ever? William kissed her neck and pulled her out of her musings.

"I have an idea. How about we meet for lunch at the ZCMI Center? I'll have James call Karen."

At five minutes after twelve, Amanda rushed through the doors at the mall, Karen standing center court.

"James called," Karen said. "They're running late."

"Goes with the territory," Amanda said. "Are we waiting for them?"

"I can wait a few more minutes," Karen answered, checking her watch.

It was only five minutes before William and James met them, their department pagers beeping. William dropped his head then trotted to a payphone.

"I'll get ours put in to-go boxes," James said. "Just another day in paradise."

Karen squeezed his hand. "It's okay. We understand."

"We gotta go, my man," William said when he jogged back. "I'm sorry, Amanda."

"It's okay. Will I see you tonight?"

"Don't know. We might be late."

She nodded as they disappeared out the doors.

"What's goin', buddy?" James asked.

"A plain clothes officer was found at Pioneer Park," William said, weaving the car through traffic. "Cap said he was beaten pretty bad. The doctor's are throwing out the option to put him in an induced coma."

"Damn! Is he going to make it?"

"Captain Kirby said he took a pretty good hit to the head, fractured the skull, but he should pull through. The officer left a couple of cassettes. Cap thinks it involves George. It's one of the dudes who's been watching that new joint on State Street."

James could only shake his head.

They pulled up to the ER, Captain Kirby meeting them under the canopy. Chief Robinson, Captain Ohlmet and Assistant Chief's Largent and Hanson stood in the hall outside the treatment room with a woman they assumed was the officer's wife.

"What do we know?" William asked.

"He was unconscious when paramedics found him," Captain Kirby answered. "He has several broken ribs, a broken jaw, his left arm is fractured badly enough it's going to require surgery and he may not regain full use of it. Multiple cuts and bruises. Both legs are broke. He was worked over pretty good. He held his own until one of them hit him with a baseball bat. He said there were three of them so he's lucky."

"Who called it in?"

"A passer-by."

"Convenient," William said before thinking.

Captain Kirby gave William a sideways glare, holding up two cassettes. "The witness hung around until the police arrived, and told them he saw the last hit and chased the men off by going after them with his truck. He gave a statement and booked. The officer came to after he arrived here and gave me these. He said they were recorded at George's. Both of them from inside the bar; one includes a short conversation behind the building. We haven't listened to them. Since you know more about the Bonner organization than anyone else, I want you to listen to them. Let me if we got anything worth anything. When he first gave them to me he mumbled something about, 'they absolved George of something'. Just listen to them and get back with me."

"And you think the muscle worked for George?"

Captain Kirby shrugged. "Who else? He was at George's bar. But we'll get 'em. They don't want a lot of people in there, so do whatever you need to do." He toyed with a rock using the toe of his shoe. "Sorry to ruin your lunch." They nodded when he looked up. "Be careful. I don't want you guys hurt, too. I just wanted to make sure you got those." He pointed to the cassettes then went back inside.

William and James climbed into the car, staring across the seat at each other.

"We still got time for lunch," James said.

"There's a reason we get along," William said, heading back to the mall.

They walked in, George approaching the girls. William opened the comm channel and locked it. This way it would record the conversation.

"I was hoping you'd be here," George said.

Both women jumped and looked up to see George.

"It was a last minute thing," Amanda stammered. "I thought you had to work the bar."

"I do get to eat," he replied. "I didn't mean to startle you, but when I saw you, I thought…maybe we could have lunch."

"Well, actually, we're expecting friends," Amanda said with a shaky smile. "It might be kind of awkward."

George took an empty chair and sat down with them. "What can I do to get you to forgive me for my previous error, princess? I thought things were working out. You come into the bar and kiss me, but now you act as if you're scared to death."

Karen glanced at Amanda, surprised.

Flashes of George in her apartment and the men in the service corridor popped into Amanda's mind, that anger issue everyone warned her about, bubbling to the surface.

"How long do I have to think about it?"

"How long do you need? Do I really frighten you that much?"

"Not really," she replied. "Only when you sneak up on me. Or I think about last year. Or when men mysteriously follow me to the restroom in the mall. Armed men."

"Amanda, believe it or not, I do not control every man in this city. When would be a good time to stop and see you? We need to have a conversation without interruption."

Karen swallowed and Amanda looked over, Karen's eyes wide.

"You said you don't know where I live." She waited, raised an eyebrow, George said nothing. "I tell you what, I'll give you my address and you come to dinner tonight? I'm going to have a few guests over. Jeremy will be there. Detective Thompson and his girlfriend…" She nodded toward Karen. "…will be there. Officer Johnson of the Salt Lake Police Department and his girlfriend will also be there. Oh, and I can't forget Detective Harrison now, can I? It would be like old home week, don't you think?"

"I think I will turn down your generous offer."

"Then I guess I won't give you that address you say you don't have. Maybe I'll see you, and maybe I won't."

George grabbed her arm, squeezing it. "Come on, girl. When will you stop again? Give me a day."

William started forward, James grabbing his arm and pulling him back.

"Give it a second," James whispered. "If he makes one more move, we're both on him."

William nodded, his lips pressed together, jaw tight.

"What day do you have off again?" Amanda asked. "I start back to work Wednesday morning. I could be there at eight-thirty. It would be three days a week. Wednesday through Friday. That's where we start."

She waited, wondering how long before he made a decision.

"Monday," he said. "I have Monday's off."

"I'll let you know. In the meantime, find a hooker."

"Amanda, don't do this," he whispered.

"You started it, George." She struggled to pull her arm free, George continuing to grasp it firmly, her anger blazing. "Let me go, George," she snapped.

Karen leaned in, eyes narrow, chin up, issuing a challenge of her own. Could he take both of them, in a crowded mall, with all these people watching?

George released Amanda, his eyes smoldering. "Wednesday it

is then. Bring your friend," he said eyeing Karen. "I would have no problem finding her a date, too."

Amanda hung her head, George walking away.

William sighed and relaxed, staring at the floor. He looked up, George disappearing through the rear doors.

"Amanda, what was all that?" Karen asked. "I don't want a blind date with any of the men he might know."

"Sorry. The man scared me half to death."

Amanda stared down the rear corridor then William dropped into the chair George had just vacated, setting his lunch on the table, James doing the same across from him. The organization's pager gave a soft snick as the comm channel closed.

"You look like you just saw a ghost," William said. "What did George want?"

"You scared me almost as bad as George did," Amanda said, clutching her chest. "He said he wanted to take me to lunch."

"He acted like he was pretty comfortable talking to you. Have you seen him before?"

"Yeah, he….uh….he stopped a couple of days ago and said hello. Apologized for being a jerk last year. He said he wants me to get to know the real George Bonner."

"You already told us that part. And that is opposed to?"

"The drugged up dealer, I guess. I'm sorry, Karen has to get back to work."

"I know you and you're hiding something," William replied.

"Like what?" Amanda asked. "I've never lied to you."

"I didn't say you lied to me. I said you're hiding something. It isn't what you've said. It's what you haven't said."

He'd caught her, but he wanted her to tell him what she had planned. She knew he didn't want her working undercover, yet here she was, working on something, when she had no idea what she was getting into. Why else would she have been in George's?

"Amanda. I have a very serious question for you."

"Okay," she answered getting this sinking feeling in the pit of her stomach. "You're not going to give me that teenage pep talk thing are you?"

"No. But I am going to expect a straight answer."

"Crap! Karen told you, didn't she?" She looked over at Karen, Karen glancing down at her lap.

"Not really. She called James because she was afraid you would get hurt."

"So…You lied to me!"

"No. I didn't lie. James was in the bar keeping an eye on you two just like you said. I only said he'd been with me all day. And he had."

"That's a technicality, William!"

"Amanda, don't start it. Let's keep this a civil conversation. Why did you go down there? Why put yourself in that position? It was stupid."

"Matter of opinion," she said. "I debated talking to you first, but then I remembered the fight at the apartment. I don't want to do that again. But, George said some things and I think he knows something about your wife's death. He mentioned it and when you talked about it at the meeting – you and James said some information hadn't been released to the public."

"What did he say that would make you think that?"

"Nothing specific," she said. "But it sounded like he knew something. How would he know if he didn't know who did it? Someone has to get him to talk and you guys can't arrest him. Not without evidence. How bad can it be?"

"And that's it?"

"Well…yeah. Then you told everybody the details and it made me think. He knows something, William."

"Amanda. Listen to me please." He looked down at what was left of his drink and thought about how he should word this. "As you know, we think George is responsible for a couple of the recent murders. We just don't want you out there getting chummy with a murderer. Do you get it?"

"That I understand," she replied. "I can help, though. I only want to stop one hour a day on my way to work and talk to him. Damn it, William!" She exhaled, holding her hand up while she composed her thoughts, James and Karen leaning back in their chairs. "I really do understand. But if I keep this to one hour a day. On my way to work. I can find out something. That is all I want to do. No dates, no drinking, just one hour a day to talk to him. And I will have the pager and my knife with me at all times. I really have tried to think this through."

"How far?" William asked.

"What?"

"How far have you thought it through? As far as Jeremy says you can work any man. Or as far as, if this goes south you could get hurt?"

She shrugged and stared at the floor.

"That's what I thought. Can you hold off long enough for us to talk to Jeremy and the other members of this team? Let us figure out something better? Do you think you can do that?"

"I can do that. When's Jeremy due back?"

"Tonight. We're going to have another meeting."

Amanda sighed. She'd only been pulling George's chain.

"I know. We heard you," William said. "With George, you are forgiven the occasional white lie."

41

Amanda watched William and James pull into traffic hitting the steering wheel with the palm of her hand. She toyed with her keys then started the car and thought again about George. How hard could it be to do this without anyone finding out?

Pulling into traffic, Jeremy popped into her mind, reminding her of her commitment to the team. This wasn't just George and William and William's late wife. She stopped at a payphone a half a block north admitting, in her excitement, she had left out the key word – team. When she finished the call, she turned back to her car, a patrolman pushing himself off the front fender.

"Good afternoon. I wanted to introduce myself. See if there's a possibility we could do dinner. Maybe stop for a beer one of these nights. I don't see a ring and Detective Harrison isn't married."

Amanda shrugged, checking his name tag, Collier, thinking about where he had seen her and what William had to do with it.

"The name's Bryce," he continued. His smile growing broader. "Sorry. I'm the officer who followed you for Detective Harrison. I have to say he has extremely good taste in women."

Amanda laughed. "Thank you. I, kind of, thought that's what

he was doing when I saw him."

"And your name?"

"Amanda. Can I let you know about the beer?"

"Of course. So.... What about dinner?"

"Not tonight," she replied. "I already have plans. I can call the station if I want to get in touch with you, right?"

"Yes, ma'am. I look forward to it." He opened the door then squatted on the sidewalk, hands on the door after he'd closed it. "I hope you don't take too long. You are a very beautiful woman."

Amanda smiled then pulled away.

Bryce watched Amanda drive off and walked to the payphone, calling the station and asking for William.

William finished the call, told James what Bryce had told him and popped the first of the two cassettes in. They listened for the next hour, each one making notes and thinking of when the man may have been discovered. No one approached him and no voices sounded close. William changed tapes, James labeling the first one and they settled in again. The last tape was just over an hour, but most of it was useless. George and his cronies were too far away to be heard over the jukebox. It was only when the music stopped that they caught anything. Then the officer signed off.

"Hope that helps," the officer said. "I need to hike it out of here before I get caught."

"I don't think our officer got out of there fast enough." James nodded toward the tapes. "I bet these are why he was worked over."

"You're right. We need to verify who the cops are, though. It just seems awfully convenient. George is out and there have been several..." William thought for a second. "....unusual occurrences recently. All involving us. But they didn't mention any names and we need something a bit more definitive than two cops."

William popped the tape and James labeled it while William

got on the phone. They also had to find out if a girl named Lori had been in juvenile recently and who had sprung her. It took almost an hour and a half, but William finally got the information and hung up.

"What did they say?" James asked already knowing it wasn't going to be good.

"There has only been one girl named Lori pulled in. Someone sprung her the next afternoon. It wasn't her parents. It was an attorney. He had all the paperwork in order so they had no reason to refuse him. And we won't find Lori. She was the girl who went off the road on Interstate-80."

They paged Jeremy telling him they would be at Amanda's at seven. And they had new info. At ten minutes to seven they were pushing the buzzer.

"What do you have?" Jeremy asked.

William took the cassettes out of his pocket and laid them on the table. "These are tapes one of our plain clothes officers got. The second one is pretty bad, most of it covered by the juke box, but in one part George is telling a girl named Lori she doesn't work for him…"

"Jeremy, Lori was the girl we caught that day at the center," Amanda said. "I'm sorry, William." She turned back to Jeremy. "Do you think it's her? Lori was working for George?"

Jeremy shrugged. "Might be."

"She's pleading for birth control pills," William continued. "Part of that one is George talking to a guy about 'two cops and a baby'. Twenty-five grand."

"There's not enough for us to go to the DA with," James said. "If they had mentioned names, we would have him. We actually have more evidence pulling George away from the teens than we have incriminating George in anything. In the one it sounds like he's ready to cold-cock Jonathan because of the girls, but someone in the background speaks up and stops him."

Jeremy reached out and took the cassettes. "May I listen to these?"

"Be our guest," William answered. "That's why we brought them."

"Do you need help finding Lori?" Jeremy asked.

"No. She's one of the teens that was killed in that accident that involved us," William answered. "But what has us concerned is the guy talking about 'two cops and a baby'. If we had gone over that barrier…."

"It would have been two cops and the girl," Jeremy said, finishing the thought. "And she was underage. Anything else?"

"The truck we saw passing the teen's car…" Jeremy nodded. "…before the explosion. The guy looked directly at me. It was a blue truck with an aluminum boat in the bed. Short blonde hair, no beard, no mustache." William paused, looked at James, James giving him a go ahead nod. "The undercover who got those…" William jerked his head at the tapes. "….was worked over pretty good this morning and is in the hospital with multiple broken bones. A passer-by happened to see it and called 911." Jeremy looked pointedly at William. "We were thinking the same thing. We talked to the responding officers and they said the witness drove a black, non-descript, pick-up."

Amanda inhaled quickly. "With electric windows?"

"We don't know, but it had Nevada plates."

"I think George Bonner is our target again," Jeremy said.

William and James nodded, trading glances before they looked at Amanda.

"Amanda," James said. "Please, explain to everybody what you are planning and why. I want everybody to hear it from you."

"Not much to tell," she said. "George approached me at the mall. One of the questions he asked was if I knew the details about William's wife's murder. It was the way he said it. He knows something. He might even know who did it. I also remember you said that shortly after her murder George broke ties with Reno. Maybe that's why George broke ties with them. I decided to see if I could get George comfortable enough to say something...."

"Amanda!" Jeremy said, surprised.

"I want to go in and talk to him in the bar where we won't be alone. I don't want to *'date'* the guy or *'go'* anywhere with the man. I just want him to think I trust him." She looked around the table recognizing the expression. No one agreed with her. "I was thinking one hour a day. I would never be completely alone with him."

"And if we don't agree?" Timothy asked.

"I told William, I will take the teams advice into consideration regarding anything, but I was asked to join this team for a reason. I don't think that reason is to sit around on my behind. If I'm going to work this team let me work. Don't hide me in the closet. If you're not going to allow me to do anything, I'll resign and give Jeremy the pager back. I'll still collate information and work the event planning side. It's good money."

"I hate to sound like the devil's advocate," Timothy said, "but she's got a point. I don't particularly like her idea any better than you guys. At the same time if she only sees George at the bar..." He shrugged. "....it might work."

"I just don't want her to end up like Olivia," William said. He met Amanda's gaze, unconsciously playing with his beer. "I want you to tell us who you called today. The officer who followed you said he saw you after you left the mall."

Amanda dropped her head then shrugged.

"Is that who you called from the payphone?"

"Damn, guys!"

"Come on, Amanda," William said. "Did you take the position at Berringer & Hardy's so you can play George on the sly?"

"I turned it down," she replied. "I decided, since I don't need the money; let someone who does, have it. But I haven't said anything to George. I really don't trust the man." She noticed the smirk on James face. "And yes, I was going to tell you. You just haven't given me the chance."

"Yeah, right," James replied. He recognized the flare of anger and raised his hands. "Sorry, but you have to admit it sounds convenient."

42

Glen was awakened by running in the hall. He jumped out of bed, threw on his clothes and checked the clock, four photos that Jonathan had given him, on the stand in front of it. Sliding them inside the waistband of his jeans, he raced up the hall to pounding on the door.

"POLICE! OPEN UP!"

"Okay! Okay! I got this!" he said to himself as he raced for the back door, footsteps echoing on the stairs. He turned and sprinted for the living room, shadows appearing on the fire escape. He cursed under his breath and ran back to his bedroom. There was more pounding at the front door and he sighed.

"Mr. Tortino. This is Detective Harrison with the Salt Lake City Police Department. We need to talk to you."

Glen threw the curtains back and stared at the street below. A patrolman pointed then keyed his portable. There was another heavy knock on the door and he started up the hall.

"Mr. Tortino. If you do not open this door, we are coming in the hard way!"

A vision of Katie lying on the cot in George's office cut Glen to the core. "COMING," Glen called. "GIVE ME A SEC!" He blew his breath out heavily then walked to the door, placing his hand on the knob. A deep breath and he exhaled as he opened it, waving them in with a butler's flourish. "I agree. We need to talk."

William handed him the warrant. "Is there anything you would like to declare before we begin, Mr. Tortino?"

"I'm going to make some coffee," Glen said. "Would you care for a cup?" He glanced between the two then went to the kitchen, dropping the warrant on the dining table in passing. James followed, his hand resting on the butt of his pistol. William gave the men their instructions and joined James. Glen pointed to the table. "Please, sit down." A couple of minutes later he sat a cup in front of each man. "Cream, sugar?" They shook their heads and he padded back to the kitchen, returning with a cup, sitting across from William. A glance in the direction of the living room then he looked back at William.

"Are you afraid we'll find something?" James asked.

Glen shook his head, laid his beefy palm flat on the table and slid it over in front of William, uncovering the Polaroid's.

"Jonathan gave me those and told me to make sure you guys got them." Glen paused as William leaned forward, taking the photos off the table. "He wanted me to make it look like George was being fingered by the boys in Reno."

"This," William said, nodding at the photos, "puts you in possession of child pornography. We can hide you inside the legal system before anyone will even know you're gone."

Glen nodded his understanding. "George killed my fiancée," Glen said. "I'm tired of hurting people. And I'm tired of people getting hurt. Let's make a deal. What can you do for me, if I help you? How bad do you want those guys off the street? Either way, you win. You have the evidence and I am the witness."

"And you could die at the hands of these men," William reminded him. "Are you willing to take that chance?"

"For Katie, yes."

"Katie?" William put the photos back on the table. "Katie Landry was your fiancée?"

Glen dropped his head. "We were supposed to get married as soon as Reno took George out. Only George found out, and he iced her. He had me dispose of the body. I acted like the good little gopher and went to Jonathan for guidance on the method of disposal."

"How could you do that to her if you cared?" James asked.

"That was the hardest job I've ever done," Glen replied, tears leaving their tracks on his cheeks. "I told her I was sorry. I promised her I would make George pay. That was the day I made the decision to do something. I just didn't know exactly what to do or how to pull it off. You guys knocking on my door made it easy." He nodded at the Polaroid's in front of William. "You just happened to find the pictures still in my possession."

"You're right, we need to talk," William said. "We'll do the search. We'll arrest you and take you in. You tell us everything. Once you give us your statement we'll go to the DA and arrange the terms of your release. Sound like something you can do?"

"How long will this take? I don't want it to look obvious."

"We might have you home tomorrow night. Unless you just want to stay an extra day for your own protection. We can keep you forty-eight hours without filing charges."

"I can live with that," Glen replied.

During the search of Glen's apartment, he directed them to a hidden panel in the bottom of one of the kitchen cabinets where they found a .38 caliber police service revolver, a fake badge and fake law enforcement ID, along with a .45 snub nose. He hadn't admitted to anything at this point, and they were fine with that. They wanted a recording of his admission.

James went to replace the bottom in the cabinet, the section next to the one he held shifted, and he lifted it out. Beneath it was a breather painted like an alien, a business card and a butcher knife stamped 'Farberware'. James picked it up and thought of the box found in the dumpster behind the dealer's room. James held up the breather. William stood, directing Glen to do the same and pulled his cuffs.

Glen stood in front of his chair, staring at James, his mouth guppying.

"You didn't expect us to find this, Mr. Tortino?" James asked.

"No," Glen said. He tried to swallow, his throat constricting. "I've never seen that before. How did it…? I mean, who …?" His shoulders drooped and he groaned, staring at the ceiling. "Why do I get the feeling I'm in deep shit?"

"Because you are," William replied.

James read Glen his rights while William cuffed him then they sat him back down. Once they'd finished the search, they took Glen downtown and settled him into an interrogation room. After they had the equipment set, they joined him, Captain Kirby in the viewing room. They identified themselves for the recording then asked Glen a few questions, prompting him to begin his version of events, being careful not to word anything so it would be construed as leading. They stopped him, asking very precise questions frequently, getting a feel for what was supposed to have taken place and to avoid any confusion.

"One more question, Mr. Tortino," William said. "Why was Olivia Holland murdered so brutally?"

"I didn't murder her," Glen answered. "I choked her. I know how to use the choke hold as well as George Bonner does." He saw the shock. "No bruises were found on her were there?"

"Several actually. And almost forty knife wounds," William answered sliding a photo of her body across the table. "She'd been stabbed multiple times."

"Olivia wasn't dead when I left her. I had a dude set to come in and stage the scene. I saw the news broadcasts, but I have no idea what happened." He directed his gaze to the far wall, refusing to look at the photo. "I never use a knife. They're too messy."

"The last place you saw her was on Park Street," James said, "and she was alive."

"No." Glen shook his head. "The last place I saw her was in her apartment. And – yes – she was alive. That was about twelve-thirty."

William leaned back in his chair. "You raped her, and then casually choke her out, in her apartment, and left her."

"I didn't rape her. It was consensual. She was a call girl. I told her I wanted a second go and was willing to pay. She agreed. I came up behind her and choked her, old-fashioned Benadryl in her drink kept her unconscious. I got dressed and left, leaving the door unlocked for the guy to come in and stage the place."

"The same guy who left Pearls on Main with you and her?"

"No again. He was only the ride. He dropped us off at Olivia's and I never saw him again. He was hired through Jonathan."

"So…" James shook his head and scowled. "Your job was to have sex with the woman and then choke her?"

"My job was to do whatever I needed to, to knock her out without leaving any marks…"

"But she's dead!" William said.

"I didn't kill her!" Glen exclaimed. "I had sex with her. That was all I did. She was a very beautiful woman. A call girl. That's what she did. She had sex with men for money." He smiled and chuckled. "Well, except choke her into unconsciousness. That does sound crazy, doesn't it?"

"According to the autopsy, she was raped," William said. "It wasn't very nice. It was rough."

"Not me," Glen said, shaking his head. "I had consensual sex with her and I choked her. She was alive and sleeping peacefully, in her bed, when I left. That's all I'm going to say."

Glen maintained his silence for the next hour, Captain Kirby finally pulling the plug. They could bring him back in, in the morning. They had thirty-six hours before they had to charge him.

William was wearing his signature scowl when they walked out. "Something's wrong, James. It isn't adding up."

"So what makes you think that? Besides the obvious."

"The obvious," William answered. "It's just too convenient. If you had assaulted those women wearing something as unique as that breather..." William locked eyes with James. "...would you direct the cops to the place you knew they could find it?"

"Nope," James answered. "And the knife. I notice you didn't mention the knife."

"Tomorrow, my man. We'll nail him with that tomorrow."

43

James had Glen put back in the room at seven the next morning. They wanted to drag more out of him before his attorney found out what happened and could spring him.

"Good morning, Glen," William said when they joined him. "We're going to go over things one more time."

William noticed the puffy eyes, debated asking Glen how he'd slept, thought better of it. The scowl and the dark circles gave William the answer.

"Let's just get this shit over with," Glen grumbled.

"Gladly," William replied. "We want to go over the alien mask again. You say you've never seen it, but it was in your kitchen in your hiding place."

"I swear," Glen said adamantly, attempting to hold his hands out the cuffs jerking them back down. "I have never seen that thing before! I told you I'd shoot straight and I am."

"And you're the only one with a key to your apartment," James said, more statement than question. "I want you to explain how it got there. Has anyone been in your apartment? Is there anything missing?"

"Nothing's missing," Glen answered. "I haven't upgraded the locks so anyone who's decent with a pick could get in. Katie had a key, but she's dead. I don't think a ghost would need a key."

"Katie was naked when she was found," James said. "What happened to her clothes? Her purse?"

"I guess George threw them away. I was too upset to even think about that."

"So, George could have a key to your apartment," James said.

"Possibly." Glen stared across the table at them. "What's so important about that mask? What did it put me in the middle of?" No one said anything, and he exhaled through his nose. "Look, I been straight with you. Tell me something."

William and James glanced between each other and William shrugged.

"We've had several rapes," James said. "One of the girls was stabbed multiple times, just like Olivia, and is dead. Three of them escaped, but had significant injuries. Cuts on the torso and faces. Two of them said their assailant wore a mask just like that one."

"Aw, Jesus!" Glen leaned back in the chair, fixing his gaze on the window then he looked back, locking eyes with William. "I would never do that." He now glanced frantically between the two. "In your search of my apartment, or my car, did you find any knives?" His voice had raised a notch, tinged with stress and panic. "I had two steak knives and a paring knife. That's it!"

"We found two steak knives, a paring knife, and…" William paused then dropped an evidence bag on the table containing the butcher knife. "…that."

"Not mine," Glen said in almost a whisper. "I swear." He looked at the door then back at James then moved his eyes to William."Where…?" He stopped, tried to swallow. "Where'd you find that?"

"With the mask," James answered. "Along with this." James laid another evidence bag on the table beside the knife holding a business card. The Landers Corporation – Reno, Nevada.

"The business card was given to me a few days ago by a dude who works for George. I remember him from last year. George called him David. I had it with the pictures on my nightstand." Glen's mouth fell open, his eyes wide. "That wasn't on the stand by my bed. I laid it on top of the pictures I gave you. It wasn't there when I picked them up."

"It looks like someone has been in your apartment," William said. "You just didn't know it."

"Who is this David?" James asked.

"Never met him," Glen answered. "He worked for George last year and I've seen him around, but I never heard his name until a few days ago. When I told George about Jonathan he was in the bar."

"And this Landers Corporation?" William asked.

"They've done some back door work for Las Vegas. I've done some side work for them, but I don't know the organizational shit. I know the goons in Las Vegas are gunning for them. Landers is cutting into the money usually collected by the boys down south."

"Is that why you moved to Reno?"

"Yeah. We were supposed to get all the dirt then Vegas would take them and the Bonner's out. No one counted on Jonathan. Everyone assumes Jonathan's a pussy, being controlled by his uncle and a bottle, but he's worse than George in some ways."

"You expect us to believe you have never met the man in charge in Reno," William stated.

"Because it's true," Glen answered defensively. "I talked to them on the phone. Vegas shipped us to Reno, ostensibly to help Reno, because we became more than a blip on the radar of the Vegas P.D. Katie and I did a couple of penny ante jobs in Reno then they loaned us to Jonathan to take George down."

"And that's why George iced Katie," James said.

"Yes," Glen said. "And I bet that's why that mask was hidden in my apartment. I should have noticed the card being gone. I screwed up."

A knock on the door interrupted them. James opened it and Captain Kirby beckoned him outside with a jerk of his head. Glen's attorney had arrived.

James stared at the captain, mouth gaping.

"I know," the captain said. "But we gotta cut him loose."

James nodded then went back in and closed the door sitting beside William.

"Your attorney's here so we're going to keep our end of the bargain, but do not even think about leaving town. We may have more questions for you."

Glen nodded.

William stared at James for a tic then recovered. "I thought you'd like to know we had that knife compared with the wounds on the women. It didn't kill either of them." Glen sighed, a deep tired moan. "My apologies. We had to make sure you weren't jerking our chain."

A patrolman entered and led him away.

The door closed and William turned to James. "How the hell did his attorney get onto this so fast?"

James shrugged and shook his head. "Don't know, but we lost him now. You know damn good and well, if we try to pull him in again, his attorney will be all over us."

Back at his apartment, Glen flicked aimlessly through the channels, his mind on the conversation with the man called David and the questions by the cops. He had no knowledge of the mask, and he had no idea who would have planted it, and he didn't want the cops showing up on his doorstep again.

He climbed into bed just before eleven, a drunk lurching into the wall by his door and a woman laughed. There was a dull thud and more drunken laughter. Paper grated on the floor as he climbed out of bed and turned the light on. He walked up the hall, an envelope peeking underneath his door. He stooped to pick it up, feeling the metal contact points too late.

Fireworks exploded in his head, pain radiating into his arm, his hand numb then there was a crash and the door blew in on him. He turned to catch his fall and was shoved face first onto the floor, a gag being wrenched around his head tight enough it cut into his cheeks, his hands tied behind his back. They jerked him to his feet, a swimmy image of two men and a woman in front of him.

"We have a message for you," one of the men snarled.

"Not here," the woman snapped. "Let's go. Check the hall."

They dragged him down the rear stairs to a waiting car, throwing him into the back seat. One of the men climbed in beside him and held his head down as he leaned over him. The second man climbed into the driver's seat, the woman plopping onto the passenger seat. A few blocks away the woman peeled off the wig and changed clothes, the man allowing Glen to sit up. The woman turned and dropped the photos Jonathan had given him into his lap, the man beside him removing the gag.

"We searched your apartment while the cops had you," the driver said. "I thought you were supposed to give those to them?"

Glen stared, dumbfounded. "I gave the pictures to the cops. That's why I was arrested." Images of the pictures on his stand, minus the business card came to mind. The cops finding the mask and the knife, with the card. David's words repeating. *'In some ways Jonathan is much worse than his uncle.'* Jonathan set him up. Glen glanced between the threesome, frantic, fighting the urge to panic. "There were no pictures in my apartment! Look…I can call the cops and let you talk to one of the detectives…."

The man beside Glen slapped him in the back of the head. Glen ducked, raised one of his legs and kicked him, leaning into the door. The man punched him, blood oozing from a cut on Glen's lip. The man struck him again, near the temple. One not meant to kill. A practiced blow. Glen's vision blurred, the man squeezed behind him, shoving Glen's face forward, his chin resting on the back of the front seat. Glen tried to push back, but the man leaned his full weight into him, the woman forcing a tube down Glen's throat.

Glen shook his head as he twisted and pushed, something bitter being poured down him. The man relaxed his hold and Glen wedged him into the corner against the seatback and the rear door, the tube still dangling from his mouth. Then the tube was yanked out. Glen coughed, gagging as the man slammed him against the door again then he was shoved onto the floorboards, a pistol held to his head. Glen remained where he lie, the man hovering over him.

"You got five minutes," the woman told the driver. "I'm not cleaning the car out. You'll be stuck with it."

When the car stopped, the men rolled him onto the ground, clouds of dust floating into his mouth and his eyes, blinding grit choking him. Glen's heart raced, his stomach reeled, pinpricks of pain erupted in his abdomen, the world fading out.

44

The team met at Amanda's, William separating two folders, sliding one to James.

"We are going to go over a few things regarding a couple of cases, and I'm going to let James begin this."

He nodded for James to take over.

"We currently have an active rapist and there are witnesses to two of them," James said, opening the folder that was in front of him. "DNA collected from Olivia points to two men being with her the night she was murdered, but George isn't one of them, and he was still at The Point then. We don't know if both men raped her or if one had been a customer. We are leaning toward the latter since we have not received anything definitive from the U yet." He placed a cassette on the table and hit record then looked across at Amanda. "Amanda, at our last meeting you remembered a man who worked for George last year named Glen. He's one of those who'd been trunking off the syndicate."

"I didn't know their names," she admitted. "As far as I was concerned they would only expect the same thing George and every other man did if we were ever alone. William called the one dude Glen Tortino."

"Do you recognize him?" James continued, sliding a picture across the table to her. "We just need you to say 'yes' or 'no'. Is this picture him?"

"Yes. He drove the limo if a guy named Frank didn't."

"Thank you." James turned the cassette off and slid it into his coat pocket. "The samples we sent from William's wife and one of the specimens from Olivia match specimens found in the DOJ database belonging to him. He worked for Las Vegas last year and he and Katie were loaned to George by Reno this year. We searched Glen's apartment and found a standard department issue .38." He went on to explain about the other items and finished with the information about Glen possibly being framed since the knife wasn't the murder weapon. "That is another reason we're worried about you following through with your plan."

Amanda nodded.

"We also found a .45 snub nose." William added. "When they ran the ballistics, the bullet fired from that gun matched the slug from my wife. Glen also said, the pictures he gave us, were given to him by Jonathan with instructions to give them to us to nail George for child prostitution, but Jonathan wanted it to appear that the syndicate was ratting George out."

"So this is where we sit," James said, taking over again. "The women from last year and the woman found in the Green River were sexually involved with the same man. And we did a DNA profile on the semen, but as we know DNA isn't admissible in court so we need to force his hand somehow. Push it hard enough, he will implicate Jonathan."

"And George is that man?" Timothy asked. James nodded. "What about Glen?"

"He gave us a statement," William replied, "but claimed no knowledge of the breather or the knife. Everything else he told us jives. His attorney bailed him out midway through the second interrogation session and Glen has disappeared. We questioned the officers stationed outside his apartment and were told a trio of drunks had gone in, but when the car left there were only two occupants so they assumed the third person lived in the building. They ran the plates as a precaution and they came back clean. Not even a traffic ticket." William paused, watching Amanda. "Amanda, this is exactly why we don't want you seeing George. Even if this was none of his doing, this is a prime example of how he works. And you are the one who would be the easiest to manipulate if George decided to use physical means to learn what he wants. Does that make sense?"

She nodded. "But…"

William raised his hand, stopping her. "Since Glen and Katie were on loan to Jonathan that means Jonathan would have been next. They were both threats to Reno's revenues. Add in George found out Katie worked for Reno and that's why he had her iced."

"Which means Glen would have been next on George's agenda," Jeremy added. "That would explain the mask."

James leaned forward, resting his arms on the table. "Before we even think about this, what do you remember about the bar, Amanda? If you go in, we need this set tight. We don't want a damn thing happening to you or any other member of this team. The time I was inside, I sat at the end near the front windows."

"There are two doors," she answered. "The taps for the kegs are at the end of a bump out where the bartender can see both doors. The old-fashioned bar and back bar sits in the front where you come in, forming kind of an 'L' running along the front of the bump out then up the north wall. At the back, behind the taps, is a wall of mirrors on the upper half with a telephone and cabinets under it. There's also a door that goes to the walk in cooler. Then there's a short piece of bar that attaches the section where the taps are to the wall. Coolers run under both sections of bar at the end of the bump out."

"What's behind that longer section in front?" Jeremy asked.

"He has coolers under it," James answered. "I also suggest – if she does this – we wire her. We need a recording of everything that is said. We can use one of my toys. Hide it in her necklace or bracelet."

They spent the next couple of hours going over things Amanda should look for. The positioning of any customers or potential bouncers. If it looked like George had a weapon behind the bar. Locations that would work for a pay station if he had a band. It would be easy to conceal a weapon there. Anything that would be of help.

"Okay. What's the verdict guys?" Amanda asked.

"Let's think about it," William said. "None of us want to jump into this feet first and find out it's quicksand. We would like you to have more back up, but Timothy is the only one who can go in with you."

Amanda forced a smiled and nodded. Without the men in agreement, she would have no back up if she went in alone.

"You don't look too happy," Jeremy commented.

"I'm not. I had hoped you guys would understand. And I don't know what else to do. I'm the one he approached."

"We only said we wanted to think about it," William said. "We may end up sending you in after all."

"I know," she answered, giving a half-hearted shrug. "It's just disappointing."

45

Amanda climbed out of the taxi and looked up at the front of the bar, turned the pager off then dropped it in her purse. She didn't want George hearing anything if William tried to call her. She approached the door, the nervous flutter threatening to overtake her. She held her hands over her diaphragm and waited. What in the hell was she thinking? She closed her eyes and exhaled forcefully, placing one hand on the door, pushing it open. Time to strut it just like she was onstage.

The hinges screeched, announcing Amanda's arrival. George looked up from where he sat at the end of the bar talking to a woman, a smile crossing his face. Amanda closed the door and he stood, his eyes locked on her. Seating herself at the end of the bar where James had sat previously, Amanda acknowledged George with a flirtatious dip of her eyes then allowed her gaze to wander. Did George have bouncers or guards inside and, if so, where?

A man sat, strategically positioned in the corner where the two sections of the antique bar met, eyeing her as she sat down. He smiled, his eyes roaming, sitting up straighter. She gave him a tentative smile, continuing her scrutiny. Across from him, at one of the tables, another man leaned against the wall where he could see the entire building. A third man sat at the far end of the bar next to the dance floor, using the bump out for his back.

"Well, hello, gorgeous," George said. "I wasn't expecting to see you so soon. Coke?"

"No. St. Pauli Girl. I took a cab tonight," she answered.

"On the house," George said, setting the beer in front of her. "Maybe we'll have more time to talk tonight."

"It looks like you have company, George. And I wouldn't want to horn in. You'll be more apt to score with her than with me."

"She won't be here long. She has clients to entertain. If you understand the meaning."

"George Bonner resorting to hookers," Amanda said, feigning surprise. "I thought you said no lady ever complained."

"Isn't that what you told me to do?" He smiled, giving her a sideways glance. "And I never said who I entertained."

A couple came in and George walked away to serve them then seated himself beside the girl. He leaned over and whispered in her ear, she glared back at him. George laughed and took her glass, drawing the woman another beer then returned to his stool.

Amanda wondered if he had dismissed her to go back to work.

Half way through Amanda's beer the old hinges complained and Timothy walked in. Pointing to the stool next to her, Timothy chuckled when Amanda rolled her eyes and took the seat ordering them each a beer.

Amanda debated changing stools, dismissed the idea and took a drink of her beer. This wasn't how she had wanted tonight to go. The idea had been to talk to George.

"William and James are disappointed in you," he whispered.

"I thought they were working late tonight?"

"They were," Timothy replied. "Key word 'were'. You didn't answer when William called so he got worried. Especially since you didn't answer the pager, either."

George brought their beers and Timothy introduced himself. Amanda took the hint and introduced herself. George frowned, returning to the hooker.

"So you were volunteered as the guinea pig?"

Timothy ignored her barb, asking simple questions like they had never met then nonchalantly slid his arm around her, rubbing her back gently before offering to buy her another beer. George's eyes narrowed, but he remained quiet. George's friend left and he moved to the end of the bar near Amanda and Timothy only leaving to serve other customers then he'd return, maintaining attention to the duo. George offered to bring another round and Timothy held his hand up shaking his head. Amanda checked the clock. Time for her to make her exit.

Timothy excused himself to make a pit stop, winking as he walked away. George followed him with his eyes, turning back to Amanda once Timothy was out of ear shot and offered her a beer. Amanda turned it down, but said she would return Wednesday morning and asked George to call a cab. Timothy overheard her, offering her a ride. George's jaw clenched and his eyes flashed but he kept quiet, returning to his stool by the taps.

In Timothy's car, Amanda was torn between her anger over William and James sending Timothy in, and her anger because Timothy felt strongly enough to do it. He had always been one to stay evenly spaced between the two sides, often agreeing with her. Until tonight.

"I know you're pissed," Timothy said, breaking the awkward silence. "But no one wants you to get hurt. That's it. Bottom line. Okay? It was either, I came in and played cozy with you, if you were there, or William was going to call in a missing persons report. Tell dispatch you were depressed, talking suicide. Then you would have been picked up and hauled to the hospital in a black and white. I don't think you'd like it in a psych ward."

"Timothy, I understand everybody's concern," Amanda said. "I am really not that dense…"

"No offense, but you were dense enough to go against our request to let us think about it. That was all we asked you to do."

Amanda pursed her lips and blew the air out, staring straight ahead, equal amounts anger and frustration welling up inside. Timothy was right, but she didn't know how else to get close to George.

"Just let me out up here," she said hotly. "I'll take a cab the rest of the way home."

"Not going to happen. I told them I would bring you home, and that is what I intend to do."

Amanda glared out the windshield fighting the urge to smash it as Timothy slowed for the light. He slowed further and she stared out the passenger window at the right lane with no one pulling up to make a turn. The car came to a stop and she threw the door open, darting for the intersecting street, racing west as the light turned green.

"AMANDA!" Timothy yelled. "Damn it!"

Timothy cramped the wheels to the right, cutting around the corner to catch her, but was met with an empty street. Not even a parked car. Stopping at the next intersection, Timothy climbed out, checked both directions and opened the comm channel. He had lost her.

"She's gone guys," he said. "I stopped for a red light and she bolted."

46

It was late by the time William and James made it back to William's apartment. They had spent hours combing the streets and alleys looking for Amanda. She wasn't returning pages or answering her home phone. Jeremy ran a search on motels and hotels, but turned up nothing. If she had rented a room somewhere she hadn't used her name. William and James had taken a picture and checked with the hotels downtown and came up empty. James called Karen and Janice, but was told neither of them had heard from her, either. Bulletins had been sent to every police department from Boise, Idaho to Denver Colorado, to St George, Utah. There was nothing more they could do tonight.

Slipping out of his clothes, William's ribs throbbed. They continued to bother him if he pushed too far, but he refused to take the pain meds. The fog would be too hard to come out of if they received a call out. He rolled into bed falling into a deep sleep, his dreams plagued by visions of his late wife. The phone dragged him awake at five a.m. They were being requested to a convenience store on the corner of State Street and Forty-Five Hundred South. Be there thirty minutes ago.

William's first thought was Amanda and he woke James then threw his clothes on, his head foggy even without the meds. Snippets of his dream floated through the haze, setting his nerves on edge. Between that, Amanda and his ribs, William tossed James the keys.

They pulled up at five twenty-five to the normal crime scene confusion. William saw the dark hair and his breath caught, his heart skipping a beat. If she hadn't been so damned stubborn. Striding to the body, William brushed the blind aside, releasing the air he'd been holding, the relief palpable, James doing the same. It wasn't Amanda.

"Same MO as the others?" William asked.

"Looks like it," one of the officers answered. "This one was well planned like the first."

James took the lead this time, kneeling beside the body, William walking the perimeter, viewing it from above. She was spread eagle; face down with her hands under her, fingers cupped over her genitalia. Streaks from her tears lined her face, creating pools where they had soaked into the mattress. She had been beaten and cut before the man stabbed her to death. Blood on the mattress near her shoulders bloomed like a flower in spring. More blood peeked from under her hips.

"Okay to turn her?" one of the techs asked.

James nodded; still amazed at the savagery some men used dealing with women.

The techs rolled her, cuts on her breasts and abdomen in full view. Marks could be seen on her arms where she had attempted to fight, but flesh was no match for steel. Her eyes were swollen and bruised, blood in a corner of her mouth. A hint at the time the man had taken with her. James turned away, visions of his sister vying for control. The man was becoming progressively more brutal with each victim.

Moving in an ever widening circle as they examined the scene, they discovered drag marks where the mattress had been hidden under a dumpster. Small drops of blood were visible between the mattress and it. William lifted his eyes, visually tracing a straight line from the crime scene through the dumpster to a spigot at the back of the building. The asphalt under it wet. William alerted the techs then he and James introduced themselves to the person who had found her.

The man was taking it hard, finding it difficult to concentrate, unable to explain what he had seen, burying his face in his hands. James allowed him his time, talking calmly using simple easy questions designed to take his mind off what he had seen. Once the man regained focus, they started introducing questions about the scene, allowing him to wander in the telling. Stories didn't always come out in a linear fashion when the teller was stressed.

"What time did you find her?" William asked.

"About three-fifteen or three-thirty," he answered. "I work at one of the bars in town and I was on my way home. I was tired and pulled in the wrong way to put gas in my car, so I drove around the building. Then I saw the corner of the mattress. I got nosy and pulled up in front of the car here." He pointed to a car parked next to the dumpster. "My headlights were pointed at the bushes and I expected to see an abandoned dog or something, but instead I see the girl. I thought she was drunk. Passed out. Maybe one of the homeless people. Then I saw she was naked. And the blood."

"Did you see anyone else?" William asked. "A person hanging around the periphery?"

"Not that I can remember. I panicked and ran inside. Told the guy to call 911. He called you guys and checked it out then leaned some cardboard over it so other customers wouldn't see her. The guy said she worked here. She got off at ten-thirty." He dropped his head in his hands again, pressing his palms to his eyes. "What did she do to make the man do that to her?"

"Nothing," William said. "Men who do that aren't human."

After they had his statement, they allowed him to go, stressing the possibility they would contact him again, and gave him one of their business cards.

William glanced up, recognizing Lloyd directing the techs and remembered their conversation at the station. Lloyd looked at them, glanced away answering a question from a tech, then turned his attention back to them.

"Hey, dee-teck-deeves! Imagine meeting you two here. What's happenin'?"

"Same oh, same oh, Lloyd," William said.

"I heard you found my breather."

"Looks like it," William answered. "We need you to ID it when you get a chance. We can't release it…."

"I know how it goes," Lloyd said. "I want you to know, I appreciate you guys talking to me first and not just accusing me of something."

"No problem." William gazed at the girl as she was loaded into a body bag unsure where to go from here. "How are the burns?"

"Doin' good," Lloyd replied, automatically raising his arms and examining them even though he couldn't see through the bandages. William noticed they covered less territory than before, angry pink scars visible in some spots. Both men were quiet a moment, Lloyd breaking the silence. "Anyway, no hard feelings, bro. You were just doing your job." He hesitated, grinning from ear to ear. "I heard you had some excitement. Glad to see you're not hurt."

"Thanks," William said. "Give us the usual. Latent's, prints, samples sent to the U. We found boot prints at other scenes. If we find any here that match, it'll give us more evidence on the guy."

They had no doubts the DNA would come back a match, but

they had to have more. They had to have something to push him far enough he would confess. The only other option was catching him in the act.

"Don't forget your famous photo shots," James added.

"Will do," Lloyd replied. He eyed William and chuckled. "I would ask if I could help you with your lady, but I didn't know if she was yours yet. How's that going?"

"It isn't full-time. You can't have her anyway, Lloyd. You're married."

"Yeah, yeah. Minor technicality, man. Minor technicality. Talk to you later."

William laughed. Lloyd was all smoke with no fire in that respect. He would never hurt his wife.

They went inside to speak to the clerk, getting corroboration for parts of what the witness had said. The woman had worked a double that day, the two to ten-thirty tacked onto her usual, six to two-thirty. They didn't get paid for their lunch, the clerk added reminding William of all the non-essential thoughts that filtered in when people were under stress. William and James took his statement then finished at the scene and headed for the unmarked. Assault number five.

"Want breakfast with your favorite partner?" James asked. "We can stop at Sambo's on State Street. Go over things. We both know we're missing something." James looked at his watch. "Well, maybe lunch."

"Definitely," William replied. "This man is sick, James."

"I hear ya."

They walked into the restaurant, grabbed a booth near the far end, ordering their food. By three-thirty they still hadn't jarred anything loose and this setting in one place was getting painful. William stretched and winced.

"You doing okay, buddy?" James asked. "You don't sound too good."

"Just these damn ribs. I guess I pushed it looking for Amanda last night. Let's go see the captain. It's almost four."

They knocked on the captain's door taking chairs across from him.

"You two look like hell," Captain Kirby said.

"Goes with the territory," William answered. "We'll just need lots of coffee."

"Learn anything from those tapes?"

"We got some good Intel on one tape about what George isn't doing," James said. "On one it sounds like George is putting a hit out on someone. Two cops and a baby. In that tape a girl named Lori is begging for birth control. Lori was one of the teens killed in that wreck."

Captain Kirby nodded as he listened. "What about the callout this morning?"

"This looks like the same dude as before," James said giving him a quick rundown on what they knew, adding it corroborated Glen's account. The butcher knife was still in lock up.

Arriving at their desks there was another folder from the U. James and William started going over the reports, hoping for something new, but they were repeats of what they already had. Even though they had been told this could happen, it was still aggravating. James tossed the reports onto his desk and shoved his chair back.

"I definitely know why detectives drink so much," James said with an exaggerated sigh.

"If that had been Amanda, I know what I'd do," William said. "I think you'd do the same if it was Karen."

"Damn right! He'd be toast."

47

Amanda climbed out of the cab the next morning expecting to find Jeremy, James and William waiting in front of her apartment, but didn't see their cars. Her clothes reeked of urine from the crevice between buildings where she had crouched for the night and she took a quick shower to rid herself of the odor. Toweling off, she climbed into bed and sighed deeply. A soft bed and clean underwear. The finer things in life. She was jerked awake later when security let William and James in. A glance at the clock and she groaned, dragging herself from under the covers. After a lengthy discussion about her actions, Jeremy showed up and now she was getting it in triplicate.

She dressed and made coffee, holding a cup up, locking eyes with each man in turn. Getting a nod from each, she poured three more cups and got comfortable at the table selectively tuning them out at intervals.

It was obvious they didn't want her doing this, but she had to get George to talk. She had to learn what he knew, or if he knew anything. If Timothy hadn't interfered last night, she might have found out something. One thing. One word, was sometimes all it took to turn things around.

"Amanda!" Jeremy said sharply, pulling her out of her thoughts. "We would appreciate it if you would include yourself in this discussion. It does involve you."

"No, thank you," she retorted going back to the kitchen for more coffee. "What I did last night wasn't handled correctly and I'll concede that. I will not sit here and listen to all three of you harp on me all day, though. I am no happier about talking to George than any of you, but no one has come up with a better idea." She stood in the door, staring between the three. "No comment? I'm impressed…."

"Amanda…"

"Oh, please, don't start it again."

"Amanda," Jeremy said, his tone firmer. "We understand your feelings, but we don't want you getting hurt."

"Oh, and I want to get hurt?"

William raised his hands in surrender and leaned back in the chair. "We only asked you to wait."

"Okay." She sighed, and sat back down. "I'm sorry. I'm tired and I'm being a bitch. I shouldn't. Please forgive me. I have already told him I would be there Wednesday morning. After that it's up to the team. Deal?"

The men exchanged glances then William exhaled. "Deal. No more undercover shit unless we all agree."

Amanda nodded. "Okay. So, what's the plan?"

William threw his hands up, rolling his eyes.

48

Wednesday morning, Amanda met George as planned, arriving before the deliveries. Cliff had coffee waiting and George had picked up bagels and flavored cream cheese from a bakery on Main Street. Since things had gone smooth, the men relented and Thursday and Friday morning's were the same.

Now, Amanda sat at the end of the bar Monday evening flying solo. Timothy was on swing. He would meet her after he got off at eleven. Listening to George, she thought about how best to steer the conversation in the direction they wanted it to go. George was talking, but he wasn't revealing anything useful. There was also the possibility George had been stringing her along, not having anything to do with William's wife's death, but she was getting nowhere fast either way.

George went to the opposite end of the bar to serve a customer and Amanda poured the last of her beer down the tap drain. There was more than one way to look like you could handle your alcohol. That was the fourth beer she'd thrown away. He hurried back, ignoring her when she told him not to refill it, setting the full glass on the bar in front of her. He walked away to serve another customer and she couldn't focus, couldn't concentrate. One of the beers had been spiked. Thank God she had poured them out.

"Are you alright?" someone asked, the voice bouncing off the wall of a tunnel or echoing inside a tin can.

Something flashed in front of her and she ducked, squinting, her mind not catching up with the movement. Her thoughts drifted to the comm channel. It wasn't open. No, James toy was on her bracelet. She looked at her wrist, her eyes not focusing and rubbed her wrist. She hadn't worn it.

"The cops will never know who ordered the hit on William's wife, precious," the voice said. "People who do that are bigger and much more powerful than me. I am but a peon in their world. They could take out half of the Salt Lake City Police Department with one wave of their hand, but they need the insiders to keep them informed. You, however, are different. You will elevate me quickly. With you on my arm, Reno and Las Vegas will sit up and take notice of George Bonner. I didn't succeed last year, but this year I will. I told you, I've learned a lot in the last year."

Except for people's tinny laughter and the reverberating crack of the balls on the pool table, the room had gone quiet and she looked up, a swimmy vision of George sitting next to her. He pulled her close and kissed her, her head lolling backwards. He ran a hand under her shirt, Amanda lifting her hand, her fingers raking his arm ineffectually. She couldn't let George find the pager. George laughed, brushing her hand away.

Another voice, farther away called as she attempted to focus. George helped her sit up, Amanda stumbled, leaning against the bar, her thoughts disoriented her mind wandering. George said something unintelligible and she nodded, grabbing the seat on the stool beside her. Hinges squawked and the voice called again. George laid her hand on the stool he'd just vacated then left to help the customer. Amanda forced her way through the haze, gripping the edge of the bar, the minutest move sending a wave of dizziness over her. Then George appeared next to her, his arm around her waist.

"Are you alright, princess? Do you need to lie down? There's a cot in my office I use if I've been here late."

"I'll be fine," Amanda mumbled. Her words fuzzy, her throat dry. She tried to swallow but gagged instead. "I just felt funny for a minute. I need to use the restroom."

Another customer called. George asked a question, but she waved him away, gripping the bar. The swimmy sensation eased and she staggered around the end of the bar, using it to steady herself. She bumped into the corner of the wall, leaning against it until the stage came into partial focus in the far corner, its shape swirling and jumpy. She had to be there. She didn't know why, but she had to reach, there.

A slow deep breath and she looked over her shoulder for George. The move sent her into the wall again, but she squinted, trying to focus, seeing him walking the opposite direction, serving another customer. Amanda peeled herself away from the wall, made a tentative step, lurched unsteadily, vertigo threatening to take over. When her head quit spinning, she took a deep breath, choked back a sob and took another step, repeating it. Then she repeated it again. As she inched her way across the dance floor, she stumbled to her left, brushing against a table and a chair, the sound loud and exaggerated. She froze and looked over her shoulder once again. This was taking too long.

Something large loomed in front of her and she staggered, bumping into one of the speaker towers. She tried to steady them, didn't hear anything fall, her shoulder meeting the wall. '*Half way there,*' she thought as she slid to the floor. She climbed to her knees, continuing to use the wall for balance and crawled toward the corner. She paused, using both walls to steady herself, her head going in circles again. A couple of deep breaths and Amanda smeared herself around the corner and along the back wall until she ran into a booth then collapsed, her head resting on the floor, the cold tile shocking her system part way back to life. A glance toward the bar and George rushed from behind it, heading for the restrooms. She had run out of time. It was now or never.

George disappeared into the hall and Amanda forced herself up, staggering around the booth, falling into the door. It took every ounce of strength she had to turn the knob then the cool air hit her, jolting her farther out of the fog, her body spinning around the edge of the door. She fell against the side of the building, attempting to orient herself, her mind in turmoil, panic thrusting its way in. She forced the fear down, inhaled a deep breath then slid her way along the wall, toward the dumpster. The odor made her stomach roil, but she pushed forward rolling around the corner of the container, stumbling into the side of another building. Leaning against it, Amanda fumbled for the pager. It was in her bra somewhere.

A door opened then closed, footsteps coming toward her. George barked orders as Amanda squeezed deeper into the crack between the dumpster and the structure, slipping down the wall until she huddled on the ground. The steps drew closer and she dragged herself under the dumpster then the steps stopped and reversed direction. The door opened, George hurling obscenities, barking more orders. The door closed the cursing fading and she rested her head on the dirt, her arms limp.

Amanda stayed where she was, unaware how long then forced her body from under the container and off the ground. A few more minutes leaning on the wall and she peeked her head around the dumpster. The alley was empty and she slid her hand under her shirt, pulling the pager out and started pushing buttons. One of them would be the right one.

"Hey, guys. I'm in trouble," she slurred.

Every alert that could go off on Jeremy's pager went off then Amanda's barely understandable message came across. All three men bolted for the door, Timothy coming across.

"What's happening?" Timothy asked.

"Don't know," William answered. "We're heading for the bar to get her."

"No. Let me take the squad. If she's coherent enough to tell us she needs help, she got outside. Is the beacon working?"

"No," Jeremy answered. "She missed that one."

"I'll get back with you as soon as I can."

Timothy flipped the lights on and headed for State Street, his partner staring at him. Timothy instructed him to show them on a missing persons call as they barreled north on State Street toward Sixth South. When they passed Seventh South Timothy turned the lights out then made a right onto Sixth. He made another right coasting into the alley, using the spotlight to scour the gaps between buildings and cars in the parking lot, finding her car wedged between a truck and a neighboring building. He turned the squad around, driving out of the alley onto Sixth. Timothy's partner caught a glimpse of movement at the intersection with Second East and Timothy coasted down the street, parking on Second East. They climbed out of the car, beginning a foot search.

At the third house, leaves rustled in the bushes. Timothy peered inside, Amanda staring back at him, glassy eyed, dirt smudged on a cheek and covering her clothes.

"Hey, lady," Timothy said. "You aren't supposed to get falling down drunk."

Amanda laughed then the tears started.

"Come on," he said. "Let's get you home."

Timothy and his partner half carried, half dragged her to the squad car, laying her on the backseat, the tears stopping as quick as they had started. Amanda sniffled then wiped her face, smearing the dirt.

"I'm going to take you to meet the guys at the hospital…."

"No," she mumbled. "No. Just get me home."

Timothy called dispatch, reporting they had found the woman and she had refused the trip to the hospital. Arriving at Amanda's, William helped Timothy get her upstairs, Jeremy helping William pour her into the bathtub and turn the water on, pulling the shower curtain shut. She sobbed, laughed, wretched, and tumbled inside the bathtub as she pulled her clothes off, slopping them onto the floor, Jeremy cramming them into a trash bag. Once they were confident she would be safe alone, both men stepped out.

William dropped his gaze, then looked at Jeremy. "Look, um…" He paused not wanting the words to sound forced. "I'm sorry for being such an ass. I just don't know how to handle her sometimes. She's a freer spirit than I'm used to."

"I understand, sir. I love her, too." Jeremy paused, the words he wanted to say a physical pain, stabbing straight through him. "I have the feeling she loves you, but hasn't admitted it to herself. I will be here if she ever needs me, but I think I need to step out."

There it was. He stared at the floor, blinked the tears back then raised his eyes, meeting Williams gaze.

William nodded and joined Timothy where he stood his hand on the knob. "Anything we should know?" William asked.

"I heard they pulled a guy over for DUI last night," Timothy said. "A blue truck with boating accessories in the back. Oars, life jackets, that sort of stuff. The driver threw something out of the passenger window and officers who searched the truck found drugs. I'm not a detective so I'm not privy to all that shit."

Thanks," James said. "We're detective and we're not privy to all that shit."

49

Amanda woke to Jeremy on the phone. From the conversation, it sounded like William. She rolled onto her side, her head spinning, her stomach heaving. Sitting up slowly, she glanced at the clock. William would be at work. She shrugged on her robe and steadied herself on the wall then slid her way to the bathroom. Jeremy hung up as she stepped into the shower.

She leaned on the cool tile, the warm water rolling over her body, closed her eyes her mind on the night before. To uncover the rest of this story, they had to work out something that didn't include meeting George. She didn't want to go in again and the team wouldn't allow it again.

She stepped out of the shower and toweled off still thinking about her next move. The fax machine screeched as she pulled her robe on and she detoured to the guest room, picking up the papers. They were for Jeremy. It stopped for a tic then began again, more information about GTB Enterprises. Amanda folded those and slipped them into the pocket of her robe then saw Jeremy striding her way. She waved the pages for him and laid them on the machine, heading for her room.

After she closed her bedroom door she pulled out the papers, skimming through pictures of the hotel in Laughlin along with a photo of a younger George Bonner. The information said George moved to Salt Lake City in early 1981, his empire already going strong. Income from GTB Enterprises being utilized to grease the gears here, that money being funneled in from three different locations. All in Nevada. Amanda thought about the 'hotel' and the stories of there being more than one. Three money sources, three hotels. She needed to trace those sources. This also said Reno played nice with the boys in the Las Vegas sandbox when it was convenient for them. But she needed more details. The puzzle wasn't complete.

In the bar George had said the people who ordered the hit on William's wife were bigger than him. That hinted at Reno or Las Vegas. Reno was closer and Reno had been the number one supplier of all things illegal in the Salt Lake valley until George arrived. Plus George had been raised in and around Las Vegas so he knew the ropes because he'd learned from the big boys.

Amanda joined Jeremy, pouring a cup of coffee, noticing the cassettes and the player sitting on the table.

"What did William want? He called awfully early."

"Just checking on you," Jeremy answered.

"Will he be late?"

"Most likely. So you, my lady, are stuck with me all day. How are you feeling this morning?"

"Ugh!" she said, pushing the coffee away. Even that turned her stomach. "Are those the tapes William left?" She directed his gaze to the cassettes. "Have you listened to them?"

Jeremy nodded, taking a drink of his coffee. "Nothing too serious, but it could prove useful down the road. Would you like to listen to them?"

"Of course."

Jeremy went to the kitchen for more coffee, Amanda gazing over the balcony rail, noticing her car parked next to Jeremy's.

"William and James picked it up for you last night," Jeremy said, following her gaze.

She smiled and nodded, her mind already working on how to get to George. The downstairs buzzer startled her.

"Expecting company?" Jeremy asked.

"No," she answered. "You?"

Jeremy shook his head as Amanda trotted over and pushed the button, Bryce introducing himself.

"I apologize for dropping by unannounced," Bryce said. "Is it alright if I come up?"

Amanda allowed him in and checked the clock on the stereo. Nine a.m. She rushed to her room, pulled on a pair of blue jeans and a t-shirt, walking out as Jeremy answered the door. Bryce glanced past Jeremy to Amanda looking surprised.

"Please, come in," Amanda said. "We were just getting ready to have breakfast. Would you care to join us?" This was awkward all of a sudden.

"I've eaten thank you," he answered, glancing between the two once more. "Coffee will be fine."

"I'll make more coffee, my lady," Jeremy said with a half bow.

Bryce raised an eyebrow; Amanda shrugged and led the way to the table.

"I'm not interrupting anything, am I?" Bryce asked. "Maybe I shouldn't have dropped by like this."

"You're fine. You just caught me unprepared."

Jeremy returned with coffee for Bryce, warmed up Amanda's cup and removed his, nodding as he backed out, moving quietly to the guest room.

"So how'd you find me?"

"It wasn't hard," he answered. "I ran a DMV check with your license number and here I am." He glanced across the space at

Jeremy's now closed door, toyed with his cup then looked at her doing a nervous tilt of his head in the direction Jeremy had gone. "Are you and....?"

"No. He uses the guest room when he's in town, but he doesn't live here. We work together. He's an event co-coordinator and I tag along as hostess. Help get things set and work with the guests. He used to work as a butler so he can be a bit stuffy."

"Okay, I thought maybe...Well, you know."

"Yes, I think I understand. What brings you're here?" She laughed when he smiled. "Right. I really hadn't forgotten."

"I decided since I had today off...What the hey."

Amanda smiled. This just might be her opportunity and those tapes were going to prove useful. "I have a couple of errands to run. How about we do lunch? Say around one?"

"Name the place."

"Let's do Harmon's on State Street. They have the best fried chicken."

Once Bryce had left Jeremy returned, pouring another cup of coffee before joining Amanda.

"That was different. Where did you meet him?"

"He's the officer who told William I had been at George's. He traced me through the DMV. What?" she asked seeing Jeremy laugh.

"A picture of you at eighty trying to outrun men in wheelchairs flashed across my mind."

Amanda stopped short of a full laugh, snorting coffee out her nose as she choked. "Jeremy, I am going to get even with you for that."

"My apologies. I'll clean this up."

"Thank you. I have a couple of errands to run this morning and then I'm meeting Bryce for lunch. I will be home about three-ish."

"As you wish," he said.

Amanda waited until Jeremy was busy in the kitchen then picked up the cassettes and the player and went to her bedroom, dropping them on the bed. Grabbing her purse, she padded to the front door.

"I have to grab a bottle of finger nail polish real quick. I'll be right back. Do you need anything?"

"No, my lady, I'm fine."

"I'll hurry back," she called, pulling the door shut behind her.

A peek into the dining area and the cassettes and the recorder were gone, and Jeremy shook his head. He wasn't blind. He had seen the mind working behind her eyes. Even after last night she was attempting to work something.

"Amanda," he said out loud, "you are going to get into serious trouble."

A quick run to a drugstore for blank cassettes, a bottle of white fingernail polish, and a portable cassette recorder, and she headed home. Safely tucked away in her bedroom, Amanda listened to the tapes, recording certain parts, placing a thin line of white polish at the end of each segment. When she had finished, she put the cassettes in the guest room for Jeremy, taking both recorders with her. She would stop at the library and avail herself of the convenient bank of payphones inside. There would be almost no background noise there.

At the library Amanda headed straight to the payphones, tucking herself away in one of the booths then dialed the bar and waited for Cliff or George to answer, making sure she had the recorders situated for easy use. When Cliff answered she asked for George, laying the receiver on the narrow ledge between the machines. When George picked up she pushed 'Record' on one and 'Play' on the second.

"Jonathan isn't answering at his apartment and I need help again," the melodic young voice wafted from the machine.

"What is your problem now?" George asked angrily, his voice

muffled through the receiver.

Amanda pressed 'Stop' on one cassette, leaving the other to continue recording.

"Who the hell is this?" George barked.

Amanda pushed 'Play', the second machine still recording.

"Look, all I need is another pack of birth control. Mom found mine and threw them out. I have an appointment tonight with a john then I have a guy who wants to score on the coke. I'll have major cash for you in the morning."

"I can't help you...." George fell silent, Amanda hit 'Stop'. More muffled voices, Amanda hit 'Play' again.

"Please, George, you gotta help me."

She hit 'Stop', the reel on the second cassette continuing to turn, recording George.

Voices could be heard again, muffled but understandable.

"I thought you iced her? Twenty-five grand? What the hell are you doing?" George asked.

"You read the reports in the paper," a man answered.

"Lori..." George said, letting the sentence fall.

Amanda set up straighter, surprised. Lori was the girl from the center. The girl who had been killed in the accident. She let the silence draw out, waiting to see what he would say.

"WHO ARE YOU?" George bellowed.

Amanda hung up and pushed 'Stop' on both machines.

Amanda met Bryce for lunch, avoiding a hustle for a beer that night and made one more stop, parking south of the bar around a corner from one of the businesses. Thirty minutes later George left, another man following a few seconds after him, going in the opposite direction. Amanda checked her watch and opened the comm channel on the pager.

"Jeremy, I'll be there shortly."

She followed George to several different locations, him not

once exiting the limo. Women, sometimes men or teenagers, approached the limo at each stop, sliding George an envelope each time. At one stop, the limo pulled up next to a black pick-up. The truck that had been outside her apartment and had followed her and Jeremy to Crystal Bay. The driver and George exchanged envelopes, the limo driving away. The limo finally pulled up outside a three story building and George climbed out, the driver pulling the car into the garage at the rear. Amanda gave George three minutes than drove to a payphone a half a block away where she had good cover and could still see his apartment, then dialed his number. George answered and she hit 'Play' on one, record on the second.

"The little one at the back door," a man's voice came from the player. "You want her iced, too?"

"Yes," George answered on the tape.

"WHO ARE YOU?" George yelled, slamming the receiver down.

Amanda rewound it to the start of the tape, fast forwarded to the point she wanted and dialed his number again. George picked up, swept a curtain to the side then let it drop. She hit 'Play' once more.

"Please, George, you gotta help me," the girls voice pleaded from the cassette.

Amanda hit 'Stop' on both machines, hung up then the curtain swung back as she retreated to her car. *'Repeat as necessary,'* she thought.

50

William and James met at the station early. They wanted to dig up some background on that arrest Timothy had told them about. They pulled up the suspects booking photo, recognizing their suspect in the assault and attempted rapes on South Temple and State Street.

According to the report, he had been pulled over for DUI and tossed something out of the passenger window. Officer's cuffed the man, placing him in the back of their squad and called in a second unit. The four officers then searched the street starting at the truck and fanning out, finding a wallet containing ID for Loretta Storey with an address in The Avenues, and a key. William and James knew Loretta Storey to be the alias for Katie Landry and wondered if the key went to Glen's apartment.

The arresting officers then searched the truck and found a stash of drugs under the passenger seat. That prompted a more thorough search and they found the make-up case behind the seat on the driver's side. The officers pulled the make-up case, revealing the bra. Those items on their own, proved nothing, but if they found DNA on either of them, they might connect a few dots. Now, to approach the captain.

Receiving the go ahead, the two drove to the impound lot. William climbed out of the unmarked car, staring at the truck he had seen on the interstate. They were only a few minutes into the search when James found a wire poking from under the driver's seat, and the seats weren't electric. He pulled on a pair of gloves and knelt down, shining a flashlight under the seat, a rectangular box coming into view wedged near the back. James squeezed into the gap between the seat and the truck body, and peered underneath, finding another smaller box, both hidden in the seat above the rail. James loosened the boxes and removed them, inspecting the wires, remembering the explosion on the kid's car and asked William to call the bomb squad. William tossed a business card across the seat to James – George Bonner, Esq.

"Esquire?" James said.

William laughed, making the call.

While they waited for the bomb squad, they drove to Glen's to see if the key found in her wallet went to Glen's apartment. They hadn't seen him for several days so, if asked, they were doing a welfare check. The key fit then William snapped his fingers, pointing to a spot just above the knob. The perfect indentation made by a ram. They slipped on gloves and went inside, signs of a struggle everywhere along with the singed corner off an envelope. William picked up the piece of paper and inspected it, finding a shred of foil adhered to the paper. James pulled out an evidence bag. A search of the apartment revealed no sign of Glen.

On their way to the station, they received a call. Another murder. A mile up Emigration Canyon Road. Teams were on scene with the County Sheriff's and State Patrol. Look for Sergeant Felton. They pulled up to the scene forty minutes later.

"Good afternoon," William said. "I'm Detective Harrison. This is Detective Thompson. We were told you could possibly have something for us?"

"Yes, sir," Sergeant Felton answered. "The victim's name is Glen Tortino. We heard you guys might be interested in the man."

"Possibly," William answered. "Who found him?"

"A couple of kids riding their bikes. It looks like it happened about a week or ten days ago."

They had reached the body and stopped, gazing down at it. It would have been better if they'd found Glen alive. Now they only had one more body.

"We found ID, cash, credit cards," the sergeant was saying. "It doesn't look like anything was taken so we've ruled out robbery. Cause of death looks like a possible overdose. Injection points in the abdomen. But we aren't finding any needles or paraphernalia. We usually find something."

"Any tracks from cars, or trucks?" James asked.

"There are several sets of tracks on the trail above. One looks like a pick-up, one is a smaller car, and two are three-wheelers. One of the three-wheeler's carried a heavier load on the way in. On the way out the track isn't as deep. There are ramp marks like the three-wheelers had been loaded on the back of the truck. We have two sets of footprints. Generic tennis shoes. The kind you can buy at any mall. Techs can tell you more." The sheriff nodded up the hill to Lloyd.

"Hey, dee-teck-deeves," Lloyd said. "You two get tagged with all the fun ones."

"You might say that," William replied. "What you got that we haven't already been told?"

"Not much. It was made to look like an overdose. I'm thinking he didn't do it. Nothing here goes with an accidental. Know what I mean? We'll know more when tox gets done. So how's that sexy thing you got hooked up with?"

"She's fine, Lloyd. Any possibility this was a body dump?"

"No, on that score, too. There's too much blood. For a three-wheeler to get the body down here and then dump it, the timings wrong. Once the guys dead the heart stops pumping." Lloyd shrugged. "The sucker may have been out, but he wasn't dead. They injected him to make it look like an overdose after they iced him. If you look at the injection points, it ain't fittin'." Lloyd knelt beside the body, showed William the marks, explaining in detail why he didn't think it was an overdose. "There's also an area up above that looks like someone big was dumped out of a car and it looks whoever it was upchucked something terrible. It's nasty! Plus the dude's got a nice split on the back of his head like he fell or was hit with something hard. That's about it."

"They can do tox screens on the residue above, right?"

"Yeah. It's foul shit to work with, but I don't have to do it." Lloyd laughed and stood. William smiled as he stood.

"So, could he have been hit by someone?" William asked.

"Possibly, but I don't think so," Lloyd said. "I think they gave him something then he was injected to cover the cause of death, but we won't know until they get those tox screens done. I think the split was caused when he fell, or was dropped, just before he died."

"Thanks, Lloyd. Send samples to the U for us again, please."

"You got it, man."

They returned to Salt Lake City and were told the boxes from the truck contained the same explosives that had been used on the teen's car.

William and James now went to Captain Kirby and told them about their desire to talk to the suspect. When they asked, they were told the U was already attempting to extract DNA from the bra and the make-up case. That magic letter every detective had received.

51

William and James had just completed the set up on the video equipment when Captain Kirby arrived. They reviewed their plan then had the suspect brought in. With Captain Kirby watching, they joined the prisoner a fashionable twenty minutes late.

"Good morning," James said. He flipped a chair around and straddled it, staring across the table at the man while hooking his thumb over his shoulder at William. "I'm Detective Thompson and this is my partner Detective Harrison. We're here to talk to you."

"I don't have to say shit," he said. "I know my rights."

"Evidently not well enough," James said. "You're already in custody. We are not re-arresting your sorry ass so we get to bring you in here anytime we feel like it."

"Maybe, but I didn't agree to talk to you."

"You can say what you will," William said, "but you're still in here and no lawyers have made a move to get you out. It looks like you're on your own."

"Now, as I was saying," James continued. "Since you're ours I'm going to tell you what we know and then you're going to tell us why you did it. It's that simple. If you don't co-operate we'll work out something else."

There was a momentary flash of anger and fear then nothing.

"Do you have anything to say before we get started? Your name's Kevin, right?"

"You know everything. You tell me."

"Good. We'll call you Kevin then," James said. "We wanted this to be quick and easy, but I guess you want to spend the whole day in here. Neither of us care there, either."

"You ain't got shit," he repeated.

"We'll see. When they searched your truck at the impound lot they found explosives. They match explosives used to put a car with two teenagers in it off the interstate and take out the police car my partner and I were in." He paused, giving Kevin a chance to speak. Kevin refused to say anything and James continued reading the arrest report. "They also found a half kilo of coke under the seat. A bra and a make-up bag behind the seat on the driver's side. Tests show the make-up case and the bra belong to two of the recent rape slash murder victims."

They continued giving him a complete run down of what, they said, they had proof of, including the murders from the previous year. They were banking on him not remembering the news from that far back. He denied everything but they could tell he was getting anxious, doubt beginning to creep in. He hadn't heard a word from his attorney and this was day two.

"Well, Kevin," William said. "It's almost noon so my partner and I are going to grab something to eat. I don't know about you, but I'm hungry. We'll continue this when we get back."

They walked out and joined Captain Kirby, Kevin yelling in the background. William waved one of the patrolmen over.

"Keep an eye on our girl scout."

It was an hour and forty minutes before they returned to talk to the suspect.

"Okay. I'm going to run down these charges one last time," James said. "We have six counts of murder. Two counts of rape and aggravated assault…."

"Six counts of murder? Where do you get six? You've been talking about this lady in the river and some runaway and a couple of teenagers! What the hell you doin' to me man?"

"….there's also Olivia," James continued. "She was raped…"

"Actually we might be able to add in these attempted rapes, too," William said.

"Nope! I didn't do those!" Kevin exclaimed. He closed his eyes and faced the ceiling, lines creasing his forehead. He sighed and looked back at them, panic showing for a split second. "Nope. You ain't pinnin' all this shit on me. Olivia and that black bitch from a few years ago, they were hits called in by the big guns in Reno. A dude named Glen did those. Glen worked for Bonner, too." He looked between the two, trying to lean back in the chair. "Come on! Ya gotta believe me!" He paused then glanced between them again. "I swear! I ain't goin' down for shit I didn't do, man!"

"For us to drop charges you have to tell us everything," James answered, glancing up at William. They both knew who the black bitch was. Maybe this hadn't been such a good idea.

"Just so you know," William said, leaning into Kevin's face. "That 'black bitch' was my wife."

Kevin cringed and ducked as if avoiding a blow.

James laid a hand on William's arm, nudging him back. "We need names, dates, everything you can tell us. If not, you're gone. You will never see the light of day again."

William's mind replayed Glen's words the day they'd searched his apartment. '*I'm tired of hurting people. I'm tired of people getting hurt….*'

"If this Glen worked for George Bonner why was he doing hits for Reno?" William asked.

"Glen only worked for George to keep the syndicate in the loop about George's plans. George knew Glen was snitchin' and decided to ice Glen. Then he got some strange ass phone calls. He thought Glen and Reno might be where the calls came from."

"And the woman they found in the Green River?"

"I don't know everything there," he answered. "George said she was a snitch, too, and I know George liked to choke 'em. It turned him on when they begged. Those teenagers. I only know George was pissed because Jonathan brought the girl in under the Bonner umbrella and she was under age. Every time he turned around she was in some kind of trouble. He asked me to off the girl…."

"Asked you, or you offered?" William asked thinking about the cassettes.

"A little of both, I guess," he answered. "I wasn't planning on her being with her boyfriend, but then I saw you guys and knew George was after you, too. George figured if he got you out of the way, the Salt Lake market would be his and he could get that one bitchin' lady he was after last year into his stable and his bed. She was going to be his Class A. She would be dessert and pay for him being sent to prison. George didn't forgive or forget. Anyone who crossed George – paid."

"I'll bet," William snorted derisively. "That's why you had the explosives? To take us out?"

"Well…No. The explosives were for other jobs that might come down the pipe, ya know? And I already set it on the kid's wheels, so I figured, why not? Two jobs at once. I'd get twenty-five grand for driving down the freeway for an hour. Sounded good to me."

"And Olivia?" James asked. "What about the dealers?"

"I don't know. Olivia wasn't a regular lady of the evening. She had more class than that. Those guys didn't snort that much normally, either. Everyone thought they did, but they didn't. When I picked them up they was straight. They said they lucked out and sold almost all of what Jonathan gave them."

"What day was that?" James asked. The cubby hole explained.

"The same night the dudes OD'd."

"What kind of car did Olivia drive?"

"Olivia didn't have a car. Neither did the dudes. They rode the bus or walked. Once in a while Glen gave them a ride in George's limo. Made them feel important."

"What about the dudes?" James asked. "You said the guys weren't high when you picked them up."

"No, man. They were straight. They told me they had almost ten grand on them."

"What kind of car was there when you picked them up?"

"None! I just told you they didn't have a car. I know one story said one of the guy's clothes had blood on them, but he was clean. I saw Olivia a couple of days later and offered her a ride, but she said she had one more appointment and then she was going home."

"Did you drop the dudes off at the same time?"

"Same time as what?" He glanced between the two, mouthed the word *'Oh'* then shook his head. "I didn't drop Olivia off. She met some guys in this bar downtown. Those dealers, I dropped them off a couple of days before she was killed."

"What time was that?" William asked. "Approximately."

"The dealers? About one. One-thirty maybe. George was letting people in for free pool while he finished fixing the place up. I remember there were two cars parked in the lot behind it when I got there and I parked beside them. One was Jonathan's. Glen and one of the other bouncers was leaving when I walked in. He said they had to run an errand. He didn't say who it was for or what it was."

William held his hand up, staring at Kevin. "Wait. Hold that thought." He opened the door and beckoned James outside. In the hall, William paused, sorting his thoughts. "So... From what he just said George was out when Olivia was iced?"

"He might have meant George had Jonathan do it. Let me try something. He already thinks you're after him. Hang tight." James went back in, closing the door quietly then sat down, watching Kevin. "Okay. We have a problem. You already know my partner is pissed, but now he thinks you're lying."

Kevin stared at James with a mix of anger and curiosity.

"You just said you dropped the guys off behind the bar and George was letting people play pool before he finished the renovations." Kevin nodded. "So... George was out before Olivia was killed?"

"Well...No," he stammered. "George was still inside. He was orchestrating everything from inside, see."

"Kevin, I don't believe you now. And if I don't believe you, no one else is going to believe you. See, I'm the sucker. I get had every single time. Now, you need to shoot straight with us, dude." He did a slight head tilt to the right, William took the cue, barging through the door and slamming it.

"I'm going to have them take the punk back to his cell," William snapped. "He's stringing us along."

"Give us a minute," James said, waving William down. He looked back at Kevin. "You know where my partner stands. What's your decision?"

"George was ram rodding the shit," Kevin replied. "He was still in the slammer. George doesn't trust Jonathan. He thinks Jonathan's a wuss, just giving everything away. Jonathan was giving us George's orders."

"One last question," William said calmly. "Why did you stab Olivia after Glen killed her? Why did you feel the need to do that much damage? She was already dead."

Kevin's shoulders sagged as he stared at the ceiling.

"Remember," James said. "We said if you help us, we'll help you. Come on, dude."

Kevin remained quiet, his lips twisted in a sideways smirk as he shook his head.

William leaned against the wall, observing Kevin, his skin crawling. "I'm going to say one more thing before we walk out this door," William said. "We have video of Olivia leaving a bar with two men the night she was iced. One of the men was Glen. The other one looked a whole lot like you."

Kevin jerked his head over, staring at William, his eyes narrowing.

"We know Olivia had sex with Glen and one other man that night. That second man has been linked to four other rapes around Salt Lake City. We have him on video for one of those rapes. He's also been ID'd by two witnesses. Think real hard about what you remember, okay?"

Kevin gave a faint head bob and stared at the table top, a look of confusion crossing his face.

William pushed away from the wall and James turned his chair around, pushing it under the table. They looked back at Kevin one last time before walking out. Joining the captain in the viewing room, they thought about how long they should let him stew. The man knew more than he was admitting.

"What do you think?" Captain Kirby asked when he saw the frowns.

"Not sure, but he knows more than he's giving us," William answered, staring through the glass. Then he looked back at Captain Kirby. "If he thinks he can con us into believing he didn't do Olivia, he'll stand on that one. He won't give in."

"You want to throw him back in?" James asked. "We can come back tomorrow and play some more."

William let the silence hang then nodded. "I guess that'll work. One more night in lock up might make him think."

They handed Kevin over to an officer, Kevin staring over his shoulder at them as he was walked away, empty hollows for eyes. No emotion of any kind. William couldn't decide if Kevin thought he'd won, or if he was issuing a challenge. He didn't like either choice. They needed Kevin to make a decision tonight so they could put George behind bars again. Then they would nail Kevin for the rapes.

"You okay, buddy?" James asked, wondering how much of William's displeasure was discovering who had killed his wife.

"Yep," William answered.

"You sure?"

"Yep."

"Cool. See you in the morning. What time?"

"Seven sounds good."

52

James walked in at six forty-five the next morning, William already there. He didn't think his partner had slept. William's eyes were dull with dark circles and bags, and he had a deeper crease in his forehead than he'd sported the night before. He wasn't dealing with this one well.

"You gonna be okay?" James asked.

"Yep," William answered, heading for the break room. "I kept going over things in my mind. Things the dude said yesterday. It all fits so I don't know if he lied or not. I usually pick up on that. I still think he knows more than he's giving us."

Pouring a cup of coffee, William lifted the cup, locking eyes with James. James nodded and leaned against the counter.

"I was thinking about that, too," James said, taking the offered coffee. "We still haven't asked him about the breather, or Loretta Storey. Want to throw the breather on the table? See what he does?"

"Don't know. Wouldn't hurt."

"How's Amanda doing?"

"Jeremy caught her up at three a.m., four-thirty a.m., and again at six, calling someone and playing portions of those cassettes we had. He nailed her about it, but she hasn't revealed who it was. I told him to handcuff her to the bed. Even offered him my cuffs."

"What did Jeremy say?"

"He said it would be too tempting to join her. Amanda was just pissed."

James laughed all the way to the video room.

By seven-thirty the suspect had been brought in, the equipment ready. Captain Kirby had returned, watching them through the glass. At seven thirty-five William started the recording, he and James entering the room, James carrying a box with the lid closed.

Kevin rolled his head to the side and gave a sigh.

"Good morning, buddy," James said cheerfully, plopping the box on the table. The thud echoed in the tight space, Kevin flinching. "We enjoyed our conversation so much yesterday we decided to go over it again. Whaddaya think?"

Whatever," Kevin replied sarcastically.

"You can drop the attitude," James replied. "We decided to give you one more chance. You help us and we'll help you."

Kevin stared, James shrugged and started going over the information from the day before, misquoting portions on purpose. Kevin corrected him every time. They were getting the same story they had previously. James stood and took the lid off the box, William behind him watching Kevin, Kevin's eyes glued to it. James pulled the breather out, dropping it in front of Kevin. There was a hint of recognition then Kevin looked away, his expression locked down. William stepped forward, taking the chair next to James. They had him. They just had to get him to admit it.

"Okay, Kevin," William said. "You recognized that, didn't you?" William glanced at the alien face staring up at Kevin. "Where have you seen it? Have you used it? Maybe in one of these assaults you say you didn't do?"

"You're fucked up, man," Kevin answered, sneering. "You're

crazier than they say I am."

"And you've been lying. You know Glen, and Glen works for Reno. Maybe you're the guy who killed that black bitch. That's how you got the job, isn't it? Did you work for Reno, too? Are you afraid George or Reno will help you retire early?"

"You guys are really screwed up, you know that?" He glanced between William and James and then shook his head. "I ain't sayin' shit."

"If that's the way you want to play it," William said. "Let's go, James. I'm tired of the games. He can rot for all I care."

"You're on the downhill side now, buddy," James said. "You want to walk out of here a free man or go to prison for crimes you say you didn't commit. We made a deal but if you screw that up, we'll put your ass behind bars again faster than you can take a breath. What's it gonna be?"

"Look. I already told you everything I know…..."

"Bullshit," James said. He slammed the breather back in the box, glaring across the table at Kevin. "You're trying to play us. I guess you don't want to see daylight again."

"What do you expect? If I snitch on Reno, I'll just sign my own death certificate," he answered angrily. "I know you guys ain't that stupid!"

"We can help," William said. He kept his voice calm keeping any emotion from bleed through. "We can bury the old Kevin and resurrect the new. It's better than a zero chance at life."

Kevin glanced at the wall and smirked then looked back at them.

"You expect me to believe that?"

"We said we'd help," James answered. "We meant it. You got five minutes."

"Okay," he said exhaling loudly. "But I go free, right?"

"We'll talk to the DA," William replied.

"Okay. George did the lady in the Green River. Glen told me."

James and William nodded, keeping their eyes on Kevin for any hint he was lying.

"Jonathan had Glen stage her like the others because Jonathan wants George out of the way. Jonathan thinks, with the syndicates help, he can grow the business bigger than George. Once he's got things running like he wants, he plans on walking away from Reno." Kevin stopped for a minute and glared across the table at them.

"And?" William asked.

Kevin stared at the wall the silence dragging out then he looked back at James, avoiding eye contact with William. "Glen did the dicks wife three years ago. And he did Olivia. They were ordered by the syndicate to pull the Bonner's in line. Okay? I don't know the head honchos name. The dealers were off'd by Glen and another associate for George. I don't know how he did it, but George gave the orders from inside. Go ask Glen. I'll give you his address."

"We can't," William replied. "Someone popped Glen."

"Fuck!" he exclaimed. "I went through all this for nothing?"

"No, buddy," James said. "We'll talk to the DA."

"If you know all this what else are you leaving out?" William asked.

Kevin remained silent.

"We'll get you back to your cell now," William said.

"You're gonna drop all the DNA crap, right?"

"No," James said. "The deal was, you tell us everything. Olivia was with Glen and one other man. We need the rest of this. Once we have that we can type a statement off this recording and you can sign it. Then it's up to the DA. But we'll talk to him."

"I don't know," Kevin mumbled.

"We need it loud enough the audio can pick it up," James said.

"I don't know," Kevin repeated louder.

There was a knock on the door and William, stepped outside.

"Both of your witnesses ID'd him" Captain Kirby said, holding up the signed documents. "I took the liberty of getting it in writing."

"May I?" William asked nodding at the papers.

"Be my guest." Captain Kirby handed the papers to William. "I was also told he works for us. He's one of our crime scene techs."

William stopped mid-reach, the memory of a tech flying out of the hotel popping up. He hesitated, attempting to remember if he had been carrying the breather. He wasn't positive, but the man had been holding something.

"You're sure."

Captain Kirby nodded.

William went back in setting the papers on the table face down. "Bad news, dude," William said.

Kevin stared at the papers, his eyes dead. "I should have known this was bullshit. You cops are all the same."

"The deals still good," William said. "If you keep your end and come clean. These are statements from witnesses. It puts you at the scene of two rapes. We have DNA that puts you at all five. Two of those women are dead. Come on, man. Why'd you do it?"

Kevin stared at the ceiling for a minute then at his hands cuffed in front of him and shrugged.

"I also want to know why you didn't tell us you work with Lloyd. You're a crime scene tech and you kept that from us."

James gasped, the atmosphere growing oppressive, as he stared between William and Kevin.

"You're a tech?" James asked, barely able to talk. "You tried to frame a co-worker?"

Kevin shrugged again. "I didn't know Glen was going to ice Olivia. I paid for her to meet us. That was all. I didn't have sex with her."

He stopped, stared at the floor for a minute. He looked back at James, his eyes dead and empty, and smiled smugly, proud of himself. William felt a chill run down his spine as Kevin laughed at some unspoken joke, the laughter stopping as abruptly as it had started.

"I wanted them to have some fun. Show them a little slice of heaven," he said. "I didn't want to hurt the ladies. But then they have to fight. They hit me. The one bitch tried to bite me. Can you believe it? Olivia tried to bite me. Ungrateful bitch!"

James blinked in disbelief then leaned back in his chair. *A little slice of heaven'*.

"Why rape them?" James finally asked. "Cutting them with a knife? What have women done to you?"

"I didn't do Olivia," he repeated.

"You just said she tried to bite you," William said, surprised. Glen's words echoed once again. *'I never use a knife. They're too messy.'* "If you didn't do her how could she bite you?"

"Glen just left her laying there," Kevin said. "She groaned and…. I couldn't let her nail me for it. I didn't do it."

"Glen hadn't been successful?"

Kevin shrugged. "I guess not, if the bitch moved," he sniped. "I had to stop her from telling on me."

"Why would she tell on you?" James asked. He straightened up, looking at William, the answers falling into place. James kept quiet, working on the wording for his next question. "Why wasn't Glen supposed to kill Olivia?"

"Because she was the best. She was Mr. Landers' favorite," he replied, the little boy from grade school who'd been sent to the principal's office coming out.

"Did you decide to get in on the action? Have some fun of your own?" William asked. "That's when she woke up, wasn't it? That's why she woke up."

"I didn't have sex with Olivia," Kevin said. "She kicked and yelled...." He stopped; his eyes growing distant then he dropped his head.

"You just said she was the best!"

"I didn't have sex with her," he repeated staring at William, his face blank. "She had sex with me. Olivia wanted me! They all wanted me! If she'd a lived, she would have thanked me!" He yelled the last two sentences, laughing loud and hard, stomping his feet.

"Yeah, right." William stood and picked up the papers.

"Then why was Olivia even targeted?" James asked. "You're dangerously close to losing this deal."

Kevin smirked and threw his head back, still laughing. It stopped as quickly as before and he stared at William, the eyes hard and cold. William recognized the smug satisfaction and a cold finger ran down his spine.

"The mighty Mr. Thomas Landers isn't as in control of The Landers Corporation as he thinks."

William had to turn away. Olivia had been a warning. And not just for Jonathan. He remembered the crime scene photos of his late wife's car. She had been shot, not knifed and beaten. His wife had been a warning for George, Olivia for Jonathan, but Olivia wasn't supposed to have died. Olivia had been Kevin's first victim and he killed her when she woke up and fought back. With his other victims he had combined the control of rape with the anger and adrenaline rush of the kill.

"You're still one sick son-of-a-bitch."

"We had a deal," Kevin said.

William looked at Kevin, doing a full body shiver. "Yep. No DNA."

It had turned into a long two days, but they had their answers. Olivia's murder hadn't been ordered by George or Reno, and the dealers murder had been ordered by George. And they had their rapist slash murderer.

William and James stepped into the hall and closed the door, Captain Kirby patting them on the back. They had closed more than one case tonight. William handed Captain Kirby the witness statements and walked to his desk.

"I need a double of every flavor of booze at the bar tonight," William said.

James nodded, silent for once.

It took several more hours to complete the reports and drop them on the captain's desk. They would work on Kevin's statement tomorrow. Outside William looked up at the stars then back at James.

"I wanted to see Amanda," he said.

"Call her," James answered. "Ask her to meet you. You know you really need to talk her, buddy. You're gonna lose her if you don't. We just need to be here early enough tomorrow to pull the warrant's together for George. We can't screw around now. Not if George is angling to get even with Amanda."

William went back inside, admitting James was right. Amanda would meet him. She always made time for him. But how long would she do that if he kept dragging his feet?

William stood in the lobby of The Hotel America, watching as Amanda drove up. She ran for him, throwing her arms around his neck, wrapping her legs around his waist, the desk clerks giggling in the background.

"We might have to hit the emergency button on the elevator on the way to our room after that greeting," William whispered.

He sat her down, shoved one hand in his pocket, the keys and coins jingling as he felt the box. Maybe this wasn't such a good idea. He was nervous. Nervous hell, he was scared to death!

"Amanda," William said. "There's something I'd like to ask

you."

"Okaaay," Amanda said. She looked up, noting the expression. He looked like he was about to be sick. "Ask away."

"This is hard," he said after a lengthy pause. "I would like to know, in front of God and everybody – well not quite everybody, it's only you, me and the desk clerks. But…" He raised the ring so she could see it. "…will you be my wife? To have and to hold, till death do us part? I don't want to waste anymore time. I really do love you."

"I'm sorry," she stammered, staring at the ring. "What am I supposed to say? William, I'm speechless."

"How about, yes?" he asked, searching her eyes. "I thought maybe…"

"Oh, William. I love you, too."

"But not enough to marry me," he said with a resigned sigh. "I was so afraid you would say no. I've been preparing myself for that for weeks now. I guess, inside, I expected you to say no. Actually, I don't know what I expected. So…I guess we're still friends? And now I feel like a bumbling idiot."

"No," she said. "I meant to say, of course I will. I wasn't expecting this tonight is all. So…Are you trying to make an honest woman out of me?"

"You know me," he whispered, slipping the ring on her finger.

"Definitely," she replied.

53

William arrived at work the next morning and dropped into his chair, his eyes burning, the light stabbing holes through them, his head throbbing. He popped three aspirin, James watching him.

"What?"

"You asked her didn't you?" James reached over and play punched William's shoulder. "I was right, wasn't I? She said yes." Then he laughed. "It looks like you partook of every flavor of booze at the bar, too."

"Not quite," William replied. "We stopped at a bottle of champagne and several shots of Tequila." He hesitated, screwed his forehead up, thinking. "Maybe some Southern Comfort ...."

"You, or you and Amanda?" James asked.

"I don't know. Remind me to stick to beer or the ale. And, yes. She said yes. Now she gets to tell Jeremy."

"Ouch!" James said.

"I offered but she refused," William said. "That's probably a good thing this morning. Now, let's get to work on these warrants. Have you talked to the Cap, yet?"

"We just have to get everything in order for the judge."

William started on the warrant for George's apartment, James working on the warrant for the bar when Captain Kirby called. Kevin had been found unresponsive in his cell. All efforts to revive him had failed.

"How?" William asked. He stood, not knowing why then dropped back into his chair, holding his head so it didn't explode. This was not the time to be nursing a hangover. "What about the warrants?" Then he groaned thinking about the inanity of that last question. "Why?"

"The warrants will be fine," Captain Kirby replied. "We have the video of the interrogation and Kevin's statement. One of the men on nightshift got bored and typed out the statement, Kevin signed it and a rookie signed it as the witness. It was on my desk this morning. As to the 'how', he hung himself from the top horizontal bar. They found him in his skivvies this morning. He ripped the elastic out of his jail clothes. The clothing was found in the sink when they lowered his body. "For the 'why', I guess we'll never have that answer."

"Shit," William said.

Too stunned to say any more, William's mind went back to the victims. What was he supposed to tell them? Kevin's confession would be a hollow victory now.

"I understand," Captain Kirby said. "Get those warrants over to the judge. Include one for his nephew Jonathan. I want both Bonners behind bars before tomorrow night."

William placed the receiver back in the cradle second guessing their method of interrogation. If they hadn't pushed so hard maybe he'd still be alive. But they wouldn't have the information they had. He looked over at James, his partner staring back at him. After he told James they finished the warrants, running them over for the judge's signature. James could only stare out the passenger window.

Once they had the warrants signed they went to Captain Kirby to plan George's arrest.

By seven forty-five the next morning spotters had been set up at three locations between George's apartment and the bar. Information told them George was in the bar by eight-thirty. Once George was inside, they would position SWAT teams across State Street and at the mouth of the alley as well as behind the bar. Extra teams would be positioned on Second East in case someone blew through the men in the alley and made it across the parking lot. When Jonathan and one of his girls arrived they would move in, positioning three men outside each door. No one knew if George had men inside with him, so they were prepared for that eventuality as well. It would only be a matter of time before George was locked up once again. And hopefully they would find enough Jonathan would join him.

William and James waited a half a block north on the northwest corner of Sixth South and State Street. At seven-fifty they received the call from the first spotter. George was on his way. They switched their radios to a secure channel and prepared to abandon their post. The next two spotters reported in quick succession. Five minutes after eight they got the call, George was inside. Everything was a go. William and James climbed out of the car, striding for the bar. James posted himself across State Street with the first SWAT team, William moved into position at the back door with the second SWAT team. Timothy, dressed as a homeless man, took up a position against the back wall of the neighboring building to help keep tabs on the rear door. Now, they waited for Jonathan. He always had a toy with him, but the girl didn't always go inside. That meant George was following some of the rules. They wanted this to be one of the times George didn't.

James was the first to see Jonathan and – true to form – he had a young one in tow. She appeared to be about fifteen or sixteen. A good-looking black girl just like the undercover on the cassette had said. He keyed the code alerting the rest of the team. Three minutes after ten, James announced team one was in position at the front door. William banged on the rear door and announced their arrival. A few seconds later someone inside yelled, 'get the girl out of the fucking bathroom'. Mere seconds and there was a single chirp on their radio. Jonathan and the girl had been arrested at the front. Running echoed from inside and George opened the rear door to find William and a SWAT team waiting for him. George tried to pull the door closed, William blocked it. Timothy and the SWAT team leveled their weapons on him. Running in the alley announced the arrival of the third SWAT team.

George took a step back, made a half turn and James and the first SWAT team had drifted through from the front after handing the girl and Jonathan over, their guns trained on George as well. Cliff shrugged impotently behind them, his hands cuffed to the bar.

George, Jonathan and Cliff were placed in interrogation rooms the girl taken to juvenile while William gave the investigators on scene their instructions. William and James took the bar. Two hours into the search, they found enough to throw George behind bars without a second thought. Combined with Kevin's statement George would disappear for a very long time. And they expected Jonathan to turn in a heartbeat. He was a drunk who had never worked a day in his life.

They were finishing the search of George's apartment when one of the officers found the safe. Lloyd walked in, glancing between William and the floor. William raised an eyebrow and Lloyd shrugged his right shoulder. William gave a tiny dip of his head. James sent the officer's for more evidence bags while they broke into the safe. Let the men think it had been left unlocked.

Lloyd sprawled on the floor, resting his ear against the dial. On the second go, the tumblers released and Lloyd lifted the door. It contained two bricks of cocaine, four hundred thousand dollars in cash and a half a kilo of heroine.

"I know why you saw the inside of those interrogation rooms now," William said with a laugh. "No wonder you left Louisiana."

Lloyd bowed dramatically as he backed out. "Back at ya bro."

They left the remainder of the search to the officers while they drove to Jonathan's apartment, beginning that search. From there they drove to the station to question George and his nephew.

George and Jonathan stood strong on their right to an attorney, but the girl turned quickly, admitting George had hired her to keep tabs on Jonathan, paying her two hundred a week. She fingered Cliff as the man who had turned her onto the job, even saying she gave him freebies now and then in exchange for turning her onto paying gigs.

The search of Jonathan's apartment produced nothing. An office had been set up, but he'd kept the business and his personal life separate. There was nothing proving the girl had been there, either. It was her word against his.

Before they completed their reports Captain Kirby called to tell them George and Jonathan were out. William dropped the phone into the cradle and stared at the phone, a low growl coming from his throat.

"What the hell are they thinking? He's a convicted murderer."

"Don't know, buddy. We need to talk to Jeremy, though."

Walking out of the station, they were handed a cassette. Both men reversed direction, going back to their desks. William popped the cassette into the player and hit 'Play'. The tape was of a few mysterious phone calls George had received at strange hours of the night. One of the voices sounded like Amanda.

"You going to nail her on this?" James asked.

"Nope," William answered. "I gotta hand her this one."

54

James watched William as they sat at their desks the next morning, glad he had walked away from Amanda. He wouldn't have been able to deal with her involvement on this team. William was a hell of a lot stronger than he was.

They finished their reports, joking about relaxing at Jeremy's with their ladies. They had worked a lot of hours and been given a few days off, both of them looking forward to playing in the pool and enjoying Jeremy's barbecue. William volunteered to grab the pages from the printer when the phone rang, stopping him.

"You're kidding!" William said. "Fuck!"

James sat up, surprised. Something had happened. His partner rarely used that word. George. It had to be.

William leaned back in his chair and listened, the anger barely held in check. He slammed the phone down and James debated saying anything, give his partner some time. Curiosity won out.

"What's going on, buddy?" James asked.

"We gotta meet Captain Kirby. Surveillance lost George."

Five minutes later they had paged Jeremy and were walking into the captain's office.

"What's up?" William asked.

"George is gone," Captain Kirby replied.

"Gone?" they echoed.

"How the hell?" James asked.

"Gone," the captain repeated, holding a hand up asking them to let him finish. "We had two unmarkeds on him. One across the street and one at the mouth of the alley behind the apartment building." He went on to explain about a drag racer and the first team calling in a black and white, then the second team being tranquilized. The entire incident had gone down in less than three minutes. "One of the men from team one called paramedics while his partner searched the alley," Captain Kirby continued. "That's when they discovered the garage door open and George's limo gone. He found a set of fresh tire tracks going north out of the alley. It matched the tread coming out of the garage. A long wide stance."

"So...George just disappeared and no one has a clue where he's gone," William said. "This just keeps getting better all the time."

"I only thought it fair to let you gentlemen know," the captain said. "See you in the morning."

"Thanks," James said as they stood.

Twenty minutes later they walked up the hall to Amanda's apartment wondering how things had gone so far south so fast. With all the evidence they had, George had been released and now he had disappeared. And they'd had him under surveillance when it happened. William paged Timothy and while they waited, Jeremy and Amanda set snack trays and sandwiches on the table along with coffee and soft drinks. When Timothy arrived they started the meeting.

"Tell us what happened," Jeremy said.

"George is gone," William answered. "It doesn't get plainer than that."

"Gone!" Amanda exclaimed. "What do you mean gone?"

"Exactly what I said. Gone. As in not there." William took a deep breath, forced himself to calm down. "Two unmarked cars were sitting outside George's apartment and he's gone. According to those involved, the car stationed on Second West was hit by a drag racer this afternoon. Two men ran from the car that hit them, but no one has found them and there were no plates and no registration on the vehicle that struck them. They ran a check using the VIN and it's clean. The original owner sold it a month ago. He had a copy of the bill of sale, but we didn't find anything under the buyer's name. The person probably used an alias when he purchased the car. Who thinks to check ID when you sell a car for cash to an individual? The second team on Ninth South was drugged when they tried to go to the first team's aid."

"Are the officers alright?" Jeremy asked.

"Officers are fine," William answered. "Shaken up a bit, but unhurt. According to lab tests the second team was targeted with a low dose tranquilizer. Enough to put them down, but not kill them."

"So someone was watching them?" Jeremy asked.

"Looks that way."

"Maybe someone didn't want killing a cop added to any other charges," Timothy added.

"Any ideas where George will go?" Jeremy asked.

"Not sure," William said. "We're running a search for any properties he may have owned." He hesitated then looked at Amanda and put a video in the VCR. "I have a question for you now."

Amanda's eyes grew wide as she stared at the video showing her disarming a man, knocking said man out then shooting a second man.

"That's you, isn't it?" James laughed and William turned a

recorder on, setting it on the table beside her. "I want to know exactly what was going on. I have to go to the Cap and tell him my fiancée is that woman, because the whole damn department is on the hunt for her. But I have to have all the facts when I do."

Amanda looked at the cassette and then at him and shrugged.

"Yeah, that's me," she answered. "That was the day George was at the mall. The day I was so flustered."

"Just explain what happened," Jeremy said.

"After George left I went back to use the restroom. Those men followed. I disarmed the first man, told him not to say a word to his friend but he didn't listen. And I couldn't kill him." She looked up. "I couldn't do it."

"That's okay," William said, holding her while James turned the cassette off. "Sometimes you don't need to kill them. FYI, the second man didn't die. He's in the hospital under guard. Now, I would like you to think real hard about anything you might have said with the latest stunt. We have the recordings of you calling George. I know it was you, Amanda. I appreciate your help, but I need to know if you said anything before George started taping those calls."

"No," she answered. "I just replayed portions of the tapes and, basically, repeated the same thing in different sequences to see if I could get him to screw up." William nodded. "Jeremy has an idea though."

"I was thinking, Amanda and I can go to the retreat," Jeremy explained. "She will be surrounded by security twenty-four seven and we can still keep in touch with you gentlemen. If anything comes across the radar – either way – we can let each other know. Of course, I would feel safer if you were with us, but I understand you have a job to finish here."

William moved his gaze back at Amanda. "What about your apartment?"

"Storage," she answered.

"According to Glen's statement, George is looking at getting even with every one of us, especially you, Amanda, so I'll talk to the leasing office tomorrow. You need to locate a storage facility and then we need to get you moved without anyone knowing. I want you out of here as soon as possible. How soon can we get it done, Jeremy?"

"I'll handle the moving through the organization so we should have everything completed by tomorrow night."

"We need to get back to the office then," William said. "We have a few more things to check before we call it a day. I'll work this out with Captain Kirby." He held the video up. "It's obvious the man was the aggressor so I doubt there'll be a problem."

"I'm sorry," she said.

"Nothing to be sorry about." He kissed her then stood, pointing at her. "Now, you, listen to Jeremy. I love you."

55

As promised, Jeremy made the arrangements. The appearance of someone moving in made the switch quick and easy. With the moving van backed up to the building, its doors propped open and ramps leaning against said doors no one saw a thing. Empty boxes went up the stairs and full boxes came down. It was a bittersweet moment as Amanda gazed around the empty apartment. She knew where each picture had hung, where each tchotchke had set, the placement of each piece of furniture. Now the place was bare. It felt like she was eleven years old and on the run again. Hiding.

Jeremy tapped her arm, prodding her to follow him. The limo with her personal belongings had already headed south. Now her and Jeremy climbed into her car and started toward the retreat, while Jeremy's men drove the truck to the storage facility to unload. As they merged onto the interstate it felt awkward. There was a discomfort here.

"Are we alright, Amanda?" Jeremy asked.

She nodded and smiled. "It feels funny. That's stupid isn't it?"

"I understand. It will work out fine, my lady. We just have to reset our boundaries. Our limits. Would you like something to drink once we get there? You don't look like you're at all tired."

"I'm exhausted, but too buzzed to sleep," she answered.

"We can get comfortable on the sofa with a glass of wine and relax a tad."

"I can deal with that." She paused, picked at her nails. "Are you and William okay? I never meant to cause any problems. I mean…" She stopped, sighed, tears threatening. "I'm rambling again, aren't I?"

"William and I are fine. I believe we have it worked out."

"I notice there's still a little tension there."

"It's difficult when one perceives someone as competition for someone they love. Now there is no need for that. You have made your decision." Jeremyscanned the highway and checked the rearview mirror, the words he wanted to ask hard to say. "Are you sure you have made the right decision, my lady?" The words sounded forced, choked and he cursed himself for not being able to hide his emotions.

"Do you mean, do l love William more than you?" she threw back at him. "No. You said yourself, I needed to make a decision. I have and now you're questioning it?"

"I am not questioning your decision," Jeremy answered, his voice raised, the words bitter, tinged with anger. His emotions still raw, too close to the surface. "I just want you happy."

They settled into an uncomfortable silence, and just south of Spanish Fork the houses thinned and farms took over, the neat rectangles appearing as shades of gray. They were so neat and organized. Why couldn't life mimic that perfection? That would probably be asking too much. The fields stayed inside the boundaries man had set; man didn't stay within the boundaries nature set. We were the ones out of sync.

"Jeremy," she said a short time later. "Is there a place we can stop?" Her words were clipped, edged by her own emotions.

"Of course. Are you alright? I didn't mean to upset you."

She sighed, pulling her emotions in line. "I know. I just need to use the restroom."

Jeremy pulled off the interstate in Payson, Amanda hurrying inside. She stood in front of the mirror and stared at her reflection. How could she have let things get so screwed up? She was the one who created this mess. She couldn't blame William or Jeremy. It was all on her.

A few towels from the dispenser moistened with cold water and she held the compress to her eyes. A final check for any sign she'd been crying and she stormed out. It might be better if she left. She had ditched Timothy so she could ditch Jeremy, too. Just hitchhike back to Salt Lake. And then what would she do? She sighed, forcing the tears back. George wasn't even in Salt Lake City.

A man wearing a clerk's smock passed her, heading into the back room, nodding as he did. Amanda scowled angrily, turning back to the front of the store. Then someone clasped a hand over her mouth and wrapped an arm around her waist. She jabbed at them with her elbow, another person grabbing her arm. There was a poke and her head began to reel, Jeremy admonishing her gently. *'Keep calm at all costs. Anger will only cloud your judgment.'* She flunked that one.

56

It was taking longer than Jeremy had expected for Amanda to use the restroom. He scanned the interior of the store and opened the channel, calling Amanda's name. Not receiving a reply, he tried again, angry at himself for asking the questions, for upsetting her.

"Is Amanda alright?" William asked.

"Just checking on her," Jeremy said. "We stopped so she could use the restroom and she hasn't returned."

A couple more minutes and Jeremy went inside and asked a female clerk if she would check the Ladies Room. The clerk returned telling him the restroom was empty. He glanced both directions, spotting the door marked 'Employees Only' and bolted for it.

The clerk grabbed at his arm. "You aren't allowed back there, sir," she said. "I'll have to call the police."

"Call them," Jeremy snapped as he pulled free, shoving past her.

The rear door lay straight ahead, cracked open. Jeremy raced for the exit, peering into a trash can as he sped by. One used syringe. Outside, a smock had been tossed aside, missing the intended dumpster. He rushed back inside, digging through bins and boxes.

The clerk had followed Jeremy and stood with hands on her hips, staring at him like he was crazy.

Finding a bin of clear plastic bags, Jeremy took two and, using one bag like a glove, picked up the syringe then turned it inside out and tied it shut. Rushing out the door, he picked up the smock by one corner and worked it into the second bag in the same way then hurried back inside where he slapped one of his cards on the desk in front of her.

"When the police arrive, give them that and these." He stabbed at the card and placed the bags with the syringe and the smock on top of the card. "If you do not and I find out…" He let the sentence drop, opening the secure channel on the pager alerting 911. They would ask the clerk for the evidence when they arrived. He locked eyes with hers and charged out, stopped then stepped back in. "Call them!"

Jeremy raced back to Amanda's car, heading for the highway, opening the channel again. How was he supposed to tell William he had lost his fiancée? This was beginning to resemble a bad TV comedy.

"Did you find Amanda?" William asked.

"I'm afraid not," Jeremy answered as the car screamed up the onramp, catapulting onto the freeway. "I'm embarrassed to tell you I lost your future wife. I suspect Mr. Bonner has her. I will take full responsibility."

"Not your fault, Jeremy. Why do you think George has her?"

"I found an empty syringe in a trash receptacle in the stores backroom."

William inhaled slowly and cursed under his breath. "I don't think he would bring her back to Salt Lake City. Not with the risk of getting caught." He paused, thinking. Where else could George take her? "If I was him, I wouldn't transport her across state lines and drive for however many hours if I didn't have to, either."

"Coordinate with James and Timothy. See if you can find any other properties George may own. Then call Captain Kirby. Fill him in on what you can. Page me if you learn anything."

"Will do," William replied. Thirty minutes later, William opened the channel. "We have a return on that property search we ran when we arrested George this time. There's a house on Bear Lake in Garden City."

"Find a motel and get a couple of rooms in Garden City. Put them under the organization's name. I'll meet you and James at your place. I'm about twenty or twenty-five minutes out. We'll go over things when I get there."

"We'll be here," William answered.

Jeremy spent the remainder of the trip trying to figure out how he had screwed up so massively. Pulling in at William's, he was still angry with himself.

"So what did you find out?" Jeremy asked. "Does he still have that property?"

"He still has the property," James replied. "He just hasn't used it recently. I think that's probably where he's taking her. There's been no activity at his apartment here in Salt Lake City. All other known properties have been sold."

"There are no other locations."

"None," William answered. "And this one's right on the water and on the main highway."

"Nothing in Julie or Jonathans names?" William frowned and Jeremy sighed. "I am sorry, sir. I didn't mean that to sound like I doubted you. What about the rooms?"

"We booked two rooms and can arrive anytime. But I want to get there early and see if we can find anything before they get the search warrants."

"And we remember where we've heard Mr. Layton's voice," James said. "The threat to Captain Jakes last year."

Jeremy groaned and leaned back in the chair. Maybe he had been working this business too long. He shouldn't have let something like that slip.

"Give yourself a break," William said. "It's been a year."

The blare of the telephone interrupted them. It was Captain Kirby. Search warrants had been requested. He would contact them again tomorrow. Would they be at William's or Garden City?

William locked eyes with Jeremy, Jeremy did a slow nod.

"Garden City," William said.

57

Amanda opened her eyes, exit signs flashing by and fought the tears. After all of Jeremy's planning she'd got angry and screwed it up. Now she was back in Salt Lake City. The exit for Twenty-Seven Hundred South floated out of view, someone stroking her hair gently. She sat up prior to the Twenty-One Hundred South sign flying by, her wrists bound in front of her with two strands of small chain and a padlock. George was taking no chances. She worked her hand under her shirt, depressing the homing beacon on the pager. She had no idea how long the pagers battery lasted, nor was she able to check it. All she could do now was hope Jeremy was behind them.

Peering around the car, two men sat silently on the opposite seat, staring out the window, George beside her. He was the one who had been stroking her hair.

The limo took the South West Temple exit, turned left onto Ninth South then took a right into an alley between Washington Street and Three Hundred West, slinking in behind a row of rundown houses. Notices had been tacked on some, advising people that the structures had been slotted for demolition, but that only served as advertising for the denizens who inhabited these streets.

A half a block north they stopped behind a two-story clapboard building. George reached toward her; Amanda recoiled from his hand, glaring at him. He pulled it back and climbed out, taking her by the arm and pulling her along behind him, the guards exiting after her.

"I'm going to let you experience something tonight, my pretty," George said. "I think you will get a better understanding of where you sit."

Amanda nodded dumbly as they dragged her inside, stopping to allow their eyes to adjust to the gloom. Urine mixed with the smell of filthy clothes and unscrubbed bodies, along with the unmistakable odors of sewage and rotting garbage filled the air.

In the far corner three teenagers huddled over a flame, a spoon held dangerously close, syringes at the ready. She turned away the guard laughing again. Amanda tried to push the picture out of her mind, but the kids haunted her, like the lines on Jeremy's chart. They should have been at home sleeping. Dreaming of school and friends, or Thanksgiving and Christmas with family, not hovering over a spoon held above a candle.

She blew the air out of her nose to dispel the odor, burying her face in her elbow. The guard laughed, dragging her deeper into the filth. A flashlight pierced the darkness and a toothless old man joined them leering at her over wire rimmed spectacles, his face cracking into a grin as he cackled between three rotted teeth.

"New meat?" he asked. "She's a nice 'un. You don't usually bring us girls like her. She'll bring in a hunderd and fifty a pop. I imagine we can run three or four men a night through her. Maybe more. For that price we'll have to fix a room up for her, though. Where'd you find her, or should I ask."

"Is the arboretum still empty?" George asked, dismissing the man's question.

"The glass room? Yeah. I was gonna move a couple of the ones with the best tits in there so guys can watch. Make a couple extra bucks. You want me puttin' her in there? We can strip 'er down and let the guys play by themselves all night."

"Leave her dressed," George said. "I imagine some of these fruits will get their jollies even with her clothes on. Do you have a new mattress in the back?"

"I got one left. I was going to give that to Janie. She's been pullin' 'em in real reg'lar lately. Want me cleanin' the room up? Some guy was so drunk he used the pond for a toilet the other day. I thought he was gonna drowned when he fell in."

"Next time, let him," George replied. "No. I want her to see exactly what happens some evenings. And keep the door locked."

"I see she's tied. You ain't afraid of her tryin' to get out? How about that room with all the cabinets? We set two men outside the doors as guards and she cain't escape."

George nodded, but didn't respond.

"I'll get it set," the old man called as he scurried away. He shuffled down the hall, jerking another man off a chair. "Come on jack ass. We got a special lady tonight. Help me get that new mattress in that pantry like room. And we cain't take the plastic off it. We don't want it gettin' dirty."

George handed her off to the guard.

"This is where the girls George can't get to cooperate come," the guard whispered. "Get them hooked on drugs and they'll do whatever you ask."

George chinned toward a large open room and they dragged her into the space. The smell here was as rank as the hall, the floor littered with filthy mattresses. Some nothing more than pads that contained occupants, a few engaged in some form of sexual activity. Others only contained bodies passed out from too much booze or too many drugs. Some didn't look like they were breathing. Amanda quickly pulled her eyes away and followed the guard through the maze, picking her way carefully along the narrow path.

The guard led her to a room with three walls devoid of any windows and a set of swinging doors that hung slightly askew. A chair sat off to the side in the hall. He shoved Amanda in, the doors meeting with an earsplitting crack, a gaping square in each where a window had once been, glass from the missing windows crunched under foot. The old man returned, him and his helper grunting as they fought the unwieldy mattress between the hinged doors. They tossed it onto the floor, and dropped a pillow and a couple of blankets on it. The smell of feces assailed her nostrils and, in the dim beam of the flashlight, a bucket materialized in the corner full to overflowing.

Footsteps echoed behind her and George walked in holding a flashlight.

"So what do you think, princess? Do you think you could work here?" George asked.

Amanda glared at him then spit in his face. "I'll die first."

"You just might," George retorted as he wiped the spittle off. "I told you I learned a lot while I was gone, but I didn't tell you what I learned. I know better than to trust you this year. I won't be afraid to have you disposed of, either. Think about it. I also suggest you listen to the house man. He won't last long enough for you to touch him, if you're worried about that."

The old man reappeared at the door, handing her a plastic bag that contained a bottle of water and a hastily thrown together bologna sandwich.

"Sorry. We don't usually feed your kind," he said. "You're pretty much on your own. Mr. Bonner said to make an exception this time."

Amanda nodded, watching him wipe his hands on his filthy pants then step back. She wondered how long it had been since he'd washed his hands then looked at the bag. That made the sandwich even less appetizing. The guard and the man backed out leaving George inside.

"I hope you learn something tonight. I'll be back to pick you up in the morning. I know you saw the restroom facilities. Do you think they'll work my pretty?"

Amanda stared at him, refusing to answer. Tears threatened, but she wasn't going to give George the satisfaction. Instead she stepped back, putting more space between them bumping into a solid wall of cabinetry. When she looked down, the counter tops were covered with rat droppings and cockroaches.

"We got the cops snooping a block away," one of George's guards called. "Let's go."

George strode across the outer room, stopping to speak to the old man and handing off the flashlight before disappearing. The man who had helped with the mattress planted a chair in the doorway, the flashlight went out and the place fell deathly silent. All noise ceased. The glow from a cigarette was visible in the frame to one of the would be windows and she thought about George's previous comment, '*let the guys play by themselves all night*'. That was a disturbing thought.

Laughter floated from the direction of the cigarettes glow, chair legs scraped on the floor and a second chair emitted a groan when someone sat down.

"Give a yell if you have to use the head," someone said. "I'll be more'n happy to help you off with those jeans lady."

Amanda remained motionless, her eyes adapting to the lack of light. A match flared on the opposite side of the door highlighting the mattress through the empty windows, cockroaches and mice skittered across the floor. As the creatures ran from the dying light she shivered. The thought of that climbing on her while she slept made her skin crawl. The person flipped the match onto the floor, a second cigarette now glowing beside the first.

Amanda turned her back on the men and lifted her jacket to check the pager. It appeared to have died. Shuffling came from behind her then the hinges scraped, the clap of the doors meeting echoing loudly down the hall, and she turned to face it. The shape of a man appeared in front of her, grabbing her and pulling her against him. The sour smell of perspiration and foul breath assailed her. She raised her arms, to cover her nose then the old man cackled and grabbed the button on her jeans. Amanda kneed him, pushing him back at the same time. Air exploded out of his lungs and he dropped the flashlight, it and him bouncing off the mattress to the floor, footsteps running toward them. Amanda dropped to her knees, fumbling for the light. Finding it, she slipped it into the waist of her jeans then she was kicked in the ribs, flying into the cupboards, one of the knobs gauging her back.

"What the fuck you doin' bitch?" one of them asked. "This is why you're here. For our pleasure. Are you stupid or what?"

Amanda leaned against the cabinet, sliding far enough to one side the knob no longer dug into her back as she struggled to breathe, waiting for the next onslaught. She had no doubt there would be more. She took the knife out of her pocket, flipped it open, one of the men inhaling loudly.

"The bitch has a knife," someone called from the door.

"Come on lover boy. All you have to do is get close," she said between clenched teeth. "I promise, I will cut you."

She pulled the flashlight, shining it on two men helping the old man stumble out then a larger man emerged from the shadows, kicking the light out of her hand. She ducked and he made an attempt to plant a second kick. She lashed out with the knife, missed and was lifted off the ground, a second man holding one of her legs. She writhed and squirmed, striking one of them with her right foot. The man holding her leg cursed loudly as he released her, something warm soaking through her pant leg then she was thrown onto the mattress the bigger man straddling her.

Amanda stabbed at him and he jerked back, doing a delicate dance, attempting to avoid the knife and maintain control of her. He leaned forward, she stabbed at him again, the point of the blade slicing through the heavy denim, something warm and sticky soaking her shirt. He screamed, pulling at her arm. A shadow appeared, grabbing her arm. The bigger man rolled backwards and Amanda arched her back sending him into his associate while she rolled the opposite direction, landing on her knees still gripping the knife tightly. She pushed herself upright then someone took her by the back of the coat, tossing her against the cabinets. Her body folded, footsteps coming at her landing another solid kick to her ribs. She twisted, striking out with the knife, stabbing an unseen object. Someone yelled, her knife jerked out of her hand clattering to the floor by her feet.

"Leave the bitch alone," the old man wheezed. "We'll tell George. He can deal with her. He don't want her manhandled."

"What about the knife? The bitch sliced me."

"If she cain't find it, she cain't use it. I doubt she'll be able to knife us all before we could overpower her, anyway. Just watch her real close like."

The men backed out and she huddled where she was fumbling along the floor, continuing her search for the knife. When she found it, she clicked it closed and slipped it into her bra beside the pager. She felt her way along the mattress to the cabinets then leaned against them, pulling in painful gulps of air. Something scooted across the counter above her head and she ducked, giving her all the reason she needed to stay awake all night.

She crouched where she was the rest of the night, alternately nodding off then forcing herself awake, listening for any sounds indicating one of the men was attempting to join her.

Daylight peeking through the uncovered windows the next

morning jolted Amanda out of her exhausted stupor and she looked around her head in a fog. George and his guard strode through the door, the old man nowhere to be seen. Him and his henchmen had left and been replaced by new wardens. George walked in and stared down at her.

"How was your first night?" he asked. He leaned over and touched her pant leg then pulled at the hem of her shirt. She followed the move seeing the blood. "It looks like there was some excitement."

"Some," Amanda murmured.

She rested her head against the cabinet, attempting to move. Her feet had gone to sleep, the tingle shocking her system as they came back to life. She leaned her head back, cringing from the uncomfortable sensation.

"Have you been like this all night, princess?"

She nodded. She didn't want to talk to him, but was too tired to fight. She was hungry, thirsty and she had to pee.

"Use the bucket," George said as if reading her mind. "Then we'll go."

"I'll pee in your limo first," she retorted.

"The head we use is next door," someone said. "It works."

One of George's men helped Amanda up, her breath catching from the bruised ribs. Once the bathroom door closed behind her, she checked it, finding it locked. She dropped the pager, but there were no signs of life. Stuffing it back in her bra, she ballooned the hem of her jacket to muffle any sound then dropped the knife, flipping the blade open. An inspection of the room brought a heat vent into view in the floor. It wasn't even wide enough to get her head through.

Examining the walls with what light filtered in a boarded up window, showed nothing useful. The window wasn't even big enough to squeeze her shoulders through. The girls would get in the way if she attempted that. She would have to get out of here before she could do anything. She sighed and closed the knife, sliding it beside the pager. She turned to the commode, finding it not much cleaner than what was out there, but the bowl wasn't full to overflowing. After she had refastened her jeans, she rattled the door then kicked at it angrily.

One of George's men opened it, taking her arm and leading her outside. The sun blinded her momentarily and she diverted her gaze to the ground, then she was sprawling across the back seat. As she struggled to sit up, George climbed in, sitting across from her, a guard on either side.

"I received a bad report on you," George said, glowering at her. "They say you fought off three of them with a knife." Then he laughed. "They also say you lost your knife. That's good."

Amanda kept her expression impassive and nodded. What he didn't know was going to come back and bite him.

They merged onto the interstate, driving north again, the signs streaking by.

It didn't take long for the soft bounce of the seat, the rhythmic flow of the car on the highway and exhaustion, to work their magic, and Amanda passed out, Jeremy's gentle voice repeating itself. *'Anger will only cloud your judgment'.*

58

The men were up early the next morning, William and James department pagers chirping the minute William's hand touched the knob. William called the station and Captain Kirby told him a limo had been spotted driving out of an alley north of Ninth South, east of Third West. Inside, they discovered a flop house slash drug den. A search of the premises and they found a ring, Amanda coming to mind. They would like him to come in and identify it.

Jeremy rode with James to the flop house while William drove to the station. William pulled up an hour after them, jogging to where they stood at the rear of the building, surveying the thigh high weeds, most of them brown and dried. Remnants of what had been a rose garden hung on by a thread next to a rotted fence. Car parts and fast food wrappers littered the ground. He hated to think Amanda had been here.

"Was it hers?" James asked.

"Yes," William answered, pulling it out of his pocket. "It was found beside a mattress in what looked like a pantry."

All three men stood to the side, avoiding the stream of officers leading unkempt bodies to waiting vans. Amanda had been here so – even though it was only a hunch – they appeared to be on the right path. Garden City was north. But, without her pager transmitting, they had nothing to guide them. Once the procession slowed, the three went inside, the stench enveloping them as soon as they stepped through the door.

They picked their way between the mats, William stopping to peer inside the arboretum, its flowers now gone, the pool brown and stagnant. He crinkled his nose against the odor and continued into a short hall, James and Jeremy following. The smell of urine and feces announced the pantry before they reached the double doors. They shined their flashlights through the empty window squares, the makeshift restroom facilities visible at the end of a bank of cabinets, the opposing wall a complete row of cabinets. A brand new mattress – still in its protective plastic – sat in the center of the floor. William pushed through the doors, sweeping the room with his flashlight then knelt beside of the mattress, blood and scuff marks on the grimy floor. There had been a fight and he hoped the blood wasn't Amanda's.

Jeremy pulled out his pager keyed in *'On Our Way'*, and hit enter. The pagers normally saved enough power for one or two emergency pages. That's what he was counting on. The beacon wouldn't work, but Amanda should still receive. William asked Jeremy the question with his eyes he was afraid to voice. Jeremy shook his head and gave a slight shrug.

"I won't know for a while, sir," Jeremy answered. "We don't even know if she still has it."

Their portables squawked and William was told to contact the captain.

"James, I'm going to find a phone. Keep an eye on things," William said, running for his car.

William pulled in at one of the area businesses and showed his badge, asking to use their phone. He called Captain Kirby praying this would be good news regarding Amanda. When the captain answered, William could tell by his tone it wasn't.

"What's up, Cap?" William asked.

"The judge rejected the initial warrant request," Captain Kirby answered.

"Damn! Why?"

"He said we need more evidence. I'm hoping you found something we can add. Anything new at the scene?"

"We're positive Amanda was here, but nothing concrete. We found blood from a struggle, but that doesn't mean it's hers. The blood could be from anybody. Let me see if I can push one of the men into giving up something. A couple of them look like they may have worked the place."

"I'm on my way. Call me on the portable if you find anything before I get there."

William pulled up behind the house, striding to one of the vans. He flung the door open, grabbing one of the men by the arm and tossed him to the ground. He climbed into the van, ignoring the angry exclamations as he waded through the occupants. One of the men's clothes were bloody, his leg and arm bandaged crudely, another's nose in bad shape, toilet paper stuffed into the nostrils. A third had a blood on the bottom of a pant leg a piece of cloth held on with masking tape peeked out below it. William found the toothless old man and dragged him out. At the van door, William jabbed one of the uniforms in the arm.

"I want you and your partner to follow me," he ordered. "You are going to be my witnesses in case this piece of trash accuses me of anything."

The officer waved to his partner. Once inside, William shoved the old man into the pantry and onto the mattress.

"First of all. Has he been read his rights?"

"Yes, sir," the officer answered.

"Which means I don't have to answer any of yer questions,"

the man threw back at William. "You can threaten me all you want and it ain't gonna work. I want a lawyer."

"You said earlier you haven't done anything," William said.

"Correct!" the man answered smugly. "And you cain't prove I did."

"And you told officer's no one runs this place."

"Yes, sir. That's correct again."

"Then I want you – in your own words – to tell me how you got this." William pulled Amanda's ring out of his pocket. "And all the cash you had on you. I want to know where it came from. And before you spout your mouth, I didn't ask you squat. I made a statement."

"And there's nothing you can do if I don't tell you."

"Yes, there is," William said leaning down. "If you aren't employed by anybody that means you're working this operation on your own. You are completely responsible for whatever we find. And it all appears to be illegal." He leaned closer and shoved the ring in the man's face. "This ring was custom made for my fiancée so I will gladly throw your happy ass behind bars for theft in a heartbeat. I would like nothing better than to watch you rot. Tell me how you got it!"

Someone grabbed his arm, William shook it off, continuing to glare at the old man.

"I have all day," William continued lowering his voice. "It might even be worth it to go to jail for a few days with you. Jail justice is much quicker and sometimes more lethal than the legal system. You would have no rights in there. Think about that."

"William!" Captain Kirby snapped from behind him.

"Don't worry, Cap," William said, holding the man's gaze. "I'm not stupid enough to hit the man no matter how bad I want to." He leaned closer. "I want to know where you got the ring and who the blood belongs to. That's it asshole."

The man avoided William's stare, attempting to scoot across the mattress away from him. William jerked him back.

"We had a girl dropped off last night. She was in this room so we could keep the guys off her. A couple of the men decided they were gonna get a little rowdy and she kicked them around pretty good. The blood's from the dude's in the van."

"Why would they get rowdy with her if you were supposed to keep her away from the guys?"

William grabbed the man's t-shirt and lifted him up so they were nose to nose.

"WILLIAM…."

"I got it, Cap!"

"Because the bitch kneed me in the jewels," the man answered.

"And why would she do that? You trying to have a little fun on your own?"

"Yeah, she was a mean bitch."

"You better know it," William answered. "Now, who dropped her off?"

"I don't have to tell you nothin'…"

"WHO dropped her off?" William asked again, hardening his tone.

"George Bonner," the man replied. "And you can't use this against me because I was fearing for my life. You threatened me."

"Yes, I can," William answered, pulling a recorder out of his pocket and pushing 'Stop'. "I have it all in your own words. And these fine gentlemen with us are witnesses who will testify that no threats were made. And there are no marks on you. Well, except maybe Amanda's. And without bruises, nothing you say will hold up." William dropped him and backed off then stepped back in. "Oh, one more thing. I'm on my way to get the lady now. That mean bitch will be testifying against you in court so you had better make sure you have your shit together. Now, enjoy your stay in beautiful downtown Salt Lake City. We boast the safest rooms in town."

William slapped the recorder in Captain Kirby's hand then stormed out and leaned against his car as they led the man back to the van. A look to his right and the captain approached, followed by James and Jeremy.

"William, you pushed it dangerously close in there," Captain Kirby said.

"You wanted proof," William said. "You got it. We're going to Garden City to see if we can find her and – with or without that warrant – once I find her, I'm pulling her out. And when I get back, I will personally hand you my resignation if I have to. Pieces of filth like them…" He jerked his head toward the vans. "…and Bonner, have more rights than we do. If you want to put me on notice, I don't care. I love my job, but I hate the politics. Sir." He looked away then glared at the captain once more. "And it shouldn't have taken this to find out who killed my first wife."

"I won't push it. In some cases, you're right," Captain Kirby said. He saluted William with the cassette as he turned to leave.

"What started that?" James asked after the captain had left.

"We get to hurry up and wait," William said. "Search warrants were requested, but the judge denied them. We needed more evidence. Now we have the evidence, but we might not get the warrants until tomorrow."

"Crap!" James exclaimed. "Bureaucracy at its best."

"You ready?" William asked looking at Jeremy.

"Most definitely," Jeremy answered.

"James, Jeremy will ride with me. We have some loose ends to clear up."

59

The limo slowed, waking Amanda. She sat up, the driver pulling expertly around the circular drive, and gazed out at the unfamiliar surroundings. George climbed out, offering his hand. Disoriented, Jeremy's prior admonishes about behaving herself repeated and she took George's hand, allowing him to help her out. A quick look around, there was a lake behind the house and a low wall in front. George cut her restraints and gave her a warning gaze before placing his hand under her elbow then guiding her up the stairs and into the foyer.

An older woman stood to the side, nodding dutifully as she reached for Amanda's jacket. Amanda folded her arms in front of her, the ring Jeremy had given her, flashing brilliantly. She took a half a step back and smiled, shaking her head. George took her hand, looking at the ring, turning it so the light danced off the facets. Amanda jerked it away then noticed her engagement ring was missing. She swept the floor with her eyes, fighting to keep the panic at bay. Jeremy floated to the surface once more. '*Keep your wits about you at all times, at all costs.*' She closed her eyes, inhaled slowly, pulling herself together.

"That's a beautiful ring," George said. "Perhaps I was wrong earlier. Did Jeremy give it to you?"

"It was a gift," she answered. "I like the way the light sparkles off the stones. It reminds me of the little girl who cleaned my rooms last year. Before you moved me to Park City."

"Sarah," George said. "She was a beautiful little girl. It's been a year and I still miss her terribly. I loved her sweet laugh."

A hint of pain crossed his face and Amanda gaped. George cared for something other than money?

George recovered quickly and directed Amanda's eyes to the woman. "This is, Chloe. She'll set your clothes out, draw your bath, make sure your bed is turned down and that your room is cleaned per your instructions. If you need anything, you see Chloe."

"You don't trust me with a butler anymore?" Amanda asked.

"No, Amanda, I don't. I have learned my lesson. Dinner will be served promptly at six and I have invited guests tonight so I expect you to make yourself available."

"Available?"

"I haven't lined you up with any clients of that nature, if that's your concern. You will be my companion. I own you."

"And if I don't feel up to participating in this dinner?" she asked. "Last night was a rather long night."

"I would greatly appreciate it if you did. You have enough time to take a nap for an hour or two before you pull yourself together."

Amanda noticed the jaw tighten and the eyes flash and looked away, biting back an angry retort. George would not be an easy adversary if angered.

"We'll see," Amanda replied.

She followed Chloe thinking about George's comments. '...you need to make yourself available... I own you.' At the top of the stairs, she eyed her left hand, turning it palm side up and then palm down, thinking about where she might have lost the ring. She had it at the convenience store. From there it was a blur. She woke up in the limo and was left at the flop house and she didn't remember if she'd had it at either place.

Amanda entered the room, taking in the space. A bed centered on the facing wall, a night table with a lamp flanked it on either side. The stand to the left held a radio. There was a window on either side of the headboard, a padded bench sat at the end of the bed, and a seating area with a writing desk to the left. Her eyes darted back to the radio. Not just a radio, a portable cassette radio. She walked to the window and gazed out onto the grounds, dropping her eyes tracing the radio's cord. A transformer lay on the floor next to the wall, Jeremy's situational awareness mantra making its presence known. '*Learn enough about your enemy and you will know him better than he knows himself.*' Maybe it would be a good idea to attend this stupid party.

A vibration in her bra startled Amanda and she stepped into the bathroom and locked the door, removing the pager. Reading Jeremy's message, she smiled and typed in, *Guards, guards, guards*, and hit enter. When she had finished, she flushed the commode, scanning the bathroom quickly. The usual, sunken tub, shower, toilet and double sinks backed by a wall to wall mirror. She couldn't say much for the gaudy aqua walls and brass fixtures, but it wasn't her choice. One more scan and something was absent.

Back at the windows, she gazed outside then returned to the bathroom. It wasn't what she saw; it was what she didn't see. No cameras. That meant she would move again or George planned on staying with her.

"Excuse me," Chloe said from behind her. "Would you care for me to have those cleaned for you?" Chloe nodded at her clothes, Amanda following her gaze.

"No, I'll rinse them out myself. Thank you."

"Is madam sure?"

Amanda nodded, Chloe looking at her as if she was insane.

"I'm sorry, Chloe. Is there a problem?"

"That's alright, ma'am. I was wondering if this dress would be alright for dinner." Chloe held up a baby blue number that left little to the imagination. "Mr. Bonner said he liked this one best."

Amanda took in the deep plunging 'V' of the neckline and the spaghetti straps and wanted to scream, but understood Chloe was only following orders.

"Is there something not quite so revealing?" Amanda said instead. "I'll apologize to Mr. Bonner for you."

"Yes, ma'am." Chloe turned back to the closet, returning with a dress that covered more and had no side slits.

"Perfect," Amanda said. "Thank you for asking."

Once Chloe had left, Amanda rinsed out her shirt and the pant leg, draping the items over the shower rod. Rummaging through the writing desk, she found a note pad and wrote a note. DO NOT TOUCH! Folding a cuff up on the dry pant leg she placed the note in it. Satisfied, she showered, inspecting the room and the grounds further.

A gentle rap on the door a few minutes before six let Amanda know it was time for her appearance. One more look in the mirror and she smoothed the skirt down over her hips inhaling then exhaling slowly, Jeremy the ever present mentor. *'Don't panic. You will only defeat yourself.'*

"And you are on," she said to the empty room. "I should win a damn Oscar for this shit."

She opened the door cautiously, an older gentleman standing in the hall, his arm at the ready. Amanda remembered the dinner at Howard's and rested her hand on his. When they topped the stairs George waited below like a nervous school boy, his eyes glued on her, anger simmering below the surface.

"George, you've been holding out on us," one of the men said.

"She's the reason for these meetings," George responded, smugly. "I want the men in Utah to know she is moving to their part of the country. She was in Reno for a short time."

"Oh, this is the exquisite young lady Jeremy had on his arm last year," another gentleman said. "I've heard about her."

"Jeremy has been working with her for me. He's done a stellar job, as usual. I can't tell you how I feel about his work."

"I'll bet you can't," Amanda said, shooting George a parting glare as she raised her eyebrows.

"And she has a sense of humor," the first person said.

An under the lash glance around the room and she counted four men, not including George, one of whom was Howard Chancellor. He did a barely noticeable head dip and smile, letting her know he had seen her. Amanda returned the move.

"Is Jeremy's training the reason we haven't seen her before now?" Howard asked.

"I had to make sure she was ready," George replied, dodging a direct answer.

During dinner, Amanda listened, scanned the room, answered questions directed specifically to her, and attempted not to act bored. Howard and another man sat to the back, observing the other two. The man seated next to Howard was younger than the rest and watched the play with a form of bored indifference while Howard kept quiet, raising his eyes as if he were making mental notes at different references. Toward the end of the meal, she took a surreptitious glance up and discovered the younger man no longer seated by Howard.

"So what do you think of all this, Amanda?" a voice said from beside her.

She looked up, startled.

"Would you care to sneak out by the pool?"

"I'd love to. Do you think we can?"

He put a finger to his lips, whispered in George's ear and nodded in Amanda's direction, leaning heavily on her chair.

George leaned toward her. "My protégé here thinks you need a restroom break. Is this true?"

"Please," Amanda said.

The younger man held out his hand, teetered unsteadily as he stepped back and led her to the rear hall, grasping items of furniture in passing to maintain his balance. Part way to the kitchen, he pointed out a half bath. When she returned, he handed her a coat then staggered to the back door. He opened it, showing off immaculately manicured grounds, the evergreens dutifully wrapped to protect them from marauding wildlife.

To one side was a large pool, the glass enclosure pulled out, steam rising inside misting the glass. Beyond the pool, waves could be heard washing against the shore, a barely discernible expanse of water past that. What appeared to be a heavily wooded parcel, a dark nothingness from here, bordered the property to the north, the telltale lights of a house twinkled to the south. She moved toward the lake and took another glance north, noticing the section closest to the house had few trees. The distance was deceiving after dark.

Amanda approached the water, slipping her heels off and lifted the hem of her skirt. She did a quick intake of air, biting back a screech, as the frigid water engulfed her feet, the waves nipping playfully at her ankles. *Must remember, wading in November is a bad idea.*

A look out over the lake and there was a ramp but no boat. A reminder that boats would be out of the water by now. Farther north along the shore sat a dark brooding hulk, a barn or a large garage. A boathouse, maybe. No matter what she did, she had to work around the guards, the lake and the highway, but still doable.

Off the sand, she slipped her heels back on, and found a chair near the pump house, sliding it closer to the building to break the wind. Once she'd sat down, she hunched her shoulders inside the coat. The wind was cold tonight, her toes frozen.

"Uncle George is a pompous ass," the young man finally said. "I detest the way he plays these games."

"Uncle George?" Amanda said. The thought of George having a family had never crossed her mind. None of their information showed siblings. But people didn't usually just hatch.

"He thinks women are only good for one thing," the man said, with a drunken slur. "Making money off of. Especially beautiful women like you. Sex is a commodity. An avenue for creating wealth."

It was quiet for a minute and Amanda wondered if he expected her to respond.

"You didn't act like you were happy in there," he continued, "so I thought you might enjoy a short reprieve."

"Thank you. I appreciate that." Amanda studied the area, the wind picking up, the temperature plummeting even through the coat. She stood, hugged the coat closer and took an unsteady step toward the house. Her feet were so cold she could barely stand. "I think we need to go inside before Uncle George comes looking for us."

"If we must," the man said, attempting to stand and failing miserably.

Amanda grabbed one flailing arm, stopping his backwards trajectory then held him a tic to make sure he was standing on his own before releasing her hold on him.

"After you," he said.

He waved his hand and steadied himself, a bottle appearing from inside his coat, and they headed to the house.

George was part way down the hall looking for them.

"Are you alright," George asked. "I didn't expect you to be gone this long."

"I'm fine. We did a short walk along the lake."

George tipped her chin up, Amanda turned her head, avoiding any possible advances, his nephew snickered in the background.

"I'll leave you to retire for the evening then," George said, his jaw tightening. "I asked Chloe to turn your bed down for you. Tomorrow one of the gentlemen will be back. He is looking for a lady to accompany him on business trips and he wants to see you in a bikini. He has to see exactly what he will be purchasing."

"I won't wear anything like that skimpy excuse of a swimsuit you had for me in Reno. I don't want to look like a cheap hooker. If you want me to act like a lady, you need to allow me to dress like one. Have a good evening."

Amanda stormed up the stairs, slammed the door to her room and found the bed turned down, a silk nightgown laid out. Evidently George had made plans. She locked the door then checked that her clothes still hung in the bathroom before going through the dresser and finding an oversized nightshirt. Tomorrow she would work on a way out of here. First she had to get past the cameras and the guards. And she had to get some rest.

The coins tumbled into the chute clinking and chiming, David apprehensive. He had never been this deep and the prospect of screwing up wasn't a pleasant one. He had no back up and no one to call. He held the last coin for a tic, prayed a silent prayer and shoved it in, the pinball sound of its freefall echoing in the tight space.

A man approached the phone next to him and laid a magazine on top of it, turning his back to David. David returned the favor and waited.

"The Landers Corporation."

The secretary answered with the same bored efficiency she had before, placing the call on hold, the stranger joking with someone behind David.

Thomas answered in a few seconds.

"I told you I would call back," David said. "Have you heard from Glen or your best hooker recently?"

"I have not. They seem to be MIA," Thomas replied. "How would you know?"

"I suggest you check on the previously named employees a

little closer," David answered. "Then we'll talk. I'll give you one hour. Have a good day."

An hour later David stood outside a Circle-K bouncing coins in his hand before feeding them into the phone. Was he doing the right thing? Should he run back to Reno with his tail between his legs and beg for forgiveness? Yes to the first question, no to the latter. He had started this with one goal in mind. That goal hadn't changed, he had just deviated from the plan. He plugged the first coin in and paused. Coins number two and three jingled through the slot, and he inhaled slowly, holding his breath. He shoved the last of the coins in hurriedly, not wanting to back out. The secretary answered, transferring the call.

While he waited two teenagers ran by, pushing and shoving each other, one of them bouncing off the neighboring phone. Thomas answered as they faded out of sight.

"Good day, sir," David said. "Did Travis have good news?"

Thomas hesitated, but only for a second. "Travis says your information is outdated. He said Mr. Bonner has been arrested again.

"Travis is correct. Mr. Bonner was arrested, but he is already out." David paused, calming his anger. This conversation was going nowhere. It was time to speed up the process. "We seem to be at an impasse so let me redirect this conversation. I know about five murders you are directly responsible for. You ordered four of the hits personally."

"You have no proof of anything," Mr. Landers replied.

"Oh, but I do," David answered. "There's a detective's wife from three years ago. She was shot with the same .45 that killed Mr. Bonner's ex-employee in Laughlin a few years ago. Then we have a call girl's unexpected murder earlier this summer and a pair of two bit drug dealers. Would you care for the details of how each was accomplished?" David chuckled when Mr. Landers's exhaled loudly. "My apologies, did I take you by surprise? You see, if I was going to turn you in, I could have done it a long time ago. Think about it real hard. I will call again in an hour."

David hung up, checked the street then walked through the convenience store, exiting the rear door and following the fence to his truck on the street behind. He hated this cat and mouse shit, but one couldn't be too careful when balancing between the cops, George Bonner and the syndicate. A thorough scan of the area and he pulled out, doubling back the way he had came. A couple of extra round-the-block tours, to make sure he hadn't picked up a tail and he merged onto southbound I-15. An hour later he was once again feeding coins into a payphone this one just north of Provo, Utah.

The secretary put him on hold again.

A hooker approached, leaning against the phone next to his, offering him her company for a measly hundred bucks an hour. In his case she'd drop it to sixty if he was interested. She winked and laughed softly. He shooed her away, hearing Thomas pick up.

"Hello again," David said. "When did you want to meet, sir?"

"That could prove dangerous."

"I understand your concern. If not done right, it would be hazardous for both of us, but I'm growing tired of the game."

"Why are you so eager to turn on Mr. Bonner?"

"Let's just say he isn't the easiest man to work for. So, tell me, when do you want to meet? My time is valuable."

"I need to check on a few things, Mr. Haus...."

"Do me a favor," David said. "Check out a body found in the Green River. I believe you will find she was your best feeder inside the Bonner organization."

"We had one girl who was invaluable," Thomas said. "We haven't heard from her in a while. That is what I want to check."

"We both know you're stalling. Your plans inside the Bonner organization backfired. Now, I'm going to give you something else to think about. So far George's plans haven't gone as desired, either, but he is a free man, and is in custody of a lady your organization was attempting to procure last year. Mr. Bonner has plans involving that lady that will make you and the boys in Las Vegas as jealous as children. You want to beat George Bonner, you need to think like George Bonner."

"Call me back tomorrow."

David hung up, checked the area once more and dropped more coins in the payphone.

"Penny's," a sultry voice said.

"I need to talk to Penny," David said.

"Penny isn't here. Can I help you? I can set you up with a personal appointment at ten o'clock tonight. What do you think, baby?"

"I think I'll decline," David said as he laughed. "Tell Penny his favorite ride called..."

"Honey, you are not Penny's type," she retorted. "I can vouch for that personally."

"Tell him..." David said his voice firm. "....his favorite ride called and is opting for the face to face. Okay?" She huffed out a breath. "If I find out you didn't relay this message, I'll make sure you don't work anywhere in Reno or Las Vegas."

"I'll get it to him," she replied in a pouty voice.

61

Amanda moved her clothes to the bathroom window to finish ridding them of the flop house odor, thankful they had dried overnight. A sudden gust of wind blew through, the frigid air wafting the smell over her and she debated her decision to wear them again.

Sitting on the edge of the tub, she took her knife and the transformer for the radio then shaved the end that connected to the appliance so it fit her pager and plugged it in. No sparks. That was a good thing. She took a shower, checking her clothes. The airing had helped.

Once she'd dressed, she walked into the bedroom, the door bursting open. George stood in the doorway, keys bouncing in his hand. Three long strides and he stood in front of her, cornering her between the stand and the headboard.

"Amanda," George said. "You and I need to talk."

"Can you give a girl a little privacy?" She looked around the room, assessing her best move.

"Not in this house," he replied. "I am the one who decides how much privacy, if any, you are allowed. As I stated last night, I own you. I decide what you will wear and you *will* acquiesce and wear it. You don't *tell* me anything. I'm not going to set you up with any appointments that include bedroom privileges, but your clients are not going to want to see their wife, or girlfriend, when they pay the amount of cash they will dole out just to have you sit with them."

"Don't worry about this afternoon. I won't let you down," she snapped angrily. "With that said, I won't wear any suit you want me to wear. As *I* stated last night, if you want me to act like a lady let me dress like one."

George nodded and she tried to squeeze past him. He grabbed her arm, slamming her into the wall.

"You really are a stubborn one," he said, his voice more of a hiss than anything. "From now on you will follow my orders. Period! Do I make myself clear? And that includes the swimsuit I have instructed Chloe to set out for today. I will also be joining you in your bed *every* night! Capiche?"

Glimpsing the surprise he leaned in, pressing his body against hers, gripping her jaw tightly. He kissed her roughly, releasing his hold, dropping his hand to her jeans.

"You also need to remember, no one knows where you are. You will obey or I will make other arrangements for you. It could take weeks to find a person in that lake." His eyes lowered, resting on her chest. "We have time for a quick taste," he said with a sadistic chuckle. "What do you think, Amanda? The gentleman won't be here until two."

Amanda slid her left hand along the wall until her arm touched the lampshade then she grasped the base firmly. With her eyes glued on his, Amanda picked it up and swung. George deflected the lamp, grabbing her by the neck, pressing her tighter against the wall.

"Excuse me, Mr. Bonner," Chloe said from behind him. "Is

this the suit you wished for me to set out for madam?"

George spun, facing Chloe who held up a suit barely wider than a string. "That will be perfect," he answered. He stroked the side of Amanda's breast then backed away. "It appears your introduction to your new life has been postponed," he said, glaring at her. "Remember, your caller will be here at two. I expect you to be ready."

Amanda massaged her neck as George strode angrily out of the room admitting she'd screwed that one up. She'd let herself think she had the upper hand, but with George – she wouldn't.

A glance out the window at the lake and she thought about George's threat. Returning her gaze to the dressing room, Chloe stood frozen in the door. Evidently Chloe had never seen this side of George.

Chloe took the suit George had wanted her to set out, placed it back in the drawer and took out a less revealing one, laying it on the bench.

"I took the liberty of setting you out a heavier cover also," Chloe said. "Even with the pool enclosure the winds off the lake can be chilly this time of year."

"Thank you," Amanda replied. "I appreciate that."

Once Chloe had left Amanda changed into the bikini, slipping her clothes under the mattress and leaned against the wall as she gazed out the window. A car pulled through the gate, a tall willowy blonde climbing out. Amanda recognized the mannerism immediately. Part of George's harem of hookers. Another scan of the grounds and it dawned on her the wall was only three feet tall. It wasn't a means of keeping anyone in or out. Jeremy thrust his way in once more. *'Appearances are everything....'* She would play today, but she would be gone tonight.

62

A soft tap brought Amanda out of her reverie, Chloe peeking inside. Her caller was here. Amanda glanced at the clock. One fifty-seven. The gentleman was punctual.

Poolside, Amanda was surprised to see Howard.

Embarrassed by the actions of George and his guest, Howard steered her to the far end of the pool.

"I'm sorry, they seem to be a little too sharing," Howard said. "I'm not into that sort of display."

"I appreciate that," Amanda replied. "Neither am I."

Amanda chanced a cautious glance over her shoulder at the spectacle the two created in one of the lounge chairs then returned her gaze to the front, even more embarrassed that she had looked.

"George said you were trained by Jeremy. It appears Jeremy has outdone himself. I have a couple of questions, if you don't mind." Howard leaned closer, whispering in her ear. "I'm trying to make this look like we've never met. It can be awkward working both sides." He paused as if waiting for her to answer then whispered again. "Jeremy paged about George abducting you again. That's why I'm here."

One of George's men approached, Howard nodded in passing then he pointed to a cluster of patio chairs. He slid two of the chairs closer together and sat down, motioning for Amanda to do the same.

Amanda took the seat and observed Howard. Why would he need an escort? He was in his late fifties, maybe, but still a good-looking man. A lean athletic build, average height. The salt and pepper hair and moustache accented his gray eyes. Then the light came on. He was the commander.

Footsteps approached and Amanda looked up to see George walking their way. She glanced at Howard with a half smile. It was time to play.

"Jeremy was always a gentleman," Amanda said. "When he started working with me he found it difficult to dance in any sort of an intimate manner. It terrified me. He worked patiently to get me to the point we could dance closely and I wouldn't panic." She looked up noting George's frown. "I appreciate you being so understanding, George. November is a bit chilly even with the pool surround out. Having Chloe set out this ensemble shows how understanding you can be."

"I hoped it met with your approval," George stammered.

Howard noticed the exchange and stood, offering Amanda his hand. "Shall we go for a short walk?" He stared beyond George at the naked woman then back at George. "I really do abhor public displays of that nature."

"I would love to," Amanda said. She gave George a veiled smirk and followed Howard's lead.

"Excuse us George," Howard said.

George nodded then stepped back, glaring at Amanda.

Once on the grounds, Howard took his jacket off and put it around Amanda's shoulders. "It's a bit chillier than I anticipated. Are you sure you want to go for a walk?"

"Yes and thank you." Amanda pulled the jacket tighter around her, her body giving an involuntary shiver.

"You're shaking," Howard said. "This was not a good idea. Why didn't you say something?"

"I'm fine," she replied. "May I ask you a question?" She didn't want to pry, but curiosity had gotten the better of her. "Why do you need an escort? I mean, you run this organization?"

"This helps everyone, my organization included. It's also a legitimate business expense. I am looking for a hostess for a few upcoming trips. My wife was paralyzed in an accident a few years ago and some of my travels just take too big a toll on her health now. In fact, it was my wife's idea to use an escort. I screen them carefully because when I go on these trips, I need someone who will conduct themselves in a civilized manner, and act like a gracious hostess. I don't want anyone like the woman we just saw.

"Plus it helps us police this side of the industry. If we come upon a woman, such as you, we pull them out, using whatever means are necessary and put the people responsible behind bars. It also lets us know who is selling ...." A pause. "...*extra* benefits. A woman working as a companion isn't breaking the law per se, but prostitution is against the law in most states. It's a fine line at times and we have to be extremely careful before accusing anyone of crossing that line."

"I'm sorry." A memory of the wheelchair lift on the stairway popped in. A single rose planted under each window. Now she understood. Howard's wife could enjoy the beautiful blooms no matter which room she was in. "I didn't mean to pry."

"You're perfectly alright," he said. He hesitated a second before looking at her. "I am not exactly sure how to phrase this next question so forgive me if it comes across a bit blunt."

Amanda smiled, giving a tiny dip of her head.

"I am very interested in having you escort me on my travels and thought it would be a nice boon to have the entire team onboard. You seem to work well together. But Jeremy is a man and I want no issues between him and William on any of these trips. I hope that came out correctly."

Amanda stared at the stone path, remembering what Jeremy had divulged at the dinner. "You will have no concerns of that nature. William has asked me to marry him."

"Congratulations!" he said, guiding her to the north side of the house. "I'm glad to hear that. And just so you know, I'm in charge of this group for a reason. It is my business to know everything. That is why I felt the need to put Jeremy on the spot."

"I understand," she said.

"I was surprised when Jeremy paged," Howard continued. "I was even more surprised when you walked into the room last night. I had actually toyed with the idea Jeremy was mistaken this time. Since that isn't the case there are a few things we need to go over."

Howard opened the door to a sunroom, directing her in. A quick inspection and she found a dark, reflective circle near a rock in one of the planters. Howard did a slight upward glance with his eyes and she lifted her gaze doing a scan of the ceiling, a shiny circle barely visible at the base of one of the sprinklers. She slid her hand under her cover and into the bikini top, Howard moving in close, blocking the camera's view. Amanda checked the pager, seeing the red light.

"There are microphones, as well as cameras," Howard said, keeping his voice low. "I don't work the undercover portion any longer, but I try to keep up with things. Please, follow my lead."

Amanda did a quick head bob.

Howard directed her to a wicker settee, draping his arm over her shoulder, pulling her close. Amanda leaned in, listening while he talked, his voice barely above a whisper, stressing they did not want her running off on her own. His presence was only to verify her being there. As soon as he was off the premises, he would page Jeremy, and the team would come in to get her. Then he raised his voice to normal tone, going over details of the trip.

"Let me deliver you back to Mr. Bonner," Howard finished. "We don't want him to get upset."

Amanda nodded.

Howard returned her to the pool and shook his head. George and his toy had migrated from the chair to the pool, clothing still an optional item.

"I will contact you later, George," Howard said.

George waved, fully engrossed in his activities.

Amanda walked to her room and changed, staring out the window as Howard departed in a waiting limo, the woman George had been entertaining leaving a few minutes after. Amanda dropped her head, heaving an involuntary sigh. She had hoped George would be occupied tonight. Avoiding him and escaping on the same night could prove tricky.

63

Amanda watched as the sun disappeared over the hills, her thoughts on the best way to work tonight. Howard had said the men would pull her out, but if they didn't know where George was.... Her pager vibrated interrupting her thoughts and she checked the screen, seeing a single word. RUN. She grabbed her coat and flung the window open, headlights and the strobing reds and blues of police cars flashing across the landscape. She lunged for the roof below her; the door to her room bouncing off the wall then George grabbed her.

"WILLIAM!" she yelled, fighting to pull free. "JEREMY!"

The cops stared weapons drawn, unable to fire. They wouldn't risk hitting her. George jerked her back inside, one of his men grabbing an arm. Amanda pushed George onto the bed, kicking and shoving the men away, in an attempt to reach her knife, the three men overpowering her.

George seized her arm, dragging her toward the rear stairs. Amanda continued to squirm in an attempt to pull free. Freeing one arm she swung. A guard blocked the blow and grabbed her jacket, thrusting her forward back into Georges' grasp. Amanda slipped a hand under her coat, grabbed her knife, activating the beacon on the pager, Jeremy calling instructions to James and William.

"She activated the beacon. They are probably taking her out the back. I'm going to see if I can intercept them. You follow from the south side of the house."

George stopped and, him and one of the guards, held her while the third man searched her. Her hand concealed the knife, fingers curled tightly around it, the pager too large to hide. The guard sneered and pulled his hand out, tossing the pager to George.

"Looks like your lady had a trick up her sleeve. What do you want to do?"

"We're going to send the cops on a wild goose chase," George said glaring at her. "Do we still have the twenty-footer in the boathouse?"

"Yes, sir. We pulled it out of the water, though."

"That's okay. Get it back in the water. Cut the ropes and let it fall if you have to. Here." George threw him the pager. "Toss this in the boat. Once it's back in the water we'll set a course for the middle of the lake. By the time they figure out we screwed them, it'll be too late. When we're out of here, we'll dispose of her. She will have served her purpose."

At the bottom of the stairs, George slammed the back door open and they raced toward the lake.

Amanda looked north, recognizing the brooding hulk of the boathouse then she was being pulled along the water's edge, stumbling over uneven rocks, her feet sinking in the wet sand. As they pulled her after them, she scanned the grounds, a familiar car headed north on the highway. A glance over her shoulder and William became visible in the outdoor lights, bolting around the corner of the house.

"WILLIAM!" she yelled.

George slammed her in the side of the head, she staggered, her ears ringing. A fist to the back of the head sent her to her knees. One of the men reached for her and she flipped the knife open, lashing out, cutting his arm. He jerked back, surprised by her move, his pistol falling. Amanda lunged forward, pushing him back as she scooped up the gun, shoving it into her pocket. The second guard dove toward her, jumping back, arms out, when she struck at him. She sliced at him with the knife once more and he dodged again. Amanda leaped up and bound for the house, folding the knife and dropping it as she attempted to slide it into her hip pocket. She hesitated, scanned the ground behind her then George jumped forward, reaching out to seize her. The second guard grabbed her arm and thrust her toward George, before sprinting on ahead.

George dragged her along the shoreline, the injured guard following. Another look back at the highway, the car she had seen earlier stopped to the north, a familiar figure drifting toward the lake.

"JEREMY!" she yelled.

George slapped her, snapping her head back, the blow splitting her lip. She could taste the blood and gripped the gun, debating the wisdom of using it. She could take him, but George and the guard were both close enough to retaliate.

George veered away from the water toward the boathouse, Amanda noticing a short section of fence between the pool house and the lake. That explained the detour.

A glance to her left and William was racing straight for them.

"WATCH THE FENCE!" she yelled, William slowing.

George punched her in the abdomen, doubling her over, air hissing between her teeth at the same time she tried to suck more in. Then there was a gasp as air rushed into her lungs. George yanked her toward him; Amanda taking in one more lungful of air before bracing her legs and pulling the pistol.

George smashed her in the side of the head once more, the force of the blow knocking her off balance. She tumbled forward, her arms thrust out to catch her, her body suddenly sailing backwards. Then she was grabbing George's arm with one hand to steady herself, holding the pistol in the other. Two more steps and she jerked away from George took a step to her left and swung, laying the guard out with the butt of the pistol.

Flipping the safety off, she took a step back and motioned with the muzzle for him to join George. The guard stood, stepped forward then rushed her, knocking the gun out of her hand. Amanda's finger was hooked in the trigger guard and it fired, fireworks exploding through her head, the top of her ear burning. The gun hit the frozen ground and she dropped, groping for it. The guard grabbed her shoulder as she picked the pistol up and jerked her backwards, Amanda aiming under her arm, pulling the trigger. She didn't expect to hit anything, but it might back him off.

The man's grip loosened then there was a thump. She looked back and he'd collapsed, hands grasping his neck, blood oozing between his fingers. She spun around, George slapping the pistol. Amanda followed the move, maintaining her grip. She took two halting steps then George yanked her toward him. She staggered, secreting the gun in her coat pocket as a twig snapped west of their location.

"JEREMY! WILLIAM!"

George snarled, hitting her in the back of the head. He struck her a second time, her head swimming, everything going black.

64

Amanda came to inside the boathouse, her arms and legs bound, a gag in her mouth. The dim light offered by a kerosene lantern revealed George and the remaining guard struggling to shove a boat into the water. The man had dropped it as instructed, the boat falling short, landing on the sandy floor. Voices filtered in from outside, still a fair distance away and they extinguished the light.

Silence descended for a short time then the sound of their straining began anew, muttered cursing audible over the scraping of fiberglass on the sand. Waves lapped against the sides of the boat then the lantern illuminated the cavernous interior again. The guard climbed into the boat, working with the controls then splashed out, him and George pushing the vessel toward open water. Once the boat drifted free of the building George pushed a button on a box in his hands, the motor sputtering to life. He maneuvered a joystick and the boat headed into the lake then he shoved it forward, the engine roaring to life propelling the craft forward.

"Set," George said, tossing the controller into the water. "They won't be able to bring it back now."

Amanda blinked several times, forcing the tears back and craned her neck to the side watching the blinking light on the boat grow ever smaller as it sped east into the darkness. George and the guard dragged her toward the interior of the building, wrapping her in a net. Then they hoisted her into the rafters until she swayed thirty feet above the ground. Laughter drew her away from her predicament, the lantern snuffed out again and a door on the far end of the building closed.

She heaved a sigh, the silence engulfing her as she took stock of her situation. She was freezing, her body shaking, her hands were numb, her jeans caked with dirt and mud from lying on the damp ground. And she couldn't move. But she had a gun in her jacket pocket. She just had to reach it. And she had to be out of here before George and the guard returned.

Another sigh and she craned her neck, attempting to rub the gag off on the net, dislodge it from her mouth, but only succeeded in scraping her skin. Amanda paused, took a deep breath then twisted her legs forward and her shoulders back, the weight of the pistol dragging the coat to the back. She wrenched her hips farther to the front, walking her fingers to bunch the fabric and pull the pocket forward. Her finger hooked in the opening and she tugged, the nylon slipping out of her grasp. After several attempts with no luck, she relaxed to catch her breath and ease the growing cramp, the net swaying.

A furtive look around the darkened interior and the faint outline of a beam came into view a few feet away. That could prove useful. What were the chances?

Two men appeared near the building opening, gazing into the lake. She recognized William's silhouette. His kinky hair and lean build. The second man was a fraction taller with a more muscular build. Jeremy. William looked at Jeremy and shook his head.

"William," James said over the portable.

William jumped, forgetting about the police radio, exclaiming under his breath.

Amanda giggled.

"William," James called again. "Everybody okay?"

"Yes and no. Did you find the body?"

"Yeah, we got it. We thought we heard a boat."

"You did," William answered. "It's heading toward the middle of the lake and Amanda is on it."

She sighed and her shoulders sagged.

"What do you mean, 'Amanda is on it'?" James asked.

"Jeremy's pager is tracking her beacon due east into the lake."

Jeremy shook his head and William released the mike.

"What? You don't think she's on the boat?"

"We don't know," Jeremy answered. "If they found her pager, it is on that boat. If they didn't find the pager, she is on that boat. We didn't see a single person before it disappeared. She hasn't answered our last page, either."

William keyed the mike again. "Disregard that. See if the State Patrol can borrow a boat. We have to verify whether or not she is on it."

"Got it," James replied. "You guys heading back? It's dark."

"We found a boat house. I think we're going to hang out and see what we can discover here."

"Want me to join you guys, or hang here?"

"Just hang there. We need someone to coordinate between us and them. You're elected. Did you find anybody willing to help?"

"A housekeeper and the guards out front. They're trying to get one of the guards to tell them where they were taking Amanda. The housekeeper is being quite helpful in other areas."

"Keep us posted," William replied.

William and Jeremy moved west along the south side of the boathouse and Amanda tried to move the net, make it swing. If she could hit that beam hard enough, she might get their attention.

The door in the end of the building opened and she craned her neck, her perch swinging, bringing the huge beam closer. Another shift of her body and the net's arc grew wider. One more attempt and she put herself in a position to kick. One more inch!

She thrust her feet out, kicking at the beam, the gun sliding out of her pocket, hanging up on the net. Her perch swung again, she kicked striking the beam with a resounding thunk that echoed off the roof. The pistol dropped, firing when it hit the ground, the explosion reverberating inside the structure. William and Jeremy dropped, turning in her direction, weapons drawn. The net swung back, her body hitting the beam and she emitted a muffled yelp. Both men looked up.

"Amanda?" William said.

She kicked at the wooden post again. Then she was falling.

"Is George coming back?" Jeremy asked.

She shrugged and used her chin to point toward the door they had just entered. Then the gag was off.

"I think so," Amanda told them. "George said by the time the cops figured out the boat was a decoy we would be long gone and once away from here they would do away with me."

"How are you holding up?" William asked, looking down at her. "You're shaking."

"I'm cold but okay," she replied.

Jeremy left William to untie Amanda, give them some time alone, while he checked the area. Once he'd freed her, William kissed her and pulled her close, rubbing her body to get some warmth back. Jeremy walked in and William helped her to stand.

"William, I want you to take Amanda and head back to the house," Jeremy said. "After you drop her off, grab a couple of men and head back this way. I'm going the opposite direction and see if I can find George and his gunman."

"Not without me," Amanda answered. "I didn't go through all this to see the man escape. I help. I stay here."

"Amanda…." William started.

"Just listen to me," she said. "We already know they plan to pop me. We just have to find something to put in that net then we hoist it up. When they return, we'll be waiting for them."

"She has an idea," Jeremy admitted. "Part of it anyway. Call James. Have him start this way with three or four men. We'll post them outside the building and we'll wait inside."

"Only if she goes back," William stated emphatically. "I'm not letting her stay. And I'm not going back, either."

"Amanda?" Jeremy asked.

She heaved an exaggerated sigh.

William opened the comm channel on the pager, his arm still wrapped around Amanda. "James, we found Amanda. She's safe. Grab three or four patrolmen and head this way. We're going to set George up. One needs to be a tall, muscle bound specimen to accompany Amanda to the house."

"On our way," James answered.

"Let's get this net set," Amanda said.

"You stay here," William said, planting her on a stool next to the wall. "Do not move."

Amanda gave William a hug, pulling his pager off. He had told her, the organization's pager was on the left, the department pager on the right. To check that she pushed the first button, Jeremy's pager chirping. Switching William's to vibrate she slipped it into her coat pocket. A slow inspection of the floor and she found the pistol. Picking it up, she made sure the safety was on then slipped it in the back of her waistband, pulling her coat over it. William turned and she held her hands out showing him they were empty.

"I'm fine," she said, his eyes narrowing.

65

William tied a large piece of canvas in several places so it resembled a body, positioning it so only a portion of the bindings would be visible then he and Jeremy loaded it into the net, hoisting the make-shift Amanda into the rafters. After James and the patrolmen arrived Jeremy explained the plan. Completing his instructions, he led the men outside, leaving the most intimidating of the officers inside. He would accompany Amanda back to the house.

After the door closed, Amanda took a metal hook off a nail on the wall, moving the gun from her waist to her jacket pocket. She gave a nod and a flirty shrug when the officer turned to check on her then, when he looked away, she lopped the heavy hook into the far corner. He spun in the direction of the sound, Amanda drifting behind the huge beam. She slid around the support post, keeping the beam between her and the officer while he made a sweep of the interior, rushing for the door when he didn't find her.

Amanda scurried to the far side of the building, creeping along the buildings northern wall, her eyes on the door as she moved. The door opened and she dropped, hugging her body tight into the shadows against the foundation. William cursed doing another search of the structure before striding out.

The door slammed behind William then Amanda climbed onto the concrete berm, her body shaking. She was wet and cold again but George Bonner was not going to win. She worked her way toward the lake, peeking around the end of the wall as William walked back in with two men and began a more thorough search of the interior. Swinging onto the ground, staying in the shadows next to the building, Amanda huddled behind a low shrub, as the remainder of the men started a sweep outside. James floated by, talking to a man three feet west of him. There were two other men farther west maintaining the same distance, working the same grid pattern.

Amanda waited until they were north of her location before moving, doing a crouching run, keeping low as she drifted toward a smattering of trees. She perused the heavier canopy to the north then glided toward it and the highway. George would need a means of transportation. If she found that, she would find George and could tell the men.

Three minutes into her excursion George's voice floated her direction, heading for the boathouse. She kneeled, peering around a tree and located a car idling on the side of the road, opening the comm channel.

"Guys," she said. "George is heading your way. He has a car on the highway north of the boathouse. Sorry, William. I stole your pager. I can't communicate without it. Jeremy, key the first button once if you heard me."

She received a single chirp and started toward the car.

"Where the hell are you?" Jeremy asked.

His irritation came across clear, but she ignored the question.

"Okay," she said. "I'm heading north. If I don't hear you've caught George, I'm going to set the beacon on the pager and throw it in the car. You follow him from there."

"Amanda…"

"Too late, Jeremy."

Amanda flattened herself against one of the trees watching the car to the north pull out then George running to intercept it.

"Amanda," Jeremy said. "Watch your back. George is coming your way. William and James are right behind him."

"I see George," she answered. "Watch the highway."

"Amanda, don't you dare!"

The car stopped and Amanda peeled from behind the tree. The driver did a double take and raised his weapon. She braced her body, elbows locked and fired, his head jerked to the side, the car coasting into a tree. Amanda darted for the road, George thirty yards back and slowing at the sight of the car. She erupted onto the blacktop, facing him, arms waving.

"YO!" Amanda yelled. "Being a bit of a coward aren't you?"

George bolted toward Amanda as she turned and raced north, sprinting up the highway. She checked over her shoulder, keeping an eye on George, the distance between them diminishing. Down to sixty feet. She had to maintain that distance or make it bigger.

The level surface gave George an advantage and Amanda examined the surrounding area, an open field to the west catching her eye. She diverted to her left, pushing the button on the pager to activate the homing beacon then opened the comm channel, tearing across the uneven terrain.

"Okay guys," she said. "George is about sixty feet behind me and gaining ground. I'm going across country. Just get your gorgeous hind ends over here. I'm heading west. Repeat. I'm heading west."

"William," Jeremy said. "Follow her. There's a road on the left, I'll catch them from there. James, follow William in case he needs back up."

William was already cutting across country, James on his

heels. All they had to do now was catch Amanda.

Amanda barreled across the field, gasping for air, fighting to keep her footing on the uneven surface, refusing to stop. Suddenly the ground dipped in front of her and she caught herself stumbling toward a ditch. Why did everything have to happen at night? An ungraceful leap and she face planted the dirt on the opposite bank. Shoving herself to her feet, Amanda continued her sprint. One more glance behind her and George had made the same jump, avoiding the face plant.

"Guys," she said, "there's a creek or a ditch up here. Watch your step."

Another look over her shoulder and George was still coming, two figures trailing him.

"Amanda," Jeremy said. "I have you in sight. Do you see the headlights to your right?"

"Yes."

"That's me. Head north. If you understand turn the beacon off. I promise we'll catch you. Trust us now."

Jeremy turned the headlights off, nosing William's car into the bushes on the side of the road. He pulled his pistol as he exited the car, keeping just inside the line of shrubbery, using it and the camouflage of darkness to move up the hill in a westerly angle.

Amanda changed direction, reaching in her pocket to turn the beacon off. Maybe she needed to start that running thing again. Her legs ached and her lungs burned, and that road looked so damn far away, but she couldn't stop. George was back there.

Then George grabbed her. He had moved faster than she'd anticipated.

"Well, shit!" she said.

"Amanda," Jeremy said. "I got you."

66

Amanda dropped her head, pulled in a mouthful of air then released a soft, steady breath, her chest heaving, working on that anger management issue and her patience. Patience was a virtue, she had been told. A virtue, she admitted, she had problems exhibiting.

"You're going to get me out of here now, my pretty," George whispered. "No one will do anything to harm you. That's what happens when ones emotions get tangled up in ones work."

"Maybe, maybe not," Amanda answered taking one more gulp of air. "I'm not the only reason they want your sorry ass gone."

William and James continued to move up behind them, George blading his body so he could watch all three men. Moonlight reflected off the pistol and William and James slowed, hands out to calm George.

"As you can see our hands are empty," William called. "Just let Amanda go."

"Stay where you are and allow us to leave," George replied. "If I go down, she goes down."

Amanda reached into her pocket grasping the pistol, releasing the safety as she pulled it out. To hell with that patience thing! George was going down. He'd hurt too many people. But the timing had to be perfect.

George maneuvered west toward a small inlet road, Amanda's neck in the crook of his arm. She stumbled to the left, choking when George tightened his grip. They continued west, George rotating his upper body every few seconds to keep all three men in view. He took one more step to the right and froze, facing north. Amanda turned her gaze the same direction to find Jeremy gone. George did another quick twist to the right, the move catching Amanda off guard. She tripped, grabbing George's arm for balance. George jerked around, two shots echoing between the hills. George twisted to his left and pulled the trigger again, her head screaming.

"AMANDA DROP!" Jeremy yelled.

Amanda shoved her pistol into the flesh under George's chin and pulled the trigger, something warm spraying her face then she dropped, pulling out of his grasp, another shot ringing out. Her body hit the ground hard, she closed her eyes as she rolled and lifted her head, Jeremy on the ground only yards away, his pistol aimed their direction, George prone in the dirt behind her a dark stain blossoming around his head and upper torso. She glanced to her right and James was kneeling beside William.

"NO!" Amanda yelled. This was not how this was supposed to go down.

"OFFICER DOWN!" James shouted into his portable. "We have three people down. One is a fatality. The officer is alive, but has been shot. I repeat the officer has been hit, but is alive!"

"Check Amanda," William ordered, between clenched teeth. "Make sure she's alright."

"Amanda's fine," James answered, ripping William's shirt to check the wound.

"Must make mental note," William said, exhaling a jagged

breath, "try harder not to get shot next time. You'd think I would have learned the first time."

Amanda stood, attempting to choke back her tears, failing miserably. They ran down her face as she started toward William, gulping in air between sobs. William wasn't supposed to get shot! Three steps and she stopped, James flipping his wrist, waving her in Jeremy's direction. She hesitated, James waved again then she reversed, sprinting down the hill toward Jeremy. Part way to him she saw the blood. Jeremy had been hit, too.

Jeremy clasped his leg, unsure what had happened. Seconds before he pulled the trigger another weapon had fired. And there had been three shots prior to that. Now William was down again. Could this go any further south?

"Are you alright, Jeremy?" Amanda asked when she reached him. "You weren't supposed to get shot. You're supposed to be saving me." She choked back a sob attempting to laugh.

"I'm fine," he whispered. "Check on William for me, please."

"James is with him. We got George, though."

"Damn the bad luck!"

"Just so you know. I don't like your idea of training," Amanda said, laughing between tears.

"I will endeavor to remember that, my lady. You must also remember I didn't set this one up. This was a Bonner creation."

Amanda pulled her knife and slit the pant leg, folding the fabric back to expose the wound. Ignoring Jeremy's orders, she cut the bottom half off her shirt, folding it to cover the hole then slapped his hand over it to zip her coat.

"Jeremy, give me your belt" she said. "This is going to hurt, but I have to slow the bleeding."

He struggled to pull it free then Amanda grabbed it, yanking it out of the loops and wrapped it around the makeshift bandage.

He cringed as she tightened the belt. "Damn! You weren't joking were you?"

"Jeremy, I lost my engagement ring. What am I going to tell William?"

"They found it, my lady," he said, sucking air in between clenched teeth. "Are you sure you know what you're doing?"

"Yes, Jeremy. You taught me. Who the hell shot you and William? Was it George?"

Jeremy nodded. "I believe so madam. We'll know when they do the ballistics."

"Oh, I have a business proposition for us. A real nice one, if you like the Caribbean."

"What kind of proposition?" He already knew. If it was in the Caribbean, it was the commander.

"Howard wants me to be the hostess on his yacht this summer. He'll need security for the trip as well, and will use you too keep things running as usual. If you're up and able."

"Funny! Where does that leave William?"

"He needs security as well," she answered, exasperated. "Did you forget already? He said he would talk to you about using James, William and Timothy. Why break up a good team?"

Emergency personnel arrived and Jeremy was placed on a stretcher for transport, William already loaded into an ambulance.

Jeremy grinned. "That could prove interesting. Three men, one woman."

"Five men," she said, teasing him in return. "James and Timothy will be there, too."

67

David exited the black and white and walked around it to the payphone, surveying the building across the street that housed the mighty Landers Corporation. Dropping change into the phone, he dialed Thomas's number. He made it past the initial conversation now it was time to go for the gold. The call was answered with the usual greeting, the secretary sending it through without hesitation.

"Good day, sir," David said. "Did Travis have good news?"

"You seem pretty well informed," Thomas replied.

"I know more than people think I do," David said, scanning the street. "I called back as instructed. Now, I expect you to give me a time and a place we can meet."

"Okay. I'll play along. But you can count on meeting your maker if I find out you've crossed me."

"I can live with that," David answered. "So, when do you want to meet?"

"Since you seem to be in such a hurry, how soon can you be here?"

"Look out the window." David stepped from behind the cover of the payphone. "See the black and white across the street?"

A drape moved and a head poked out, a man gazing down at the street. "Yes."

David waved. "I can be in your office in five minutes."

"You're pretty sure of yourself," Thomas said. "I like that. Come on up Mr. Haus."

David hung up, walked across the street and the lobby to the elevator, second guessing his decision. He might not make it off that elevator alive, but it was a chance he had to take.

On the second floor the elevators whooshed open and Travis stepped in.

"Good afternoon, Travis," David said. "I didn't expect to see you here."

Travis nodded, standing between David and the door, his back to David. An upward lurch and Travis inserted a key, giving it a turn, stopping the elevator. He turned and faced David.

"How bad do you want to work with us?" Travis asked.

"Bad enough to put my life on the line by walking into the lion's den," David replied. "From what I've heard, you carry a lot of weight. You're number three in line. Is that why you're here? A member of the board of directors here to make the tie breaking vote?" David chuckled.

"Number two," Travis said correcting him. "Or I will be soon. Answer my question."

Something had changed. The tension palpable. A sensation so thick David could almost taste it. He pointed to the door with his chin, his mind repeating Travis' words. *'Number two. Or I will be soon.'* His stomach tightened, coiled into knots, the implications threading through.

"Once out of here, will I be caught up in something I don't want to be caught up in?"

Travis smiled. "And if you say anything your compadres will think you did it all on your own. Are you still in?"

"If I say no?"

"You're dead. This organization is going to go to even greater heights, Mr. Haus, and you are being given the opportunity to come along for the ride." Travis chuckled. "As the number three in command."

"I assume I will get more of an incentive that way?"

"Of course. Mr. Fielding will explain it to you."

"Mr. Fielding?"

Travis' smirk broadened, but he remained quiet.

"Then let's get this show on the road," David said, directing Travis' gaze to the key.

Travis turned the key and the elevator continued up, the doors sucking open when it stopped. Travis stepped out, one of Mr. Landers's men reaching for David's revolver, Travis watching from the hall.

David blocked the move, keeping one hand on the buffer, the doors bumping open when they hit his hand. His eyes had gone cold, his voice harsh.

"That stays. Understand?" David said.

The man nodded and backed up, tipping his head to the right, directing David past the secretary. David walked out of the elevator, Travis moving in behind him and his body hit the floor, his revolver being pulled from its holster. He rolled onto his back, the secretary leaning over him, a stiletto on his chest and a gun in his face. There was the signature crack of his service weapon and Mr. Landers man went down, a hole through his neck. Two men appeared from the far end of the hall, dragging the body away. David exhaled. Less than sixty seconds and he'd been screwed.

The secretary motioned for David to stand with the muzzle of her gun. He obeyed. Travis handed David his weapon, directing him toward the door. David hesitated then took the pistol and holstered it. If he took out Travis, the secretary would take him.

Once inside Thomas's office the door closed and David looked behind him, expecting to see a gun pointed at him, but Travis stood perfectly still, just inside the doors, his hands clasped in front of him. He chin pointed David to the desk and the man on the phone behind it. A second man stood behind the desk to the left, arms clasped in front of him like Travis'. The man on the phone pointed to one of two chairs, studying David, his eyes resting on the firearm. David took a deep breath and moved closer, the man reaching across the desk to shake David's hand and introduce himself.

David thought about Thomas' calm then noticed the quiet. The room had been soundproofed. No doubt so those outside wouldn't know what happened inside. Today it would work the opposite. Thomas had no idea he was being had.

"I appreciate that," Thomas said, studying David. "My appointment is here. I'll call you back." He hung up and stared across the desk. "I get the feeling you knew Mr. Bonner better than Travis here did." He diverted his gaze beyond David for a tic then looked back at him. "You said Travis would underestimate George. How did you know he would play Mr. Bonner the way he did?"

"I've worked with George for several years," David answered. "Travis hasn't. Travis played the game as usual. George knew those rules."

Thomas sat unmoving, continuing to eye David. "I don't know why, but I trust you, Mr. Haus. Is there any reason I shouldn't?"

"No, sir," David answered. "I understand the uniform can put one off."

David dipped his head, hands out in a modified half bow, two shots ringing out in quick succession. David dropped to the floor pulling his weapon as he rolled under the desk. He looked up, Travis' pistol pointed at him. Travis flicked the muzzle up. David took the hint and stood, Thomas Landers body already being wheeled out.

David holstered his gun and held his hands out to his sides. Far enough to be non-threatening, but not far enough he couldn't reach his pistol if need be. The man behind David slipped his gun into his waistband and perched on the front corner of the desk. Travis holstered his and walked out.

"Sorry for the disturbance," the man said, "but I have to make sure you don't cross me. Everything that just happened has been recorded. If you attempt to pull anything, certain…." He paused, choosing his words. "…portions will be released by us to the Reno P.D."

A growing sense of dread tightened its grip on David. An understanding of just how easily he had allowed himself to be taken advantage of landing like granite. The door opened then closed, Travis dropping a plastic bag with a single spent cartridge in it on the desk.

"You didn't have to be so melodramatic," David said. "You have plenty of men close by. I saw them."

"You are very observant."

"I have to be. A man in my position won't last long if I'm not."

The man did a slow nod then locked eyes with David. "Now, what can *I* do to make sure you become a long lasting member of *my* team?"

"I make the same requests of you that I did of Mr. Landers. Meet those and I'll happily join the family."

"Sit down Mr. Haus."

He walked behind the desk, a chair magically appearing at his bidding. He laughed at some hidden joke and raised an eyebrow as he stared at David.

"What is your going rate for a hit?" he asked. "Every pro has a set fee. Usually it's more than an organization's agreed upon payment. One has to leave some room for negotiation, doesn't one?"

David hiked his left shoulder. "I don't do hits, but I have a few '*friends*' who will do the work for a fair price."

"The name's Robert Fielding," the man said. "You have six weeks to prove you're not going to stab me in the back. If you do, you die. Fair?" Robert reached out to shake David's hand.

"Fair," David answered, exhaling slow and quiet, returning the handshake.

"Welcome to The Fielding Corporation." Robert reached into the top drawer of the desk and pulled out a thick manila envelope, dropping his gaze to the finger on David's right hand, nodding in its direction. "Is the late Mr. Bonner the cause of your injury?"

"Indirectly," David said with a laugh. "When you're ready for me to begin, let me know. I would like nothing more than to show you what can be done with the Salt Lake City market."

"David," Mr. Fielding said as David stood. "As a show of faith I'm going to give you a bit of an incentive."

David stopped, still facing Robert.

Robert tossed him the envelope. "That should be ten grand. Your job starts today. No strings attached, except you terminate your employment with the Bonner's. Is that agreeable?"

"Yes, sir," David said catching the envelope. "I'll keep a close eye on things for you. In the meantime, if you are in need of anything, you have my number."

"Expect the same every month. Plus commissions on your proceeds."

"And Jonathan?"

"Keep us informed for now. We're going to dig him in a little deeper." Robert grinned. "Of course, we'll give him a chance to straighten things out along the way."

David did a half smile, saluting Robert with the envelope then turned to walk out. He was in, Robert's words an echo. '*You have six weeks… you die*'. David knew it would be longer than six weeks. He would be watched every single day he was inside. And the uniform would only add to Robert's paranoia.

The door closed behind David and Robert turned his gaze to Travis.

"See what you can find on Officer David Haus. I want to know how many times he passes gas in a day. Call me at home. We have to be out of here tonight."

"Yes, sir," Travis answered, striding out of the office.

David climbed into his cruiser and drove to a strip mall a couple of miles away to use a pay phone. A quick scan of the parking lot and he recognized the telltale Lincoln two rows back, the occupants still inside.

David walked into a restaurant and out the back, doubling around to a payphone on the corner, calling one of his favorite numbers.

"Penny's," the woman breathed into the phone.

"Tell Penny his favorite ride is in."

He hung up and reversed direction, exiting the same restaurant, a to-go box in hand and climbed into his car. He started the engine and watched his new friends while he ate. Now it was time to learn the other half of this dance. He couldn't sell the drugs or do hits, especially members of law enforcement, but he would have to guide the employees and order those hits, except members of law enforcement. They had to be spared no matter the cost.

"Touché, Mr. Robert Fielding," David said, his mind rerunning the set up outside the elevator. He couldn't allow himself to be had like that again.

68

James walked into William's hospital room grinning from ear to ear, playing with three cassettes, a manila folder under one arm. A bleary eyed plain clothes officer trailed. James placed the cassettes along with the folder on the bed table then the officer laid a cassette player on the table beside them. William reached for the folder. James and the officer each pulled up a chair and got comfortable.

"What have you got here?" William asked.

"A present for you dudes," the officer said.

"Our trusty plains clothes guy here got some good stuff, buddy," James answered.

William looked at the officer. "You look like hell."

"Thank you," he replied. "I will take that as a compliment."

"So what did you find?"

"I ran into one of Bonner's flunkies. A David Haus. Officer David Haus of the Reno P.D."

"David. Isn't that the name Glen gave us?" William asked.

James nodded.

"The report is the normal chasing the guy from phone to

phone," the officer continued nodding toward the file William held, "until we got to Reno. Then it got a little interesting."

"You followed him to Remo?" William asked surprised. "You could have got your ass in trouble."

"Yeah, I know," the officer admitted. "I didn't think about it then. I was on the trail of something hot and I could feel it. The nerves were janglin'."

"Because you were running on empty," James interjected.

"You're probably right there," he answered. "But he was into something and I knew it. I could feel it. He worked for Bonner last year, but no one has seen him much since George went to the slammer. Until now." The officer laughed a little too loud. A tired laugh. "I conned a hooker and a couple of teenagers into helping me. That cost me sixty bucks, but this is going to be worth it. The dude has his own black and white…"

"His own black and white?" William looked up to see James' grin. "Do we have anything on him?"

"Not much," the officer replied. "He's a little on the slippery side. I saw him at Main and Second South and he parked and headed for a payphone. I just had a feeling about the dude, man. Especially after not seeing him for so long. One of those hunches you get. So I decided to see if my recorder would work in the open."

"So you have three conversations on tape," William said.

"Three one sided conversations. He made three phone calls, an hour apart, from Salt Lake City then hightailed it to Reno. So, I stayed low and followed. Once in Reno he did a couple of round the block tours to ditch anybody then parked behind a bar."

The officer continued, explaining how the man had backed his pick-up into a narrow driveway between a garage and the bar and hooked up to an enclosed car hauler. Once he'd pulled the trailer out, he unlocked the doors then loaded a black and white into the trailer.

"I wrote a note about the door skins and roof identifiers. They're Reno P.D. The car carried law enforcement license plates, too. I put all that plus pictures and addresses in the report. I spent the rest of the night writing my report and making copies of the tapes. Then my partner and I got side tracked. A couple of drug stings. Haven't slept for a day or two."

He answered a few more questions, then excused himself. He needed some sleep. Even caffeine wasn't helping any longer.

"Do we know this is legit?" William asked, after the officer had left. "I mean – is Officer Haus a real cop?"

"Cap thinks he's an undercover. The chief called Reno, got pushed around a bit by higher ups and decided not to force the issue. Reno wouldn't tell us anything anyway. It would be suicide to out the undercover. Even to another law enforcement agency. And he doesn't want to blow it for them. I gave Jeremy a copy of everything. The organization is already working on it. It would be vague and circumspect in a court of law, but it's a start. What do you think?"

"What about the address in Reno?"

"Dead end," James answered. "Reno went by and found a room above the bar, but it's already been rented. Prior tenant was a John Smith." He laughed when he saw William's smirk. "They traced the number we had on those business cards, disconnected."

William sat up straighter.

"The phone company checked call logs and discovered the day after our officer got these recordings…" James nodded at the tapes. "…a call was received at the disconnected number from a payphone across the street. The office had been rented at one time to The Landers Corporation. Reno P.D. searched the office and found trace amounts of blood on the carpet outside the elevator and in the main office. Someone tried to clean it up, but missed a particle or two. A hiker called 911 last night and reported finding two bodies in the hills near Ruby Valley. One has been identified as Mr. Thomas Landers, former head of The Landers Corporation and suspected head of the syndicate in Reno. The other was a known flunky for Mr. Landers."

"So they had a coup."

"Looks that way."

"What about the financials of The Landers Corporation?"

"Funneled into a phony company and funneled out again. So far no word on its final resting place. They ran a trace on Mr. Landers and information came in that solidifies Reno's idea that he headed the syndicate at one time. Since we tied up the other cases between Kevin and Glen, and with Mr. Landers dead…."

"And Glen's cause of death?"

"Lloyd was right. It wasn't an overdose. He was poisoned. But the Cap says we're golden. He said to take a nice long vacation."

"How long's long?"

"Not that long," James said, laughing at William's grin.

69

Jeremy's injury had been a flesh wound. No bone or major arteries involved. Bled like hell and burned like mad and he left for Cedar City berating himself for getting involved with one of his charges. He drove through the gates at his retreat, the emptiness oppressive.

Inside, he sat at the breakfast bar where he and Amanda had shared so many morning memories, glancing down at his left hand. She hadn't noticed his ring. Or if she had, she hadn't mentioned it. He took it off, thought about giving it some time. Just to see if there might be someone else out there, but that was laughable. There would never be another Amanda. He slipped the ring back on.

He walked through the house, a tightness filling his chest he had never felt before, Howard's words floating through. *'What will you do if William asks her to marry him before you get your head out of your duff?'* Definitely successful in this business for a reason.

Jeremy wandered to the room Amanda had occupied, her perfume lingering in the air, a ghost taunting him. He closed his eyes, visions of her eyes wide open laugh, the sun shining on her face, bombarded him. He could still feel the warmth of her cheek against his chest when she'd told him she was marrying William. That had been the last time he'd held her. Something wet traced its way down his cheek and he cursed himself for being so blind. He wiped the tears away and walked to his office, pulling up his computer.

He took out the pager, keyed in 'Downtime' and hit enter then began the end of op reports. Fax tones pulled him away from his work and he turned to the papers it was spitting out.

Glad you're back. How are you and William healing?

I thought I would give you the ballistics report. Two shots struck Mr. Bonner. One from Ms Granger's weapon and one from yours. The bullet that struck William, and the bullet that struck you, were fired from Mr. Bonner's. Another round, which we assume was meant for James, was found a few yards beyond William. Also from Mr. Bonner's weapon.

Now for the bad news. We have another bad apple in Salt Lake City. He's connected to the trunk, trying to kill the root. All signs show the poison may be coming from Reno again. Continue to monitor things closely.

Jeremy smiled, laying them on his desk. He had information to gather, training to set up and a wedding to plan.

Lightning Source UK Ltd.
Milton Keynes UK
UKHW021146260620
365567UK00007B/1312

9 781646 691371